Lynda Bellingham

tell me tomorrow

**SIMON &
SCHUSTER**

London · New York · Sydney · Toronto · New Delhi

A CBS COMPANY

First published in Great Britain by Simon & Schuster UK Ltd, 2013
A CBS COMPANY

1 3 5 7 9 10 8 6 4 2

Simon & Schuster UK Ltd
1st Floor
222 Gray's Inn Road
London WC1X 8HB

www.simonandschuster.co.uk

Simon & Schuster Australia, Sydney
Simon & Schuster India, New Delhi

A CIP catalogue record for this book
is available from the British Library

Hardback ISBN: 978-1-47112-856-1
Trade Paperback ISBN: 978-1-47112-996-4
Ebook ISBN: 978-1-47110-282-0

Typeset by M Rules
Printed and bound by CPI Group (UK) Ltd, Croydon, CR0 4YY

To mothers everywhere

ACKNOWLEDGEMENTS

I would like to thank Suzanne Baboneau for her support and belief in me; Joan Deitch for her invaluable contribution to the words; Gordon Wise, my agent, who adds joy to my life; my sister Jean for her kindness; and my dearest husband Michael for his IT skills. And finally, YTL for their beautiful hotels, which provided me with a joyous place to write this novel.

'A mother's treasure is her daughter'

ANON

PROLOGUE

Spring 1995

The tiny violet flower slipped from between the faded yellow pages of the prayer book and wafted gently to the floor. Anna watched the drop of mauve, like a lilac tear, intrigued. She brought the prayer book up to her nose and inhaled the smell of age and leather and just the faintest trace of violets. She then bent down and picked up the flower, careful not to break the petals. It was almost like holding a butterfly without the wings.

Placing it on the dressing-table, with the other dried flowers that had been pressed between the pages, she turned to the front of the prayer book and read the inscription written on the flyleaf.

> *To my dearest daughter Mary.*
> *God bless you and keep you safe forever.*
> *Your loving mother,*
>
> *1910*

Anna was overwhelmed by a sense of sadness she could not explain. There was something so tender in the neat, spidery handwriting that it tugged at her heart. Who did this prayer book belong to, she wondered. She found more writing on the next page.

1

Dear Jane,
You will always be in my heart.
Be kind and strong, and keep safe.
Love, Mother,
1944

Anna realised that the Jane in question must be her grand-mother. There was more to come, as another inscription was written below this.

Dearest Meredith,
When in doubt,
Be kind and think good thoughts.
With all my love, Mummy, xx
1963

Anna smiled to herself. How weird was this? One by one she replaced the dried flowers inside the prayer book then went to find her mother.

Meredith Lee was sitting at her desk in the study of their cosy cottage in the Vale of Health, a leafy sanctuary in the heart of Hampstead, North London. She was typing furiously. She always complained that she was never able to type fast enough to keep up with her thoughts.

'Mum, you never told me about this.' Anna came towards Meredith, holding up the prayer book.

'What? Anna, please don't interrupt me, I have to get this done tonight,' answered Meredith, peering at the screen.

'But this is part of my heritage, Mother, to be passed down through the years. When were you going to write something in it and hand it over to me, your darling daughter?'

Meredith stopped typing and looked up. 'What on earth are you blabbing on about?'

2

'This, Mommie dearest.' Anna handed her mother the prayer book and waited.

Meredith turned it over in her hands very gently, as if she knew there were flowers inside. She opened the book and read the loving inscriptions – and suddenly, she was transported back to her childhood. She could smell her mother in the room, that special scent of her Yardley lipstick and Bourjois Rouge powder.

'Oh my goodness, where on earth did you find this?' she asked, her deadline completely forgotten.

'In the attic, under a pile of photo albums. I have been looking for photos of the family for a project we are doing for GCSE History. Isn't it lovely? I have decided I am going to write about the importance of the mother figure through history.'

'I think that is a lovely idea,' said Meredith, holding the prayer book in her hands and remembering so clearly how much it had meant to her. How much it had meant to her mother Jane and, in turn, Jane's mother Mary.

'It is very important to celebrate motherhood,' she went on. 'Your great-grandmother Mary would be proud of you.'

Meredith let her thoughts drift back half a century, to her own happy childhood.

'I used to love going to church on Mothering Sunday,' she said, smiling to herself. 'I even sang in the choir, can you believe it? All the mothers were given flowers by their children as part of the service. It made us feel very important. Your gran had loved doing the same thing for her mother, Mary. It goes right back to Mary's mother, Alice. Look – that's her handwriting there. But there is such a sad story connected to that first inscription by Alice.'

Meredith reached out to take Anna's hand and her eyes sparkled with tears.

'You see, she was dying, Anna. In fact, she died on Mothering Sunday 1910 and these were the last words she ever wrote . . .'

PART ONE

Chapter One

Hertfordshire, Spring 1910

John and Alice Charles had three sons, loud, strapping lads always up to mischief, but only one daughter. She was called Mary, and she was the youngest of the family. John was the vicar of St James' Church in a small village called Allingham, not far from the historic town of St Albans in the county of Hertfordshire.

It was on a church outing to St Albans that Alice Cooke entered the young would-be curate's rather lonely life, and love blossomed. Alice was the daughter of a wealthy landowner in Buckinghamshire, and her marriage to John was deemed a drop in the social scale. Once it was clear to Alice's parents that she was determined to marry beneath her station, they sent her packing, albeit with a quite substantial dowry. However, Alice never saw her parents again. They regarded her as feckless, and a disappointment, and concentrated their hopes and ambitions on their two sons instead. As the only child of elderly parents who died when he was embarking on his career in the clergy, John was alone in the world. Alice was now abandoned, so the two young lovers made their world themselves, and thanks to

Alice's optimistic nature and goodness of heart, between them they created a loving family.

Their daughter Mary had the advantages of being brought up with three brothers – and the disadvantages. She was protected and spoiled, but also very innocent, and unaware of life outside her family. But she had a lively mind and had inherited her mother's warmth and optimism. She loved to learn, and if truth be told she was the brightest of them all. However, life in those days was ruled by the men. Mary had to play a secondary role to her brothers even though she often taught them herself, as school was not something they went to willingly. There was many a day when cries could be heard from the scullery as one or other of the boys was beaten for playing truant.

But not today; nobody was going to be shouted at today. It was Sunday, Mothering Sunday to be precise, and it was a beautiful morning, with the promise of spring in the air. Mary had been waiting for this special day to arrive for ages. She had made a card for her beloved mother and helped her brothers to make one from them. The back door of the scullery was wide open as the girl searched the garden for early snowdrops and budding daffodils to put on her mother's breakfast tray. She could hear a lark showing off in the field behind the house, and paused to listen to the clear notes soaring above her. It was hard not to enjoy the promise of the day, outside here on the step.

But Mary was under a dark cloud that morning. Her mother, Alice Charles, lay upstairs grievously ill with pneumonia.

Mary was only ten years old but was already taking on the household chores. With her father and three brothers in the house, the work never ended. Mrs Edge came in every day to help. She was a lovely round lady who lived in the village. Her duties covered everything from cooking a hearty tea for Mary and the boys, to arranging all the flowers in the church and leading the ladies of the village in the cleaning of the brass. She was a great comfort to Mary as her mother's illness took hold. The little girl was very much alone as John Charles did not seem able to cope at all with his wife's decline. He had always been a rather distant figure to Mary. He worked very hard, dividing his time between the church and his parish duties, and spent hours shut away in his study. He always had time for his wife, of course, for Alice was the light of his life, and she tried to ensure that the house was calm and tranquil. Not an easy task with three sons around. Now Mary was trying to ease the burden of her mother's care, so that her father could write his sermons, and perform his pastoral duties. But the house had lost its brightness since her mother had taken to her bed.

Mary had spent most of the night beside her mother, tending to her and trying to keep the fever at bay. She had just changed the bed-linen and Alice's nightgown. Having washed the other sweat-soaked sheets by hand and stuffed them through the mangle, she was hanging them out in the morning sunshine to dry. She felt a little faint from lack of sleep but paid no heed. Time enough to sleep when her mother was on the mend.

Back inside the kitchen, she put her posy of flowers in a tiny glass vase and placed it on the tray. Then she went to the range to pick up the heavy black iron kettle that was boiling on the top. She made some tea and spooned plenty of sugar into a cup. Mrs Edge said sweet tea could cure anything. This would make her mother feel better. She was not supposed to touch the heavy kettle, but these were difficult times, and all the child knew for sure was that she had to do her very best. She cut a slice of bread very carefully, with the sharp bread-knife threatening to do her mischief at any moment, and spread some butter and jam on the extra thick slice. How she loved the sweet-smelling sticky jam her mother made. It smelled of summer and strawberries and fun.

9

She carried the tray upstairs to her mother's bedroom. The curtains were closed and the room was dark and stuffy, and it smelled sour. Mary put down the tray and tiptoed to the bedside. Alice was propped up against the pillows, her eyes closed, breathing with great difficulty. The little girl took her hand and squeezed it gently.

'Happy Mothering Sunday. I've got your breakfast, Mother. A nice cup of tea, and some bread and jam. Now you must eat it all up to make you strong.'

Alice Charles opened her eyes and smiled wanly at her daughter. 'You are a wonderful nurse, Mary,' she managed to whisper. 'I'll have it in a minute. But first, will you open the drawer in my bedside table, please, dear?'

The little girl did as she was told. Inside the drawer were some lovely lace hankies and a lavender pouch. Mary picked it up and smelled the wonderful fragrance. As she did so, Alice tried to turn her head but the effort was too much. She breathed hard and it caught in her throat as a gasp. Mary was frightened by the sound.

'Mother, please be still,' she implored. 'Please get better.' And she tried in vain to stop the tears that were desperately forcing their way down her cheeks.

Alice drew herself up, praying silently for the strength to do what she had to do, and said, 'Mary, dear, now don't cry. It is going to be fine. Inside that drawer you will find my prayer book. Please pass it to me.'

Mary found the book and put it in her mother's trembling hands. Alice opened the book at the first page and showed it to her daughter.

'Look here – see? I've written you a note. Promise me you will keep this prayer book with you always, and every night when you go to sleep, you will say your prayers and think of me. I'll be watching over you all the time, my dearest daughter. You will have a lot to do, but your father and your brothers need your help. Please don't be sad, I will be with you always in your heart.'

The dying woman made a last superhuman effort as she gasped, 'Now be a good girl and go and call your father to come quickly. I need to speak to him.' Then she fell back on the pillows, exhausted.

To Mary it seemed as if she had fallen asleep.

'Mother, please wake up, you haven't eaten your breakfast.' She shook her mother's arm and it dropped heavily off the bed and just hung there. The little girl slowly backed away from the bed and a scream rose in her throat.

'Father! Come quick!'

The funeral service seemed very long to Mary. She tried hard to sing all the hymns well for her mother, but she wanted to cry all the time. As she sat in a pew with her prayer book clutched in her hands, and her eyes screwed tightly shut, she prayed and prayed to God to make her mother come back. But He didn't. Mary would often talk to Him at night, after that. She never gave up asking, and she always kept her prayer book close by, along with the card she had made that day for her mother.

Mary now became a mother to her brothers even though she was the youngest. It was a lonely life, for her father could offer her little comfort as he was grieving himself, and the boys were busy growing into men. Mrs Edge still came in every day and helped with the chores, but it was clear to everyone in the village that the vicar wanted to be left alone. He performed his duties with care and diligence, but the spark of life had gone out of him.

Mary never really had time to make friends at school because as soon as the bell went, she was off home to cook and clean for the household. But it was not all bad. There was a farm just up the road from the vicarage owned by a couple called Ernest and

Olive Cooper. They had two sons of their own who went to school with the Charles boys, and all the lads loved to play on the farm. Haystacks and cowsheds made great hiding places, and every summer the boys would spend long hot days in the fields. For Mary it was a magical place to go and be with all the animals. She loved the smell of Olive's kitchen where there was always an animal of some description in front of the range. Cats, dogs – even baby lambs. One afternoon there was a sheep giving birth and Mary sat with Olive who was keeping an eye on it, because it had been having difficulties. At last the lamb dropped to the ground as Mary watched in awe. The farmer's wife picked up the lamb and placed it under the mother's nose, rubbing it with the afterbirth.

'They need a bit of help sometimes, to understand what it is all about, God bless 'em!' she explained to the little girl.

But the ewe did not want to know. She butted the still wet and bloody lamb, and walked away. Mary was so distressed to see this that she burst into tears.

'Don't fret yourself, dearie,' said Olive kindly. 'I will take the lamb indoors and put it by the fire, and you can help me feed it by hand.'

Sure enough, they carried the lamb indoors and soon it was lying in Mary's lap in front of the fire, while she fed it from a glass baby bottle. It was love at first sight. Mary was round at the farm every minute she was free. The lamb grew bigger and bigger each day. Mary called her Alice after her mother. Her brothers teased her mercilessly and ran round her singing the old nursery rhyme:

'Mary had a little lamb
Its fleece was white as snow.
And everywhere that Mary went
The lamb was sure to go.'

She even took it to school one day to show her class. Mary could never quite get over the way the mother sheep had rejected and abandoned her baby, but the farmer's wife was very matter-of-fact about it. She said it happened quite often.

'But how could you not love your baby?' whispered Mary.

'Well, there are some women as have the same problem, dearie. There's naught you can do about it though. You can't *make* people love you.'

Having three brothers meant that Mary was always learning all sorts of things, not all of them good either. They taught her to spit and she was really good at it. In addition, she could skim a stone across the pond with the best of them and ride a horse and drive a cart like a champion. Her happiest memories were of sitting on the hay cart at the end of a hot summer's day. The sun would be setting as they rolled back to Coopers Farm full of fresh air and cider and homemade pies. The boys would be fighting and scrapping on top of the hay like young lion cubs. She would sit up front with her eldest brother Joseph, lulled by the swing of the horses' rumps in front of her and the jangling of the harness and the screeching of the bats swooping around them in the dusk.

As they reached the farm gates, the last streaks of the red sunset collapsed on the horizon, and darkness would fall. The boys would walk Mary back to the vicarage and then they would go to the pub. The landlord of the Wheatsheaf in Allingham was well aware that the boys were not only too young to be drinking but also the vicar's sons, so the boys were given non-alcoholic ginger beer and big plates of shepherd's pie. At home, Mary would creep in and check on her father, who was usually sitting at his desk preparing a sermon or writing letters to do with parish matters. Sometimes she would find him fast asleep with his head on his arms. The Reverend Charles made Mary feel a little frightened because he was

13

always sad and often stern with them. He just could not give his children the affection they needed, and while the boys had each other for comfort, it made the girl miss her mother so much, especially at bedtime when she could remember so vividly her tender embrace as she tucked Mary in, with loving words to help her dream wonderful things. Just before she fell asleep, Mary would remember her mother's words and slip out of bed to kneel on the floor and say her prayers, because she knew her mother was watching.

One morning Mary got out of bed and was horrified to see blood on the bed-sheets and on her nightdress. She checked herself all over for cuts and could find nothing wrong. In the bathroom, she suddenly felt her stomach contract in pain. She sat down on the lavatory and bent over to ease the cramps, but felt a rush of liquid between her legs and heard it splash into the bowl below. Looking down, she cried out in panic as the water in the bowl turned pink. Sobbing now with fear and disbelief, she grabbed a flannel and held it between her legs. What was happening to her?

There was a knock on the door and she heard Joseph's voice outside. 'Mary? Come on, girl, we want our breakfast. What are you doing in there?'

Mary tried to rise from the seat, but another trickle of blood stopped her in her tracks. She called out, 'Joe, something dreadful has happened. I am bleeding and I think I am dying. Please fetch the doctor.'

As a young man of nineteen, Joseph had already picked up a good deal of knowledge about the opposite sex. However, it was one thing to discuss the female anatomy with his friends, but quite another to speak of such delicate matters with his sister.

But he knew someone who could help. Telling his sister to

stay calm and to hold on for a few minutes while he fetched help, Joseph sped off to Dr Jeffreys' house two streets away, and banged on the door. The doctor's wife, Lorna, answered his knock. She was a trained nurse and often stood in for her husband when he was too busy to deal with minor ailments that arose during surgery hours.

Blushing, Joseph explained to her what he thought was Mary's problem. Lorna Jeffreys was very understanding, and quite impressed by this young man's grasp of the sensitivity of the situation. Fetching her coat and hat, and an old but clean sheet, she followed Joseph back to the vicarage, where poor Mary was still closeted in the bathroom. Joseph led the nurse upstairs and tapped on the door.

'Mary, dear, don't panic,' he called. 'Mrs Jeffreys is here to help you. Please open the door. I will go downstairs and make us all a cup of tea in the meantime, and don't worry about breakfast. I will see to everything.'

Once Mary had heard her brother go downstairs, she opened the bathroom door and Lorna was soon attending to her, helping her bathe, showing her how to cut up and make a cloth pad and fetching her clean clothes from the bedroom. At the same time she was giving the poor girl a welcome lesson on the female anatomy.

'You must think me very foolish,' said Mary, as Mrs Jeffreys explained about her monthly cycle. 'I am so sorry to cause you all this bother. I just had no idea what was happening to me. Mother died two years ago now and my education mostly consists of housekeeping and reading books that my father suggests to me. There has been no room for girlish talk or another friend or their mother to teach me about such things.'

'Oh, you poor child,' said Lorna. 'Please don't apologise. It is a very natural thing to be worried when you start your cycle. But all is well now – and if you ever need to ask me anything again,

15

anything at all, please do not hesitate to come and see me. I am very happy to talk to you at any time.'

With that the doctor's wife packed her bag and was gone, leaving Mary feeling as if her life had changed forever, and she was still not quite sure why.

Life went on and Mary toiled from dawn till dusk in the vicarage. She was quite content with her life, however, and loved nothing better than to see everyone round the table of an evening, eating the food she had cooked and laughing and animatedly discussing things going on in the world. She still visited the farm all the time to see Alice, her pet sheep. Mr Cooper suggested they might let her ewe have a lamb of its own one day soon.

The Charles boys were finding their feet now. Brother Joseph had been away in London studying to become an accountant and would come home on his rare leaves full of stories of drinking all night and dancing till dawn. Joseph was the only one of the three boys who had left home, albeit temporarily. Reginald was still at school and studying very hard. He had a rather serious side to his nature and his father had great hopes that he would follow him into the Ministry.

John Charles remembered his own years of study with great fondness, even though he had lost his parents so young. His meeting with Alice had changed his life completely. Not just because of her sunny disposition and warm and caring spirit, but due to her inheritance. Although John vowed he would never touch his wife's money, Alice had persuaded him to buy their first home – a small terraced house in St Albans – as a means of securing their future. When they left to take up residence in the vicarage at Allingham, the couple did not sell the house but found a lodger and his family. And to this day, the rent still provided extra income for the family – a welcome boost to the Reverend Charles's modest stipend.

Alice had turned the sombre vicarage into a house full of light and joy, and the sound of happy children. John Charles missed his wife with every fibre of his being every day of her passing.

Stephen was the youngest of the boys and closest to Mary. There were only three years between them. He shared her love of animals and the two of them spent all their spare time at Coopers Farm. Recognising the lad's love of farming, Ernest Cooper encouraged him to learn all he could about animal husbandry. One day, as they were sitting in the farm's big welcoming kitchen, Stephen announced that he wanted to be a vet when he left school.

When he told his eldest brother of his hopes and dreams, Joseph gave him a friendly punch on the arm and said, 'That's a fine ambition to have, young Stephen, but beware you don't get led astray like me and spend too much time in the pub instead of attending to your studies.'

Their father had just quietly entered the room and overheard this – and they fell silent, waiting for a reproof. But he hardly seemed to see them and just turned and went out again without a word. Mary ran after him to make sure he had everything he needed. She hated to see her father so lost. When she returned to the kitchen, the boys had already forgotten the interruption and were laughing and joking as Joseph continued his tales of life in the big city.

One day, Joseph came home with a friend called Henry Maclean. Henry was in the Army and talked about how there was going to be a war soon, with the Hun, and everyone would have to fight for their country. All the brothers sat round the kitchen table listening to him and drinking beer, which Mary served them. She could only feel dread at the thought of a Europe at war, but the boys were bright-eyed and full of plans to join up. She was secretly entranced by Henry, who seemed different from her brothers somehow. More sophisticated and well-groomed. He had beautiful sandy hair that flopped in his eyes, and he had to keep brushing it out of the way as he talked. His voice was very mellow and he was well-spoken, but not too posh.

When Henry left that night, to return to his regiment, he squeezed Mary's hand and gave her a kiss on the cheek. The spot burned from the touch of his lips. She was so young, but already she felt the catch in her belly, the tightness in her throat – and the pain in her heart.

Henry Maclean was proved right. War did come – and it spread across Europe like a huge black cloud, covering every-thing in a net of death and destruction. Hundreds of thousands of lives were lost. Stephen Charles was killed in battle, blown up in a German attack on his regiment, three months after he arrived in Passchendaele. Joseph somehow managed to survive but came home a broken man. The carnage he had witnessed left him shell-shocked and staring into a bottle of whisky. Reginald took all the pain and suffering as a sign that he should follow his calling and enter the Church – much to the delight of his father. The Reverend John Charles went straight to his wife's grave to share the good news with her.

Although devastated by the news of Stephen's death, John had somehow found a new strength during the war. He had worked tirelessly, travelling from village to village to take serv-ices in times of need; many of the clergy had joined up to provide spiritual support for the soldiers and to work with the wounded. Often with Mary at his side, Reverend Charles would seek out bereaved families and offer his help and comfort.

Mary herself felt that she had been pretty much deserted by everyone. She mourned her brother's death and prayed for his soul to that same God who had taken her beloved mother from her. She shed many bitter tears. But life had to go on and there was so much to do and so many people in need that she had to push her own hurt to the back of her mind and just get on with life. She worked with the Red Cross, helping to care for wounded soldiers, and she also taught classes in the village school when necessary. She grew up very quickly, as did so many young people at that time.

One summer evening in 1919, Mary was picking strawberries in the garden when she heard a motor car. This was a rare occurrence. She knew no one who owned a car except the doctor. She ran out to the front of the house and saw Joseph, looking very much the worse for wear, slumped in the front passenger seat of a Bentley. At the wheel was Henry Maclean. He looked just the same as always, if a little tired and lined around the eyes. Mary's heart skipped a beat. Joseph stumbled out of the car and staggered up the garden path, waving his arms in the air and attempting to sing 'It's a Long Way to Tipperary'.

'Joseph, calm down! What are you doing here? Whose car is that?' she asked, dancing excitedly round the two young men as they walked into the house.

'Got any of that homemade sloe gin, Mary?' Joseph hiccupped and fell into the nearest chair.

'I think you have already had quite enough,' she retorted.

'Oh, come on, old girl, don't be such a killjoy. Poor Henry here needs a drink. He has fought a war, for God's sake!'

Mary turned to Henry, who was standing in the doorway with his hat in his hand looking rather bemused.

'I am so awfully sorry,' she said shyly. 'Please do come and sit down. Of course I will fetch you a drink, and some food maybe? You look like you could do with a good meal inside you.'

'That would certainly be very welcome. Thank you, Mary.' He gave her a huge smile and her legs went quite wobbly.

An hour later, Henry and Mary were tucking into homemade

19

soup and bread and cheese, followed by bowls of strawberries just picked from the garden.

'Oh my God, this is heaven,' said Henry through mouthfuls of food. Joseph was sprawled on the sofa now, practically asleep. He was red-eyed and unshaven and stank of whisky.

'I have made a bed up for you in Stephen's room. If you don't mind, that is, sleeping in his room because he . . .' Mary stopped and felt the tears fill her eyes. She hurriedly left the room and went into the kitchen to compose herself. She was leaning on the sink wiping away her tears with her apron when Henry came to find her.

'Please don't worry,' he said gently. 'It is so hard for everyone. We have lost so many of our friends and loved ones. Joe only gets drunk because he is grieving so much.'

Mary looked into Henry's eyes and could see the pain. 'Was it very bad?' she whispered. Henry didn't answer for a long moment and seemed to be fighting with himself for control.

'Yes,' was all he said, and then he took her in his arms and kissed her. Long and hard. Needing to feel her softness, her goodness and her innocence.

They stood absolutely still, holding each other. Mary wanted the moment to last forever, but it was broken by the sound of Joseph's snores from the other room.

'We'd better get him into bed,' she said, gently breaking away from Henry's arms. 'Would you be kind enough to help me?'

'Of course, come on.' Henry led the way and the two of them hauled Joseph off the sofa and somehow managed to push and heave him upstairs to his room, where Henry virtually threw him onto the bed. Joseph moaned and turned on his side and was fast asleep again before they had reached the door. They laughed and turned to go downstairs. A moment held between them. What now?

There was a bang from the front door downstairs and the

Reverend Charles called out, 'Hello? Anybody home? Mary, where are you?'

Mary quickly moved away and went to the top of the stairs, calling out, 'I am here, Father. Henry and I have been putting Joe to bed.' She ran down to give her father a hug and turned to indicate Henry as he came down to join them.

'Hello, my boy, good to see you home safe and sound,' the minister said. 'Terrible business – thank God it is all over at last. Are you staying the night? Has Mary fed you?'

'Mary has done us proud in every way, sir. She has kindly offered me a bed, and if you will excuse me, I will retire to it now. It has been a long day. Goodnight, Mary, and thank you for everything. Goodnight, sir.' He turned to go up the stairs and Mary put her hand on his arm.

'Wait, let me get you a towel.' She went to fetch it and her father moved off to the kitchen in search of his supper.

Mary came back with a clean towel and handed it to Henry, her eyes never leaving his face.

'Thank you.' He leaned in and softly kissed her on the lips before turning slowly and climbing the stairs. He might have been going to the moon. Mary felt so bereft. What could she do to keep him close?

'My dear, have you got my dinner ready?'

'Coming, Father,' came her reply.

After he had finished his supper, John Charles left the table, kissed his daughter goodnight, and retired to his study, where he shut the door.

Mary cleared away the dishes and went out into the back garden. It was a beautiful summer's night. The sky was so clear she could see every single star.

'Twinkle, twinkle little star ...' Mary whispered to herself and she looked up at the window of Stephen's bedroom, as if she could transport herself to where Henry lay asleep. At the thought of him, a tremor ran through her entire body. She felt as if she was on fire. What was happening to her?

Sensing movement behind her, she turned – straight into Henry's arms. He held her very close and she could smell him. Touch his skin with her lips. She caught her breath and tried to look at him but that meant pulling away, and she didn't want to do that. She wanted to stay close to him forever. Oh, but what about her father? She let out a little gasp of fright.

'What is it?' Henry asked.

'My father is in his study. He must not see me this way.'

'He just went to bed. I heard his door shut. I was lying awake thinking of you. I couldn't sleep, Mary. I had to hold you once again.'

Henry took her chin in his hand and slowly pressed his lips to hers. Oh so gently, did his tongue prise her lips apart, and play against her teeth. Oh so gently, did his tongue go deeper, teasing her tongue to respond. She seemed to be melting into his arms her body pressed into his, as he lifted her up in his arms and carried her towards the little summerhouse at the bottom of the garden. Never letting his lips leave hers for a moment, he lowered her onto the garden seat and started to unbutton her dress. Mary could feel nothing but the beating of her heart and a sound like rushing water in her head.

As he kissed her, Henry's hand moved down to touch her breast and then her nipple. He teased it between his fingers, making it hard, and Mary let out a moan of pleasure. Could anything be more wonderful than this? Henry had lifted her dress now and was exploring beneath it. He ran his fingers, feather light, up the inside of her thigh, pausing to stroke the soft skin above her stocking top. Her body jerked involuntarily as he found her secret place. She could not control the waves of ecstasy and opened herself to his fingers as they gently pushed into her warm moist self. With this exquisite sensation, her head lost the battle for logic or reason; her innocent young body responded naturally to his touch, to his closeness, and her very being demanded to be satisfied.

Her legs fell open to take Henry's body between her thighs. Her hands instinctively found his hard erect penis and fondled it. The anticipation was unbearable. She was gasping with need. And suddenly he was inside her, pushing urgently into her warmth and wetness. There was no pain, just the pleasure of being full up with his manhood. He moved and she moved with him. It was so natural, both these young bodies wanting affirmation of life after so much death. As their passion grew, their lovemaking became more intense and he penetrated deep and hard into her, touching her to the core. She followed his rhythm, and felt him spurt into her, her muscles clasping him as if her life depended on it. She let out a cry of pure joy and held him to her until they were spent. He looked down at her and smiled to reassure her all was well. She took his face in her hands and kissed every inch of it, laughing and crying all at once.

Eventually, Henry got up and dressed himself, then helped Mary gather herself together. They did not speak a word as they walked back to the house, under the starry sky, holding hands. Henry kissed her lightly at the kitchen door and went to his room. Mary stood at the kitchen sink drinking a cup of water and feeling every bone and muscle in her body tingle. This was what it felt like to be alive, she knew it! She wanted it to last forever.

But it was not to be. The next morning, when Mary woke up, Henry had gone. Joseph explained to her that he had made his apologies, but said he had to drive back to London to attend a job interview with a City bank. He sent his thanks to Mary for everything, and hoped they would all meet again soon. Mary had to run out of the room, so as not to give herself away. She raced into the garden and was violently sick under a hedge. A terrible blackness swept over her as she seemed to understand her fate.

Three months later, she was sat in front of Dr Jeffreys, white-faced and trembling, as he gave her the results of her night of passion. A baby, due to be born in the spring. Mary left the surgery in a daze. Despite the warm summer sunshine she was shivering and her legs felt weak; she had to sit down on the bench outside the doctor's house.

'Hello, Mary. Are you feeling all right, dear?' Lorna Jeffreys was looking down at her. The doctor's wife remembered so clearly their shared secret of all those years ago – Mary's ignorance of her body. Now she could see the naked shame in the young woman's eyes and her heart went out to her.

Putting her arms round her and lifting her up, Lorna said quietly, 'Come on, let's go and have a cup of tea, shall we?' She led Mary round the side of the house to the living quarters at the back of the surgery.

Neither woman spoke until they were sitting at the kitchen table with their tea in front of them.

Lorna broke the silence: 'Do you remember all those years ago, when I said that if ever there was anything I could do to help, you should call on me?'

Mary sighed deeply and searched Mrs Jeffreys' face. The woman had obviously guessed what was wrong, but there was no reprimand in her voice. No disapproval in her gaze. Mary started to cry. She felt so alone and so ashamed. What could she do? She was a fallen woman. This news would surely kill her father.

Charles had grown quite frail in the last few months, so much so that they had called Reginald down from his Theological College in Hendon in North London. The family hoped that it might be possible for Reginald to do his curate training with his father, at St James' Church in Allingham. The Reverend John Charles was highly regarded in the Diocese, and the Bishop of St Albans was a close friend. The proposal had been discussed, and as things in the local parishes were still a little disordered since the war ended, it was agreed that John Charles could do with the help, and to have his son close by was the best thing to do for all concerned.

It was a comfort to think that her father would soon have Reg to support him. As Mary's tears slowly subsided, she was able to drink her tea and think more clearly.

'Is there anything I can do to help you?' asked Lorna, taking Mary's hand.

'No, not really. But thank you for all your kindness to me. I don't deserve it.' Mary stood up and made for the door. Turning, she told Mrs Jeffreys, 'I am going to talk to my brother Reginald; he will know what to do for the best. Thank you again. Goodbye.'

Mary walked home, consumed with her guilt and shame and fear. Her father must never find out. How could he ever forgive her? She thought of her dear mother and the tears sprang afresh. How could she have been so foolish? Reg would be coming home in the next few days to make arrangements for his training, and until then, she would have to keep her own counsel.

On reaching the vicarage, Mary went straight to her bed, telling her father that she had a headache. She hated to tell him a lie but needs must. Yet another sin to add to her long list. Before getting into bed, Mary prayed to her mother and begged her forgiveness. She held her prayer book to her heart and fell asleep with it in her hands.

'It's all right, I will help you. We will get through this together,' Reginald told his sister as he handed her a cup of tea; he and Mary were sitting in the front parlour. The vicarage was empty as John Charles had gone to visit a sick parishioner. Mary had poured out her story to her brother and was now once again collapsed in tears in her seat.

Although Reginald had always been the most serious of the

brothers, he possessed a very kind heart. Deep down, there was a romantic streak inside him and he was currently in the throes of falling in love, thanks to a meeting with a girl called Leonora Matheson, who came to his college for Bible Studies. But now was not the time to confess these feelings to his poor dear sister.

'Leave things with me and let me have a think,' he said, handing Mary a large handkerchief so she could blow her nose. 'I have an idea already that could be a solution but I need to find out more. Take heart, dear Mary. God will find a way and He will forgive you. Now stop crying and go and make yourself busy.'

Mary did as she was told, but nothing could take away her deep shame and sense of foreboding. What did life have in store for her now, she wondered.

Chapter Two

Two weeks later, Mary had a gentleman caller named Alfred Hughes. Alfred was in Insurance and lived in St Albans. He was a few years older than Reginald, but they had gone to school together and kept in touch through a mutual love of history. Living near an historical town like St Albans had given both men a keen sense of the city's architectural gems, and its links with days gone by, in particular the period of Roman occupation. Over the years they had met up for a drink, and a discussion, and even visited other local areas of interest. Alfred had never married, and although a good deal older than Mary, Reginald felt that the man would make a suitable husband for his sister. She in turn would be a dutiful and caring wife.

He persuaded Alfred to meet his sister, having first gathered his courage to explain the rather unusual circumstances. Reginald had decided to persuade Alfred with the promise of the deeds to the terraced house that his father still owned in St Albans. He had discussed this with Joseph, of course, who was also a beneficiary of their father's will and would be losing his share of the sale of the house if this arrangement were to go forward.

'So you and I would both give up our inheritance, then?' said Joseph, sitting in the Wheatsheaf one night with his brother.

'Yes, that would be the idea. I appreciate it is a lot to ask, Joe, but we cannot let Mary down. She is a good girl, and has made a terrible mistake that will haunt her for the rest of her life. You make a good living as an accountant – well, you would, if you didn't pour it all down your throat,' he added.

'Yes, yes, all right, no need to start the lecture,' Joseph replied irritably, ordering another pint. 'But what will you tell Father?'

Reginald had thought long and hard about this, and prayed for guidance. His father was not a well man and they all knew he was not long for this world. Reg had discussed the issue with Alfred, who was quite happy to wait for things to take their natural course. Once John Charles passed away, and the will was dealt with, the two brothers would sign an agreement handing the deeds over to Alfred. Reginald had applied to take over his father's parish, so he would be able to continue to live in the vicarage. This was the only way they could save their dear sister from shame and destitution.

When Mary was presented with the plan she was horrified and appalled, but as Reginald made clear to her, she really did not have any other options. She prayed and prayed for God to give her another way out, but His silence was deafening. So eventually, she agreed to marry Alfred Hughes.

The couple were married by Mary's father in St James's Church. Shortly after the ceremony, the newlyweds moved to St Albans, and John Charles found that he missed his daughter's quiet presence deeply. Mrs Edge's own daughter now came in to 'do' for him as her mother was suffering with arthritis in her hands.

Within weeks the Reverend had faded in body and soul; he died in his sleep shortly before Christmas 1919. The village all turned out for his funeral, and Alfred and Mary joined Reginald and Joseph at the graveside. It was a bitterly cold day, which was just as well, as Mary was bundled up in a huge heavy coat and long scarf and shawl. No one knew she was five months' pregnant. The couple excused themselves from the wake afterwards, as Alfred had to return to St Albans for a business meeting that could not be avoided.

The two brothers and their sister said their goodbyes outside the church. Joseph held Mary tight and whispered, 'Keep your spirits up, girl. It will all come right in the end. Alfred is not such a bad fellow, and as for that bounder Henry Maclean, I've a mind to give him a damn good hiding next time I see him.'

Mary said immediately, 'No! Please, Joe, promise me you will never mention any of this to Henry. It is my sin, my problem. Please – I am begging you!'

Joseph could feel her hand gripping his arm; could see the panic in her eyes. 'Calm down, I will not do anything, if that is your wish. Please try and make the best of things, dear Mary. Look after yourself.' As the young man turned away, sadness overwhelmed him. He had lost a mother, a father – and now his sister. Life was just so hard. No wonder he needed a drink from time to time.

Reginald organised the transfer of the deeds on the house in St Albans, and Alfred and Mary set up home. Their baby daughter, Jane, was born in April 1920 and was christened by her uncle, the Reverend Reginald Charles in St James's Church. If anyone in the village had cared to count the months, they might have been surprised. But Mary was too well loved in Allingham for anyone to question her integrity.

Mary spent the first few months of her pregnancy trying to make amends for her sins. She knelt in the cathedral in St Albans, clasping her prayer book, beseeching her mother and God to forgive her. The majesty of the enormous cathedral seemed to add to the enormity of her transgression. Thoughts of Henry would creep into her head but she would push them away, frantically attempting to purge him from her mind and body. She could hardly bear to look at herself in the mirror, and as her belly grew, so did her sense of panic. What would happen to her? Would she be able to love this baby? It had been conceived in sin. *Her* sin. The poor child would be damned by her transgressions. What kind of life could she make for it?

Her brother Reg tried to calm her fears, and reassure her that God was kind and forgiving, but she would not listen. Once again, she felt so alone. Even her pet lamb had died of old age now. She thought about the day it was born and how awful it had been to watch the mother butt her baby and walk away. Would she want to abandon her child like that? Could she love the child despite the fact that Henry had betrayed her? She must love the baby. She *must*. What else could she do? Alfred had been kind enough to marry her and save the family name. Her dear father had been spared the horror of her disgrace and had died peacefully. God rest his soul. She hoped her parents had finally been reunited.

As for Alfred, he was attentive, but kept his distance. He had little understanding of how he should behave towards his bride, who was pregnant before his wedding night with another man's child. He pushed these thoughts to the back of his head, and concentrated on the positive side of the arrangement. Mary was a good and hardworking wife, and she had come with a considerable dowry, which meant that he would eventually reap his rewards on earth as well as in heaven. Her domestic abilities were so good that they saved money on a housekeeper's wages ... and once the baby was born, Alfred decided, he would teach her the other wifely duties that were owed to him.

Mary was able to keep Alfred at bay until Jane was born, but then once she had recovered from the birth, he demanded his conjugal rights. He was a brusque man who did not express emotion easily, but he was not unkind, and did seem to accept that for Mary, this marriage was going to be a struggle. She kept a good home and was an excellent cook, and Mary herself had hoped this would suffice to keep him happy. However, one evening after she had put the baby to sleep and was preparing to retire herself, she was dismayed to find Alfred waiting for her at the top of the stairs with a glass of sherry in each hand.

'I thought we might celebrate the birth of your – *our* – daughter.' He handed her a glass and led her towards their bedroom, where they had twin beds.

'My dear Mary,' he went on, 'I hope I have shown some degree of sensitivity towards you. However, I am a man, and your husband, and would hope we may begin to embark on full and proper marital relations very soon.' He threw back his glass of sherry then grabbed her hand and drew her to him as he sat down on the edge of the bed.

Mary had dreaded this moment, but she had known it must come, and was pragmatic enough to realise that it had to be dealt with sooner or later. She drank her sherry and felt the warm liquid trickle down the back of her throat. Sadly, the sweet wine was not enough to lubricate the tightness in her throat, never mind any other part of her.

Alfred took her hand and placed it on the buttons of his fly. 'Perhaps you would do the honours, my dear,' he said thickly.

Mary could hardly bear to look him in the face as she fumbled with the buttons, only too aware that each time her fingers grasped at the buttons they rubbed against his manhood. He was getting hard very quickly, and his breath was now coming in gasps. He pulled at her dress and then tried to lift her skirt. She felt herself go rigid. How was she going to get through this? She stepped further away to take off her clothes. At least she could have the dignity of undressing herself without him pawing her. Watching her undress aroused him even more, and

31

he struggled to get out of his trousers and long johns, only to realise he still had his boots on. Cursing under his breath, he sat down again on the bed like a naughty schoolboy, to untie his laces. Mary thought it would have been comical, were it not so tragic.

She walked round to the other side of the bed and lay down naked beside him. Trying to keep her breathing calm and even, she waited for him to free himself from his clothes. He turned to look at her, and what he saw must have pleased him because his flagging manhood revived with a vengeance; he climbed upon her and proceeded to force entry. She was completely dry and it was quickly apparent that he had no idea what to do except to keep battering at the door. She sat up and said, 'Please, Alfred, have a little patience. This is not going to work.'

His apparent lack of success was making him angry.

'Well, that's rich. You could do it with some man you hardly knew, and do it enough to get pregnant, but you can't do it with your lawful husband. Well, we will see about that, won't we, my dear?' And before she could get away, he pinned her to the bed and entered her brutally. She let out a yell of pain which seemed to inflame him more, and he began to thrust up inside her.

Mary desperately tried to think of something else to take away the horror on top of her. Oh God, how different it had been with Henry. Suddenly, she seemed to lift herself above the bed. It was as if she was floating above the terrible scene below her. She could feel Henry inside her, feel her body relax and open up to him. The pain became less and less as her body took over and released her mind from the torture. Gradually she felt herself floating back into herself, becoming aware of the weight of Alfred's body on top of her but not hurting any more. He was withdrawing. Oh thank God! The blessed relief!

He sat on the edge of the bed for a few moments, and

seemed to gather himself together. Then he went to the bath-room. Mary lay with her eyes closed, waiting for him to finish and go to his bed. Instead, he went downstairs and she heard the living-room door close. She tiptoed to the bathroom and washed herself, surprised that she did not feel more sore than she did, after all his pushing and shoving. But thank God there did not seem to be any damage. She went to check on baby Jane, who was fast asleep, with her little fingers clutching the blanket. How beautiful was her baby! She would die for her. Any sacrifice was worth it for her child's safety and happiness.

She crept back into bed and fell asleep immediately.

In the morning, Mary rose early, fed Jane and then prepared breakfast for Alfred as usual. He had the same breakfast every morning: a lightly poached egg on toast, with another slice of toast and butter and marmalade to follow, and two cups of tea. His paper was delivered, and he folded it very neatly into a quarter, in order to read it while he ate his breakfast. This morn-ing, Alfred came downstairs at eight o'clock on the dot as he always did. He nodded a greeting, but ate in silence and read his paper. He then picked up his briefcase and his umbrella, and stood in the hall in front of a tallboy with a mirror. Here, as every morning, Mary took a clothes brush made in the shape of a woodpecker and brushed his overcoat.

This was all done in complete silence, then suddenly, just as he was about to open the front door, Alfred turned to Mary and said, 'Thank you,' and kissed her on the cheek!

From that day, the couple managed an uneasy truce. Mary realised she owed Alfred a good deal and did her utmost to be a loving and loyal wife. As far as the physical side was con-cerned, she did what she had to do with good grace. Her baby was all the incentive she needed.

Then one day she fell pregnant again, and nine months later gave birth to another girl. They called her Pamela after Alfred's late mother. He was beside himself with pride and joy and became obsessed with his daughter. Mary was pleased that her husband was happy, but concerned for her own daughter's place in the family. Unfortunately, it would always be Pamela first.

As she grew up, the child was spoiled rotten by her father, and learned that she could get away with being rather cruel and manipulative towards Jane. She made the older girl run errands for her, right from when she was tiny, and ensured that Jane took the blame for any pranks that she instigated if they went wrong. Despite this, Jane adored her sister. Right from the start, Pamela was the leader even though she was the younger. Mary would watch the two little girls in the garden as they played. Pamela would dress them up as nurses and doctors – herself as the doctor naturally – and would demand that Jane do everything her way. Dear Jane would trot behind her sister, happy as Larry.

In fact, Jane loved pretending to be a nurse so much that Mary made her a proper costume so she could act out her fantasy. She would line up her dolls and spend hours performing operations on them. Alfred had bought Pamela a beautiful china doll one year for her birthday. It was so delicate, with clear blue eyes and a pink porcelain complexion. Pamela was not at all interested in the doll, but one day while Jane was playing with her toys, Pamela brought the doll down to the kitchen.

'Do be careful with that doll or you will break it,' said Mary, rolling out the pastry for an apple pie.

'Oh, it's fine, Ma, don't fret so,' her daughter said airily. 'Anyway, Jane can mend her if she breaks. She is such a good nurse!' Pamela laughed and skipped off with her doll to look for Jane. She found her in the dining room under the table.

'What are you doing under there?' Pamela asked. 'My doll is very ill and I need you to make her better.' She knelt down and handed Jane her doll.

Taking the patient, Jane laid her on the carpet and started to examine her. Pamela watched for a few minutes and then got bored.

'Oh, never mind, Jane, give her back to me. I don't want to play this game.' Pamela bent to snatch the doll back, and as she pulled it from under the table, she hit its china head on the wooden edge, and immediately it cracked into several pieces.

'Now look what you've done, you naughty girl!' screamed Pamela. 'You've broken my doll. Ma, Jane has broken my doll!' And she ran into the kitchen.

Jane crawled across and gathered up the broken pieces of china. The doll looked so strange, as the top half of her head was still intact and she seemed to be staring at Jane with her big blue eyes. Jane laid the doll on a makeshift bed that she had created under the table, covered her with a blanket, and gave her some pretend medicine with a teaspoon. Then she put the pieces of the doll's face back together again like a jigsaw. All the while she talked to the doll like a patient.

Mary came in with Pamela, who was still snivelling.

'What has happened?' Mary asked her daughter. 'Did you break Pamela's dolly?'

'No,' came the reply. 'Pamela knocked its head on the table by accident but I have made her better. Look.' She showed her mother the doll, lying there with its face all lopsided but basically intact.

'She looks horrible,' cried Pamela. 'I hate you, Jane! You have broken my dolly and now she looks horrible and ugly just like you!' She ran off upstairs.

'I didn't break her, Mummy, really I didn't. It was an accident but I am a good nurse and I will make her better.'

'I am sure you will, dear,' Mary sighed. 'Come on, love, let's go and find some stronger medicine for the doll.' She took Jane's hand and led her into the kitchen to look for some glue.

They spent the next hour painstakingly putting the doll's face back together. Fortunately, the china had broken in quite large pieces so it was much easier to stick. Of course, they could do nothing to hide the cracks.

Jane took the doll upstairs to Pamela, who had all but forgotten the whole incident by now. When she saw the doll she just pushed it away, saying, 'Oh, I don't want it now. It's ugly and broken. You can keep it.'

When Alfred came home that night, Mary waited for the inevitable reprisal from him. Pamela ran to hug him at the door and to lead him into the parlour for his tea. It was her habit to babble away at him, taking his hat and coat which she dragged across to her mother. Then she would sit on his knee and tell him the day's adventures.

Today, sure enough, it was not long before she said, 'Jane broke my china doll today, Daddy.' Alfred looked up to see his elder daughter standing in the doorway holding the broken doll. Before he could speak, Jane walked up to them and held out the doll wrapped in a blanket.

'No, I didn't. It was an accident and I made the doll better. Look. Pamela doesn't want the doll now, so I will look after her until she is better. That is a good thing to do, isn't it, Daddy?'

Alfred looked up at Mary and realised the truth. The little girl was innocent. He would not gain anything by being angry with Jane. However, he was not going to be angry with his darling Pammie. Standing up, he said, 'Yes, Jane. You look after the doll. Now come on, sweetheart, show me where my tea is and be a good girl for your dad.' He took Pamela's hand and she skipped off with him through the door, turning briefly to stick her tongue out at Jane and Mary.

Jane said solemnly, 'Accidents do happen, don't they, Mummy? Pamela was naughty to say I hurt her doll. Why does she tell fibs sometimes?'

'I don't know, dear,' answered Mary, giving her a hug. 'But don't worry, she loves you very much, and so do I and Daddy. Now come and have your tea.'

That was the pattern of their daily lives. Mary spent most of her time keeping Alfred happy in all ways conjugal, while at the same time standing guard between her two daughters in an attempt to keep Pamela from completely destroying Jane. And yet the two girls seemed to love each other in a strange way. Perhaps because they were both so different, they got on.

In 1930 Alfred decided he wanted to move out into the countryside. Mary was happy to comply as the girls were growing up fast, and it would be nice to have a larger house with an extra bedroom. After much deliberation Alfred found a charming four-bedroom cottage just a few miles from the centre of St Albans, near a lovely old town called Redbourn. The house was in a tiny hamlet called Burslet, surrounded by glorious countryside. There was a bus service to St Albans and a very good village school and a secondary school further up the road on the way to Berkhamsted.

The girls were thrilled, and Jane especially was happy, because she could go and visit the local farm and see the animals, just as her mother had done when she was young.

Jane grew into a very practical girl while Pamela longed for a life she had only read about in magazines. Although Jane would tease her about this, and try to bring her back down to earth, she would still help Pam by making dresses for her and doing her hair in the latest styles. Pamela was ambitious, and all through school she chafed at the bit, wanting to leave as soon as she could and go to London. Alfred was torn between not wanting to lose her and his pride in his daughter's ambitions. He wanted the best for her.

'But at what cost?' Mary would say.

Jane did well at school, and by the time she was fifteen in

1935 she had made her mind up that she wanted to train as a nurse. She wasn't at all envious of her younger sister's dreams for the future. Pamela had announced that she wanted to be a dancer, and after weeks of badgering her mother and getting nowhere, the girl went to Alfred, who gave in as usual and agreed to pay for tuition at the local dancing school in St Albans. However, it soon became clear that Pamela did not have the necessary talent or dedication. She couldn't be bothered to practise, and as time went on, her appetite increased – to the point at which Miss Bunce of the Bunce Academy for Dance had to tell Mary that she really did not feel that Pamela was cut out to be a dancer.

'Too big, dearie,' she whispered behind her hand.

Too big she may have been for the dance, but Pamela's figure was already attracting the attention of the local boys, and attention was Pamela's stock in trade. Boys became top of her list.

Jane, meanwhile, had met a boy when she was sixteen. George Lee was the same age as her and a farmer's son. His father, Donald Lee, ran the Malthouse Farm a few hundred acres just up the road on the outskirts of Burslet. Jane had been going there since she was a little girl when they first arrived in their new home, but she paid little attention to George; she was much more interested in the piglets and lambs. Both children went to the same school and became firm friends on the bus home. It was good to have someone to walk with from the bus stop on a cold dark night.

Jane even got a Saturday job, working with George's father on the milk round. She would get up before daylight, and make her way to the farm, where she'd find Donald in the cowsheds milking his herd of Jersey cows. They were such beautiful docile creatures with huge brown eyes, and were renowned for producing the creamiest milk and thickest cream on the market. Jane would help bottle it up and stamp the silver and red tops on, or the gold tops, and stack the crates on the cart. Then Donald and she would set off in the pony-cart to deliver the milk.

The first time she went to leave milk on someone's doorstep she was chased by a very fierce-looking sheep dog. She ran out of the garden gate screaming at the top of her voice. Mr Lee was killing himself laughing and pointed to a sign that said *Beware of the Dog.*

'Why didn't you tell me!' exclaimed Jane. 'I could have been eaten alive!'

'No, I know that dog – he is all bark. You don't really think I would have let you go in there if you were going to get bitten, do you? I just wanted to show you that you need to be on your guard when going to folks' houses.' Donald chuckled again and said, 'Let's face it – you won't do that again in a hurry, will you?'

Jane became like one of the family, so by the time she was sixteen and a schoolfriend suggested that George was her boyfriend she shrugged it off with, 'Oh no, it's not like that. I am not in love or anything.' She based this on her knowledge of love and passion as she read it in books like *Wuthering Heights* or *Jane Eyre.* There was no room for smouldering passion in her life. She and George were quite simply 'best friends'. When Pamela went on about all the shenanigans in the back row of the cinema, Jane really couldn't see what all the fuss was about. She tried to talk to her mother about it but Mary seemed too embarrassed to divulge anything of note. When Jane told Pamela that she had asked their mother about sex, her younger sister hooted with laughter.

'For goodness' sake, Janie! How could you ask Ma? She knows nothing.'

'Well, she must know something, because we were born,' replied Jane rather observantly.

'Well, yes I know, so that proves they did it twice. But she and Father have separate beds, don't they? And have you ever seen them kissing? Ugh, what a thought!' and she screwed up her face. 'You wait and see, Jane, by the time we are old enough to have sex, things will be like they are in Hollywood.' Pamela launched into a song that was very popular at that moment on the wireless, called 'Let's Do It'. Jane burst out laughing, it was so cheeky. Certainly, Pamela was very different from herself and she was quite happy to let those differences be. She and George would stay friends forever, she hoped.

Chapter Three

By 1937 there was great unease in England, as people followed the rise of the Third Reich in Germany. Alfred Hughes said things were looking grim, and that business would suffer. War was on its way, he predicted, but luckily for him he was now too old for conscription.

Jane had been working at the local hospital gaining valuable experience and saving up to enrol at one of the major Schools of Nursing in London. But Mary was so concerned about the possibility of war, she begged Jane to stay home for the time being. The girl was happy to oblige. She loved her work at the hospital, and her relationship with George had blossomed into love. The young couple were well and truly stepping out, and both sets of parents gave them their blessing.

Pamela was quite a different matter. Ever since childhood she had had ideas above her station. Mary used to try to drum some common sense into her, but then Alfred would come along and fill the girl's head again with all sorts of fancy ideas. Then one day, one of Alfred's colleagues at work suggested there might be a job going for a well-brought-up young lady in an office in Barnet, which was only just up the road really, a few miles from Burslet. The company was a client of theirs, and dealt with property and construction. The MD, Myles Harrison, was looking for a bright, ambitious young woman to act as his personal assistant. Well, it might not be the West End of London, but as far as Pamela was concerned it was a move in the right direction. With no serious experience, and a complete lack of typing ability, she amazed everyone by landing the job.

Myles Harrison had been bowled over by Pamela's self-assurance and confidence. He also found her extremely attractive – and the feeling was mutual. The two of them recognised like souls and fell in love. Pamela was canny enough to keep the relationship under wraps, for the time being at any rate. She was given a room above the offices where she lived during the week, and she went home at weekends. This changed within six months to a rather nifty one-bedroom apartment, which she and Myles nicknamed the 'love nest'. Needless to say, Alfred and Mary had no idea what was going on.

The affaire went on for nearly two years, until war with Germany was declared and everything changed. Myles went and joined the Navy, and was away for nearly four years, until he returned with his legs shot to pieces by a torpedo attack on his ship. Pamela had earned her stripes throughout this time by holding the fort in the Barnet office, and learning the construction industry inside out. Jane and George faced other problems. George had applied to enlist, against all Jane's entreaties, only to discover that he had a weak heart. Jane was relieved, but he was devastated.

'I wanted to fight this war,' he said, as they sat at the table with the letter from the Army in front of him.

'I know you did, but you and your family will be doing your bit on the farm, won't you? Remember, an army marches on its stomach.' Jane's relief soon turned to a nagging worry at the back of her mind about George's heart problem. How serious was it? Would it affect them getting married maybe? Having children? *One thing at a time*, she told herself. *Let's get through this damn war first.*

Mary was distressed by the idea of another war in her lifetime. All the loss and heartache that she and her family had endured in the Great War had seemed more than enough to bear. Alfred was determined to support the war effort in any way he could. Even though he was too old for service, he joined the Reserves and loved every minute of it. Mary worked on the farm with Donald and Louise Lee. She was back where she belonged, working with the animals and on the land. The farm and its crops were invaluable to the war effort. Jane worked in the hospital and on the farm too, whenever she could. Although times were hard, they had a wonderful sense of community around them.

Mary's big worry was for Pamela, who was up there in Barnet. Stories of bombs and the Blitz gave her many sleepless nights. But on the odd occasion when her daughter did deign to visit, she was adamant that she would not return to Burslet. She hinted to her mother that she and Myles were a couple, and that she was waiting for him to return from the war. Then in 1941 she turned up on the doorstep with her fiancé. Myles Harrison had proposed and she had accepted and had come to ask for her parents' blessing. They were to be married as soon as possible, as Myles had to return to his ship.

Mary and Alfred were rather taken aback, and slightly in awe of the rather suave gentleman in their front room.

'I am sorry it is such a fleeting visit,' explained Myles, 'but needs must in times of war. You are more than welcome to come and join us for a glass of champagne at the Ritz, but I fear it might be too dangerous for you. Perhaps we can have a family celebration when this god-awful war is over.' He threw a smile around the room, scooped up his bride-to-be and they were gone before anyone could utter a word.

Alfred was distraught. To lose his baby, his little girl, was one thing – but to lose her to a smooth-talking sailor was another. Mary tried to calm him, but she was secretly a bit shocked at how Pamela had turned out. There was a veneer about her. A hard gloss, and it wasn't just the red nails, or the immaculately coiffed hair. Her daughter seemed to be dancing with the devil, in more ways than one.

Time passed . . . they rarely heard from Pamela now she was a married woman, although they always worried about her . . . and then a letter arrived in the summer of 1944, begging Jane to come to London. Pamela had given birth to a little girl, but the child had been born prematurely and was still being cared for in a private clinic. Pamela desperately needed someone to help her cope, and the only person she really trusted was Jane.

The latter knew she had no choice but to answer her sister's cry for help.

That night she met George in the Scarecrow public house and explained that she would be going away for a few weeks. She didn't dare say 'months', but in fact had no idea how long she would need to stay with her sister and niece. George was not best pleased, but he loved Jane very much – probably more than she realised, if truth be told. He had been intending to ask her to marry him in the near future. The war had caused havoc in everybody's lives, and dreams were lost every single day. But life was so precious – and if you were spared, and had something or someone you cared about, George thought, then you learned to hang on to them. The idea of his Jane being up amidst the perils of war-damaged London filled the young man with horror.

That night in the pub, they sat in the snug holding hands and stealing a kiss. When she had first met George, Jane had been far too young to think about him sexually. They were best friends for ages. She just knew he was kind and gentle and trustworthy, and gave her all the affection that Alfred had with-held from her but had lavished on Pamela. As time went on, she instinctively began to feel things were changing between them, until one day George plucked up the courage to kiss her.

It was one night when they were on their way home from the village hall. They had been to a barn dance, and had a whale of a time. They were laughing and joking and stopping to do dance steps along the deserted, moonlit road. George had his arms around Jane's waist and they were twirling round and round, until she begged him to stop before she was sick. George slowly came to a halt, but instead of letting her go, he drew her to him and kissed her on the mouth. She responded – and the kiss developed into a full-blown passionate clinch that left them both gasping for breath.

They walked the rest of the way in silence, busy with their own thoughts. Obviously they both reached the same conclu-sion – about how good it felt – because from that moment, a good deal of kissing went on: whenever the opportunity arose, in fact. But as for actual intercourse, it was never really men-tioned. George did not push the subject, and seemed very happy with the way things were, until the week before Jane had to leave for London. They were at the pub, sitting next to each other outside in the garden as it was such a beautiful summer evening, and Jane was wearing a cotton frock with her legs bare. George suddenly leaned across to Jane and kissed her and ran his hand up her leg under her dress.

'George, stop it! Someone will see us. What are you thinking of?'

'I'm thinking of you and how lovely you are, and how I don't want to lose you up there in London.'

'Oh, don't be so daft. I am going to look after Pam, not have a good time.'

'Well, that's as may be, but you are still lovely, and any man

45

would be glad to have you. What about the bombings? You might get hurt in a raid.'

'Oh, thanks for that, George. Now I really feel better. The war is nearly over and the Jerries are in big trouble everywhere. What's got into you tonight?'

'Nothing.' George took her face in his hands and looked into her eyes. 'I just wanted you to know I love you, Jane Hughes, and when you come back I want us to be married. And so you don't forget me, I want you to wear this.' He brought out a box and handed it to Jane.

She opened it to find a perfect Victorian gold ring, with tiny garnets set in the top, and little seed pearls at each end.

'Oh, George, it is beautiful! Where did you find this?' She took out the ring and held it up.

'It was my gran's, and my mother said I could have it. She knows how I feel about you, and she loves you as well. We all love you, Jane. Will you do me the honour of becoming my wife?'

'Oh yes, George. Nothing would make me happier!' She held out her finger and he slipped on the ring.

They kissed, slowly at first and then more eagerly. Jane pulled him close against her and she could feel his heart beating.

'Now, now, you two, remember where you are. Cool down or I will have to fetch a bucket of water!' The landlord of the Scarecrow was standing in front of them. They sprang apart, embarrassed.

'Sorry, Amos,' George said sheepishly. 'We got carried away. You see, I proposed and Jane accepted: she has agreed to be my wife!'

'Congratulations! Well done, the both of you, that is wonderful news. Let me go and get some sparkling wine to celebrate. It is elderflower, I made it myself and it is delicious.

Just the thing for a celebration. Come on, let's go and tell the wife.'

And with that they all trooped into the snug. An hour later, George and Jane practically stumbled out of the door and made their way home. Jane felt wonderful, and the warm glow that enveloped her was not just due to the wine. She knew that George was a kind and decent man who would take good care of her. She also knew he had another side to him. A passionate and deep side . . . and she wanted more.

'George, hang on a minute. Don't let's go home just yet. Give me another of those kisses like before,' she said daringly.

He stopped and looked at her and his eyes had gone very dark.

'I am not sure we should, Jane. I don't know if I can be trusted to behave like a gentleman after all that wine.' He smiled at her and she felt her heart soar. She felt so good and so wanted and so loved. She moved up close to him.

'Please, just one little kiss,' she whispered, and offered up her lips.

George took her in his arms and kissed her. She could feel his body against hers, so hard. She wanted to melt into him with her own soft body. Wrap herself around him. She could not quite understand what was happening to her. She seemed to be losing control of her limbs. Her stomach was churning and there was a sweet pain between her legs. She tried to pull away and catch her breath.

'Stop a moment, George. What's happening to me? Why am I trembling?' Jane looked at George, who was bent over with his hands on his knees and groaning.

'What's the matter?' she asked, scared. 'Is it your heart? Are you ill? Tell me!'

Suddenly he stood up, and laughed a deep throaty laugh that shook his whole body.

'Jane Hughes, you will do for me, you will. God, I want to make love to you so much! Never mind that you're trembling, I am as hard as a rock and bursting with love. But we are going to wait and do this right my dear, dear love. So come on, no more of this courting tonight, or I will not be so strong the next time. Let's go home.'

So saying, he took her hand and started to run up the lane, with a protesting Jane dragging behind him. That night, alone in her room, Jane relived the kiss and touched herself. She was still warm and wet, and the sweet pain had returned. Well, one thing was for sure, she and George were going to have fun when she got back from London. Jane would miss him, of course, but there was a part of her that was rather excited to be going to London. She had never been, and there was so much she wanted to see. And she couldn't wait to cuddle her baby niece, whose name was Sylvia.

Myles Harrison had spent the first two years of World War Two in the Merchant Navy, during which time he made several trips across the Atlantic to New York. He was young and keen to make money, and dipped in and out of various schemes, one of which proved very lucrative in a bizarre way: the import of bird seed. Wars come and go, but people and their pet budgies remain, and the price of bird seed in England rocketed during the war. Myles would import it from the States at ten cents a bag – and then sell it for a pound a bag. It was rumoured that he then moved on to diamonds.

He had worked his way up through the Navy to the highest level as a Black Cap, where he was in the ultimate position of trust, and could come and go as he pleased. This made smuggling an easy option, with the right contacts and strong nerves. Myles had those in spades. By 1943 he was a wealthy man, and when his ship was torpedoed mid-Atlantic, he was lucky to escape with two broken legs and a pocket full of diamonds. Using them to fund the expansion of his construction business in North London, he then proceeded to clean up in the building trade. His old contacts brought him new contacts, and he quickly became the number one property developer in bomb-stricken London.

After his marriage to Pamela, who had waited for him so patiently and worked so hard to keep his business affairs in order, he bought a beautiful Georgian house in St John's Wood. They moved in to start their married life together.

Pamela was perfect for Myles. He needed a classy, good-looking wife at his side, but had realised very early on that because of his lowly roots, no girl from the upper classes in Britain at that time would consider him as husband material. It was a tight-knit circle, still reliant on old money. However, towards the end of the war, society began to loosen up and it became a question of who you knew, and where you spent your money. Pamela had that peculiar mix of middle-class gentility and good taste. She was bright and eager, and willing to learn. She had proved her worth in those years they spent apart, and then when he was finally invalided out in 1943 she was thrilled to be rewarded with a huge house to run and furnish, with money no object. She had to hold fire until the war was over, but there was plenty to keep her occupied, especially when she unexpectedly fell pregnant. When the baby was born – premature and sickly – she knew she needed help, and the only person who could do that was her sister Jane. She had never been what one would call the maternal type, but in some ways this baby secured her position as Mrs Myles Harrison; in other ways, however, it left her vulnerable to attack from outside predators. And boy, were there predators!

Myles was a very attractive man, and although in the first few months of their marriage he was very attentive, Pamela was quick to spot his roving eye. It was part of the attraction really, to get the man every woman wanted. In those early days she was confident that she could handle him. She was young and sassy and ambitious. Now, however, she was lying in bed with a flabby tummy and inflated leaking breasts, and a sore fanny. This was not attractive. She needed to get back up to speed as soon as possible. Myles had already complained that she looked terrible and should pull herself together; he would not come anywhere near the bedroom. Oh, he adored his daughter and would spend hours watching her in her incubator at the hospital. Pamela could not breastfeed due to the circumstances and as the baby was so poorly at first, the clinic had sent the mother home and kept the baby under observation.

Until now. Very soon, baby Sylvia, as they had decided to call her, was coming home! The nursery was ready, and sister Jane was standing by to help.

Jane had been overwhelmed by the enormous house. She had arrived by train at King's Cross and taken a taxi to St John's Wood. She was surprised how busy the streets were in the city centre. Every now and then, they would pass an underground and she was reminded of the dangers. Big posters reminding you to wear your gas mask. Signs indicating ways into the underground when the sirens went off. As she had come out of the station there was a booth offering information about becoming a volunteer, and Jane had taken a leaflet.

She still wanted to pursue her ambition to become a nurse, whenever this terrible war came to an end. She was twenty-four now and time was rushing by. All along the route, there was evidence of the devastation left by the bombing raids. Poor London had certainly taken a beating. Buildings empty and burned out. Huge potholes in the road, and paving stones sticking out at weird angles. It must be so dangerous in the dark, she thought. Nothing like the country lanes at home. The worst thing that could happen there, in the dark, was to trip over after too many ciders and land in a ditch.

The taxi interrupted her thoughts and pulled up outside a huge gate. The house behind was very imposing, made even more so by the blacked-out windows. It seemed to loom over her almost threateningly. She shrugged off her gloomy thoughts, paid the taxi driver, took a deep breath and rang the bell. She stood there for ages, until finally the door was opened by a rather grumpy-looking man. He was wearing a collarless shirt, waistcoat and black trousers, and his shoes were incredibly shiny.

'Can I help you?' he enquired. Jane thought he was rather like a bad actor who had been given the part of the butler in a comedy play.

'Good afternoon. I am Jane Hughes, Mrs Harrison's sister, and have come to stay and help,' she announced herself. 'I assume you have been expecting me?'

'Of course we have, dear Jane,' came a deep baritone voice from behind the door. 'Bert, open wide the door and let our sister in.'

Myles Harrison stepped forward and proffered his arm. Jane took it and allowed herself to be led into the house. The entrance hall was magnificent. There was a huge domed ceiling, which was a skylight; from this hung an enormous chandelier over a circular mahogany table, on which was the biggest arrangement of flowers Jane had ever seen in her life. It was an entire garden in a vase! The floor consisted of black and white tiles; it shone like a dance floor. It quite took her breath away.

'Goodness me, what a beautiful house you have, Mr Harrison!'

'Please call me Myles. After all, we are related, albeit by marriage. Bert, please take Miss Hughes's luggage to her room.'

Jane giggled at the word 'luggage' and looked at Bert, who forgot himself and nearly smiled. 'Hardly luggage,' she said. 'I only have my case,' and she indicated the little brown leather case she was holding.

'No matter. Give it to Bert, and he will put it in your room, while I take you up to see Pamela. She is so excited you are here.'

He started to make his way up the staircase – favouring his left leg, Jane noticed – so she passed her case to Bert with a smile and took off after him.

The staircase was wrought iron, intricately crafted, and wound round and round and up to a single landing, with a corridor going to the right and left. Myles turned right, and, limping slightly, strolled down the thick carpet to a door on the left. He opened it with a flourish, and announced, 'Voila, my sweet, your guardian angel has arrived. Welcome Sister Jane!'

Jane followed him into another vast room with an incredibly high ceiling above a bed that would have held an entire village. Sitting up in the middle of it was a tiny figure surrounded by pillows and bolsters: her sister Pamela.

'Jane, darling. Thank you so much for coming. Give me a hug!'

Jane was trying to do just that, but the bed was so big that her arms could not reach, and she had to scramble onto it in a very undignified manner to get anywhere near enough to give her sister the requested embrace.

'Thank you so much. Oh Jane, it has been awful! I was so frightened, and the pain . . .'

Myles interrupted this tirade with, 'Well, I will leave you two ladies to talk. I have a lot of work to get on with before dinner. Till then, Jane.' He turned and crossed the room and once again Jane noticed the limp.

'Take off your shoes and come and sit beside me,' Pam urged. 'Would you like anything? A cup of tea, maybe?'

'Oh, yes please. A cup of tea would be lovely. Mother made me some sandwiches and a flask of Camp coffee, but that feels like ages ago.'

Pamela tugged a long brocade bell-pull by the side of the bed. Within minutes a young girl appeared at the door.

'Hetty, could we have tea for two, please, and some of those rock cakes in the tin?'

'Yes, ma'am,' said Hetty with a bob, and left.

'Pammie, you have got servants! This is extraordinary. You never wrote and told us about all this, did you?'

'Well, I didn't want to boast, and Mother would have tried to take me down a peg or two. You know how she is.'

'Oh, I think you are being a little unfair, Pamela. Mum would always be happy for you to do well.' Jane felt a need to defend Mary, who had always tried to give the girls a balanced view of life. Certainly, she had helped Jane to take things with a pinch of salt, especially when Alfred had so favoured Pamela.

'I suppose so,' sighed Pamela. 'Daddy would certainly be proud of me, wouldn't he? How is everyone? God, this war has made keeping in touch so difficult, and I have been run off my feet. How's George? It is still George, isn't it?' She nudged Jane. 'Have you done It yet?'

'No! Really, Pam, you are terrible. Anyway, it is none of your business. Now be quiet and tell me about the baby. What happened?'

The girls spent the rest of the afternoon happily catching up. Pamela was so relieved that Jane would be there to help, by taking the baby off her hands while she was recovering. There was no mention of Myles and his desire to have his wife back, nor of Pamela's feelings for the new baby. Jane was so excited about seeing Sylvia that she did not really register any coolness in her sister's attitude to motherhood.

After tea was cleared away, Pamela settled down to have a

nap. Hetty came to fetch Jane and led her back to the top of the staircase, then along the corridor the other way to a door on the right.

'Here you are, miss. I have put your case in the cupboard and left your nightdress on the bed. There are towels and anything else you may need in the bathroom. Please let me know if you have any other requirements.' Hetty pronounced 'requirements' as though it was a foreign word which she had carefully learned how to pronounce. Obviously training was still taking place.

Jane smiled, thanked her and shut the bedroom door after the girl had left. She leaned against the frame and took a deep breath. Gosh, this was so different to what she had expected! She had always known that Pamela would do well in life, but this was far beyond anything she could have imagined. It was strange, because although she could see how grand everything was, and how expensive, she was not at all envious. This was not what she wanted for herself. She thought of George and his family and their farm. The huge kitchen range, the heart of the kitchen, where they would all sit round and eat their supper. She had spent so many happy hours with the Lee family, who had been especially kind to her when her own father had rejected her. She knew how hard her mother tried to shield her from his prejudice towards her, but she was an intelligent girl and had understood what was happening. However, the reasons why her father preferred Pamela would always be a mystery to her. What had she ever done to upset him?

She crossed the thick cream carpet and sat on the edge of the bed. It was high, like Pamela's, and very hard. The cover was silk and the pillows were pure cotton. Crisp and cool, and so white! As her fingers traced the pattern of the needlework round the edges of the pillow cases she thought how much her mother would have loved this. She decided to inspect the bathroom and gasped as she saw the size of the bath. It was standing in the corner on a plinth, with lion feet proudly holding it up. The basin was as big as their scullery sink at home where they did all the washing. The chrome taps gleamed. A china dish held a bar of soap shaped like a rose. Jane put it to her nose and inhaled the sweet, musky scent of summer. The towels were white and inches thick, and so soft. This was indeed another world. She looked at a row of bottles on the shelf above the basin. Each one was labelled. *Shampoo, Face Cream* and *Eau de Cologne*. How exquisite. There was even a tube of toothpaste and a new toothbrush beside it.

Jane felt a wave of fatigue pass over her. It had been a long day. She went back into the bedroom and lay down on the bed. What would it be like to live like this? What about George? How would he like the high life? She thought about his kind eyes and the way he held her hand when they walked out together. Then she thought about their kisses, and shivered.

Pamela had always been more adventurous with her love-life. Jane thought about her question: 'Have you done It yet?' *It?* What a strange way to refer to making love to someone. She had always believed that when she gave herself, it would be as a virgin on her wedding night. However, just lately, she had felt tempted to give herself to George before then.

Thinking about George now as she lay on this huge bed, she wished with all her heart that he was beside her. Then she turned over, and the minute her cheek touched the soft pillow, she fell deeply asleep.

'Please, miss, wake up, it is dinner-time.' It was Hetty, tugging at her arm. 'Mr Harrison says you are to come down to dinner. Sorry to wake you, miss.'

'No, don't worry, Hetty. Please tell Mr Harrison I will be down in five minutes,' Jane yawned.

Shaking herself awake, she went into the bathroom and splashed cold water on her face. She looked in the long mirror in the bedroom, and realised she looked very crumpled. She only had one other blouse and skirt with her, but at least they were not creased, so she changed and brushed her hair, and put some of the Eau de Cologne on, and made her way downstairs. When she got to the bottom she had no idea which way to go.

While she stood hesitating, Myles's voice rang out from a room to the left, where the door was ajar. She followed his voice and arrived at a huge dining table, with Myles seated at one end, half-hidden behind an enormous silver candlestick. It would appear she was supposed to sit at the other end as she could see a place setting, but that seemed such a ludicrous idea, to sit half a mile away.

And where was Pamela? Why wasn't *she* here?

Chapter Four

'Take a seat, my dear,' boomed Myles, indicating the other end of the table. 'It's just us, I'm afraid. Pamela never feels well enough these days to eat with me.'

'Well, thank you. But if you don't mind, I will come up to your end. It seems a bit daft, us shouting down the table to one another, don't you think?' And with that Jane gathered up the knives, and forks, and napkin, and glass, and set up camp next to Myles.

He roared with laughter and said, 'I am going to like you, young lady. It will be fun to have some company at the table.'

'Easier to pass the salt too this way,' said Jane, emboldened by his response.

Myles laughed again and passed her the salt.

The dinner *à deux* became a bit of a ritual over the next few weeks. It was a strange set-up at the best of times between Myles and Pamela, Jane thought. They seemed to get on perfectly well, but never spent any time together. Myles went out in the mornings and did not return until six or seven at night, and sometimes not at all – or certainly not until well after Jane, and the rest of the household, had gone to bed.

Pamela, by contrast, did not rise until late in the morning, and sometimes not at all. Jane tried to talk her into coming out for a walk, but she would have none of it.

'I need to recover,' she told her sister. 'I am so stiff after the birth. Believe me, you have no idea of the agony I went through. It was hell.'

Jane could not even persuade her sister to visit the baby in the clinic. The very suggestion sent Pamela into a tizzy. 'Please no! Jane, I hate hospitals and clinics, they make me feel ill. Leave the visiting to Myles – he loves it. I need you here with me to prepare for baby Sylvia's homecoming.'

Jane felt like saying that it was odd that so many millions of women had been through exactly the same experience, and were out of bed the next day, and back to work not long afterwards.

To fill her days before the baby was allowed home from the hospital, Jane went and signed up for volunteering with the Red Cross. She was fascinated by all the work involved in keeping the people of London safe, and the way that medical supplies were moved around the city. She attended several incidents over those first two weeks, when V1 and V2 flying rockets had caused terrible injuries and destroyed people's homes. These new stealth weapons were greatly feared: with their silent approach there was no warning time to make a run for it.

That day, she had gone down to South London where the worst-hit areas were, and helped to clear away the rubble and find shocked people some shelter. It was heartbreaking to see, but everyone was so kind and helpful. There was a fantastic sense of the power of the human spirit, and making the best of things. The poverty in some parts of London, even without the bombings, was unbelievable. It was so hard for Jane to take in, after the quiet of the Hertfordshire countryside. Nobody there was particularly wealthy, but somehow, being outdoors in the fresh air, able to grow vegetables, keep chickens and have a ready supply of eggs … all such simple things that she had always taken for granted, now seemed like major luxuries compared to life on a street off the Old Kent Road.

It was also a far cry from St John's Wood, and returning there in the evenings made Jane aware again of just how far up the ladder her sister had climbed. But did Pamela appreciate her good fortune?

Jane would try to discuss various topics with Myles over their evening meal together, but he would not be drawn into any kind of political discussion. With reference to the bombings, he would merely say that his company was working all hours to repair and restore many of the damaged houses, which had to be a good thing, surely? Jane just could not help feeling that he was benefiting from other people's misfortunes. Myles did not strike her as a man who did anything for nothing. Pamela was always going on about the charities she supported, and how much time she spent on various committees as a Chairwoman. So maybe someone gained something from these people.

Jane would sometimes write to George, describing some of her experiences, but playing down the danger. The Harrisons had a bomb shelter in the garden that was large enough to accommodate them all, but Jane sincerely hoped they would never have to use it. They were certainly not immune from German raids. If a bomb 'had your name on it' as people liked to say, then 'your number was up, mate'.

Finally, now she was thriving, baby Sylvia was allowed home.

The whole household was there to greet her; even Pamela was up and dressed, and at the door.

Sylvia was carried in by her very proud father, then taken up to her nursery and deposited in her new cot. Jane knew no more about babies than Pamela, but she had oodles of common sense, and she had made a friend of the cook, who had three young children under five, so got plenty of tips from her.

In those first few days she tried very hard to get Pamela to bond with her daughter, but it was not easy. The minute the baby cried, Pam would call for Jane to take the little monster away.

'But Pam, if you could just pick her up and give her a cuddle, she will stop crying. She just wants her mummy to hold her,' Jane said, to no avail.

'I have too much to do,' Pamela snapped. 'Just take her away.'

'What are you going to do when I am no longer around? Leave her to cry?'

'Don't be so dramatic, Jane, of course I won't! I am going to get a full-time nanny organised. In fact, you will be relieved to hear that it looks as if you will be able to go home next month. I feel much better and more able to cope, and thank God, I can now fit into my clothes again. You have been marvellous, Jane. Myles tells me he will miss your little dinners together. I had better start coming down to those, hadn't I? Can't have my husband enjoying your company too much, now can I?' Pamela arched a perfect eyebrow.

'Oh please don't be so pathetic,' Jane retorted. 'It's not like I have any choice who I eat my dinner with, is it? In my opinion you should have left your bed weeks ago!'

That evening, the three of them had dinner together, and it was enormous fun. Jane felt as if she was in the middle of a tennis match as the banter went back and forth across the table. What she did notice that night was just how much they both drank. Pamela was chucking back the gin, followed by red wine all through dinner. Then Myles suggested they all had a night-cap in the study. Jane was exhausted by this time and declined with the excuse that she might be woken in the night by Sylvia. She said her goodnights, and went to her room.

Later on, she was woken up by raised voices – the low drone of a baritone and a high-pitched shrieking.

A glass was smashed at one point then finally silence. She quickly fell asleep again and thought no more about it until Pamela called her into her room the next morning.

'Jane, would you mind meeting this new young nanny that Myles has found, and tell me what you think of her? I feel we should have someone older and more experienced. I have asked her to come here this morning so you can meet her.'

Jane was rather taken aback. What on earth did she know about nannies? On the other hand she adored Sylvia, who was thriving under her love and care, and she certainly wanted to make sure her niece would be in safe hands. Nodding, she said, 'Well, if you want me to I will, though I am hardly an expert in these matters.'

'Please, Jane, just do it for me, will you? And if possible, try and persuade Myles to have someone older. The last thing I need in my present condition is some floozy wafting around the house.'

'Floozy, what do you mean? I thought we were talking about a nanny. Pamela, what is going on?'

To Jane's amazement her sister burst into tears.

'Oh God, Jane, I am at my wits' end! Men are all animals. All they think about is sex. Myles is making my life impossible at the moment, because he is constantly coming to me and demanding I make love to him. He wouldn't come near me before the birth and made me feel like an elephant, but now, apparently, since I am back to normal, in his eyes at least, he says he wants his conjugal rights. But what about my rights? I am a woman who has just had a baby. My poor body is ruined. It may take weeks before I can begin to contemplate sexual relations. My God, what if I got pregnant again? I would kill myself. He just keeps on and on, Jane, and when I refuse he threatens to go elsewhere.' Pamela sobbed. 'How can he be so cruel? The trouble is, there's an army of women out there ready to offer themselves to him, and he knows it.'

Jane sat down on the edge of the bed and tried to digest all this.

'Did you and Myles have a row last night?' she asked.

'Yes. He came to my room and demanded that we have sex. I threw a glass at him and sent him packing.'

'Don't you have the same room, then?' Jane had been wondering about this ever since she had arrived. Myles always turned left at the top of the stairs when he went to bed, and she knew Pamela's room was to the right. So that was another mystery solved.

'Good God, no! That would just about put the kibosh on it. Jane, you have a lot to learn about men and women and marriage. Trust me. Anyway, the last thing I need now is for this young nanny to come into my house and tempt my husband. He is easily led, believe me. Always has been. There is always someone on the horizon.'

'But he is not actually unfaithful to you, is he?' Jane could not believe she was having this conversation.

Pamela suddenly paused and looked at Jane searchingly. A shadow crossed her lovely face and her eyes went very dead.

'Oh yes, dear. That is the price I pay for being Mrs Myles Harrison, and believe me I can handle it normally, just not right now.'

Jane was indignant. 'But what kind of marriage is that, for goodness' sake? Leading separate lives like this, it's wrong. Does he love you at all?'

'Yes, in his way, but he is a man with needs, and I can't always meet them, and now there is Sylvia to think about as well. I didn't really want any children, Jane. I am not in any way a maternal person. How am I going to live with this child in my life? At least Myles adores her, that is something I will have over the other sluts in his life – and I will never divorce him, never!'

This last was a cry of anguish. Jane felt real sadness for this woman that she really did not know at all. They were like chalk and cheese. How could they ever have been born sisters?

There was a knock on the door and Jane went to open it. 'Yes, Hetty, what is it?'

'A young lady to see Mrs Harrison. I showed her into the drawing room, miss.'

'Thank you, Hetty, I will come down immediately.' Jane closed the door and turned to her sister, who was quietly weeping. 'Don't worry, Pam, I will meet her and see what can be done.'

She left and made her way down to the drawing room. What she found there gave her quite a start. Certainly the young woman standing in the middle of the room was not obvious 'nanny' material. She was tall and blonde, and what could only be described as 'well-endowed'.

'How do you do. I am Jane Hughes, Mrs Harrison's sister. And you are?'

'Gloria Smith. I am interested in the job of nanny for the Harrisons' baby. I have already met Mr Harrison and he seemed very happy with my credentials.' Was that a smirk on her face?

'I see,' replied Jane. 'And what exactly are your credentials?'

'Well, I have two younger sisters that I have always looked after, and my neighbour has just had a baby boy. I have been babysitting for them, so I know what I am doing. My mum used to clean for several of the gentlemen at Mr Harrison's club and there have never been any complaints about me, so she spoke to Mr Harrison about me coming to work here.'

'Well, that is very interesting, Gloria. I am sure you are absolutely marvellous with children, but I think that Mrs Harrison is really looking for someone with more experience for the early years of her baby's life. So thank you very much for coming to see us today, but I am afraid to say we will not be offering you the post.'

'Well, that is charming, I must say,' pouted Gloria, all pretence of a respectable nanny going down the drain. 'Bloody marvellous! I come all this way over here and don't get the bleeding job. Didn't want it, anyway. Bloody kids, who'd have 'em!' And with that she was gone in a flurry of temper, and cheap perfume. It would have been laughable were it not so scary. Poor little Sylvia! What was going to happen to her? Jane was in two minds whether to apply for the job herself, until she thought of George, followed by an image of Myles, and realised it was definitely not the job for her. But she did realise that the sooner she got this problem sorted out, the sooner she could go home.

That afternoon, Jane borrowed the cook's bicycle and went to an agency she had spotted in the high street, advertising home helps and nannies. One of the good things about St John's Wood, and neighbouring Swiss Cottage, was the fact that they had a big Jewish population and everyone knew each other. There was a real community spirit and people looked out for one another. They were also very family-orientated. Sure enough, the lady in the agency, Mrs Freed, could not have been more helpful. She understood the situation perfectly.

'Always such a worry with a young baby,' she asserted. 'Got to be so careful. But don't worry, I have several candidates who I think will suit you perfectly, dearie.' She gave Jane a list of five names and made arrangements for them to come into her office that afternoon, to meet her. This was ideal as Jane did not want to bump into Myles before she was ready. She wanted to present him with a fait accompli, so there could be no arguments. Whoever she picked could come to the house and meet Pamela and Sylvia, and they could take it from there.

It was nearly two o'clock and there was no point in going

back to the house so Jane bought herself a salt beef sandwich from the Deli. Another good thing about a Jewish community, she thought to herself, lovely food! She took her sandwich and cycled to Regent's Park to eat it. It was such a beautiful park. The flowerbeds were immaculate and the lawns and shrubs abundant. She just loved it here. Everywhere she looked, people strolled happily in the sunshine. Who would have thought there was a war on? Then she stopped short, as she remembered what the implications of being Jewish in this war would mean to so many families here in London. Oh my God, how could she forget, even for a moment, the horrors that Jews were suffering, every day that Hitler continued to live. She sat on a seat by the boating lake eating her sandwich, and silently said a prayer for all the victims of Nazi persecution.

By the time she got back to the agency, Mrs Freed's office was full to bursting with ladies. Jane felt rather nervous of her newfound responsibility as an employer. The things she did for Pamela!

The first lady was lovely but spoke no English at all. Jane did not know what the language was that she did speak until afterwards, when Mrs Freed explained that it was Yiddish. Well, you learn something every day, thought Jane. After two hours of talking to the first four candidates, Jane was exhausted and deflated. None of them were suitable, in her opinion. Poor Sylvia's future was in her hands. This brought back her determination to succeed, and she invited in the last applicant with a renewed sense of purpose.

Mrs Lehman was well-dressed and well-spoken, if a little reticent. She explained that she had recently been widowed; her husband had been killed in action. She had a son of six and welcomed the thought of filling her days with hard work, and the joy of a baby to take her mind off her loss. There was no trace of self-pity or bitterness at her situation, just acceptance and a desire to keep going. Jane guessed that whatever grief she was feeling, she had learned to conceal for the sake of her son. He went to a local school, so all she required was time to take and fetch him, and also, she hoped it might be possible for him to remain with her sometimes, when she worked, because she had no one other than friends to help her with her childcare. Jane thought it sounded like the perfect solution for everyone and arranged for her to come to the house the next day to meet Pamela.

Vivian Lehman arrived the next morning, and within two hours was running the nursery like clockwork. She had even managed to get Pamela up and busy at her desk, organising a charity lunch for war widows as introduced to her by Vivian. It was a marriage made in heaven. God knows, she needs something to help her through her own marriage, Jane thought, as she watched Mrs Lehman encouraging Pamela to play with Sylvia. All she had to do now was tackle Myles.

Jane decided to catch him before dinner, before he had had too much to drink. So when she heard his not-so-dulcet tones ringing round the hall about six o'clock, she quickly slipped downstairs and followed him into his study, where he was already pouring himself a large scotch.

'Jane, to what do I owe this pleasure? Will you join me in a drink before dinner?'

'No, thank you, Myles. Not just now. I wanted a quick word with you about the nanny situation.'

'Well, Gloria Smith is coming next week,' he answered with a shrug.

Jane took a deep breath. 'Well, actually, I have told her not to come. I know just how much Sylvia means to you, Myles, and I want to be absolutely sure, before I go home, that she has the best possible care. In my opinion, Gloria Smith is a thoroughly nasty piece of work, and I wouldn't trust her to come within an inch of my beautiful niece. You and Pamela lead very busy lives and I know how important it is for you to have a wife who can be by your side at all times, to support you and give you what you need' (you animal, she thought). 'You do not want to be continually concerned about your daughter's welfare and safety. So I have taken the liberty of finding you someone slightly older' (*and* without a huge bosom), 'who has heaps of experience and is very discreet. The perfect addition to your household. You can lead the kind of life you want without jeopardising the safety of your daughter' (you selfish man).

Myles stood regarding her for several minutes, to the point where Jane began to feel uncomfortable. Then he said, 'Well, Miss Hughes, you are really quite something. You come here and take over my house, and my daughter's welfare – and even *my* welfare, it would seem. You talk as though you know all about me and my wants and needs. Can this be possible?' He paused and held her gaze again challengingly, but Jane did not look down.

'Very well,' he said finally. 'I will be guided by you in this matter. I have no doubt my wife will be delighted. I take it this new woman is not going to win any beauty pageants?' Without waiting for an answer, he lifted his glass in a toast. 'I wish you all the best, Jane, and good luck in the future. I think you will do very well. Are we dining tonight?'

'No. Unfortunately, I am unable to join you tonight as I am on duty with the Red Cross.'

'Goodness me, will it be Saint Jane before the night is out?' Myles took a large swig of his black market whisky. 'Be careful, it is still dangerous out there. The Germans haven't given up quite yet, I regret to say. Could you pass on a message to my wife and tell her I will not be in for dinner either? I have a meeting at my club. Goodnight, see you tomorrow.'

She was dismissed. Well, that was fine with her. She went to

67

find Pamela to give her the good news about the nanny. Later on, just before she was ready to leave, she found Hetty in the nursery with Sylvia.

'Thank you for standing in for me tonight, Hetty,' Jane said. 'Once Mrs Lehman the new nanny starts here, you will not need to do the extra work. Night night, Sylvia.' She bent and kissed the baby's head.

'Oh, I don't mind at all, miss, she is such a good baby. I love her to bits. We all do. You take care tonight, miss. Good luck.'

It turned out to be a long hard night. Jane went to visit several families in the East End who had been made homeless by the raids. Medicines were in short supply and it was sometimes a difficult choice as to who got what. About 10.30 p.m. she had started to make her way back, when the unit she was with was suddenly diverted to Baker Street, where there had been an incident. The information was sketchy, but as they got closer, someone reported that a young woman had gone into labour in the underground, and needed assistance. Jane and another girl called Julie took the call. They left the Red Cross unit, and carrying their emergency kits made for the entrance to the station just as the sirens started to go off. An air raid. What appalling timing.

'Come on, Julie, down the hole!' Jane shouted to her colleague. 'We must find that poor woman.'

She pushed through the crowds already streaming into the underground, holding up her Red Cross pass to clear the way. They had been given instructions to look on the Northbound Bakerloo line, Platform 1. Jane dashed down the steps two at a time, followed by Julie. They were hampered by people coming the other way. Jane shouted to them as she passed, to stay put as there was an air raid going on, then hurried on down into the bowels of the underground. There were an awful lot of steps. Finally she arrived on Platform 1 and saw a crowd of onlookers, grouped in a circle.

'Red Cross – make way, please. Move away, please, let us pass. Thank you.'

Jane kneeled down beside the young woman who had collapsed. Someone had propped her head up against the wall. She was leaning against it, panting.

'Hello, my love. My name's Jane, and this is Julie. We've come to help you. What's your name?'

'Mabel,' she gasped. Then: 'I think the baby is coming.' She moaned and clasped her stomach.

'That's OK, Mabel, try and relax. Just forget about everything else. We will make you as comfortable as possible. Is the baby due about now or is it early?' Jane needed to get as much information as she could, as quickly as she could, in case the girl lost consciousness.

'No, it's not due for another two months. I don't know what's happening. Please don't let me lose my baby!' She clutched Jane's arm and let out another cry. The crowd had retreated out of respect, and the three women were huddled against the wall, surrounded by a sea of humanity all crushed against each other, waiting for deliverance. There was hardly any noise; no one talked much.

'Listen to me, Mabel, I am going to examine you and try to see what is going on. So we are going to lay you down flat and cover you with a blanket.' Julie had already taken it out of the emergency kit bag. 'Now, if you can bend your knees for us ... Do you remember how you do it for the doctor?' The girl nodded, and whimpering, lay down. 'That's lovely, well done, Mabel. Julie, give her your jacket as a pillow, would you? That's it. Now bring your knees up and try to relax, dear. I know it's hard for you, but concentrate on breathing slowly in and out. Try counting ... one ... two ... three.' All the time she was talking to Mabel, Jane was gently removing the girl's under-clothes, and she was shocked when she saw the amount of blood. The poor girl was haemorrhaging. She was going to lose the baby.

She tried to signal to Julie how serious the situation was; eventually, her partner got the message and moved out of earshot with her radio to try and get help. But this was an impossible situation. They were in the underground in the middle of an air raid. Julie passed Jane the two towels from their kits. They were woefully inadequate to staunch the blood. Jane took the girl's hand and tried to soothe her.

'The baby is coming so we shall have to improvise,' she told her. 'Julie is calling for an ambulance but as there is a raid on, I am afraid it may take a while. Now you must be very brave. Keep up the breathing – very good … but push when I tell you, all right?' Mabel stared up at Jane and registered her words, but Jane could see she was getting weaker by the minute. She tried to breathe but the effort was too great; she seemed to shrink away from Jane.

'I don't want to lose my baby.' It was only a whisper now, and Jane had to lean in to catch the words.

'Come on, love, you can do this. Push now. Don't give up on me now. *Push!* Give me your hand.'

Mabel reached out, but her hand fell as she tried to catch her breath, which stuck in her throat like a tiny snore; then her whole body seemed to let out a sigh as she gently passed away.

Jane was frozen on the spot. Disbelief and shock took over. Mabel couldn't die! Mabel was having a baby, Mabel was … Jane felt a hand on her shoulder and looked up to see Julie standing, staring down at the bloodied towels, and her grip on Jane's shoulder became like a vice. Jane lifted the blanket and groaned in horror at the sight that greeted her. A tiny mangled form nestled between the dead girl's thighs. It was bloodied and twisted but still recognisable as human, with little hands and feet visible in the bundle of flesh and bone.

'Oh God, oh God, help us. Oh, sweet Jesus ... Julie, help me, please!' But Julie was on her knees a few feet away, being violently sick into a dressings bag.

Jane stifled the desire to do the same thing. She stood up, her hands balled into fists with the effort of stopping herself from thinking, or seeing, or feeling. She quickly covered the bottom half of the body with her jacket, then knelt and closed Mabel's eyes. She did not linger in case she broke down, but got up and immediately turned to the people around who had begun to move in to take a look.

'Right, ladies and gentlemen, move back, please, as far as you can. Show some respect. Just keep calm and wait for the ALL CLEAR. We would appreciate your co-operation. Thank you. Move back, please, sir.'

Julie had managed to pull herself together, and was standing guard by the body.

'There is nothing we can do until the ambulance gets here,' said Jane, coming to join her. 'Please God it is soon.'

Suddenly, their prayers were answered, and the ALL CLEAR sounded. The crowd dispersed remarkably quickly, and the two girls were left on the platform with their tragic bundle of assorted coats and towels.

'I suppose we should try and identify her,' said Jane, and turned to find Mabel's bag. She located her ID in a wallet with a photo of a very handsome and smiling RAF pilot. Written on the back was: *I will always love you, Mabel, don't you ever forget.*

She put the things back in the wallet, and held the bag ready to hand it over to the ambulance crew, who arrived a few minutes later. Jane explained what had happened and showed them the body. She could not bring herself to look down again at the carnage of the tiny human being.

71

One of the crew was an older man and he could see the effect the whole thing had had on these two girls. He gave them both a rough hug and said, 'You've done well, you girls. Try to forget this. Don't dwell on it. Life is cruel and we have to deal with it as best we can. Pick ourselves up and get on with it. I know that must sound hard and uncaring, but this is the only way we can carry on and help others. You did a good job, the pair of you. Nothing else could have been done. Now get yourselves home. You'd better take your jackets. Will you be all right, or do you want someone to go with you?'

'No, thank you. We will be fine, honestly.' Jane turned and saw Julie picking up her bag. 'Julie, shall we walk a bit together? We go the same way, don't we?'

Julie nodded, and the two girls linked arms and left the platform, making their way slowly up the steps and out into the night. It was pouring with rain.

'Oh blimey, this is all we need. Blackout and rain. Come on, let's hurry!' Julie set off and Jane quickly followed her. Neither girl spoke. There was nothing to say and anyway, all their efforts were concentrated into stepping over puddles and potholes, fast filling up with water. It was bad enough in the daylight, but now in the pitch black it was downright dangerous. There had been an article in the paper recently, about a man who had tripped and fallen at night, having had one too many, and landed face down in a large pothole, left from a raid, and drowned.

Jane was grateful to have Julie's company, at least until they got to the Finchley Road, where Julie left her to head on up to Swiss Cottage and Jane turned off towards Abbey Road. She finally reached the front door and stumbled into the hall of the big house in St John's Wood, soaked through to her skin. She left a trail of dripping water all the way up to her room, where she peeled off her wet clothes and wrapped a towel around herself. She was too tired to have a bath, but decided to have a good wash and then get herself a hot drink. She made her way back downstairs, aware of how silent the house was … God knows what time it was.

She stopped at the foot of the stairs as the door to the study opened, and there was Myles standing in the half-light, a large glass of brandy in his hand.

'Well, well, who's a dirty stop-out then? Come and join me for a nightcap.'

Jane was about to refuse, but then realised that a brandy was probably just what she needed; and although Myles might not be the kindly uncle one might wish to talk to, he was at least another human being, and right now she needed company. She took the glass he offered and sank into the enormous sofa in the study, staring into the remains of the fire. As the warmth enveloped her, and the brandy relaxed her, she started to tremble, and the tears began to fall as she related the horrors of the night.

Myles was surprisingly solicitous, and poured more brandy. Jane was beginning to feel a little light-headed, and then suddenly Myles had his arm around her, and was whispering in her ear. It tickled, and she wanted to brush him away … but he was pushing her back into the sofa, telling her to take it easy. Suddenly, this did not feel right. Where was everybody? Her head was pounding now, and she was feeling sick. She tried to get up, but Myles was on top of her, an immovable weight, and now the towel was slipping away from her. She plucked at it desperately, to hold it in place, but then she could feel Myles's hands moving up underneath it. He was whispering things all the time, and as she focused on the words they were no longer kind and comforting.

'Bitch, come on – you know you want me. I bet you have a hot cunt. Come on, Janie, show that sister of yours the way to do it.' She was naked now, and he pinned her down with one

73

arm across her neck so she could hardly breathe. His knee had forced her legs apart, and Jane did not seem to have any strength to stop him. Her muscles were like jelly, yet every nerve in her body was screaming out against this violent attack. She tried to scream but no sound emerged. All she could do was turn her face away from his brandy breath, and then she could feel the spittle on her cheek, as he hissed abuse and filth at her.

'You're all the same, you girls – bitches and sluts who want to be fucked. Oh yes, you want this! Open your cunt and feel a man's cock.'

He rammed up and into her, but was frustrated by her dryness. He withdrew, and stuck two fingers inside her and pushed, and probed. Jane tried desperately to clear her mind. *Please God make him stop.* He had started to enter her again and was shoving his way in, up to the hilt. His breath was coming in grunts now, faster and faster, as he reached his climax. His guttural cries grew louder and louder in her ears, like the sound of bombs falling. He let out a yell as he spurted into her, and the noise was all around her. The ominous whine of an air-raid siren, the crash of falling masonry as a doodlebug reached its target – and Mabel's screams as her baby fell out of her onto the platform ... And there was blood everywhere.

Jane closed her eyes and could only see red swirling behind her lids. Slowly she started to drift away. She was floating above the sofa; all she could feel was a blessed release. She was drifting away into darkness and nothingness. Her last thought was, *Where is George?*

When she came round, she was lying by the fireside on her towel, and the fire was almost out. Just the last flickering sparks on a log. Her head was pounding, and as she tried to sit up, it felt as if it was going to crack open in two. She fell back on the towel and lay there, trying to remember what had happened. Slowly the truth dawned, and without realising it she let out a sob, a heart-rending sob, from deep within her soul. Her hand went down between her legs and stopped as she felt stickiness, and then the bruised feeling, and then the pain took over. Not just a physical pain in the secret parts of her body, but a terrible pain of horror at what had happened. She frantically tried to gather herself up. She must get to her room and hide. She must have a bath. Oh God, what was going to happen to her?

Jane staggered up the stairs. The house was in complete darkness because of the blackout. She was like a blind woman as she felt her way along the corridor. She stopped at one point because she could hear whimpering. Was it a cat? Was it Sylvia? No. Oh God! It was her. She could taste the salt of silent tears running down her face. Terrified that Myles might come back, or that Pamela would wake and find her like this, Jane went straight into her room and closed the door. She was too exhausted to run a bath, so she went straight to the basin and filled it with hot water and washed herself all over very slowly and meticulously. Holding the flannel between her legs, she let the warmth of the water soothe her rawness. Finally, when she could hardly stand any longer, she dried herself very gently and climbed into bed, and let sleep bring a tainted oblivion. Tomorrow would come soon enough.

Her final image was of a small mangled baby as it fell into the world amidst tears, death and the hellish din of war raging overhead.

Chapter Five

Jane packed and left London the next morning. She tiptoed into the nursery in the dawn light to kiss the baby farewell. She could not bear to see Pamela, and the fear that Myles might find her again made her feel physically sick. She just wanted to get away from this place!

Jane sat huddled on the train back to St Albans, her cheek against the cold window pane, trying to be invisible. She felt so sore and ashamed. Luckily she managed to get a taxi home from the station. It was early and people were still waking up to another day. As she stepped into the parlour, her mother was just clearing away the last remnants of breakfast. Thank goodness her father had left to go to work.

Jane ran to her mother and burst into tears. Mary held her tight while she sobbed her heart out. Finally, when she was exhausted from crying, Jane let her mother take her to the kitchen table and sit her down. Mary then bustled around her making a pot of tea. She placed a cup in front of her daughter and waited.

'Mother, I am so sorry,' the girl wept. 'I had nowhere else to go. Please forgive me. I am so ashamed. Something terrible has happened and I just don't understand how it could all have gone so wrong.'

'Now there, my dear, just be calm and tell me all about it.' Mary took her daughter's hand across the table and squeezed it.

Jane drank some tea and was instantly comforted. She took some deep breaths and started to tell her mother everything, from the shock of seeing Pamela in the big house, to the horror that had occurred in the underground last night, to the other horror that awaited her when she reached St John's Wood. When she had finished, she closed her eyes and slumped back in the chair. Mary sat for a few minutes, and then without a word she stood up, took her daughter's hand and led her upstairs to her room. She sat Jane on the bed, then went to the bathroom and started to run a bath. She fetched fresh lavender from her cupboard and sprinkled it in the water, then selected the biggest, softest towel she could find and went back to Jane's room, where her daughter was still sitting on the edge of the bed.

Mary bent down and took off her shoes and stockings, and then Jane stood up and let her mother remove her skirt and blouse. She lifted her arms above her head just like she used to do as a child. Finally Jane removed her underwear and handed it to Mary who took the bundle of clothes as she led Jane to the bathroom. The room was filled with steam and smelled of lavender. Jane eased herself into the warm water and looked up at her mother.

'Thank you,' she whispered.

'Everything will work itself out, my love. You are home now. Just take it one step at a time. But first you need to sleep. When you have finished your bath, get into bed and I will bring you some food. Don't worry, dearest, you are safe now.'

Jane lay back and closed her eyes. All her thoughts were jumbled up, and she was beginning to feel so tired. She soaked for a while and then as she felt herself falling asleep she got out, dried herself and went to her room. Mother had laid out an old nightie on the bed, and the reminder of her childhood days made her weep quietly. It felt so soft and smelled of roses. She climbed into bed and let the pillows close around her and the covers envelop her aching body. She fell asleep immediately. When Mary came in with a bowl of soup, she took one look at her daughter and tiptoed out again.

In the week that followed, Jane slept most of the time. Alfred seemed very pleased to see her, and wanted to know all the news of Pamela and the baby, but under instructions from Mary he agreed to wait for the answers to his questions until his elder daughter had rested.

One morning as Jane came down for breakfast, her mother handed her a bowl of porridge and said, 'Eat up, it will do you good. Then we need to talk, Jane. George called by last night as he had heard you were back. Bless him, he was so eager to see you, but I explained you were very tired after your experiences with the Red Cross in London, and needed a little time to yourself. But at some stage you will have to decide what you are going to tell him, dear.'

'Do I have to tell him anything at all?' Jane was dreading the inevitable moment when she had to face her sweetheart.

'Well, you can't leave it like this. I certainly don't think you should tell your father, mind. He is not a man to understand these things.'

'I can't see George yet. Please, can't you tell him I am ill?' Jane began to weep.

'There, there, now. Come on, love, it is going to be fine. Time will heal all. I will go to see George today, when I am in the village, and say you are still not well and will be in bed for a few more days. Now eat your porridge and cheer up.'

By the end of the week Jane did, indeed, feel much better. She realised she must write a letter to her sister with some excuse for her abrupt departure. As for George, she would try to see him this coming Sunday after church. She hadn't been to a service for so long, and suddenly she felt a deep need to pray. She remembered the prayer book that Mary had given her when she left to go to London. Her mother had explained that her own mother, Jane's grandmother Alice, had given it to her the day she died. It had made Jane feel so sad and yet even closer to her mother. She had kept it by her bedside in London. Suddenly panicked that she had left it behind in her dawn flight, she was deeply relieved to find it in her bag. She took it out and held it against her.

It was a mellow autumn morning as the congregation filed out after the service. Burslet was only a hamlet but had its own lovely old church. Reverend Simms lived between Burslet and Redbourn, and gave services in both places, alternating the morning and evening services. Jane thought back to her childhood and to St James's Church, where her father had preached. Sometimes Mary and Alfred would visit Reginald, who had taken over at the vicarage in Allingham. Reg had made a great success of his parish and Leonora had proved the perfect partner for him. The couple had three children, who filled the old family home once again with noise and laughter.

Jane came out of the church and saw George across the road with his mother and father. She felt a flood of love for them all. The Lees were such good people. She crossed the road and gave Mrs Lee a hug.

'Hello, Louise, how are you? It's lovely to see you again – and Don, you look so well.' She gave him a kiss on the cheek and then stopped in front of George. 'George, it is so good to be home.' She was suddenly struck by enormous shyness and could hardly look him in the eyes.

Beaming all over his face, George stepped forward and said, 'Shall I walk you back to the house?'

Jane was flustered. 'Yes, yes, thank you.' She turned to the Lees and with a huge effort managed to flash them a bright smile as they all said their farewells.

George and Jane walked in silence for a while. Jane was frantically trying to put her thoughts in order. She wanted so much to make George know how deeply she loved him, but how could she marry him now, without telling him the whole truth?

'I missed you.' George broke the silence.

'I missed you too. But to be honest, I was so busy trying to sort out my sister and the baby, and I was volunteering with the Red Cross, and that took up all my spare time. It was all so new and different and parts of it were extremely daunting. I hardly had a moment to myself.' Jane ventured a sidelong glance towards him.

'Too busy to write and tell me?' He caught her look. Was he angry, she wondered.

'Oh, George, I did try to write more but the time just flew by ...' Jane began to panic. George squeezed her arm.

'I am only teasing you. Don't worry. I didn't really expect any letters, and I was grateful for the news you did send me, because I was so worried about you with the air raids and everything.'

'Oh George, it was horrible sometimes. I went to a call in the underground at Baker Street.' Jane told him the story of Mabel. It was still so vivid in her memory, and in a way it was easier to relive that horror and let it take over her thoughts, than to dwell on the nightmare scene that followed when she got home. George listened intently. They slowed down as they approached her house.

'I had no idea you had seen such tragedy,' he said sombrely. 'No wonder you needed some time alone. I thought you didn't want to see me.' He smiled ruefully and took both her hands. 'I still love you, Jane, and I just hope we can pick up where we left off.'

'Oh George, I am sure it is going to be fine. Just give me a little more time to adjust.' Jane was starting to panic again. She just didn't know what to say, and she was sure that George could see right through her.

However, he did not pursue the issue, just kissed her on the cheek and said, 'I am here when you are ready.'

She watched him turn and walk down the lane, and she longed to run after him and give him a big hug, but she couldn't trust herself not to break down.

Over the next two or three weeks Jane gradually fell back into a routine. She helped her mother in the house and ran errands for her father. She saw George just enough to keep him from asking questions but she could feel his frustration at never being alone with her. He tried to talk about their wedding plans, but she fobbed him off, saying it was nearly Christmas, and they needed to get that out of the way first. She heard nothing from Pamela although she had sent a letter ages ago.

Little by little, Jane was able to lock away the memories of that night until one morning she woke feeling dizzy and sick. At the same time, it dawned on her that she had not had her monthly period. Memories returned of Pamela sitting on her bed telling Jane what it had been like when she had been late, and then realised she could be pregnant. Although it was terrifying, Pamela had seemed to enjoy the drama. To her it was like a game. But it wasn't a game.

With a creeping sense of dread as each day went by, Jane began to withdraw into herself. She couldn't face her mother or George, and certainly not her father. She secretly went to see a doctor in St Albans, who confirmed her worst fears.

'Mother, I am pregnant.' Jane stood in front of her mother in the kitchen.

'Oh dear Lord God in heaven.' Mary sank into a chair. She

had almost sensed this, had dreaded this after the rape of her daughter. How could fate be so cruel? Was this her punishment for her own transgression? But she had paid for that, surely? She had brought up her two daughters and done her duty as a wife to Alfred the best she could. Why this now?

Alfred must never know. Whatever happened, he must not find out the truth. All these years they had never spoken again of Mary's night of passion with Henry. But it was always there, even when Pamela came along to divert her husband's attention from Jane. A few years back, her brother Joseph had been killed in a car accident after drunkenly driving his car into a wall – and Mary had feared that Henry might turn up at the funeral. To her great relief, he had not put in an appearance, and Mary was able to lay her thoughts to rest with her beloved eldest brother. Now this had happened to Jane, and she could not bear to think Alfred could ever have a chance to say: 'Like mother, like daughter.'

Mary pulled herself together and gave Jane a hug.

'Oh you poor girl, life is cruel! But we will manage. We will do this together. No one will ever know, least of all your father. You must never tell him the truth, Jane. Never – do you hear me?'

Jane was shocked by the vehemence in her mother's voice. Why was she so adamant that her father must never find out?

Mary knew that she had to tell her daughter the truth about her own birth. Although she had not been raped by Henry, it had still been an assault: she had been so young and innocent, and Henry's betrayal of her had had life-changing repercussions.

Taking a deep breath, Mary began her story. Jane did not interrupt her but could hardly take in what she was hearing. Her whole childhood flashed before her eyes. It all became so clear – her father's coldness, her mother's reserve.

And most of all Pamela! No wonder they were so different.

How did people live with these lies? Now she was creating another lie. There was just too much to take in.

Jane looked at her mother sitting there, and she seemed so small and sad.

'Well, at least you gave Alfred what he wanted, didn't you?' she said, unable to call him 'father' any longer. 'When Pam was born he must have been over the moon.'

'Oh yes, and it did help the marriage in many ways, but it was so unfair on you, I'm afraid, dear. Pamela was the apple of his eye. He spoiled her rotten, and created a thoroughly selfish human being, I am sorry to say. I wanted to protect you, and look how I failed.' Mary broke down in tears. Jane had never seen her mother cry. She had always seemed so strong and capable.

'Please don't cry,' she said tenderly. 'It's not your fault. I am a grown woman and I have my own choices to make. George is a wonderful man and he is already helping me to heal. Everything is going to be fine.' She hoped she sounded more confident than she felt.

Mary looked at her daughter across the table. 'You must go to George and tell him everything,' she declared.

'But how can I tell him something like this? How do I explain the rape and everything? He will hate me!'

'No, he won't. I honestly think he is a bigger man than that, Jane. He loves you very much. He was lost when you went to London. He used to come and sit here with me sometimes, and talk about you, and how you would be married and live on the farm together. He was so full of dreams and plans for you both. I really think you should go and talk to him. Tell him the truth and be done with it. What have you got to lose?'

Everything, thought Jane. Even if he still wants me, how can I love him now the way he deserves? I don't want this baby. Oh God, it is Myles's child. Not only has he taken my life away, he has destroyed any chance for me to make George happy. No, she was not going to let him win! Suddenly, something inside her changed. She felt it in her womb, as if the baby was trying to make her see sense. This baby was innocent. She would not let Myles corrupt her life, or the baby's, or George's. Between them they were going to create something good and strong and lasting that would destroy all trace of Myles Harrison.

The next day, Jane went to Malthouse Farm to see George and tell him her story. When she arrived at the farmhouse, his mother Louise was there.

'Jane, it's wonderful to see you, dear. How we have missed you. I'm so sorry you have not been well. You still look a little pale, but don't worry. We'll soon put some roses in your cheeks. There is nothing like a bit of home cooking, and fresh air.' She put the kettle on and got out a Thermos flask. 'George is up on Meadow Hill, doing some fencing. Do you want to walk up and see him? I'll give you some bread and cheese, and a flask of tea, and you can have lunch together. Hang on a minute.' And with that the busy woman was off into the pantry to fetch supplies.

Fifteen minutes later, Jane was trudging up the hill. The dogs saw her first and came running to meet her, barking their greeting. George stopped working and looked up and waved to her. She waved back and quickened her pace. Onwards and upwards, she thought, and said a little prayer for strength of purpose.

Taking their lunch, they sat together in the little shepherd's hut that had been built there, years ago, for the lambing season. It was quite cosy and George had lit the fire. After they had eaten, she said she had something to tell him, and that he must not interrupt until she had finished, or she would lose her courage.

The story tumbled out and George sat still as stone. Even

when she described the rape he did not move a muscle. She finished and waited, her head bowed, for his response.

George stood and came over to her, kneeled down beside her and took her hands in his.

'I loved you then and I love you now, Jane. I pledge to protect you and your baby for the rest of my life. I will make you happy, and the Harrison name will never be mentioned again in our house.'

Jane sobbed with love and relief, and threw her arms around his neck. They held each other so tightly that Jane had to pull away to catch her breath. They gathered up the picnic and made their way home across Meadow Hill, arm in arm.

Chapter Six

George and Jane were married almost immediately, and at Mary's suggestion the wedding was held in Allingham, so that Jane's Uncle Reginald could perform the service. For Mary the day brought back so many memories, many of them sad ones. But she thought of all the years now passed, and how she would not have wished to be without her daughters, especially Jane. The woman was full of hope for her daughter's future. George was a fine man, and his love and strength would see them through this early hiccup in their marriage. Her one great regret was that Alfred had decided he wanted to move to the seaside. The war was in its last throes, and he wanted to make a fresh start: he was going to take early retirement in a few months' time, and, without discussing it with his wife, was looking to buy a house near Brighton. Mary was dismayed by the prospect. Not only would she be on her own with Alfred, but she'd be far away from her new grandchild, and her family and friends.

'You will soon get used to the idea,' announced Alfred. 'I have only just started looking for a property. Plenty of time to get to know the baby before we leave, and it is only a train ride or two. A couple of hours at the most. You can visit them, for goodness' sake!' Her feelings were dismissed, and Mary kept her thoughts to herself after that.

Meredith Lee was born on 1 June 1945. George was a wonderful father from day one, and Meredith was a very happy baby, which amazed Jane, bearing in mind her traumatic conception. Life was so full and busy. Jane worked alongside her husband in the fields as well as in the house. Donald had been building a cottage nearby for his ultimate retirement, and he and Louise decided that now, with their son married with a new family, it was the right time to hand over the majority of the farmwork to George, and take up residence in their new bungalow.

Everyone felt a new lease of life upon them. There was a real buzz in the air after the war ended. People were filled with hope for the future, determined to make it a better one. It couldn't have been a better time to be farming. Produce was in demand and prices of stock were down. He could build up a fine head of beef cattle, and run a dairy herd, and sheep. Later he adapted with the times and turned to arable products like wheat and barley. Malthouse Farm was thriving.

The farmhouse was turned into a beautiful home, thanks to Jane's practical and wifely skills. Marriage had made her bloom and she loved being queen of her castle. She would spend hours sewing curtains and covering chairs, while the baby played on the rug beside her. As the seasons passed, she and Mary would scan the hedgerows for blackberries and elderflowers, and between them they made pots and pots of delicious jams and chutneys – not to mention wine and sloe gin. Mary spent so many hours with her daughter and her grandchild that Alfred was often left to his own devices. But he was happy enough scouring the newspapers for properties, and planning his retirement. A prudent man with finances, he was in no hurry to make the change but would do it when the time was right. He never ceased to congratulate himself on having become a man of property, through marrying that fallen woman, Mary Charles.

Jane had always loved the idea of growing her own vegetables, so George allocated her half an acre at the bottom of the garden for her own use. She would go out there in all weathers, and dig and hoe and rake until her hands were raw with blisters. Slowly the patch took shape and by the end of the first year they had their own supply of potatoes, onions, beans and carrots. Jane was so proud of her efforts.

George did everything in his power to make his wife feel loved and secure, and Jane was happier than she had ever been in her life. She wanted so badly to respond to her husband positively in every way, to show him how much she loved him in return, but there was a wall between them in the bedroom. However much she tried to overcome her horror of being touched, she could not relax and let George make love to her.

Once the baby was born, and she was fully recovered, physically at least, she became aware that George was desperately trying to hide his need for her. She would catch him watching her with longing in his eyes. A huge wave of love for him would engulf her and yet she felt dead inside. Jane thought about what her mother had been through when she was born. Poor Mary! Jane could not imagine marrying a man she did not love at all.

One morning, after she had rocked Meredith to sleep in her pram, Jane strolled over to see her mother and suggested they walk to the village as it was such a lovely day.

As they walked, Jane broke the contented silence and said, 'Mum, I need some advice. I have no one but you I can turn to, and I am sorry to pry into your life, but I am at my wits' end.' She took a deep breath and ploughed on. 'George and I ... well, we don't, he hasn't ... I just can't bear to let him touch me,

Mum. I just panic at the thought of the whole business and freeze up. But George deserves better. He has been so kind and loving towards me, and I do want to love him back, but I just can't get beyond a hug. What shall I do?'

Mary stopped walking and took Jane in her arms. 'Oh, dearest girl, it must be so hard for you. I can only imagine your pain. But listen to me, it will pass with time.'

'But I haven't got time, Mum. George won't wait around for ever. I need to break down this block I have inside me!'

Mary walked on in silence for a bit and then started to talk, quietly at first, as if to herself.

'You know, a woman's body is the strangest thing. I had so little understanding of it as a girl, and there was no one in our family to teach me. When I gave in to Henry I really didn't understand what had overcome me. I just knew I wanted him to hold me and love me. I didn't even know what I meant by love. I was still full of grief for my mother, so very lonely, and I needed some kind of physical contact with another human being. My father was very wrapped up in his world and he was never very affectionate anyway. After my mother's death he missed her so much and he just shut down. To the boys, I was like another brother really, and they didn't hug each other or anything. So when Henry kissed me, all those pent-up feelings just flooded out and became sexual – well, he made them sexual. Had it been someone else, I wonder sometimes, maybe we would not have made love at all.'

She turned to Jane. 'But he also had a need for love and warmth. The war was so cruel to those boys, Jane. They saw terrible things and they must have had to learn to shut out all their emotions. Suddenly, there we were in a beautiful garden at night, and I was so full of passion for life; he somehow turned that into passion for him. It was a wonderful moment and I will never forget it.'

Mary paused, allowing herself to enjoy the memory after so many years.

'But then I fell pregnant and suddenly my youth was lost for ever. My body was no longer my own to discover and learn about in the natural passage of time. I had experienced a wonderful sensation but now it was gone, and I was left feeling sick in my stomach and my heart. Not quite the same horror of violent rape as you went through, my darling, but in a strange way we both ended up in a similar position. I, too, found myself unwilling to sleep with my husband. I had no interest in him at all physically, and like you feel now, I was numb, dead. The thought of his touch repelled me. But as soon as he thought I had recovered from giving birth to you, he more or less took me by force. That first time, my whole body recoiled. I didn't want him, Jane. I was dry and he forced his way into me.'

Mary started to cry at the memory. Jane felt so guilty for making her mother relive this unhappiness.

'Please, Mother, stop. We don't have to talk about it. I am so sorry I asked you.' Jane rummaged in her bag to find a handkerchief.

'No, please, it is good for me to talk about it because looking back, I realise it was the best thing that could have happened. Women are fantastic creatures, Jane. We adapt and change. We are also much more passionate and sensitive to our feelings than society would have us believe. My body responded to the intrusion in a way I could never have imagined. In the end, it was stimulated, despite my mind trying to tell it otherwise. You could say it let me down by responding the way it did, but it saved the day because Alfred felt wanted, and in return became kinder to me. Our marriage was never very passionate, but after that initial disaster we found a way to accommodate each other. Having you helped me, and then when Pamela was born Alfred used most of his emotional content up on her, so I was never really important to him any more. Oh, I know that sounds terrible but we managed, and I will always be so grateful to him for taking me on. It is bad enough these days to give birth to an illegitimate child – imagine what it was like for me, a vicar's daughter! It would have killed my father. Things are changing so fast these days, and maybe one day there will be no shame in having a child out of wedlock, who knows?'

Mary reached out to straighten the baby's blanket, concluding: 'All I am trying to tell you, dear, is that the mind is a powerful thing, and sometimes we have to trick it, to stop it controlling our emotions. Find a suitable moment for you and George to spend some time together. Go out somewhere and have a few drinks, I will look after Meredith. Let him touch you, and slowly your body will return those feelings naturally. Just relax, and let it happen. There is no shame in real love between a man and a woman.'

Jane hugged her mum and felt such love for her. She was such a wise woman.

'I will try, Mum. Thank you.'

As it turned out, fate took over from any of Jane's best intentions. A few weeks later, George was up in the top field hedging, when the wire-cutters slipped and took his thumb off. He staggered into the kitchen as white as a sheet, saying, 'Jane, love, get me to Doctor Wright as quick as you can. I have cut myself badly.' He then promptly fainted.

Jane got the horse and trap harnessed, and managed to bundle George in the back, while she placed Meredith in her carrycot on the front seat beside her. She arrived at the surgery in record time. George had to lose his thumb but the doctor was able to stitch it and close the top over the knuckle.

'That will be very sore for a few days, I am afraid. But as long as you keep changing the dressings you should be as right as rain in a couple of weeks. Good job your Jane is such an excellent nurse.' Dr Wright had heard all about her work with the Red Cross during her visit to London.

Jane managed to get them home, and after putting Meredith to bed in her cot, she settled down to give her husband some loving care and attention. She cooked him a special tea and opened a bottle of the infamous sloe gin.

'Blimey, this is strong stuff, love!' said George, taking a swig. 'There'll be no germs left after this goes down.'

Jane laughed and took a swig herself. It tasted wonderful, so warming. They sat on the sofa eating her homemade steak and kidney pie from plates on their laps, drinking sloe gin until they were both nearly nodding off.

'Come on, you, bed. What a terrible nurse I am, giving my patient alcohol.'

Jane got his arm around her and they staggered upstairs to bed. They fell into the room and managed to get themselves on top of the bed. All the while, George was holding his bandaged thumb up in the air away from harm. It made Jane burst out laughing, and they both got hysterical when they tried to undress.

'Here, let me,' said Jane, as she saw George struggling with his trouser buttons. It set them off again into gales of tipsy laughter. 'You will have to learn to do this all over again now without your thumb.'

And she was so intent on her activity she did not notice George's arms go round her; suddenly he was kissing her, and the kisses were getting more passionate. She almost pulled back and then remembered her mother's words. 'Just relax and let it happen.' It was good to feel his lips on hers. She had forgotten what a good kisser he was, slow and probing. It was exciting to taste him again. He groaned a little and she tried to pull away.

'Is your thumb hurting?' she whispered.

'It's not my bloody thumb that's hurting, girl. Oh, God, I love you, Jane. Please don't refuse me. I want you so badly.' George tilted her chin and searched her eyes. 'You are so beautiful, oh wife of mine. Don't be afraid. I will be very gentle and fill you up with my love.'

Jane loved him so much at that moment her whole body relaxed. The only thought in her head was to give herself to this man, to drown in his love, and shelter in his embrace. His arms were around her and she felt safe at last. This was the only place she wanted to be.

George undressed her as best he could in the circumstances. His injury made life very difficult for him so, giggling, Jane took over. Once naked, she lifted the bedclothes and slid beneath the sheets, holding them up for George. He was trembling with passion and trying so hard to control himself. He kissed Jane again, slowly, and then harder as his tongue found hers, and they teased each other with their kisses. Tenderly George touched his wife from head to toe as if trying to remember her from his dreams. He was so hard against her stomach that Jane fought back a moment of panic. He waited a moment as he felt her tense, then very gently he began to caress the inside of her thigh, his touch, featherlight, cajoling her into opening her legs for him. She shuddered with desire, surprising herself at how much she wanted him. She pulled him in to her and lifted her legs around him. Slowly, agonisingly slowly, George entered her. It was so wonderful to feel him at last, and her whole body felt warm and soft and pliant. As he started to move inside her she let out a gasp of pleasure. It was such a relief to realise she wanted him as badly as he wanted her. They made love in perfect harmony. It was passionate and loving and completely satisfying.

Jane turned to face George as he lay back on the pillows and gazed at her husband.

'Thank you, thank you, George, for waiting for me. I love you so much and I will spend the rest of my life making sure you are happy.'

'I am happy now, Jane. I will always be happy as long as I have you beside me. Just think, I have lost a thumb today but gained a wife!' They laughed and made love again, and slept the sleep of the truly happy.

Three years later in 1948, Jane gave birth to a son and he was christened Frank Donald. The family was complete and George was the happiest man alive. For Jane it was a joy and a heartbreak, as by now, her mother and Alfred had sold their house in St Albans and finally moved to Hove. She missed Mary so much, especially in those early weeks with a newborn baby. She really had her hands full with a babe in arms and a lively three-year-old Meredith. Her mother came to the christening with Alfred, but they didn't stay as Alfred was keen to get back to his new life by the sea. Jane told her mother she was welcome to come any time and Mary promised she would. She already felt so cut off down in Hove. She spent a good deal of time alone, as Alfred had joined a Bowls Club and spent hours with his cronies, either playing or drinking in the club. Mary soon knew the train timetables off by heart, and would leave food in the cupboard and a tin of homemade cakes, and set off on her train journey to happiness.

Meredith was a little put out at the arrival of her brother. This new bundle of joy seemed to be a possible threat to her domain. But she soon understood she was still Daddy's girl. George would sweep her up onto his shoulders and take her out with him to the cowshed. Meredith loved to watch the cows being milked. Her dad would squirt warm milk at her from the cow's teat, and she would shriek with delight, and clap her hands. She loved it when her Grandmother Mary came to stay

94

because she could go out with her and play for long hours. In the spring when the lambs were born, Mary taught Meredith the nursery rhyme 'Mary had a little lamb'. She told the child about her pet lamb Alice, and when George brought a sickly lamb into the kitchen one day, he watched with a smile on his face as Mary showed her granddaughter how to feed the lamb, making the little girl sit on the floor by the cooker, placing the tiny animal in her lap. It was a touching sight, and Jane was happy that her mother could enjoy these special moments.

Meredith loved feeding the lamb. She giggled at the feel of its rough tongue as it sucked and pulled on her fingers. Outside in the rickyard she would play for hours if she could. There was always a smell of hay, warm milk and animal sweat. She liked to build tunnels and camps. As Frank grew older he became her playmate and very best friend, and she especially loved him because he did whatever she told him to do.

Meredith and Frank had the perfect childhood. In the winter, they would come home from school to a cosy kitchen, with toast and homemade jam waiting for them. In the summer, Jane would bring them a picnic in the garden with fresh lemonade, and chocolate sponge still warm from the oven. Meredith learned to bake with her mother, as Jane had often baked with Mary. Jane made a lot of pastry for pies, as farmers were hearty eaters, so there would always be some left over for Meredith to roll out and cut into different shapes with the pastry-cutters. She liked to make jam tarts and give them to her father for his pudding. Or she would take some in a box to her Grandad Lee, just up the road.

She loved visiting Nanny and Grandad Lee, because children were allowed to do whatever they liked in their bungalow. Sometimes she and Frank would go to tea on Sunday and they watched TV. This was magical, because they didn't have a television yet in their house. They had tea on their laps, while watching the black and white pictures flicker in front of them. In 1953 when Queen Elizabeth II was crowned, the Lees had a big party and all the village came and practically swamped their front room trying to catch a glimpse of the royal occasion on the screen. It was exciting, and Meredith was given a little silver Coronation carriage and horses from her school to mark the occasion.

Meredith also liked it when her Grandad Lee took her out in the pony-trap. He would drive up to the top field, and they would chase the old bull all the way back down to the yard, and into his pen. Nanny tried to make him stop as she thought it was dangerous, but Grandad was having none of it, even though he had once been gored by a bull. Meredith would sit beside him and listen to his stories in awe. He had a big white moustache, and at home he would sit with his feet up on the mantelpiece, his toe poking through a hole in his sock.

'You put me to shame, Donald Lee,' Louise would scold. But he took no notice. He was the boss, and they all knew it.

Sometimes Meredith would sit with Nanny Louise under a huge cherry tree in the garden, and pod peas. Then there would be the cherries. So many cherries! In pies, in jam, or straight off the tree in handfuls, just like the marbles she and her brother played with all day long. What a collection he had, hundreds. He would spread them out on the grass, and they would compare size and colour. He always had the best, and the best conkers too. When it was time for the conker season, Meredith could never beat her brother.

'That's because I'm a boy,' Frank would tell her proudly.

Visits to Granny and Grandad Hughes were a different matter. Looking back, it seemed to Meredith like gazing into a silver-framed photo of Victorian life, with her Grandmother Mary sitting stiffly on a chair and her Grandfather Alfred standing behind her, a heavy hand on his wife's shoulder. The couple lived near the sea in one of those endless roads of dark brooding houses full of repressed secrets, Meredith would comment, later in life. How right she was, as it turned out. Trips to this house were never looked forward to, but often ended on a happy note. Looking back as an adult, she realised she must have gone several times on her own when her mother had given birth to Frank, and needed some rest.

Her grandfather was notoriously grumpy but to Meredith, who was such a sunny, well-adjusted child, he was just another grown-up to be won over. And win him over she did. He was really quite taken with her, and decided one holiday that he was going to teach her to swim. Every morning they would set off for the local baths. A strange sight, the elderly man and the little girl clutching her water ring. Meredith loved the swimming baths. She was deposited at the ladies' changing room, and a jolly lady called Doreen would take her through and help her change, and put her clothes in a locker. Then she would skip through to the other side and find her grandfather waiting by the side of the pool. He never got into the water, but would stand at the side shouting encouragement and tips.

Sometimes he wouldn't notice that the poor child was practically blue with cold, until Doreen would pop in and call out, 'Mr Hughes – time to come in now or the little mite will catch her death.' Then Meredith would run into the changing rooms and Doreen would rub her hard to stop her shivering. She would struggle into her clothes, still cold, and they would stick to her. But slowly she would start to feel warm again, and as soon as she got her big treat, which was a hot chocolate with cream on top, all was right in her world. Her grandad would also sometimes take her to his Bowling Club, and she would sit outside on the veranda with a beaker of lemonade watching him play with his team.

Mary loved having Meredith to stay, of course. She would plan for weeks before she arrived, things to do and what to eat.

She knew that the house held little joy, but she did her best to make Meredith feel at home. And to be fair, Meredith handled it quite well. If she felt homesick she would go to her room and find her favourite doll called April, which was kept at the Hughes's house, and sit and talk to her until she felt better. Sometimes she would wander upstairs and see her grandmother at her dressing table as she passed her door, which was always ajar. One time Meredith watched spellbound as Mary let down her hair, and began to brush it out. It went right down to her waist and was jet black. Meredith had never seen such beautiful hair. Mary turned to her and waved to her to come in.

'Do you want to brush it for me, dear?' she asked. Meredith nodded solemnly and took the proffered hairbrush. It was a Mason Pearson with a shiny black back. Meredith never forgot it. The memory belonged with those things from one's childhood that are so evocative. She would never forget her mother Jane's Yardley lipstick, or her Bourjois Rouge pot, and the smell of face powder and lavender cologne.

The little girl stood behind her grandmother and started to brush.

'I do a hundred strokes every day, you know,' Mary told her. A hundred strokes! That would take all day.

Meredith pulled the brush through the thick hair, very careful not to tug on any tangles. The rhythm of the strokes lulled her into a kind of daze. The room was very warm and smelled of violets. It was like being in a trance. She stole a peek at her grandmother and saw that Mary's eyes were shut. The silence was as heavy as the velvet curtains at the window. Suddenly, a sharp tone cut the air and made the little girl jump.

'What's going on in here?'

'Meredith is brushing my hair, Alfred, can't you see?'

'Well, she must stop it now. This is no way to behave, Mary. Get downstairs and prepare my lunch, if you please.' He turned and went into the bathroom. Mary shook her head slowly, and looked at Meredith in the mirror.

'Men don't understand anything, do they, dear?' She took the brush, and put it on the dressing table. Then she twisted the cascade of black hair into two plaits, and pinned them round her head. Meredith watched this manoeuvre, transfixed, and Mary smiled at her reassuringly.

'Shall we go and make Grandad's lunch?' she asked. Meredith nodded and ran off downstairs.

Mary sighed. Poor Alfred; he always felt threatened by any suggested intimacy, even from a child. Still, she had managed, despite everything, to create a life for her family. She was proud of what she had achieved. Her thoughts turned to Pamela and she wondered if she would ever get to know her other granddaughter, Sylvia. She always sent a card for the girl's birthday, but no reply was ever forthcoming. Alfred occasionally made the trip up to London to take Pamela out to lunch – without inviting Mary to join them – but he always returned rather subdued, and she never liked to ask how everything was in Town.

Mary and Alfred had continued to maintain their uneasy truce after his retirement, and life was almost agreeable. Once their daughters had left home there was the inevitable gap. Coming to live in Hove had been a terrible wrench for Mary, but she had made the best of a bad job as usual. She paid frequent visits to stay with Jane and George, who always made her feel so welcome, and she had to admit that Alfred's association with the Bowling Club kept him out of the house and from under her feet. She enjoyed reading and walking on the beach, and had joined the local Women's Institute. She found the community spirit of these ladies rather encouraging. Having had a lonely childhood with three older brothers, it was quite a novelty to be with a group of women and to feel so at home.

She enjoyed following their recipes and trying out the crafts, and it gave her a sense of herself she had never had before. Sometimes a tiny voice in her head suggested that her life had been wasted, and yet she knew this was untrue. She tried hard not to imagine what her life would have been like if she had not fallen pregnant. Still, Jane had been a joy to her, and even Pamela had had her moments. She did worry about her younger daughter though. Somehow she glittered too brightly for her own good, and it hurt Mary that Pamela chose not to include her in her life. Jane was happy at last though, and despite the horror of her rape by Myles Harrison, she had found happiness with a loving family. Thank the Lord it had all turned out right.

One summer in the early 1950s, a couple of years after they had moved to Hove, Mary decided to write to Pamela and invite her down, with Sylvia, when Meredith would be with them next. After all, there was only a year or so between the two girls and they might enjoy each other's company. She gave Pamela the dates of Meredith's stay with them, and waited with interest to hear the response.

About two weeks before Meredith was due to arrive, Mary received a letter from Pamela.

> *Dear Mother,*
> *Lovely to hear from you. It really has been too long, I know, but life just flies by and there is never any time. I think it is a wonderful idea to have your two granddaughters to stay. Could we bring Sylvia down next Tuesday?*
>
> *Fondest love,*
>
> *Pamela*

Mary put the letter away. This was a turn-up for the books! She went to break the news to Alfred.

'Do we really need this inconvenience,' he muttered behind his paper.

'Well, I thought you would be delighted to see Pamela and Sylvia. Meredith will be here anyway, and it is just as easy with two, as one. It will be so lovely to see Sylvia, dear, don't you think?'

There was no reply, just an irritated rustle of the *Daily Telegraph*, but Mary was undeterred and soon set about baking cakes and preparing the girls' room.

When Jane arrived on the Sunday night, Mary was in a high state of excitement, and a little nervous about how her daughter would react to the news.

'Oh, Mother, why?' Jane said immediately. 'Why have anything to do with the Harrisons?'

'Well, it's not the child's fault, is it, dear? You don't have to see anyone, unless you want to come and visit, and see Sylvia after all these years.'

'No, thank you. I have no desire to see her. I know it's not her fault, and she is innocent of her foul parents, but that is a step too far for me. Just make sure Meredith is not left out. You know what Father is like.'

Mary waved goodbye with Meredith at the front door, then took the little girl into the kitchen to have some cake. Whenever her mother left, Meredith fretted for the first hour. Distraction worked well, Mary discovered, and cake was an easy option. She also kept the doll called April in the cupboard for Meredith to play with whenever she stayed. It had become part of the ritual of the visit to get April out, and make her a new outfit. Either Mary made a dress, or knitted a cardigan or some such. Meredith loved April, and the doll always had pride of place on her bed.

Tuesday arrived, and Mary and Meredith prepared for Cousin Sylvia's arrival. Meredith had not even known she had a cousin until this week. She was excited to meet her new friend. Towards midday, a large car drew up outside and a woman stepped out, looking amazing in a black and white polka dot dress, nipped in at the waist with a full skirt. Her trim ankles were encased in white calf high heels and she wore a huge sun hat and white sunglasses. Meredith had never seen anything like this except in her mother's magazines. A young girl popped out behind this vision, looked around, then caught Meredith's eye and ran towards her.

'Hello, Meredith. I am Sylvia.' A pretty child with lots of blonde curls and big blue eyes, she was wearing a frock of printed cotton, with white socks and patent shoes. The two girls ran into the house and Mary hugged Pamela.

'How lovely to see you, dear, it has been such a long time,' she said, letting out an involuntary gasp, as over Pam's shoulder she saw the imposing, tall figure of a man coming towards her. This could only be Myles Harrison. She had only met him once before, very briefly that time he was introduced as Pamela's fiancé, but there was no mistaking the man. He came forward and shook her hand, firmly, and she felt herself draw back at his touch. He was smiling but his eyes were cold. Poor Jane, she thought.

'Good to meet you again, Mary,' he said.

'You too, please do come in.' She turned and led them into the house. Myles seemed too big for the hall and loomed in the front door like a spectre.

'I have only made a light lunch, I hope it will be enough for you,' said Mary, as she showed them into the front room. 'Please do take a seat. Can I get you some squash or tea perhaps?'

'Look, I brought some wine,' announced Pamela, producing a bottle from her oversized bag. 'Just get me a corkscrew,

Mother, and we are away. You do have a corkscrew, I presume?'
And she flounced off into the kitchen.

'Do sit down,' repeated Mary, feeling Myles towering over
her. 'Or perhaps you would like to go in the garden as it is such
a lovely day. The door is through here.'

Myles went out into the sunshine and started to light a cigarette. 'Lovely garden,' he muttered and turned away from
Mary. She went to find Pamela in the kitchen.

'Why didn't you tell me he was coming?' she asked Pamela,
in a whisper. 'I have prepared such a paltry lunch, it is embarrassing. What will he think?'

'Who cares what he thinks?' answered Pamela, taking a swig
of the wine. 'Don't fret so, Ma, it will be fine. We have to get off
fairly quickly anyway, as Myles needs to get back, so a snack is
ideal.'

Mary heated up a tin of tomato soup and buttered slices of
bread from a loaf she had made following a WI recipe, then put
some salad and a slice of corned beef on each plate. She laid the
table and called to the girls, who were upstairs. Alfred was not yet
back and she couldn't keep them all waiting for their lunch. They
all sat down round the table. Sylvia made to grab a slice of bread
and butter, but Mary stopped her with, 'No, dear, not until we
have said Grace.' She bent her head and recited 'For what we are
about to receive, may the Lord make us truly thankful.' She lifted
her head and passed the plate of bread and butter to the little girl.
'Please, help yourself, dear. And be careful – the soup is very hot.'

Sylvia took a slice very tentatively, as if she was expecting it
to jump up and bite her.

'Eat up, everyone,' said Mary, and passed the plate to
Pamela, who was already halfway through the bottle of wine.

'Oh, not for me, thank you, Mother. Got to think of my
figure, haven't I, darling?' And she threw a look in Myles's
direction with a big smile.

'No need to worry on my account, my darling. You have the perfect figure,' he replied. Then he turned sharply to Sylvia and reprimanded her with, 'Don't bolt your food, girl!'

The girl spluttered, and sprayed tomato soup across the white tablecloth. Meredith started to giggle and so did Sylvia. They were both stuffing their napkins into their mouths.

'Stop that at once,' scolded Myles, but it just made things worse and the girls simply could not control their giggles. Myles stood up and went round to the back of his daughter's chair.

'Get up, Sylvia. You must go to your room until you stop this nonsense.' He pulled her out of her chair and dragged her to the door. Meredith was on her feet in a flash and standing in front of Myles, defiantly.

'Don't be so mean! She couldn't help it, she choked. Come on, Sylvia, I will come with you.' She seized the girl's arm and off they went together. Mary almost expected her to stick out her tongue, as Pamela had once done after the incident of the broken doll.

Now, Pamela laughed and said, 'Myles, don't be so hard on the child – it was an accident.'

'She has to learn manners,' he retorted. Then, 'I apologise for my daughter, Mary.'

'It is quite unnecessary,' replied Mary. 'Sylvia meant no harm, I am sure. Shall I go and get them to finish their lunch?' Myles hesitated a second, then nodded his assent.

Mary went to find the girls, who were in their room still giggling. They stopped as she entered the room, and looked at her guiltily.

'Sorry, Granny,' said Meredith. 'We didn't mean to laugh, but it was funny.'

Mary smiled conspiratorially at them. 'I know it was, but don't tell your father, Sylvia. Now come downstairs and finish your lunch. But first you must say sorry.' She took their hands and they made their way downstairs.

The two little girls went to the head of the table, stood in front of Myles and said in unison, 'We are very sorry, please may we sit down again?'

'Yes, you may,' came the reply, and lunch passed without further incident. Mary had reheated the soup for the children and everyone ate heartily, apart from Pamela.

An hour later, Myles and Pamela were on the doorstep saying their farewells.

'Your father is going to be so upset he missed you. Can't you stay a little longer? He was planning to be back for lunch at one o'clock – I've got no idea what has detained him. We didn't realise you wouldn't be staying.' Mary dreaded what Alfred would say – but it was his own fault. He should have joined them at one o'clock as promised. She did her best to make Pamela wait longer, but to no avail. The couple climbed into the waiting Daimler, and disappeared round the corner in a flash.

The girls helped their grandmother clear the table and then ran off to play. Half an hour later, she heard Alfred's key in the door. She went to meet him.

'You missed Pamela, dear. She and Myles only stayed an hour because he had to get back for an appointment.'

Alfred took off his coat, his face like thunder, and walked into the parlour muttering, 'A likely story. Well, good riddance. Is the girl here?' He sat down and took out his paper.

Mary made a pot of tea and put the cup in front of him with a corned-beef sandwich. 'Yes, she is playing with Meredith. She seems very sweet.'

When Mary went to find the girls a bit later on, they were engrossed in playing with April, and chatting very happily. Meredith asked her, 'Is Grandad going to give us an egg hunt, please?'

'I will go and ask him,' replied Mary, fearing what the answer might be. She found Alfred in his greenhouse tending his tomato plants.

'Sorry to interrupt, dear, but your granddaughters would like you to give them an egg hunt. Would that be acceptable to you? I know you must be tired but they would love it so.'

Mary was surprised as her husband turned round and said, 'Of course I will. Give me five minutes to organise it.'

Mary breathed a sigh of relief, and went back to tell the girls the good news. They danced round the kitchen table whooping with delight.

'Please calm down, your grandfather does not like lots of noise,' chided Mary gently.

Just then, Alfred himself appeared at the door. 'Now then, girls, away you go and find your egg for tea. They are hidden somewhere out there.' He was positively jovial. The girls ran past him shrieking with anticipation, and he actually smiled. Wonders will never cease, thought Mary.

After their tea of boiled eggs and soldiers, the girls went to have their bath, and while Mary was clearing up the watery mess they had left behind, they got ready for bed. Meredith kneeled down beside her bed and began to say her prayers.

'What are you doing?' asked Sylvia.

'Saying my prayers, silly. Don't you say your prayers?'

'No, we don't say them in my house,' replied Sylvia. 'What are they, anyway?'

'Well, you have to say them otherwise Baby Jesus won't love you. You say them like this.' Meredith put her hands together and recited very carefully: 'God bless Mummy and Daddy and my brother Frank, and Nanny and Grandad Lee and Granny and Grandad Hughes and all my friends and now my cousin, Sylvia. Thank You for all the lovely things You give me. Good night, Baby Jesus.' Meredith then stood up, and went to get April, the doll, from Sylvia's bed.

Her cousin ran over and pulled the doll away from her.

'I want the dolly,' she said.

'Well, you can't have her, she's mine,' retorted Meredith, grabbing the doll back.

'No, she's not. She belongs to Granny, but I want her tonight. Give her to me!' Sylvia screamed and tried to seize the doll again.

Mary heard the commotion and rushed into the room. 'What on earth is going on in here? Both of you stop this at once!'

'Sylvia took April,' complained Meredith. 'She can't have her, she's mine. I always have her when I go to sleep.'

'Well, yes, that is true,' agreed Mary, and turned to Sylvia. 'Do you mind very much if Meredith has April tonight as usual?'

'It's not fair,' Sylvia wailed. 'Why can't I have the doll? I am the guest. Meredith should let me have April.'

'Meredith, dear, shall we let your cousin have April tonight as she is a guest? It would be so kind of you if you could lend it to her.' Mary smiled encouragingly, and crossed her fingers. Meredith closed her eyes and thought very hard, and then finally opened her eyes and relented.

'All right, just this once, but remember – she is my dolly.'

Sylvia scuttled off to her bed with the doll, triumphant.

As Mary tucked her beloved granddaughter into bed she leaned in to give the little girl a kiss and whispered, 'You are a very kind girl, and always remember, Jesus loves you.'

'Well, I don't like my cousin, and she is not kind, Granny. April is *mine*.' And with that she snuggled under the covers and went to sleep.

PART TWO

Chapter Seven

The Lee family prospered through the 1950s. George worked tirelessly, and the farm did well and doubled its production. Jane kept a wary eye on her beloved husband. Thank God, the problem with his irregular heartbeat was monitored by Dr Wright, and there had been no problems so far, but she never quite forgot the threat was there.

Jane and George were a great team and worked alongside each other happily as the years passed and their two children grew into teenagers. Jane loved to spend hours in her vegetable garden, and by helping her and having their own patches in which to grow simple things, Frank and Meredith learned everything there was to know about seeds and planting. She also continued to cook with her daughter, and sometimes even Frank would join in, though he did think it was a bit cissy for boys to put on an apron. He would much rather spend time with his dad, learning to drive a tractor. Meredith, however, loved cooking and Jane could hardly keep her daughter out of the kitchen. The family were subjected to all sorts of weird and wonderful concoctions. Cooking had become the girl's favourite hobby.

She also loved school, unlike her brother who had to be

bribed, threatened and cajoled on a daily basis to get out of bed and join his sister at the bottom of the road to wait for the bus. Meredith's best friend from her primary-school days was Eva Hamlin, whose family was very wealthy, and lived in Long Moor House, a mansion with a huge estate just up the road. The fact that the two girls came from very different back-grounds did not seem to affect either of them. Eva was very flamboyant and wanted to be an actress, while Meredith was quite happy to work backstage and sew costumes. Which was just as well when it came to the school plays, as there could have been unwanted rivalry between them. Meredith was very happy to let her friend be 'the star'.

One morning, when she was about twelve, Meredith announced to her mother, 'I think I want to be a nun.'

Trying not to show her surprise, Jane replied, 'That's nice, dear, what made you decide that?'

'Oh, Gran and I were just talking, you know. She is very reli-gious and always telling me about Jesus and how much He loves me. She said she thought about being a nun once, when she was young, and thinks it would be a lovely thing for me to be, maybe.'

'I see,' said Jane, making a mental note to talk to Mary. It was not the most helpful advice she could be giving her young granddaughter. 'Come on, get your coat now, and we will talk later. Dad is taking you to school this morning.'

'Oh no, why?' whined her daughter.

'Because I have to take your brother to the doctor to have his ear checked.'

'Oh, he is always going to the doctor, stupid boy,' she said as Frank came into the kitchen.

'Who is stupid?' Frank asked suspiciously.

'You are, you little monster,' said his big sister.

'That is not the attitude of someone who wants to become

a nun, Meredith,' scolded Jane. 'I am sure Jesus would not be very pleased to hear you talking like that to your little brother.'

'Well, I am very sorry, I'm sure,' Meredith snapped as she flounced out of the door.

As Jane walked Frank to the local surgery she thought about her mother. Sadly, Alfred had died a couple of years ago – quite suddenly, of a heart attack at the Bowling Club after playing a lengthy match in the full sun. It had been quick, at least, but Jane had worried about her mother, all alone in that awful house in Hove. When George had suggested she move back and live in one of the farm cottages, it seemed the ideal solution. It meant that she was close to her family, but retained her independence.

Pamela, naturally, had not proffered any support at all. She had turned up for Alfred's funeral alone, with neither Myles nor even Sylvia, saying her husband was too busy and a funeral was no place for a child. It was a very bleak affair; hardly anyone came apart from the family and two or three colleagues from the Bowling Club, and a former associate from work who had also moved to Sussex. It was not really surprising, as Alfred had not been a particularly pleasant man, but nevertheless it was rather sad. Mary told herself that he had stood by her in her time of need, and she would always be grateful for that. These days, the past seemed as vivid as the present, and she spent many hours praying earnestly to God to forgive her for her sins.

Fortunately, her suggestion to her granddaughter did not take root, and as her teenage years overtook her, Meredith forgot about being a nun and spent more time trying to emulate her rather flashy friend. Jane was not thrilled by this either, but realised the more she tried to put Meredith off Eva, the more fascinating the other girl would become. The friends were inseparable, and when they reached the Upper Sixth at school, they started making big plans to go to London together and share a flat. Eva had applied to RADA to study drama, and to her delight was accepted, and Meredith had a place at Le Cordon Bleu School in Marylebone Lane to take a cookery course.

Sensibly, they decided to go up to London in their summer holidays before term started, to find somewhere to live. Both girls had been to London several times with the school on trips to museums and art galleries, and by themselves to go round the shops, so the big city was not a shock to them. Meredith found it exciting and such a contrast to life in a country village. They took the train up to St Pancras one sunny morning, arranging to go their separate ways and enrol at their respective colleges, then meet at Meredith's college to begin their hunt for somewhere to live. They set off to the first address with high hopes. But these hopes were soon dashed. Most of the places were little more than slums.

'How can people live like this?' wailed Eva. 'We are never going to find anywhere, Merry. This is so depressing!'

Both girls were used to the comforts of home, but as she looked round the one-bedroom dingy basement flat, Meredith thought to herself that this was worlds away from anything they had ever experienced. The furniture was stained and battered, and there was an all-pervading smell of gas and boiled cabbage. She felt tired and disheartened, as well as irritated by her best friend, who was useless in a crisis. Eva had no stamina, and caved in at the first sign of defeat. Well, not Meredith Lee.

'Come on,' she said, 'we are going back to Le Cordon Bleu. There was a really nice boy there called Oliver who seemed to know everything about everything. Let's hope he is still around.'

They found him in the college canteen with a group of other students.

'Excuse me, it's Oliver, isn't it?' interrupted Meredith, flashing him her brightest smile. 'My name is Meredith, and this is my best friend Eva. We are looking for rooms in a flat, if possible. You don't know of any going, do you?'

'As a matter of fact I do, my dear,' replied Oliver with a big grin. 'I have managed to find a three-bedroomed pad in Marylebone High Street, just round the corner, no less, and I'm looking for a couple of people to share with. The place needs a bit of tender loving care, but you look like the kind of girl who doesn't mind getting her hands dirty. Can't say the same for your friend, though.' He looked Eva up and down as she posed on a stool, flashing reams of leg, and tossing her mane of golden curls.

Meredith burst out laughing. 'You have got that right, Oliver. But trust me, she is not as useless as she looks, and she makes a mean cocktail.' Meredith had been introduced to alcohol at the Hamlin house. She loved the different concoctions that Eva would devise at her parents' cocktail bar. They were a far cry from her mother's elderflower wine. 'Could we look at it now as we need to get our train home soon?'

The girls loved the flat. It was at the top of three flights of stairs, with a little terrace that looked over the rooftops. Meredith thought it was the most romantic place she had ever seen. Oliver had taken the biggest bedroom, naturally, but the other two bedrooms could hold a single bed and a side table and a wardrobe.

'That will never take all my clothes!' cried Eva.

Meredith was investigating the kitchen. It was tiny but had everything they needed and the window opened onto the roof.

'Look, Eva, we can sit out here in the summer. It's perfect.'

The living room was heated by an old gas fire, fed by a meter.

'What does that mean, for heaven's sake?' asked Eva.

'Girls, you are so naïve. True country bumpkins,' mocked Oliver.

'All right, Mr Know-it-all, there's no need to be rude,' said Meredith. 'Just give us the gen, all right? We learn quickly, us country girls.'

Oliver explained that they would have to keep a pot of shilling pieces to put in the meter. 'Which brings us neatly to the money situation,' he announced. 'The rent is £7 a week each, for you two, and as I found the place, I get away with paying a pound less – £6. All bills are split three ways. Term begins in three weeks, so how about you give me twenty pounds now, as a kind of deposit, and then that covers you till then. Does that sound fair?'

The girls agreed and the deal was done. Meredith arranged to meet Oliver for a cleaning and decorating day in a couple of weeks. Eva couldn't come as she was going away with her parents to the South of France.

'Oh, you poor girl,' came Oliver's sarcastic response and Eva pulled a face at him.

'OK, OK, stop taking the mickey. I can't help it, but I will ask my mum for some extra dosh to buy us a nice new sofa, to make up for not being here to help: does that sound good?'

'Perfect,' laughed Oliver. 'Just what the doctor ordered. I can tell we are going to have a great time.'

Meredith and Eva spent the journey home making plans.

'Do you think he's handsome?' said Eva. 'I thought he was quite flirty.'

'I didn't really notice, but please, Eva, don't start anything. We are flatmates and we do not need any complications.'

'I know, don't worry. Gosh, Merry, just think – our very own place! Think of the parties we can have.' Eva's eyes were sparkling at the thought.

'Yes, I suppose,' Meredith said doubtfully. 'But we must make sure we do all our work first.'

'Oh, Merry, you can be stuffy sometimes,' retorted Eva. 'But I adore you, and you are my best friend ever.'

Meredith and Oliver spent a long and happy day cleaning and painting the flat. After eight hours it was transformed.

'I can't wait to go and buy some paintings and bits and pieces. Only from junk shops – you know what I mean,' said Meredith.

'I will take you to this amazing market called Portobello. You will love it,' enthused Oliver. 'It sells everything you can imagine! But listen, you should choose your room: you get first choice as you have done all the work.'

Meredith chose the smaller of the two bedrooms because the window opened onto the same flat roof as the kitchen. She would be able to sit outside and watch the sun go down over this part of Central London.

Her mother had given Meredith some bed-linen, and made both girls beautiful embroidered bedspreads. Meredith was staying the night as it had been such a long day, so before she and Oliver fell into their beds, they opened a bottle of fizzy wine and drank a toast.

'To friendship and sharing,' proposed Oliver, clinking his glass against Meredith's.

'And to success,' she added.

A week later, Meredith and Eva were standing on the platform at St Albans station with all their worldly goods. Meredith hugged her mother and promised to write, or phone, at least once a week. Jane and George had been somewhat apprehensive about Meredith sharing a flat with Oliver. It was not quite what they had hoped for, and George especially was suspicious of the boy's motives. Meredith had laughed at this.

'Oh Dad, don't be so daft! Oliver is my friend and Eva's. It's not like that at all. But it is nice to have a man around to do stuff for us, and look after us. He is going to come here for the weekend as soon as we are settled, if that's OK with you, so you will be able to see for yourself how nice he is.'

So they had reluctantly agreed, and now here was Jane saying goodbye to her only daughter and trying not to cry.

'Make sure you phone when you arrive, please, and let me know you are safe,' she said.

'Have we got a phone in the flat?' asked Eva, who was having the same conversation with her mother further down the platform.

'Yes, but I forgot to write down the number. Don't worry, Mum, I will ring as soon as we arrive.'

'This is to wish you luck,' said Jane, pressing a small parcel into Meredith's hands. 'Open it when you are alone. Goodbye, dear, and good luck, and don't forget to phone, any time.' She kissed her daughter and turned away to hide the tears welling up.

'Thanks, Mum, for everything. I will come home as soon as I have got settled, and bring Oliver to meet you. Don't worry, I'll be fine.' Meredith turned and struggled up the platform with her case, and bags full of nonsense. It made Jane smile through her tears.

By the time the girls reached the flat it was late afternoon. They staggered up the stairs, having to make several journeys. Oliver was on hand to help and he had also cooked them supper. It was wonderful to sit in their new home with a glass of red wine eating spaghetti bolognese by candlelight.

Later on, as Meredith was unpacking, she found the parcel her mother had given her at the station. She sat on the edge of the bed as she unfolded the tissue paper, to find a small leather prayer book inside. There were several flowers pressed inside the leaves of the book and a mauve petal escaped and floated to the floor. Meredith picked it up very carefully and put it back inside the book. The pages were so thin and faded but she could still make out the inscriptions on the inside, dated 1910 and 1944.

This prayer book must have belonged to her mother and her grandmother before that, Meredith thought, awed. How wonderful that Jane had entrusted her with it now. She read her mother's special message to her:

Dearest Meredith,
When in doubt,
Be kind and think good thoughts.
With all my love, Mummy, xx
1963

Meredith was very touched, and vowed to keep the precious book safe and pass it on to her own daughter one day. God, that was a thought! Would she ever have children? She fell asleep dreaming of baby lambs for some bizarre reason.

It was hard work, those first few weeks. There was little spare time between classes and general everyday grind. Eva quickly adapted to the London party scene, though. When Meredith tried to tell her to slow down and concentrate on all her classes, Eva airily fobbed her off with, 'Darling, you have to speculate to accumulate. I am making lots of contacts. In my business it is all about who you know.'

Meredith and Oliver both had practical cooking to do and would sometimes cook together in the flat. Meredith was so impressed by her flatmate. Oliver was a natural and quickly established himself in the class as a potential first-class chef.

119

There was a little French restaurant just off Marylebone High Street, Le Garcon Bleu – owned by a lovely French lady called Madame Broussard. She took Oliver on at weekends as a general dogsbody in the kitchen and he adored it there.

'I am learning so much, Merry,' he told her. 'The chef is real old school French regional cuisine, and brilliant.'

Meredith was enjoying her cookery classes, especially the ones on Patisserie. But she had also started to spend some of her spare time going to exhibitions on contemporary design. It became a passion of hers. There was so much to see. The innovations in furniture design and lifestyle were very exciting. It was a fabulous time for the arts and fashion. In 1964, a young designer called Terence Conran opened his first store called Habitat. It revolutionised everyone's attitude to home furnishing. Then Biba opened, and fashion just took off. There was a 'Biba' look. Meredith could not quite bring herself to wear the plum lipsticks, but she sometimes wandered round the famous store in Kensington absorbing all the different colours and styles. She loved some of the fabrics inspired by the Aubrey Beardsley posters, and the whole 'Hippy' thing, although she was a little frightened by the free love and acid trip mentality.

There was a huge cult following for the Rolling Stones and Jimi Hendrix, which seemed to go with the 'pot smoking' lot. Meredith herself preferred the Beatles, who seemed healthier somehow, and more normal. Those four boys with their shiny haircuts and Liverpudlian accents appeared less threatening and more accessible to the likes of Meredith, and she made sure to buy all their LPs as they appeared. Eva and Meredith were frequent visitors to the King's Road in Chelsea. Like Carnaby Street, it represented trendy London – centre of the 'Swinging Sixties'. Hundreds of young people flocked there. At college, the female students told each other where to go to be prescribed the new contraceptive pill: free love was the order of the day. Eva was already taking the pill, but Meredith didn't even have a boyfriend and her upbringing had made her wary of behaving so irresponsibly.

For her, the designs were endlessly thrilling. She loved to watch as hippies with long skirts, long hair and jangling beads jostled in public fashion parades with girls in short white dresses, initiated by a French designer called Courrèges. Then 'hot pants' arrived, and girls who were lucky enough to have good figures would swing along the pavement wiggling their pert derrières. Meredith would never have had the nerve to wear them herself. She preferred the designer Mary Quant, who had produced gorgeous short A-line dresses which were so chic worn with knee-high white boots. Even the men were becoming style-conscious, wearing ridiculously tight velvet trousers called 'loons' and high-heeled boots.

It was life on a shoestring most of the time, but so colourful and full of optimism that being broke didn't matter. They managed to eat well, thanks to Oliver's creativity, and the flat looked fabulous, thanks to Meredith's eye for a bargain. Eva's contribution was endless hysterical stories about would-be actresses and their exploits. Hours of gossip, in fact, until Meredith and Oliver were screaming at her to shut up!

'OK, OK, keep your hair on, guys. But listen to this! I have got a part in a commercial. I get £75, can you believe it? So I am taking you both out to dinner next week, on me.'

The three friends dressed up the following week and went to a little bistro in Kensington called Alexyei's Café. The restaurant was owned by a mad Russian who claimed to be related to the Romanov royal family. He was obviously madly in love with Eva.

'Aren't they always?' remarked Oliver as he threw back another vodka.

'Well, it does have its advantages, Olly,' replied Meredith. 'Lots of free vodka.'

They all got rather tipsy and then, at Eva's suggestion, they adjourned to a nearby club.

The music was thumping and the crush of writhing bodies was claustrophobic. The air was heavy with the sickly-sweet smell of pot and sweat, and it made Meredith feel sick. The three friends managed to find a booth to sit in and Eva went off to organise the drinks. It was impossible to have a conversation over the noise of the music, so Oliver and Meredith settled down to watch the dancing. Eva came back with a suave man in tow, in a white suit. He seemed very struck with Eva, and they went off to dance. Then Oliver was dragged onto the floor by a girl in an impossibly short skirt. Meredith laughed and waved him good luck.

Not wishing to be a wallflower, she decided to go exploring. By pushing her way through the heaving mass of flesh, she came out into a little garden at the back. It was blissfully cool out there, so she sat down on a chair and got a cigarette out. Before she could find her lighter, a hand appeared with a very expensive gold Dunhill and lit her cigarette.

'Allow me,' said a very sexy voice. Meredith looked up into the face of an extremely suntanned man with a huge gold chain round his neck.

'Thanks very much,' she replied. Now what? she thought.

'Do you come here often?' he asked, sitting down beside her.

This can't be for real, thought Meredith. Nobody actually says that line, do they? She tried not to laugh out loud.

'No, never, actually,' she replied. She started to get up, but he was up before her and blocking her exit.

'Such a beautiful girl like you cannot be on your own, surely?' He tried to take her hand. Meredith noted that his accent had something foreign about it.

'Oh, believe me, I can. Will you excuse me? I have to find my friends,' and she pushed past him and practically threw herself back into the melee of bodies on the dance floor. She looked over her shoulder and saw that Mr Smoothie was following her. Oh help! She found Oliver back at the booth, with the blonde in the short dress practically sitting on his face.

'Olly, I need your help to get rid of the creep coming up behind me, right now.' As Meredith said this, the white suit was at her elbow, and whispering in her ear, 'Would you like to dance, Beauty?'

'No thanks, we have to go now,' replied Meredith. Grabbing Oliver's hand, she pulled hard. He half fell on the floor and the girl was left hugging the cushion on the sofa. 'Come on, guys, let's split,' she shouted.

Thank God Oliver got the message, and pulling himself together, he clasped Meredith by the elbow and steered her towards the door. The blonde lunged at Oliver's other arm and hung on for dear life. Mr Smoothie watched in amusement as the three ducked and dived their way to the exit. Meredith managed a wave to him as they fell out of the door.

Once outside, Meredith could see the funny side and burst out laughing.

'I'm so sorry, everyone, but he was a real drag. I was desperate to get rid of him. Sorry to spoil your fun.' She then hailed a taxi, saying, 'Special treat, on me. It's too late to get the tube and too far to walk in our platform shoes.'

When they got back to the flat Oliver disappeared into his room with the blonde, and left Meredith to go to bed contemplating life in Swinging London. Not all it was cracked up to be, in her opinion. She was feeling a bit the worse for wear now she was home, and as she fell asleep she vowed to go easy on the vodka in future.

Meredith woke up with a hangover. It was still early, and as she got up to fetch an aspirin, she decided to go home for the weekend. She had an overwhelming desire to see her family. She checked her timetable and was pleased to see that on Monday she was free, so she could come back Monday night, which gave her longer at home. She was out of the flat and onto the train in no time, and spent the next hour sleeping off her headache. By the time she reached home she was feeling much better.

Her mother was thrilled to see her walk into the kitchen. 'Goodness me, what a surprise! To what do we owe this pleasure?' she said, giving her daughter a big hug.

'I missed you all.' Meredith kissed her mother on the cheek. 'Where's Dad?'

'He's muck-spreading, I think. He will be back by four when it gets dark. Sit down and I'll make you some breakfast; it is still quite early, isn't it?' Jane went to put the kettle on and get the eggs out of the fridge.

The two women spent the next hour at the kitchen table and Meredith regaled Jane with stories of life in London. They were in fits of laughter when the door suddenly opened, and George came in.

'How's my favourite girl? Haven't forgotten us then?' He gave Meredith a bear hug that lifted her right off the floor.

'Dad!' she screamed with delight, feeling like a little girl again. 'Put me down. I missed you.' She kissed him, noting the winter cold on his cheek. 'Where's Frank?' she asked, expecting to see her brother come in behind his dad.

'Ah, Frank has other fish to fry,' winked her father. 'He is courting now, you know. Getting quite serious, I think.' He sat down and started to take off his boot. Meredith grabbed the heel and started to pull.

'Wow, I can hardly believe it, my little brother!'

'She is a very nice girl,' added Jane. 'She's going to be a teacher when she finishes her training. Her name is Jenny. You will meet her tomorrow as she is coming for Sunday lunch. Now, tell me what you are doing home so early, George?'

'I felt a bit tired, to be honest, love, and thought what the hell? I'll come home for lunch. Frank was going off into town with Jenny anyway, to do some shopping, so here I am.' He got up and went over to give his wife a cuddle. 'I must have known my two favourite women would be here. Come on, put those eggs away, Janey – I'll take you to the Wheatsheaf for a pub lunch.'

The three of them had a lovely lunch in the pub, and when they got back Meredith and her dad both fell asleep on the sofa, while Jane made a steak and kidney pie for supper. The week-end flew by. Lunch on Sunday, which Meredith helped to cook, was full of laughter. She thought Jenny was adorable and found a moment in the kitchen to tell her brother how pleased and proud of him she was. For once she wasn't teasing him.

'She's great, isn't she? I really like her,' he said shyly.

'Well, go for it, little brother. Can I be a bridesmaid?'

Frank threw a tea-towel at his sister and ran from the room.

By the time she was back on the train on Monday night, Meredith was full of homemade pie, cake and wellbeing. She could face the world again. Throughout her life, and especially over the next few years, Meredith would always find strength in her family. They were her rock, the one place she really felt safe.

Chapter Eight

When Meredith arrived back on Monday night, Oliver was waiting for her with supper.

'Why did you run away on Saturday morning, before any of us were up?' he asked, spooning out the chilli.

'I didn't run away, I just wanted to see my family,' Meredith told him.

'I thought I might have upset you because of Tania,' said Oliver, tucking into his food.

'Tania? Oh, you mean the blonde girl in the mini-dress? Why would she upset me?'

'Er . . . because I thought you might be a bit jealous.' Oliver was eyeing Meredith across the table and she burst out laughing.

'*Jealous?* Oliver, what are you on about?'

Oliver was looking very sheepish. 'Well, I popped my cherry,' he announced proudly.

'Ooh, you dirty little devil. How was it?' Meredith asked.

'Good. Well, amazing actually. So you're definitely not upset?' he said.

'Don't be so daft. Apart from Eva, you are my best friend and I am delighted you have lost your virginity successfully.' Meredith leaned over and gave him a kiss.

'Your turn next then?' he ventured. 'Anything I can do, you can do better.' He sang the words from the song and laughed.

'Well, I was hoping for some sort of romance to be involved. Fall in love first, at least,' said Meredith.

'Oh, that's really square,' replied her flatmate. 'It is the Age of Aquarius, don't forget – free love and all that.'

'You carry on, Olly. I am quite happy, thank you. It will happen when it happens.'

Eva was busy practising free love all over the place. Meredith hardly saw her any more. She got back late, if at all, and was never out of bed when Meredith left in the morning. The inevitable result was a tearful Eva announcing that she had been thrown out of RADA.

'Bastards said I was not committed enough,' she grumbled, opening a bottle of vodka. 'I'll show them, you wait and see. Have a drink with me, Merry, help me drown my sorrows.'

Meredith sat down with her and threw back a shot. 'What are you going to do, Eva?' she asked. 'Your father will go mad.'

Eva's parents were very wealthy, but they believed in their children fending for themselves, to learn the value of money. Eva spent money like water and was always sponging off her friends, but at least she had a grant. Now that would be finished and there would be no cash.

'What are you going to do for money?' Meredith asked her.

'Oh, don't worry, I have got that all sorted. I have joined an escort agency,' Eva said airily. And when Meredith could not hide her shock: 'Oh, don't fret, it's not that kind of agency. All I do is escort blokes out to dinner and things. There is no hanky panky.'

'Let's hope they know that,' muttered Meredith.

'Anyway, it won't be for long because my other news is that I have got a proper theatrical agent, and he has put me up for a part in the next James Bond film! Can you imagine that? Hollywood here I come!'

'That is fantastic news, Eva, well done!' Meredith hugged her friend and they danced jubilantly around the room.

They went down the road later to tell Oliver the good news. He was now a sous-chef at Le Garcon Bleu and Madame Broussard was delighted to see them. She fed them steak and frites by way of a celebration.

Oliver was the star pupil now, in college. Meredith basked in his reflected glory. She also got extra tuition from him, which was just as well, as the end-of-year exams would soon be upon them. Meredith had to create and serve a dinner for six people. She spent hours looking at recipes, and discussing dishes with Oliver. He promised to do a practice run with her nearer the time. She trawled Portobello Market for table linen, and found some fabulous Victorian wine glasses and even a dinner service for six. Feeling optimistic, she vowed she would create a table never seen before at Le Cordon Bleu College.

The week before the big day, Oliver took her through the menu and gave her three stars! But sadly, he was not going to be around on the night as he had promised Madame Broussard he would do some extra hours in the restaurant.

'But you are my date!' wailed Meredith. She had carefully chosen her four other guests from people at college, but had wanted Oliver to be her date so he could keep an eye on things.

'I am so sorry, Merry, I really can't. There must be someone else you can ask.'

Meredith thought about asking Eva but she was so unreliable, and Meredith did not want to have to worry about her on top of everything else. There was a guy in the year below her who might be a possibility. He was the same age as Meredith and studying to be a chef. He was very good-looking, which had made Meredith a bit nervous at first, but he seemed very keen to get to know her, and he was always coming up to her in the canteen and offering to buy her a coffee. She had been slightly dismissive of him, as it was considered 'uncool' to talk to anyone in the years below. But now it was a case of needs must.

She found him in the canteen as usual.

'Hi, Tony, how are you?' She sat down. 'I have got a huge favour to ask you. Would you come and make up the numbers for my exam dinner tomorrow?'

Tony looked stunned. 'Oh wow, that would be fantastic, Meredith, I would love to. Thank you for asking me.'

'Great,' said Meredith, standing up. 'You have to be ready to eat at 5 p.m., suited and booted, in the Executive Dining Room. Is that OK?' Tony nodded enthusiastically. 'See you there, then.' Meredith gave him a winning smile and left.

The next afternoon he appeared on the dot, looking very smart in brown cords and a white ruffled shirt. Meredith couldn't help noticing he looked very hunky. But she had no time to dwell on Tony's sex appeal, as the exam board was calling.

Her table looked fantastic with all the lace napkins and Victorian glassware, and she had borrowed silver candelabra from Eva's mother to complete the effect. Tony turned out to be the perfect host, and kept the conversation going between courses while Meredith was busy serving up. It was a triumph, and after everyone had gone, he even stayed behind to help her clear up.

'That was amazing, Meredith. Every course was just right and cooked to perfection. Do you fancy a drink on the way home? It's still early.'

'I can't think of anything nicer, I could really do with one, to be honest!' Meredith laughed and they set off for the pub. It was a mild evening and they sat outside in the garden. The Carpenter's Arms was one of the few pubs around that actually served decent wine. Tony ordered a bottle, which was impressive on a student grant.

He walked her to her front door and kissed her lightly on the cheek, thanking her again for a superb meal. 'Perhaps we could do this again? Not the whole dinner bit,' he smiled at her, 'but a film, maybe? I would love to see the new Roman Polanski movie, if you fancied it?'

'Yes, that would be lovely,' replied Meredith.

'What about Friday?'

She nodded.

'Great, let's meet in the same pub, shall we?' suggested Tony.

'OK – see you then.' Meredith went into the house, holding her breath. She shut the big front door quickly and leaned against it. A date! It was her first since she had arrived in London. Wait until Oliver heard about this!

'Well, who is he? Can I meet him first?' demanded her flatmate over breakfast the next morning.

'Who do you think you are – my mother?' retorted Meredith through a mouthful of toast.

'I just want to make sure he is OK. What do you know about him?'

'Oh for goodness' sake, Olly, it's a date, that's all. This is 1964, remember – and I am a liberated woman.'

Oliver could not think of a suitable riposte, so kept quiet, and finished his breakfast.

By Friday, Meredith was a bag of nerves.

'This is ridiculous,' she said to Eva. 'I mean, it's no big deal, is it? It's a date, that is all.'

'I wouldn't know,' her friend replied mischievously. 'You tell me.'

'Oh shut up! Don't you start, please. I have had enough with Oliver going on at me. You would think he was my father!'

When Meredith got to the pub, she was relieved to find Tony already waiting for her at the bar.

'Hi there,' she said gaily, plonking herself down on the stool next to him.

'Wine?' He held up a glass of white.

'Yes, thank you,' she said, taking it.

They had a lovely evening. The film was a bit scary, and Meredith had clutched Tony's arm at one point in the cinema. He didn't seem to mind.

They walked back to the tube hand in hand, and when they got to the top of the steps, Tony turned to Meredith and gave her a long, tender kiss.

'Thank you,' he said, gently brushing some hair off her face. 'You are something else, Miss Lee. May I see you again?'

Meredith smiled inanely, and scurried into the underground. She was trembling as she sat down in the carriage. Gosh, he was so gorgeous! Could this be love at last?

For the next few weeks Meredith was walking on air. She lived for her dates with Tony. She couldn't concentrate on anything else, so it was just as well she had finished her exams for the year. Oliver was hardly around as he was working double shifts at Le Garcon Bleu and Eva was off filming her one line in *Thunderball*, the latest Bond film.

Meredith had no one to talk to or ask for advice. She knew the moment was fast approaching when sex would rear its ugly head. What should she do?

She was meeting Tony tonight at his place. He had suggested he cook her dinner. She decided to wait and see. The idea of things being premeditated was not appealing. She wanted to live in the now. She was in control of her destiny.

Tony's flat was small but classy. He had lots of books around the living room and an easel in the corner. Meredith looked at the drawing pinned up there while Tony was fixing drinks in the kitchen.

'Oh, please don't judge me by that,' he said as he walked in and saw her looking at the picture. 'I am always very nervous about people seeing my work.' He handed her a glass of white wine.

'I didn't even know you could draw,' said Meredith. 'You are so good. Why do you want to cook for a living when you could be an artist?'

'I don't really think I am good enough, to be honest. But it is my first love. I must paint you one day, if you would let me, that is.'

Meredith was aware of him standing very close behind her. She turned and took a gulp of wine.

'What's for dinner?' she asked, to break the moment.

'Pasta con Vongole, followed by strawberry mousse. Come and sit down.' Tony took her hand and led her to a little alcove. There was a table set for two with candles flickering, making shadows on the wall.

'How lovely,' remarked Meredith. And very romantic, she thought to herself.

The dinner was delicious. Meredith had never eaten seafood like this before. The little shells in the garlic and cream sauce were absolute heaven. Tony was the perfect host, once again, and talked so easily about everything from the latest films to new books. After they had finished eating they went and sat on the sofa and Tony poured out two large Cognacs.

'Blimey, I'll never find my way home after this lot!' joked Meredith.

'Well, I was rather hoping you wouldn't bother.'

Tony was kissing Meredith before she realised what he had said. She started to pull away, and then thought, To hell with it, go with the flow! He was a talented kisser, slow and smooth. She felt her whole body begin to relax into his. Slowly, he found her shirt buttons and flipped them open, then her bra catch, and gently freed her breasts, cupping each one in his hands and teasing the nipples with his tongue. Meredith gasped. All these new sensations were overwhelming. She was trembling and a little frightened by the intensity.

'Hang on a minute,' she managed to blurt out. 'I am a … I mean, I am not sure … I have never done this before, Tony.' She searched his face for reassurance.

Tony pulled away and took her hands, and then gently leaned in and planted kisses all over her face and down the side of her neck. It tickled and made her smile.

'Relax, baby, I would never hurt you. You are so beautiful and I want you so much. This is right for us. Just trust me.'

He kissed her passionately and pulled her clothes off and then his own. She shuddered as her skin touched his. She had never felt so alive. Tony then knelt in front of her, taking her breasts and softly kneading them, and brushing her nipples with his thumbs. The sensation hit the pit of her stomach and she pressed into him. His hands traced the outline of her waist and then moved across her stomach down to her navel, and slowly down between her legs. She moaned with pleasure as he leaned forward and slipped his tongue inside her. It was an unbearably exquisite feeling and she cried out, holding his head in her hands and pushing him into her. He pulled her down to him, and started kissing her on the mouth so she could taste herself. Meredith was losing all sense of her surroundings. She just knew she wanted this man, wanted him inside her to relieve this ache.

'Please, Tony, make love to me,' she whispered, forgetting she was not on the Pill, forgetting everything but her need. He moved on top of her, kissing every part of her. She was going mad with wanting him. She opened her legs and wrapped them round him as he entered her. She could never have imagined the pleasure as he thrust inside her. Slowly at first, and then more urgently as she joined his rhythm, matching his need. Faster and faster until he cried out and suddenly withdrew, and fell onto her gasping.

'That was close,' he panted. 'Are you OK?'

133

Meredith could not understand what was happening. 'Why did you stop?' she whispered, feeling cheated.

'Sorry, baby, but I am assuming you are not on the Pill and we can't take any chances now, can we? So it's down to good old coitus interruptus.' He kissed her, and got up and went to the bathroom.

Meredith sat up and looked at the sticky mess on her stomach. So this was love? One minute she was flying high in Paradise, the next she had been dumped unceremoniously down to earth. She pulled on her pants and found her bra and shirt and started to get dressed. She was trembling and needed a ciggie, so she found her bag and sat on the sofa and lit up.

Tony came striding back into the room saying, 'Sorry about that, baby. You were so terrific I got carried away. Listen, I have to get up early tomorrow, so do you mind if I call you a taxi to take you home?'

Meredith nodded. 'That's fine,' she said quietly, putting on the rest of her clothes.

Tony took her outside and hailed a cab. As he helped her into the back he kissed her one last time, and whispered, 'You were far out. See you later, baby.' He banged the door and the cab moved off. Meredith turned to catch a glimpse of him through the back window, but he had already disappeared through the front door.

When she got home, Meredith was relieved to find everyone asleep. She washed herself and put on her pyjamas and made a cup of tea, then sat in bed and tried to control the sinking feeling in the pit of her stomach. This was not how she had imagined it would be the first time. Did Tony love her? She knew the answer deep down, and was overcome with a terrible sense of guilt and shame. What had she done? She put down her mug, and noticed the prayer book that her mother had given her that day on the platform. She picked it up as the tears started to fall.

The next day when she got to college she saw Tony coming towards her down the corridor. He was with a group of students.

'Hi, gorgeous!' he called as he passed. He did not even slow down. So that was that. Meredith got the message loud and clear. She had been had. The Age of Aquarius and free love! She could only think how gullible she had been. What an idiot! Tony must have had such a laugh. Would he tell everyone? Oh no, please, not that humiliation as well. Thank goodness it was the end of term and she would not have to face him for two months.

That night, at home, she told Oliver the whole sordid story and sobbed on his shoulder.

'Oh, Merry, don't cry, please. It's not the end of the world. Forget about the bastard and put it down to experience.'

Meredith did lock it away, in her drawer of life. She had devised an escape from anything she did not want to think about and it was that drawer she kept locked in her head. Inside it, she stuffed all the bad thoughts, to be dealt with at another time, like a stack of unpaid bills.

At the end of term, Olly and Meredith donned their backpacks and set off for France. Eva was away making a commercial for hand cream so the two of them went together and had a ball. Oliver was a fantastic travelling companion because nothing fazed him. They had no idea where they were going to stay when they got to France, but on the ferry going over to Brittany, Oliver made friends with a group of girls who were going camping and they gave him an old tent. It was full of holes and you could hardly sit up straight inside it, but the pair of them managed somehow, and laughed so much it hurt. They hitched down to the south and found a cheap *pension* in Cannes, stuck up a little alley, and spent three days cruising up and down the Croisette pretending to be film stars. By the time they had arrived back in St Malo to catch their ferry home, Meredith was her old self again.

On their last night, Oliver suddenly said, 'Merry, I do love you, you know.' He looked very serious.

'And I love you, you daft devil. What's the matter?'

'Oh nothing, I am just being silly.' Then: 'Do you think we should have sex?' he said.

'You and me, you mean?' Meredith looked at him. 'But why would we want to spoil our friendship by doing that? Honestly, Olly, it would ruin everything.'

'I suppose so.' But he didn't sound entirely convinced.

Meredith gave him a hug. 'Believe me, if I ever have sex again, I will have it with you before anyone else. That's a promise. Come on, let's go home.'

Their friendship was sealed forever.

Chapter Nine

The time was fast approaching for the three flatmates to face the big wide world. College was nearly over. Eva, of course, had been out in the cold for some time, but she was doing OK. She had had a couple of decent parts on television, but her big break was still eluding her. Meredith was worried that she mixed with the wrong people and would end up in trouble, somehow. But her friend was buoyant.

'Merry, I am fine, honestly. Please don't worry about me.'

Oliver had no worries about what he was going to do when he left college, as Madame Broussard had secured his loyalty with the promise of becoming head chef at Le Garcon Bleu. So it was just Meredith who needed a job, and it turned up from an unexpected source.

Meredith and Eva had been invited to a Private View at a gallery in Mayfair. The owner of the gallery knew Eva's mother well. Always on the lookout for pastures new, Eva persuaded Meredith that an evening of culture would do her good. They arrived at seven for the champagne reception. The gallery owner was there to greet them, and introduce them to her newest protégé, Guy Meadows. The young artist was very tall and thin, sporting round granny glasses *à la* John Lennon, and had long flowing locks. It turned out he had been at Harrow public school with Eva's brother Simeon.

'Hi guys, thanks for coming,' he said. 'This is my girlfriend, Sylvia Harrison.'

Meredith stopped dead in her tracks. 'Sylvia Harrison? Are you Pamela and Myles Harrison's daughter, by any chance?' she asked, taking in the rather attractive girl standing next to Guy.

'Yes, for my sins. Who, pray, are you?' The girl looked Meredith up and down.

'Your cousin, Meredith Lee, can you believe it?! What a coincidence, meeting you here.'

'Wow, far out,' replied Sylvia. 'Unreal! God, Meredith, do you remember the doll – April, wasn't it?'

Both girls burst out laughing and they spent the next hour catching up. Sylvia met Eva, and they all decided to go to a club. Eva certainly didn't need asking twice, she had had her culture trip and was ready to groove. They had a great evening, though Guy did not have a lot to say for himself. Meredith thought he looked stoned. But it was obvious that Sylvia was entranced by him. Meredith felt sorry for her. She was the typical poor little rich girl – a bit spoiled, and paying for everyone as a way of making herself popular. Guy was onto a good thing, Meredith suspected.

At the end of the night the cousins agreed to keep in touch and swapped phone numbers.

Eva could not stop talking about Myles Harrison all the way home.

'You have to get me an introduction, Merry. I can't believe he is your uncle, for God's sake. Surely you must know he is a big producer?'

'How would I know? I haven't seen him for years,' replied Meredith indignantly. 'I thought he was a builder or something.'

Two days later, Sylvia rang and invited Meredith to dinner at her parents' house in St John's Wood. Meredith was curious to see what her aunt and uncle were like; after all, Pamela was her mother's sister, and yet Jane never mentioned her at all. Whenever Meredith got a card from them on her birthday it would have cash in it, but her mother could not be persuaded to talk about that side of the family. Even her grandmother was tight-lipped. All she would say was: 'All families have secrets, dear. Your mother will tell you when she is ready.' Which left the girl no wiser.

When Meredith told Eva about her invitation, her friend pleaded, 'You *have* to get me an invite. Please, Merry. Myles Harrison is one of the producers on that film I auditioned for last week. If I could just meet him face to face, I know I could persuade him to give me a part in the film. I can't afford to miss this chance. Please!'

Meredith looked at her friend, standing there imploring her, and shrugged. 'I suppose I can but ask,' she said. 'Hang on, I will go and ring Sylvia.' She went out to the hall table and picked up her address book, found Sylvia's number in it and dialled.

After a couple of rings the phone was answered by a sleepy voice demanding brusquely, 'What do you want?'

'Oh, I am so sorry, I must have the wrong number.'

As Meredith went to hang up she heard the voice say, 'Is that you, Cousin Meredith? Hi, it's Guy, you remember? Hey, baby, it's your cousin.'

Meredith heard rustling and yawning, and then Sylvia's voice saying, 'Meredith, is that you? What time is it, for God's sake?'

'Please, go back to sleep, I am so sorry to have woken you. I can call ba—' Meredith was stopped by a hand on her arm, and Eva whispering furiously in her ear, 'No! Ask her now, please, Merry. I have to know I can go!'

'Um ... Sylvia, are you still there? Only I have a favour to ask you.'

139

'Yeah sure, honey, shoot.'

'Would it be possible to bring my friend to dinner next week?'

'Oh cool, Meredith, I didn't know you had a guy. Of course you can bring him. The more the merrier. It's very informal, just me and Guy, and a couple of Dad's friends, taking advantage of Dad's chef, and drinking some of his amazing wine that he will only hide away in his cellar forever.'

'Actually, it's not a guy, it's my flatmate, Eva. If you remember, you met her the other day at Guy's Private View. She is an actress, but she's resting at the moment.'

'Oh yeah, right on – that's cool. Daddy will like that. He loves pretty actresses, doesn't he, Guy?' There was a grunt in the background. 'Bring her along. Ciao, baby!'

The phone went dead, and Meredith turned to see her friend leaping up and down with excitement.

'Thanks, Merry – you are a true friend. I will have to go and "lift" something from Biba to wear for the occasion. You can come with and advise.'

A week later, the two girls set off from home to walk to the Harrisons' house in St John's Wood. They had decided to walk because it was such a lovely evening, and the tube fares would go towards a taxi home, if needs be. They had pooled their resources as the budget was tight, as always.

They arrived at the gate of the very imposing Georgian house, and rang the bell.

The door was opened by a rather fearsome woman in a dark grey suit and crisp white shirt.

'Do come in. I am Susan Armstrong, Mr Harrison's PA. Will you follow me, please?' She led them across an enormous expanse of tiled flooring, under a huge chandelier, towards some double doors.

Eva nudged Meredith and let out a little squawk of excitement.

'I am sorry, did you say something?' Susan Armstrong stopped and faced them.

'No, sorry, no, no nothing,' stammered Meredith, giving Eva a dirty look, then tried not to giggle. Susan opened the double doors with a seasoned flourish, and stood back to let them pass.

Meredith hardly had time to take in the sumptuous décor of the beautiful drawing room before she was confronted by her uncle, towering over her, or so it seemed. Myles was tall, but not unusually so; his presence, however, was overpowering. He was handsome for his age, which Meredith reckoned must be about fifty, with a full head of sandy hair which gave him an almost boyish quality. His eyes were brown, and although he was smiling, there was a coldness behind those eyes. There was a wariness about him too. He leaned down and kissed Meredith on both cheeks.

'Well, well, this is a surprise. How lovely to meet you again after all these years, my dear niece. Where have you been hiding, Meredith?' He held her by her shoulders as he waited for her reply.

'I haven't exactly been hiding, Uncle Myles,' Meredith said politely. 'I am at Le Cordon Bleu School of Cooking. Thank you so much for having us. May I introduce my friend and flatmate, Eva Hamlin.'

Meredith made to step back to introduce Eva, but her friend had already positioned herself neatly between them, and was now reaching up to kiss Myles on both cheeks. She was so close Meredith could smell her perfume. Eva was in her element. She laughed, tossed her curls and stood back to give Myles a better view of her beautiful figure.

'A Continental kiss is *sooo* much more interesting than a stuffy English handshake, don't you think, Myles?' She gave him the full beam of her Hollywood smile, flashing her perfect white teeth, only recently straightened at great expense, and

141

paid for by her doting mother. Myles took her hand and brought it to his lips in a rather exaggerated display of hand-kissing.

'An Englishman is never threatened by a Continental kiss, my dear. Delighted to make your acquaintance. You are very welcome in my house. Can I offer you a glass of champagne?' He placed his hand firmly in the small of her back and steered her towards the bar, leaving Meredith stranded, to make her own way into the room.

She was joined by her Cousin Sylvia who gave her a hug, saying, 'Hi again, great to see you. Guy is over there.' She indicated across the room to where her boyfriend was sprawled across a huge cream sofa.

Meredith nodded a greeting, and looked around the rest of the enormous room. It was so elegant, with floor-to-ceiling French doors all along one side, leading out to a walled garden. These doors had been opened to let in what little breeze there was on that warm summer night. The drapes were all heavy cream silk, with braided edges, and huge tiebacks of twisted silk cord. Two sofas stood facing each other, with an incredible coffee table in the middle. It was all chrome and glass and very modern, but it somehow fitted with the elegance of the furnishings.

Her gaze caught movement at the bar and she looked across at Eva, who was laughing. Myles noticed Meredith watching them and called her over.

'Come and get a glass of champagne, my dear.' She took the proffered glass and then went to join Sylvia, who was sitting on the sofa with Guy. The two of them seemed rather incongruous in this setting. Both were dressed like hippies, with lots of beads, and Sylvia had a flower-power chain of daisies around her head.

'Where did the daisies come from?' Meredith asked her, for want of anything else to say.

'I made a daisy chain in the garden. It's really cool, isn't it? We love to be outdoors, don't we, Guy? We hope to find somewhere to live down in the West Country, so we can both paint. Once we have a base we can go travelling for a bit, you know? India, Nepal, Marrakesh . . .' She leaned across and gave Guy a long, lingering kiss. Meredith felt rather embarrassed by this obvious show of affection. She would never have done that in front of her parents.

She turned away, wondering where her Aunt Pamela was in all this. Myles joined her and lifted his long-stemmed, crystal flute in a toast.

'Cheers! Here's to family reunions!' They chinked glasses, and then he turned and lightly tapped Eva's glass.

'And new friends,' she purred, gazing into his eyes.

'Oh yes, Myles loves new friends – especially female ones, don't you, darling?'

The double doors had opened, and leaning against the door jamb was Pamela Harrison. Well, Meredith assumed it was her aunt, not having seen her since she was a child.

Pamela strode unsteadily across the room and gave Meredith a peck on the cheek. 'Hello, dear, how you've grown! Doesn't time fly when one is having fun? Don't you agree, Myles? And who is this adorable creature?' She slid smoothly between her husband and Eva, in order to scrutinise the intruder.

Eva held her ground, as a good actress should, and extended her hand with a big smile. 'Mrs Harrison, it is such an honour to meet you. You have a beautiful home. I am Meredith's flatmate and best friend. We both went to school together, in Hertfordshire.'

'Fascinating.' Pamela had already lost interest and moved towards the bar. She took a glass of champagne, then sashayed across the room to stand in front of her daughter.

'Sylvia, darling, whatever are you wearing? You seem to have half the garden lawn around your head.'

143

'Please, Mummy, don't exaggerate. It's a daisy chain I made with Guy. Why don't you sit down, before you fall down.'

'Don't be cheeky,' Pamela scolded. 'Now, Guy, how is the painting coming along? When are you going to paint me?'

Meredith watched the scene unfold, taking it all in. There was an air of expectation in the room, as if something was going to happen at any minute. Sylvia seemed uneasy with her mother, and Myles too was surreptitiously keeping an eye on his wife, even while he appeared to be engrossed in Eva's tales of life as an actress. Meredith meanwhile was quietly amazed at the difference between her aunt and her mother. Two sisters whose lives had gone in completely different directions. Jane was such a quiet soul, buried out in the country with her husband and with the farm routine to fill her days. She was a real homebody. Yet here was her sibling, dressed in a slinky red number and made up to the nines, knocking back the champers. How did that come about?

Her thoughts were interrupted by Susan Armstrong announcing the arrival of Mr Jack Blatchford and Mr David Ferrante. Two very attractive young men had entered the room, bringing a welcome breath of fresh air.

'Myles, how are you?' Jack Blatchford said cordially. 'May I introduce you to my lawyer, David Ferrante? He is also helping me find the funds for our latest development. Pamela, you are more beautiful every time I see you!' As he said this, Jack Blatchford kissed his hostess on both cheeks.

Myles poured two glasses of champagne and brought them across to the young men.

'Jack, you are incorrigible, but my wife adores you, don't you, darling?'

Pamela was lighting a cigarette. 'Indeed, I do,' she replied, blowing a thin line of smoke elegantly into the air as she smiled at the newcomer.

144

'Jack and David, let me introduce you to our other guests. This is the lovely Eva, a budding actress, and her good friend and also my niece, Meredith Lee. You know Sylvia, of course, and this is her latest squeeze, Guy ... I am sorry, young man, but I do not recall your surname.'

Still sprawled on the sofa, looking utterly wasted, the boy grinned inanely and said, 'No need to get uptight, man, it's not important,' then sank back into his pot-fuelled haze amongst the huge silk cushions. Meredith had caught the expression on Myles's face harden briefly, and then she found herself facing Jack Blatchford – who had the most incredible blue eyes.

'How do you do,' he smiled at her. 'So, a long-lost relation, eh?' He had a soft burr to his voice that made him sound like a character from a Thomas Hardy novel.

'Not really lost, more never looked for. My mother and Pamela are sisters, but lost touch with each other about twenty years ago. I bumped into Sylvia quite by chance the other evening, and she invited me to dinner.' Meredith was very aware of this man's presence near her, of how good he smelled. She reminded herself that Tony the rat had always smelled good as well.

'What do you do?' she asked rather abruptly.

'I am a property developer – well, apprentice property developer really. I have just got my first real opportunity, thanks to your uncle. I am a builder by trade.' He smiled his dazzling smile again and Meredith felt the need for more champagne.

'Could you get me a refill, please?' she mumbled, blushing slightly.

'My pleasure.' He took her glass and went in search of champagne.

At this moment the doors at the far end of the room opened to reveal a dining room and table laid for dinner. Susan Armstrong was showing Myles a bottle of wine and Pamela was sweeping towards the table, calling everyone to 'Take your seats for the bun-fight.'

As Myles made for the head of the table, Eva slipped deftly into the seat on his left. Meredith saw Pamela note this, but instead of making a direct comment, she took the seat at the other end of the table, calling to Jack, 'Come here, you gorgeous man, and sit next to me. David, please take Meredith round to the other side of my dear husband, and you may sit beside her. Guy, can you manage to find the chair here by me? Lovely. Now, Sylvia, you can sit the other side of Jack, and you might learn something interesting, for a change.'

Meredith allowed herself to be escorted to the table by David. He was also very charming, and actually quite attentive throughout the dinner, as there were only the two of them on that side of the table, but she found herself constantly looking across to Jack. Their eyes met several times during the evening, and each time her heart gave a little jump. So stupid, especially as during dinner she discovered that he was about to get married! How depressing was that? The man was definitely from the same mould as Tony the rat.

The table was beautiful. Meredith took in every detail for future reference, from the black and white table linen and mats, to the clear lines of the Swedish cutlery and the stylish heavy glasses. Everything was expensive and in good taste. There were modern stainless-steel candle-holders at each end of the table, with black and white candles casting a soft light on all the faces of the diners. Eva was on fine form, telling excellent jokes and anecdotes. Her laughter was very infectious, deep and throaty. The men were entranced. Sylvia seemed rather taken with David, and poor Guy spent most of the evening resembling the dormouse in *Alice in Wonderland*, waking up intermittently to a conversation that was halfway through. Meredith felt sorry for him, although she did notice that he

146

made sure he got everything that was on offer in the food and beverage department.

The dinner was divine, and Meredith made a mental note to get the recipes from the chef. The first course had been avocado and prawns. Meredith had seen avocados in the market, but had no idea how to eat them. They were a relatively new addition to the British menu, and certainly not available in St Albans. The main course was breast of chicken stuffed with butter and garlic. 'Chicken Kiev,' announced Pamela, chosen by her after she had tasted it at the Savoy recently. Dessert was a Black Forest Gateau consisting of lots of chocolate and cherries, with layers of cream.

Once Pamela had discovered that Meredith was doing a cookery course, she was at pains to take her through every recipe in detail, and promised her a tour of the kitchen, and an introduction to her chef, who was Austrian. Meredith thanked her aunt, who promptly cast her eyes back to everyone's glasses and called for more wine. One thing was certain, Meredith thought: Aunt Pamela was a great fan of the grape.

The conversation had ranged from new films to racial equality. At one point, Sylvia had launched into a diatribe about the British being racist, and how they should take note of what was happening in the United States, and all about the amazing rise to fame of Martin Luther King. Myles coolly interrupted her mid-flow, by asking Jack how the deal was going on the block of flats he was trying to buy, and thereby completely eliminating his poor daughter from the conversation. The rest of the table then had to listen to property speak for a few minutes, until suddenly, Pamela stood up and announced that as Miss Armstrong was taking her time, she was going down to the cellar herself to fetch some more wine.

'Haven't you had enough already?' Myles said tersely.

'No, I haven't,' replied his wife, slurring her words slightly.

'Anyway, I am sure Jack would like another glass, wouldn't you, darling? Just because you are a boring old fart, Myles, doesn't mean the rest of us have to suffer.'

There was an awkward silence, and then Jack stood up and said, 'Now come on, Pamela, my lovely, don't be naughty. Let's go for a stroll round the garden and then I can have a cigar.' He took her hand, and she stood up slowly, and allowed herself to be gently propelled towards the French doors, and out into the garden. There was an almost audible sigh of relief from the table, though Myles hardly raised his head from the conversation he was now having with Eva. Meredith watched with a mixture of admiration and dismay as her flatmate wove her magic spell, placing her hand on Myles's sleeve as he spoke, or leaning in closer to catch a phrase, or her naughty chuckle at a risqué anecdote.

David had also been entertaining, and made Sylvia and herself laugh a good deal at his tales of courtroom dramas. Jack was very attentive to Pamela, and Meredith realised he knew all the ins and outs of the family, and avoided all the pitfalls. It was not easy for an outsider to know which way to jump. Pamela veered from charming hostess to Cruella de Vil in the flap of a batwing!

There had been a wonderful moment when Pamela, back at the table, had asked Eva if she had ever slept with a director for a role.

'No, never, because everyone seems to be queer!' had been her response. 'It is so difficult to find any straight men in my business.'

'Don't find many straight lawyers either,' joked Jack. 'David is about the only one I know – bunch of shifty bastards the lot of them!'

They all laughed, and David responded with, 'Well, sorry mate, but we are a necessary evil, and you know it.'

Meredith asked Sylvia which art school she was at, and Sylvia explained that she had been at Chelsea for a year, but decided she wasn't really good enough, so was hoping to study History of Art at a private college near Bath.

'That's why we want to find somewhere to live down there, and then once I have a degree, Guy and I hope to travel the world, and sell his paintings as we go, and possibly end up in Paris. Maybe buy a little apartment there as well.'

Myles left his tête-à-tête with Eva for a moment, to chip in with: 'As long as you don't expect me to fund this little caper, Sylvia. I am not paying for you, and Picasso there, to drift around the world getting stoned.'

'Oh please, Daddy, don't be so dreary. Guy will sell his paintings and we will be self-funding. Why do you have to be so negative all the time?'

Pamela, who seemed to have sobered up after her sojourn in the garden with Jack, now homed in on her niece.

'Tell me, Meredith, how do you intend to earn a living from your cookery course?'

Meredith explained to her aunt about her plan to work her way up through a hotel, learning the trade from every angle, and then to get financial backing to open her own restaurant. That was her dream.

'You should talk to Jack here. He is a man who is going places. Maybe he will invest in you. What do you think, Jack? Does she look like the kind of girl who could run her own business?'

Jack smiled at Meredith and said, 'Well, to be honest, that is what girls want these days, to be equal and independent, so good luck to you.'

'Hear, hear!' chimed in Sylvia. 'Equal rights for women.'

'Is it true you are all burning your bras and demanding free love for everyone?' asked David.

149

'Steady, mate,' laughed Jack. 'You are opening a can of worms now!'

'Have you seen that new film *Darling*, starring Dirk Bogarde and Julie Christie?' asked Eva. 'She is amazing in it. Everyone says she will win an Oscar.'

'Isn't it all about sex and orgies?' retorted Pamela. 'Whatever happened to romance in the cinema?'

'Well, yes, it is quite sexy, but it is also about romance. Or lack of it,' replied Eva. 'It is all about being liberated as a woman and having choices, even if we make the wrong ones.'

'Myles would love women to be more liberated, if it means he is offered more sex. Isn't that right, darling?' Pamela's voice had risen a tone and she was leaning on the table now, clutching her glass, eyes diamond bright.

Jack took her hand and kissed it, saying, 'Oh Pamela, now come on, you don't have to worry about Myles and his wandering eye. You know all there is about how to keep a man happy. Myles adores you.'

Meredith smiled, trying to look interested, but was transfixed by the huge diamond on her aunt's finger. It was like something Elizabeth Taylor was always flaunting in the magazines, when she was being photographed with Richard Burton.

'Yes, dear, I was going to be a dancer,' Pamela said, 'but Myles put an end to my career when he married me.'

'Only because I wanted you all to myself, darling,' responded Myles, and Meredith had seen the flash of anger in his eyes as he looked down the table at his wife. 'Pamela, my little flower, why don't you shut up and we can move on to dessert.'

Myles then rang the bell, and the plates were removed in silence. Meredith desperately tried to think of something to say to change the atmosphere, but it was Guy who managed to break the mood. He suddenly stood up, announced that he felt sick, and stumbled from the room. Sylvia hurried after him.

Jack swiftly turned to Meredith and, in order to establish normality at the table, said politely, 'So Meredith, you are a budding career woman, then? What about marriage and kids?'

Before she could answer, Myles interrupted her. 'Eva, what about you? Do you have someone special in your life?' He smiled as he spoke, with all the charm of a panther about to leap on a young doe.

Eva took full advantage of the moment and paused before she answered, taking in the table. With perfect timing, she lowered her eyes demurely and said, 'Oh no, Myles, I am too dedicated to my career. All my energy goes into my work.'

Meredith suppressed a snigger into her napkin, and when she looked up she caught Jack's amused gaze on her. He leaned across the table and whispered, 'Now that is what we call in the trade, a load of bullshit, if you will pardon my French.' Meredith laughed out loud and turned to David, who had also been chuckling and remarked, 'He is not shy of speaking his mind, is he?'

'Why all this mirth, may I ask?' Pamela was back up to speed, and pulled her guests to attention. 'Please share the joke with the table, Jack.'

'I was merely remarking that Sylvia's young man might not be up for dessert any time soon,' replied Jack, with a wink to Meredith.

'Quite so,' agreed Pamela. 'Now, shall we adjourn to the drawing room – and tell dirty jokes?'

The dinner was over. Meredith was keen to leave before anything went seriously awry. She made her excuses.

'Aunt Pamela, forgive me but I really must be going as I have an early start in the morning. It has been a lovely dinner. Thank you so much for having us. Please tell Sylvia I will ring her.'

Meredith looked across at her friend. 'Are you ready, Eva?'

she said pointedly, willing her not to make a fuss. Eva got the message and stood up to make her exit.

'Thank you so much for the wonderful dinner, Mrs Harrison, and Mr Harrison, thank you for your hospitality. It has been a fabulous evening.'

'Actually, we ought to be making a move too,' said David Ferrante. 'Maybe we could give you girls a lift somewhere?'

Before Meredith could decline, Eva pounced on him and took his arm, saying, 'David, you are my knight in shining armour. Thank you so much.' She whisked him away without further ado. Meredith and Jack followed behind.

By the time they reached the flat David was completely smitten by Eva's charms. As Eva skipped up the steps, David followed behind, pen and paper at the ready to take down her number.

Jack took Meredith aside. 'Listen,' he said, 'it was really good to meet you. I am sorry in a way that it couldn't have been under different circumstances, but that's life, isn't it? I wish you all the happiness and success you deserve. Goodbye.' He kissed her gently on the lips and then the two men got back in the car and drove away.

'Ooh, I think you pulled, you dirty girl!' Eva was at her side, laughing.

'Oh, don't be so daft. We are not all like you, you know. Wasn't it a weird night?' Meredith sighed as she kicked off her shoes. 'I thought there was going to be a massive row at one point. My aunt definitely has a drink problem and my uncle is very creepy, but you certainly got on well with him. He was practically drooling at the mouth by the end of the evening.'

'Mmm,' Eva said dreamily. 'I think he is rather dishy.'

'Oh, come on – he's practically old enough to be your father. And may I remind you that he is married to my aunt!'

'I know. I was only kidding. Goodnight, Merry, thank you so

much for getting me the invite. I think I am home and dry now with the part. Myles has told me he is going to talk to the director for me.' Eva went off to the bathroom to take off her warpaint, happily humming the Beatles' hit, 'I Wanna Hold Your Hand'.

Meredith sat on the sofa and thought about Jack Blatchford. He had certainly been dishy. Far too smooth for her liking though, and getting married soon. His poor wife-to-be! She heard a key in the front door and went to welcome Oliver home from a hard night in the kitchen. Bless his little cotton socks!

Chapter Ten

College finally came to an end and Meredith decided to leave London and go home to the farm for some R&R. She had been away too long. Oliver was up to his eyes at Le Garcon Bleu renovating the restaurant, and preparing for his debut as head chef. Eva was off being very indiscreet with Myles Harrison, much to Meredith's disgust. She and Oliver had decided it might be in everyone's best interests if Eva was encouraged to go and live elsewhere. She was a very disruptive influence in the flat, and enough was enough. Oliver and Meredith were so close now it was almost like a marriage. Meredith had caught herself several times in the last few weeks, wondering if their relationship might grow into something more permanent. She was so comfortable with him, and they got on so well, it seemed the logical conclusion. Well, she would pop that thought in the drawer and think about it another day. Now, she just wanted to chill out with Mum and Dad, and decide what to do next.

She arrived home to great excitement because her brother Frank had become engaged. Meredith was thrilled for him and Jenny.

'Will I be asked to be a bridesmaid, do you think?' she asked.

'Of course you will, stupid!' replied Frank. 'We are having

the full church wedding, you know.' He was puffed up with pride.

Her mother was already discussing the cake. 'I will be making it for them, naturally, and the sooner I get the fruit base done the better. You can help me, now you're home.' Jane was faffing around the kitchen.

'Blimey, how soon is this wedding? She's not in the club, is she?'

'Meredith, be quiet! Don't be so crude. Your brother is a gentleman. No, the wedding is next spring, but the base will taste all the better if it has rested a few weeks.'

'Rested?' giggled Meredith. 'By that time it will have fallen asleep! Sorry, sorry ...' She ran from her mother's wooden spoon.

The summer weeks were always the best on the farm, and Meredith went out every day with her dad, to help with the haymaking. She slept soundly every night, and slowly began to feel the benefits of fresh air and good home cooking. She went to visit all her old chums from school, many of whom were already married now, with kids.

When she went to visit Eva's parents, she was shocked to hear that the Hamlins were thinking of selling up.

'Life has changed so much since the war, and we have lost a good many of our investments. We can't afford to run the estate as it should be run. We are considering selling the house and building a smaller one in the grounds, and farming some of the land,' Mr Hamlin explained. 'We've made no firm decisions, and it doesn't need to happen right now, but we shall see how things go.'

'So what are you hoping to do now, Meredith?' asked Mrs Hamlin. She was such an elegant woman and had always inspired Meredith, who had loved the furnishings and splendour of Long Moor House. Mrs Hamlin had enjoyed giving her tips on flower arranging, and such. Jane used to laugh at her daughter's delusions of grandeur.

'I would love to see the day you are living in a house like that, my dear,' she would say, but she was not unkind about Meredith's aspirations – she encouraged them.

Meredith explained to Mrs Hamlin about Oliver, and Le Garcon Bleu, and how Madame Broussard had let her be a waitress there, and taught her all kinds of things about running a business. She would love to open her own restaurant one day, maybe, or even run a catering company at some point, but for the time being she was just biding her time and trying to get as much experience as possible.

'Well, that is absolutely wonderful and quite the right approach. Well done. Actually, I may be able to help you there. We happen to have a very good friend who runs an advertising agency, and they are always in need of in-house caterers. Shall I see what I can find out for you?' offered Mrs Hamlin.

'That would be fantastic. Thank you very much,' said Meredith gratefully.

A week later, Mrs Hamlin phoned to say that her friend Nigel Tubbs, the MD of the advertising agency Tubbs, Steele & Lane, would be delighted to meet her. Thrilled, Meredith made an appointment for the following Monday. She went up by train, having rung Oliver to say she would be coming back to stay at the flat that night – so if he was free, they could have dinner together.

'I will make sure I am free,' he promised. 'Good luck, I know you will knock 'em dead!' She smiled as she put the phone down. Dear Oliver, he was always so supportive.

Tubbs, Steele & Lane had a suite of offices in Mayfair, in a huge brand new building of glass and steel. The reception area was about an acre in size. Meredith walked across the marble floor feeling very small and insignificant. There was an incredibly well-groomed girl on the desk who could hardly move, her skirt was so tight. Her lips just about moved as she asked who Meredith had come to see.

'Please take a seat,' she purred, and indicated across the waste-land of floor to a huge leather settee in the corner. Meredith sat down and leaned back, only to find that the sofa was so deep, her feet left the floor. She hauled herself up, quickly looking around to make sure no one had seen her. *Stop being so pathetic,* she chided herself. *It is only an office, for goodness' sake.*

The clothes-hanger was waving to her across the shining sea of marble; hurrying over to the desk, Meredith was instructed to take the lift to the top floor. She made her way to a bank of lifts and waited to be transported on high. A commissionaire materialised from out of the lift and stood back for her to enter. He pressed a button and they rose swiftly, leaving her stomach behind. She recovered in time to walk out of the lift with her dignity intact, only to lose it once again at the sight of yet another gorgeous being coming towards her, across yet another expanse of flooring, this time of soft glowing wood.

Swallowing hard, and putting on her most confident smile, she said, 'Hi, I am Meredith Lee. I have an appointment with Mr Tubbs.'

'Yes, of course,' caressed the voice of this vision of loveliness. 'Please follow me.' They walked together to a huge door, which seemed to open as if by magic. Nigel Tubbs was seated behind an edifice disguised as a desk, in front of the most amazing windows which stretched the length of the room. Beyond lay a panoramic view of the city.

'Wow, that is some view!' Meredith blurted out, unable to stop herself.

'Yes, indeed it is. You must be Miss Lee. How do you do? I am Nigel Tubbs. Please take a seat.' He pointed to a leather triangle. Meredith nervously perched on the edge.

'You come very highly recommended by Laura Hamlin. Have you known the family a long time?' he asked.

'Since I was a child, actually; I owe whatever good taste I may possess to Mrs Hamlin.'

'Well now, Meredith – may I call you Meredith? Tell me what you have in mind for yourself.'

Meredith outlined her master-plan for Nigel Tubbs. To run her own catering company, or restaurant.

'Here at Tubbs, Steele & Lane we have our own in-house catering,' Nigel Tubbs told her. 'We also have home economists for our commercials that involve any food or cookery. I would like to suggest that we take you on in the catering department for three months, and see how you get on. How would that suit you?' He waited for her reply.

Meredith was thrilled but tried not to show it too much.

'What would my starting salary be?' she asked.

Nigel Tubbs smiled. 'That's what I like to see – a girl who knows her worth. Shall we say £100 per month?'

Meredith managed to keep her cool. £1,200 a year! 'Yes, I think that would be fine. Thank you.'

'Good. So why don't you start on the first Monday of next month, and we shall look forward to a long and happy association.'

He stood up, came round from his desk and held out his hand, and Meredith shook it, noting it was cool and smooth. No rough work for Mr Tubbs. He then turned back, walked behind his monument of a desk and sat down. She had been dismissed.

Meredith managed to walk out, reasonably elegantly, from the room and across to the lift. Once inside, she let out her breath and as she left, she blew the surprised doorman a kiss. Yes, she had done it! Got her first real job!

She couldn't wait to tell Oliver her good news, and on the way back to the flat she bought a bottle of champagne. It was strange coming here after being in Burslet. The flat didn't feel like home any more. But as she waited for Oliver, she wandered around picking things up and remembering all sorts of things from their shared time here, and she realised how much she had missed Oliver the past three weeks.

The door banged, and Oliver came through into the room and lifted her up with a whoop of delight. 'Merry, I missed you!' He swung her round and they fell on the sofa in a heap. 'How did it go?' he asked.

'I got the job and a £100 a month!' She fetched the champagne from the fridge and started to open it. 'Olly, we are on our way, you and me. It is so exciting.' She popped the cork and filled the glasses, and they drank greedily.

'Right, we are going out tonight,' Olly announced. 'I am sick of cooking. Come on, bird, get your glad rags on. We are going Up West, as they used to say. Let's do the Ritz!'

The friends had a fantastic evening, and got completely hysterical when the bill came, because it was so expensive.

'This is a month's rent, for God's sake,' giggled Meredith. 'We will be bankrupt before we have even started. By the way, have you spoken to Eva at all about leaving the flat?'

'No, I haven't had a chance, but I will before you come back. I know it is awkward for you because of her parents and everything. Just leave it to me. How much longer are you going to stay on the farm?'

'Well, only another two weeks because I start the job at the beginning of next month and I'd like to have a few days to get my act together and buy some new clothes, et cetera. Olly, you should see the women in those offices. They are impossibly gorgeous.' Meredith let out a sigh. 'I must go on a diet,' she added.

'No, you must not!' retorted Oliver. 'You are dead fanciable as you are. Now eat up your last petit four as they are too expensive to leave.'

Back at the flat, they finished off the champagne and cuddled up on the sofa. This was perfect, thought Meredith. *They* were perfect. She lay with her head on Oliver's lap and he was stroking her hair. Suddenly, he leaned over and kissed her tenderly.

'I really missed you, Merry,' he whispered. She looked up into his eyes and saw such love there, that she kissed him back with equal tenderness. Oliver helped her from the sofa and led her to his bedroom.

'Is this wise?' she murmured, not wanting to break the spell.

'Oh yes, I think it is the wisest thing in the world,' he said very definitely, and they fell onto the bed.

They woke up next morning and made love again. It felt so natural to them both. There was no embarrassment or angst, and while it may not have been the most earth-shattering sex in the whole world, it felt right, and satisfying.

'I can't believe it has taken us three years to get here,' said Oliver, buttering a huge slice of toast. 'Do you have to go home again, my sweet pea?'

Meredith laughed. 'You sound like an old married man,' she said.

'Well, why not? Shall we get married? Marry me, Meredith, and have my children.' Oliver went down on one knee and took her hand.

'Oh, don't be so daft! We are perfectly OK as we are. And I don't want children – well, not yet anyway. We have to make our fortunes first, so get up and finish your toast and get to work. I will be back on Sunday.' She gave him a big kiss and skipped out of the door.

Meredith spent the next few days at home helping her mother with the chores. Her Grandmother Mary was delighted to have her come and read to her and do some shopping for her. George got her driving the tractor, and Jenny and Frank asked her opinion on wallpapers and decor. They were going to live in the other farm cottage which had been empty for a while now and needed a proper overhaul before they could move in. There was a lot to do before the wedding to get it shipshape. By the time she left to go back to London, Meredith was exhausted. Her mother dropped her at the station.

'This is just like it was when I left home, do you remember, Mum? By the way, did I ever thank you for the prayer book? It is really lovely, and I will always treasure it.'

'I hope, one day, you will have a daughter to pass it on to,' her mother said softly. 'Be happy, Meredith. Don't work too hard so you have no time for other things in your life. How is Oliver, by the way?'

'What made you ask?' Meredith said, getting the feeling her mother had second sight!

'He is a lovely young man and a good friend to you, isn't he, dear?' Jane Lee said. 'I had always hoped that one day you might end up together.' She hugged her daughter. 'Time will tell, eh?'

Meredith thought about her mother on the way back in the train. There was always a certain reserve about her. Meredith couldn't put her finger on it, but somehow she knew that Jane had been badly hurt at some stage in her life. She wondered what had happened – and would she ever find out?

She got back to London to find that the problem of Eva and where she was going to live had been sorted by Eva herself. She announced that she was off to the States to find her fortune. She had broken up with Myles, who had proved to be, in her words, 'cruel and heartless'.

'Well, I hate to say I told you so,' said Meredith.

By coincidence, Meredith got a strange call a couple of days later.

'Is that you, dear? This is your Aunt Pamela. I wondered if you could do me a small favour.' The woman sounded very fraught, thought Meredith.

'I will do my best,' she promised. 'What is the problem?'

'It's Sylvia, I'm afraid. She has gone off to live in a squat with that loopy Guy boy. She had a huge row with her father and now he won't give her a penny and I am so worried about her.'

'What do you want me to do, exactly?' asked Meredith.

'If I give you the address, could you just go and visit her and make sure she is OK?' said Pamela.

'Yes, of course, what is the address?' It was somewhere in Camden Town. Very salubrious – not!

'Thank you so much, dear. I am very grateful. Please give my love to your mother,' Pamela said in a choked voice and hung up.

Well, there's a turn up for the books, thought Meredith. She decided to go on the next Saturday morning, when Sylvia was more likely to be around. When she told Oliver about her proposed visit, he said, 'Be careful, Merry. It can be a bit rough round there.'

When Saturday came around, Meredith took a cab so she didn't have to waste time finding the place. The squat was in a rundown terrace of Georgian houses, all in serious need of a lick of paint; half the windows had been boarded up. She went up the steps of number 39 and looked for a bell. She tried the door, but it was locked so she banged on it as hard as she could and waited. Nothing happened for a good few minutes, then she heard noises from inside. She pushed the letterbox and it opened just enough for her to shout through.

'Hello! Is anybody there? Can you open the front door, please?'

She stood up and waited. Suddenly, a bolt was shot back and the door opened a little way on a chain. A very hirsute face peered at her, saying, 'What do you want? Are you trying to score?'

'I would like to speak to Sylvia Harrison, please. Is she there?' Meredith recoiled from the smell of stale cider and cigarettes.

'Dunno, you'd better come in,' said the face. He opened the door just enough for Meredith to squeeze through the gap and then shut the door again quickly and bolted it.

'Can't be too careful,' he chuckled. 'Bloody pigs will get you. You're not the fuzz come to bust us, are you?' He suddenly looked frightened.

'No. Nothing like that,' Meredith reassured him. 'I am a relative of Sylvia's. I just want to make sure she is OK.'

The young guy started to cough without covering his mouth and Meredith took a step back.

'Are you all right?' she enquired.

'Yeah, nothing a fag won't cure. Have you got one, by any chance?' He waited for her to open her bag. I will probably get robbed now, thought Meredith, but he was quite happy with the cigarette and wandered off into the gloom.

'Do you know where I can find Sylvia?' she shouted after him, and was rewarded with an arm waving in the direction of the upstairs landing. Meredith gingerly climbed the stairs, expecting someone to jump out at her at any moment. On the landing there were three doors. It's like a game, she thought. She tried the first door, and a gruff voice shouted, 'Fuck off!' She shut the door quickly. What now? The second door was locked, so she went for the third door, which was ajar. She popped her head round and peered into the dusty depths. A figure was sitting on the floor, rocking backwards and forwards, snivelling. The place stank of pot and patchouli joss sticks.

'Sylvia, is that you? It's me, Meredith. Your cousin, remember?' She stepped into the room cautiously.

Sylvia stopped her rocking and stared at her, as if trying to focus Meredith in her mind's eye. Then: 'Meredith? Oh wow, it really is you. Am I glad to see you!' She tried to stand up but slipped down again onto the mattress, which covered most of the floor-space.

'What is the matter with you?' asked Meredith. 'Your mother asked me to come and make sure you were all right. Where's Guy?'

'He's gone, the bastard. He's left me here on my own and gone off with his sodding mother, the wimp. I loved him, you know? Bastard has gone.'

'Calm down, Sylvia. Where has he gone?' asked Meredith. 'And why has he gone off with his mother?'

'Because she is a bitch and she never liked me and she was always trying to break us up. She has taken him to rehab and he's left me here.' The girl started to cry again and then had a coughing fit which left her wheezing and croaky. Her nose was running. Meredith got a packet of tissues out of her bag and handed them to Sylvia. Her cousin was in a really bad way.

'Look, why don't you come with me and I will take you home. Your mum is really worried about you,' said Meredith.

'Don't be fucking ridiculous! She doesn't care about me. If she cared about me she wouldn't have let my shit of a father stop my allowance. I have got no money and Guy wouldn't stay with me without any money. And now he'll get clean and I will be stuck with a fucking habit. Can you believe it? Meredith, please help me. Lend me a couple of quid then I can get myself sorted.' Sylvia was starting to whine now. Meredith knew enough about heroin to know that giving her cousin money was the last thing she should be doing. But how to get her out of here?

'OK – come with me and I'll see what I can arrange. You don't want to stay in this dump on your own. Come back with me, please.' She bent down to take the girl's arm.

164

'Don't you fucking touch me, don't touch me!' Sylvia crawled into the corner of the room and crouched there like an animal.

Meredith was shocked. 'Please yourself,' she said, overwhelmed by the situation and having no idea how to handle it. 'I was only trying to help.' Then she added more strongly, 'I can't stay here all day, so make up your mind. Are you coming or not?' And she turned to leave.

'Wait! Don't leave me!' That whine again. 'I am so sorry, Meredith, thank you for coming. Have you got a fag? I could kill for a ciggie.' Sylvia hauled herself up and started to stagger towards Meredith.

'Yes, you can have a cigarette when we get outside. Come on, Sylvia, give me your arm. There you go.' Meredith took her arm. The girl was so thin she could practically get her hand round the top of her arm!

She managed to half-carry, half-drag her not-so-sweet-smelling cousin out into the blessed sunlight. Sylvia was sniffing and snivelling again. Meredith lit a cigarette and put it in her mouth and then hailed a taxi. The driver did not look thrilled at the thought of a passenger who was drunk or sick or both.

'Please take us to Marylebone High Street as quick as you can,' ordered Meredith, and flashed the cash. Sylvia perked up when she saw the money.

'Oh, bless your heart, Merry, lend us a few quid just to get me sorted out then you can call my parents and tell them I will be home later. Not that they care. They have never cared, you know. Mum thinks I am a pain and Dad is disappointed in me because I can't make money. Well, I am an artist. I could have been a painter but I chose to look after Guy instead. I was his patron – I used all my money on him. Oh God, the bastard! How could he leave me? How could he do that? Now I am all fucked up.'

This went on all the way back to the flat. Meredith was worried that Oliver would not let them in. He hated anything to do with drugs. She hauled Sylvia up the three flights of stairs to the flat and pushed her down on the sofa, feeling exhausted.

'Sit there a minute and shut up, Sylvia.' Meredith left the room to make some tea and put lots of sugar in Sylvia's mug. When she carried it through to the sitting room, she found her cousin passed out on the sofa. It was a blessed relief in a way. Christ, what am I going to do with her?

Meredith decided to ring Pamela.

'The Harrison residence, who is calling, please?' said a voice she recognised – that of Susan Armstrong.

'Hi, can I speak to Pamela, please? It is her niece, Meredith Lee.' She heard the line go dead, then a minute later: 'Yes, hello, is that Meredith? Have you found my daughter?' It was Pamela.

'Yes, I have, and she is in a pretty bad way. Do you want to come and pick her up from my flat?' Meredith had a horrible feeling that was the last thing this woman wanted.

'Um – well, no. You must think us awfully heartless, but this is the third time she has skipped rehab. We cannot go on enabling her to do this. The doctor says we must resort to tough love. If she has no money and nowhere to go, she will have to pull herself together eventually.'

'I see,' said Meredith. 'Fine, but Sylvia is here on my sofa and what do you suggest I do with her?' You stupid, selfish woman, thought Meredith.

'I really don't know what to suggest, my dear. I appreciate what you have done for me. Perhaps you could put her in a hostel somewhere. I will reimburse any expenses you might incur.' Pamela then hung up! The woman hung up!

Meredith heard the door of the flat open and close, and went to tell Oliver the bad news before he was faced with the body on the sofa. He listened to the story and then went to see the damage for himself. Sylvia was curled up like a little cat in the corner of the sofa. There was nothing of her.

'What a mess!' he said. 'Look, we'd better keep her here tonight and then take her to a hospital or something in the morning. I don't know.' Like Meredith herself, he was at a loss.

Meredith spent the evening trying to clean Sylvia up and feed her. It was like dealing with a very stroppy child. One minute she was sniffing and crying pathetically, the next she was screaming abuse. She finally fell asleep again, and Meredith and Oliver went to bed worn out.

'What are we going to do with her?' were Meredith's last words before she fell asleep.

The next morning she was woken up by Oliver standing at the foot of the bed.

'Our problem has gone away,' he said.

'What do you mean?' Meredith yawned.

'Sylvia has gone. She's left with the contents of your purse, unfortunately. Did you have much in there?'

'Oh Christ, how stupid am I? I should never have left my bag lying around. It doesn't matter about the money, Olly, but will she be safe? She'll have gone straight out to a dealer, and what if she ODs or something?'

'Who knows? Look, you did your best. She may even turn up back here, and then we'll think again.'

A week passed, with no sign of Sylvia. Meredith had fretted about her absence, but in the end had had to accept that her cousin was a law unto herself. Then out of the blue, there was a phone call. She picked up the receiver, but no one spoke.

'Sylvia, is that you?' asked Meredith – and then she heard a heart-rending sob and braced herself; she was already afraid of what would come next.

'This is Pamela Harrison. I am sorry to have to inform you

that Sylvia is dead. She died of a heroin overdose and was found on the tow-path by the canal in Camden Town.' Pamela hung up.

'Oh Sylvia, I am so sorry. Please forgive me,' wept Meredith.

When Meredith rang her mother to break the news of Sylvia's death, she was prepared for Jane to be utterly distraught, and had warned Oliver that she might have to go home and see her. But Jane hardly reacted. Her reticence spoke volumes. What the hell had gone on between the sisters, all those years ago, to cause such a rift and unspoken bitterness?

All Jane said at the news of Sylvia's death was: 'She was such a beautiful baby.' Nothing more.

'Mum, are you still there?' said Meredith. 'What about the funeral? Shall we go together?'

There was a sigh then Jane answered: 'No, I don't think so, dear. It is too late now. Too much time has passed. I just can't face them. I am so sorry, love, please forgive me.' The silence on the end of the line was deafening!

Meredith decided to phone her grandmother and see if she could be more illuminating on the subject.

'Gran? It's me. Meredith. How are you?'

'How lovely to hear from you,' Mary said warmly, 'I don't see nearly enough of you these days.'

More guilt, thought Meredith. 'I know – and I am truly sorry, Gran, but work is full on at the moment. Gran, I have a favour to ask you. It's about Mum. Can you tell me what the problem is between her and Pamela?'

'Oh, now that is a difficult one. I am not sure you should be asking me. Why do you ask?'

Meredith took a deep breath. 'Because Sylvia is dead, Granny. She died of a heroin overdose. It is so tragic, but Mum won't come to the funeral and I just don't understand why not.'

Mary heard the words from a long way away. How could this

have happened? Sylvia was dead? That poor girl had never had a chance of a normal life. She remembered the night in the bedroom with the two girls fighting over the doll and felt a profound sorrow at how life gave us these terrible blows. Poor Pamela, poor Jane. All these lives touched by tragedy, all the lies that had been told. She thought of Henry and Alfred, of the links in the chain that had brought them to this point. She pulled herself upright and gripped the phone.

'Meredith, my dear, I cannot talk to you of these things. You must ask your mother to tell you. I am sorry, but there are just some things that have to remain a secret until they are ready to be told. Now be a good girl and leave things be.' She put the phone down, and sank into her chair and wept for the first time in a long, long time.

Meredith let out a frustrated expletive and accepted defeat. She would go to the funeral on her own and be damned. She tried ringing Pamela but there was never anyone there, and then suddenly she got sent to a TV festival in the South of France with the agency. By the time she returned, it was too late. She sent a note of condolence to the Harrisons but never heard another word.

Chapter Eleven

Meredith decided it was time for a break. In the last two years she and Oliver had worked non-stop.

'We have no life,' she complained one morning when they were actually both at home, at the same time, having breakfast. 'Olly, it is ridiculous that you and I never meet; we have no social life, no friends even.'

'Speak for yourself, my darling. *I've* got lots of friends!' he replied, preening in the mirror.

'Oh please,' Meredith sighed. 'Well, anyway, I think we should go for a holiday and re-ignite our passion.'

'Did we ever have passion in our relationship?' asked Oliver.

'What is that supposed to mean?' asked Meredith, throwing him a look.

'Well, don't get me wrong, but passion was never our number one priority, was it? I love you dearly, and we are happy in our way, but I wouldn't say our love-life bore any resemblance to *The Perfumed Garden* exactly.'

'I didn't know you had read that book?' Meredith gave Oliver a sidelong glance. 'Is it any good?'

Oliver laughed. 'If you like that sort of thing,' he answered. 'Don't worry about it, Merry. Our love-life is fine.'

Meredith thought about it for a moment and decided to let things be, but by the time Oliver went to work he had agreed to take a week off. She then sat in the kitchen trying to pin down her thoughts. The issue of their relationship was something that had dropped out of the drawer in her mind, and was not necessarily very welcome! Over the last couple of years she had been so busy she had not really given their relationship a thought. Living with Oliver had just been a progression from their college years. Their sex-life had certainly never had the passion of *Lady Chatterley's Lover*. She smiled at the thought of Olly dressed as the gamekeeper Oliver (!) Mellors! But had she let him down in some way? Had she failed in that department? Ever since the episode with Tony the rat, Meredith's attitude to men had become almost indifferent. At work she was surrounded by Alpha males who could only respond to women as sexual objects, so her way of dealing with them was to ignore them. She never let the situation spread over into anything too personal. It was always business first.

If she was honest with herself, maybe she had shut down altogether. Her love for Oliver had really always been platonic. The sex was intermittent, at best. She decided they would discuss this while sitting in the sun with a large cocktail . . .

The plane landed with a bump at Nice airport. Meredith looked out of the window at blue skies as the stewardess finished her spiel '. . . and the temperature is 71 degrees. Thank you for flying with British Airways. Have a pleasant stay.'

They had decided to fly first class and were being picked up at the airport and taken to the hotel Olly had booked.

'Oh, this is the life,' murmured Meredith. 'Sunshine and limos.' The car sped into the centre of the town and pulled up outside the hotel. They were whisked through registration at the desk and followed a cute bellboy up the grand staircase to the first floor where he showed them into a huge suite.

'This is fantastic!' gasped Meredith. 'Olly, how did you manage this?' She ran across to the enormous windows and stood looking down on the Promenade des Anglais.

'Madame Broussard has a cousin who is a manager here. I got a special rate,' he told her, looking pleased with himself.

'*Voilà!*' announced the bellboy who had finished opening the shutters. '*Merci, monsieur.*' He smiled broadly at his generous tip, and closed the door behind him.

Meredith danced into the bathroom. It was top to toe in marble, with glistening chrome taps and a huge shower that could have accommodated an army!

'I love it! Well done, you clever man.' She gave Oliver a big smoochy kiss.

'Come on,' he said, 'let's get down to the hotel beach. Race you to the sea.' And he was off.

They had dinner that night on their balcony watching the world go by below them. Now that she had actually stopped running around, Meredith began to feel exhausted. She climbed into the king-sized bed, sank into the crisp cotton sheets and fell asleep as soon as her head hit the duck-down.

Oliver was already awake and sunning himself on the balcony when Meredith opened her eyes the next morning.

'Blimey, you're keen,' she said bleary-eyed. 'Have we ordered breakfast?'

'*Mais oui, madame.*'

The moment the words were out of his mouth, a knock came on the door, and a rather small waiter staggered in behind a rather large tray. It was piled high with café au lait, slices of baguette and croissants, and French butter and jams. Meredith thought she had died and gone to heaven. She was still eating when Oliver appeared from the bathroom fully dressed.

'I am just going to get some francs from downstairs and have a stroll. I will bag us an umbrella right opposite and see you there, my little sunflower.' He kissed her and was gone.

Meredith joined him later and they dozed and read all day, with the occasional pit-stop in the tanning process for a cool drink or two.

'I have found a lovely little bistro round the corner for tonight,' announced Oliver. 'Eight o'clock, is that OK for *madame*?'

'*Bien sûr*,' said Meredith, checking her tan lines.

Dinner could not have been more traditionally French. Snails in garlic, steak and frites and green salad, washed down with a bottle of local wine.

Meredith snuggled up to Oliver that night, whispering, 'Fancy a cuddle?' He responded with a grunt. 'That'll be a *non* then,' she sighed, and turned over and joined her sleeping partner in the Land of Nod.

The week was very soon over. Meredith felt rested and revived, but a little disturbed by Oliver's behaviour. He seemed withdrawn and had gone off several times on his own during the past few days, with some excuse or other. Then on their last but one morning, as Oliver went off for his usual stroll along the promenade, Meredith left him outside the hotel and walked in the opposite direction to find the shops. Having wandered around for a couple of hours she was returning to the hotel when she spotted Oliver across the street. She lifted her hand in a wave, but he didn't see her and disappeared into a small bistro. She crossed the road, hurrying to catch him up, but as she arrived at the door she could see Oliver embracing a young guy inside and moving through to the back. She instinctively ducked out of sight and stood on the pavement for a moment. Then she walked round the block and found the rear of the bistro. She could just about see over the wall through the trees at the end of the little garden. Oliver was sitting outside at a small table, deep in conversation with the boy – and they were holding hands!

Meredith backed away up the alley, trying to comprehend what she had witnessed. How could it be? There must be some mistake, an explanation.

She leaned against a wall and tried to catch her breath, suddenly aware that she had been holding it. Her body slumped as the truth dawned on her. Oliver, her friend, her lover . . . no, he was not her lover. Had he ever been hers? How could she have been so stupid, so blind, not to have seen this coming? Same old same old, she thought. Stupid, stupid, stupid! Meredith Lee is a stupid selfish woman who cannot see whatever is in front of her. She started to cry. Oh please, not self-pity. Come on, Meredith, for Christ's sake get a grip.

She stood up straight and walked back to the front of the restaurant. The street was bustling with beautiful people, all enjoying the sunshine. Life goes on. The smell of coffee drew her attention to a café on the opposite side of the street. She made her way towards it, like a man coming out of the desert and finding an oasis.

She sat down under an umbrella and ordered coffee and a Cognac. She longed for a cigarette, the first time she had wanted one since she gave up a year ago.

And then she waited. An hour and a half she waited, by which time she was icy calm. The sense of betrayal was still there, however. Why did these things always happen to her? Oliver was her soulmate – how could he keep this from her? Why?

She sat up as she spotted Oliver coming out of the restaurant, followed by his friend. She felt sick. They were kissing on the pavement. Kissing in broad daylight! No one took any notice.

Well, this was France, she thought. Then, before she realised what she was doing, she had run across the road and was hitting Oliver on the back. Pummelling him with her fists.

'How could you do this to me?' she screamed. 'You bastard! You liar!' She then burst into tears as Oliver managed to grab her wrists.

'Meredith, stop! Look at me! Stop this, please. Let's go back to the hotel.' He kept hold of her and said something in French to the boy, who flounced off down the street.

They marched back to the hotel in silence. Once in their room, Meredith collapsed in a chair. She felt so empty. Her thoughts just whirled around in her head. Oliver seemed like a different person. He was a stranger to her. All these years of knowing him, and yet she knew nothing.

'I have been trying to tell you for ages, but there never seemed to be a good time. We have both been so busy, and I suppose I kept hoping I would get over it.' Oliver looked wretched.

'Get over being queer? How the hell do you suppose you could do that?' Meredith spat the words at him. She wanted to hurt him, humiliate him as he had humiliated her. 'How could you betray me like this? You said you loved me. You asked me to marry you, for God's sake! Was that all a con, a cover-up for you being queer? Would we have had children and *then* you might have told me? Broken it to me gently over dinner? "Oh, by the way, darling, thanks for everything, but I need to tell you something now. I am a poof!"'

'I did love you,' Oliver said sadly. 'I do love you, Meredith. I wanted to love you in the right way and I tried, but I just couldn't. I have fought this for so many years. You have no idea what I have been through. I have felt so alone most of my life. I couldn't tell my parents. I couldn't tell you ...'

'Why the hell not? Why couldn't you put me out of my

misery? When did you know for sure? How could you treat me this way?' Meredith shouted at him.

Oliver suddenly screamed back at her, 'For fuck's sake shut up! It's not all about you, for a change. This is my problem, my life, my crisis! I am going crazy, can't you understand? Do you have any feelings for me? We have been friends all these years and I am still the same guy you supposedly love and care about. I am frightened, Merry, and I am hurting so badly.' He started to cry. Tears were rolling down his cheeks and he sank onto the bed with his head in his hands.

They stayed like that for ages. Meredith in the chair, and Oliver on the bed, and this chasm between them. Finally, Meredith stood up and went over to the bed. She looked down at her friend who was like a crumpled pile of laundry waiting to be swept into the laundry basket, and touched his arm.

'I am so sorry, Olly. Forgive me. You're right – I am a selfish cow. This isn't about me. Please let me make amends. I do love you, and I am your best friend in all the world, and I want to help. Come on, it's not so bad. We will always have each other. I couldn't live without you, Oliver.'

Meredith sat down beside him and took him in her arms and rocked him like a baby. He sobbed and sobbed, until he slowly ran out of tears. Then he pulled away and searched her face.

'Meredith?'

'It's all right, Olly. I love you and I understand. You are not alone and we will get through this together. You're quite right – you are still the same Oliver deep down. You are my best friend and my soulmate and I am a bitch!' She grinned and Oliver allowed himself a shaky laugh.

'Yes, you are, but I won't tell anyone. No one will ever know except maybe a few holidaymakers who happened to be passing when you attacked me in the street!'

Meredith groaned. 'Oh, don't remind me! Oh God, what

about that boy, your friend? Who is he, by the way? You have only half-confessed to me. I want the whole sordid story now.'

Oliver stood up and went to the window. 'He is a waiter at Le Garcon Bleu. His family live near Nice and when I said we were coming for a week's holiday, he took a week off as well. It is nothing serious really, but he has been very sweet to me over the past six months.'

'Six months! Does Madame Broussard know about it?' asked Meredith.

'I think so, but we've never discussed it and I'm very discreet. I can't quite get used to the idea myself really, Merry. This is not how I imagined my life would be, you know. I always wanted a wife and family. It is hard to come to terms with the whole caboodle. My parents will be devastated, but I must tell them because I can't live a lie any more. It has been bad enough hiding the truth from you.'

'OK, that's enough. Go and find your friend. What's his name, by the way?'

'Jean-Paul,' Oliver replied.

'Well, go and find Jean-Paul and tell him we are going to celebrate tonight. You are coming out of the *placard, mon ami,* in style!' Meredith gave Oliver a hug and added, 'It is going to be all right, my friend. I will always love you.'

Two years ago, Meredith had taken Tubbs, Steele & Lane by storm. Her contract had initially been for three months, but by the end of the first year she was Head of the Catering Department, and had even formed her own company, called 'Extra Helpings'. She just loved the work and meeting so many different types of people. Towards the end of her second year Nigel Tubbs summoned her to his office.

'Meredith, I have a proposition for you. We are going to open a production arm of the agency to make our own commercials, and I would like you to be Head of Food. We think your input would be invaluable. Not just from the point of view of cooking the food, but also presenting it and selling it. You would work alongside the Art Department. What do you think?'

It was exactly what Meredith wanted. She could see just from being around these creative guys, that there was a whole new world to enter and exploit in media and commercials. She was already thinking about how she could market Oliver and his cooking. Maybe put him on TV. So this new job opportunity would get her foot in the door.

'I would be really interested, Nigel. Thank you. How do you want to set it up?'

'Well, I will announce your new job description and it is up to you to make yourself known to the Art Department and take it from there. You will have your own office, of course, and a secretary and more money, naturally.' He smiled at her from across his desk. 'Subject to your approval, I would suggest five thousand pounds a year?'

'Done,' Meredith said immediately, and she grinned broadly from ear to ear.

The other big change in Meredith's life concerned Oliver. Since he was now well and truly out of the closet, they had decided that it might be better for them both if they lived apart. Both of them were making good money now, and it seemed foolish not to think about investing in their own homes. Property was going through a slow period at the moment, and Meredith had seen some fantastic bargains around.

Oliver was in the throes of his first real romantic attachment. He had met Michael at the launch of some recipe book or other. Michael was a literary agent, and very successful. Oliver was thinking about moving in with him, so his property plans were on hold. Meredith was so happy for her friend and just a tad envious. Would she ever meet anyone, or was she destined to end up an old maid? She put the thought away in the drawer and concentrated on house-hunting, eventually finding a beautiful apartment on the ground floor of a substantial Edwardian house in North London. There was a garden with lots of mature plants and shrubs, and a little shed at the bottom tucked away under a spreading fir tree. It was perfect. She put in an offer and spent the next weeks on tenterhooks, until the solicitor rang her one morning and confirmed that she would be exchanging contracts by the following Monday. Almost to the day, Oliver announced that he was moving in with Michael, who had a large house in Notting Hill Gate.

'Oo! There's posh!' said Meredith. 'But what are we going to do about our little love nest?' Their flat in Marylebone High Street had been the backdrop for so many important stages in their lives. Meredith was going to be so sad to leave it.

'Guess what?' Oliver beamed triumphantly. 'I have persuaded the landlord to sell it to me. The thing is, Merry, I need some kind of investment like you. Moving in with Michael solves my emotional life but is not a practical solution to my long-term security. I need a place of my own, a bolthole. So I am going to buy Marylebone and then rent it out for the time being. Not just a pretty face, am I?' he smirked.

'Not even,' quipped Meredith. 'I think that is very sensible of you and very grown-up,' she teased.

The two of them spent days clearing out the old flat, wading through boxes of old photos and memorabilia, and reminiscing over times gone by. Meredith had hardly heard a word from Eva, and hoped her schoolfriend was safe and well. Oliver tried to throw stuff away, but Meredith kept changing her mind and retrieving stuff from the bin. When the big day finally arrived, the two friends greeted the removal men with a rendition of 'My Old Man Said Follow the Van' ... and it was downhill all the way from then on.

Meredith was in her element decorating her new home and spent hours at her favourite haunt, Portobello Market. It was so close to Michael and Oliver's house that she would shop first for bargains, and then go and have lunch or dinner with them afterwards. Meredith got on well with Michael, and the two of them were trying to get a book off the ground for Oliver, not to mention a TV show, which was slowly, but surely, coming together.

Life finally seemed sorted out. However, as time passed and the busy years followed on from one season to the next, Meredith was only too aware that she was the wrong side of thirty and on her own, with no man on the scene, not even on the horizon – but that was the price she had paid for choosing a career over her love-life. She thought briefly about her long relationship with Oliver. Those had been wasted years, in a way, as she had removed herself from the marketplace. Still, she couldn't blame Olly for that: it had been her choice of lifestyle, and he had fitted in very nicely at the time. It had suited her not to commit to a man who would demand her full attention and want her to have babies. She had looked at her schoolfriends and seen how they had cut short their careers and compromised on their ambitions once the babies had arrived. You couldn't have both. Resigned to her future as a crabby old maid who drank too much, Meredith vowed that she would surround herself with lots of vibrant young people and become the fascinating eccentric that everyone wanted to talk to at parties.

Having accepted her fate and settled down to her life in her new home and enjoying the fact that everything was going smoothly, life chucked her a bombshell.

Chapter Twelve

George Lee was only fifty-nine when he died very suddenly of a heart attack. He had been mending a fence in one of the top fields with his son Frank. It was a mild autumn day and the men had been at it all morning, only stopping at lunchtime to have a flask of soup that Jane had made for them, and some big doorstep ham sandwiches – George's favourite. The two men sat on the tractor trailer feeling the warmth of the sun on their faces as they enjoyed the food. The collies Star and Dolly were lying at their feet eagerly waiting for a scrap to come their way. George always saved the last crust for the dogs. Suddenly, he gasped and bent forward.

'What's the matter, Dad?' Frank jumped down from the trailer and put his arm out to his father.

'Christ knows, son, got a bloody awful pain though. God, it hurts.' He leaned forward too far and toppled off the edge of the trailer into Frank's arms, and they both sank to the ground.

'Dad, please, you're scaring me,' pleaded Frank. 'Come on, get on the back of the trailer and lie down and I will take you home.'

His father was gasping for air and clutching his chest. 'I am sorry, lad, I don't think I can move,' he panted. 'Just leave me here and go and get your mum. It's probably only indigestion. Go on, son. Be quick about it!'

It was a good couple of miles back to the farm and Frank knew it would take him a while even if he ran all the way. He tried once more to get his dad up on the trailer but George was a dead weight. Frank wasn't prepared to leave him any longer than necessary, so he decided to take the tractor. Before leaving, the younger man took off his coat and laid it tenderly over his dad. George was lying on his side now and groaning quietly.

'Dad, just lie still and keep warm, and I'll be back in two shakes of a lamb's tail. Don't you worry, mate. Dolly – stay! Stay with the master, there's a good girl. Star – sit!'

He started the tractor and bumped off over the hill, looking back every few minutes until the hunched figure of his dad was just a tiny dot.

The ambulance got there too late. George Lee was lying on the unforgiving soil with his two dogs beside him like sentries.

Oblivious to the wind, Jane knelt by her husband's body and howled with grief. Frank had never seen her so much as shed a tear in all his life. It frightened him, to see his mother like this. He tried to prise her away from the body so the ambulance crew could do their job.

'Come on, Mum, please. Let them take Dad. Please, come on.' He took the sobbing woman into his arms, and slowly managed to help her to rise. 'Let's get you back to the house. That's the girl.'

Frank led her to the car and assisted her into the front seat, while the dogs jumped in the back. He had to pick Star up because the dog would not leave the body. The ambulance crew then made ready to move and the sad convoy made its way over the field, disappearing into the afternoon dusk.

Back in the kitchen, Jenny made them all some tea. The three of them sat round the table in stunned disbelief.

'My poor George,' whispered Jane. 'Dying all alone out there with no one beside him.'

'Mum, I had to leave him. He couldn't move and I had to get help!' Poor Frank was consumed with guilt.

'Of course you did, my love. You did the right thing.' Jenny took his hand and gave it a squeeze.

Jane took his other hand and held it. 'Yes, of course you did the right thing, dear. I am not criticising you at all. I am just so sad for George. We knew he had a weak valve in his heart, but I just always hoped it would be fine. He was still so young – why did it have to happen!' She started to cry again. 'What are we going to do?'

Poor Frank looked so miserable and lost, Jenny took over.

'Come on, Mum, I am going to make you something to eat. No, no point in protesting, you must eat something. Frank, you feed the dogs and light the fire in the snug while I cook the tea.'

And there they were, the unhappy trio, eating eggs and bacon and baked beans by the fire until they fell into bed exhausted by grief.

The next few days passed in a haze of sadness. Jane was completely unable to cope. Meredith had come as soon as they had rung her, having cancelled all immediate commitments at work. She had never seen her mother at such a loss. She put away her own grief for her dad until later. Filed it away in that drawer. It was what she always did with any big problem in her life. Now her mother needed her, and Meredith was not going to let her down. With Jenny, who had been amazing, Meredith organised the funeral, and the food and drink for the gathering afterwards. She could have done with some support from Oliver, but unfortunately he was away in France on a work project and could not get the time off.

Jane did all the invitations, and seemed grateful for the diversion. There was only one strange moment as she and Meredith

183

were going through the numbers for the church service, when Jane stopped and said, 'Must I invite your Aunt Pamela, do you think?' She looked at Meredith, searching her face. 'It's not as if we ever see each other, and we have never been close. George didn't really like her and he had absolutely nothing in common with Myles.' It seemed to her daughter that she shuddered as she uttered Myles's name – but thought it must be her imagination.

Meredith thought back to her visit to the squat in Camden Town to find Sylvia and just how badly the Harrisons had behaved towards their own daughter. Meredith had never got to the bottom of why Jane had been adamant that they would not go to Sylvia's funeral. She had always felt guilty that she had missed the funeral in the end, because no one had bothered to return her calls and tell her where it was to be held. She went away to do a job because she was contracted, and had still hoped to come back in time. Pamela and Myles never bothered to contact her again. Now here was her mother trying not to invite her sister to her brother-in-law's funeral. Bloody families!

'I think you ought to really, Mum. After all, she is your sister and she did lose her daughter in terrible circumstances. Haven't you spoken to her since then?'

Jane looked uncomfortable. 'Well no, to be perfectly honest. It does seem very remiss of me, I agree. But time goes by so quickly and your dad and I ...' She stopped and tears welled up again. 'I can't believe he has gone.'

'I know, Mum.' Meredith blew her nose. 'Please don't cry now, or you will start me off. I wonder if they ever found out exactly what happened to Sylvia.' She asked the question more as a diversionary tactic than anything else.

'Yes, that was terrible.' Jane wiped her eyes. 'I looked after Sylvia for a few weeks when she was first born, did you know that? She was very poorly to begin with, but then she grew stronger and oh, she was such a lovely baby. It was a nightmare really. It was during the war; I had to go up to London to stay with Pamela when she was recovering from the premature birth, and George and I were stepping out together. He didn't want me to go and then . . .' She suddenly came to a halt.

'Stepping out! What a lovely phrase, Mum, how sweet. How long did you . . . Mum, what's up?'

Jane had gone very pale and was staring into the distance.

'Mum, what's the matter?' Meredith sat down and took her mother's hand. It was cold and clammy. 'What is it?'

Jane jumped and looked at her. 'Sorry, love, I was miles away. Another time. Another life.' She gave her daughter a wan smile. 'I'm fine, really. It's just that sometimes memories return unbidden and unwanted. It doesn't matter now. Bless you, Meredith, you are doing sterling work organising everything for me. Thank you. I don't know what I would have done without you and Jenny. Poor Frank is all over the place, isn't he? Jenny says he wanders round in a daze, poor boy. Still, at least he has the farm to keep him busy.' She looked into Meredith's eyes and studied her daughter. Then she dropped her gaze and whispered, 'I am so sorry. I haven't been much of a mother to you, have I?'

'Oh, don't be daft, Mum. You have been a fantastic mother! You and Dad are the best parents a girl could ever have, I promise you.' Meredith started to get up because she could feel herself beginning to crack. *Not now*, she told herself sternly. *Save it till later.* As a matter of fact, her mother was right in a way: she had never really given Meredith the kind of affection reserved for Frank. Meredith had always put it down to mothers and their sons. She hadn't really minded because she had been a daddy's girl. Oh God, what would she do without him?

Pulling herself together, she went out into the garden to gather some vegetables for lunch. George had given Jane the veggie patch for herself, but he always helped her with it when he could. He had shown Jane how to grow asparagus, long before it became

185

fashionable. He had taught her to grow runner beans and sweet peas together, so they shared the same sticks. Meredith wandered across to the greenhouse, which was looking very sad in the autumnal greyness, but how wonderful it had been to go inside and smell the tomatoes in the summer. George was in charge of the salad, and his lettuces were his pride and joy. 'There's nothing like the smell of fresh lettuce,' he used to say.

'Lettuce doesn't smell, Dad,' retorted his little daughter one day.

'Oh yes it does, my girl. Smell that,' and he had pulled an impossibly green lettuce from the ground and held it to her nose. It did indeed smell of earth and water and fresh air, if that were possible. She could not describe it, it just smelled wonderful.

Meredith let out a sob and looked around hastily, to make sure she was alone. One of the dogs, Dolly, had come to find her, and she gave the friendly animal a hug and followed her back to the house.

The funeral of George Lee took place on a damp, misty morning. Meredith, Jane, Jenny and a lady from the village had done the flowers. George had loved wild flowers but they were rather sparse in late September, so they had decided to make the most of the harvest festival theme and used straw and greenery and seasonal vegetables. It was unusual for a funeral but Meredith found it ideal; her father had loved everything about the countryside. Jane was happy that her vegetable patch provided some of the produce.

They had made the beautiful little Norman church look warm and welcoming. They had lit dozens of tea lights all around the window-ledges and placed many more candles up the aisle and round the altar. There were baskets of greenery everywhere you looked, glowing in the candlelight. The leaves were so shiny they looked as if they had been polished.

Although the Lees were not particularly religious, they were very much part of the community and attended the church on high days and holidays. Meredith's Grandmother Mary was well known in the church. She was seventy-nine now and quite frail, but she led the mourners with her head held high. George was a popular man in the village and there was a big turn-out to see him off. Meredith had helped her mother choose the music, but Jane had insisted the coffin be brought in to Elgar's 'Nimrod', from the *Enigma Variations*.

'Your dad loved him because he was so English,' she explained tearfully.

As Meredith and Jane came down the aisle she felt her mother's body stiffen ramrod straight.

'What's the matter?' she whispered.

'I can see Myles Harrison in the pew,' her mother answered, and seemed to falter in her steps.

'It's all right, Mum, you are doing fine. Keep strong,' Meredith said firmly. She looked up to acknowledge her uncle, and her gaze took in his imposing frame; next to him was a very glamorous creature in a huge hat. This must be Pamela, and then next to her ... Oh my God, Jack Blatchford! What the hell was *he* doing here? She looked down to hide her confusion, and she and her mother seemed to totter down the aisle forever. They finally made it to the front pew and sat down gratefully. Jenny was there, saving a place for Frank who would arrive with the coffin as he was a pallbearer.

Meredith dared not look round in case she caught Jack's eye. She could not understand what he could possibly be doing here. How many years ago was it since that dinner party? Ten years? More? She noticed that her mother was searching for her hanky, and by the time she had found it the organ had started to play, and the congregation was rising to receive the coffin.

The wake was a success – if one could say that about a wake.

Everyone seemed to enjoy themselves. Meredith had placed her mother by the Aga in the kitchen, because she knew that was her comfort zone. Mary was in a chair in the living room holding court. She had grown more lively as time went by, and always loved a gathering, albeit this was a rather sad occasion. First through the door to offer her condolences was Pamela. Like a battleship, she had cut a swathe through the tide of mourners and made straight for the vodka on the sideboard, poured herself a hefty slug, then cornered her sister.

'Dear Jane, I am so sorry. How very sad. He was no age, your George, was he? God knows, they say the good die young but no one should go before their time. How are you coping?' She took a large swig of vodka. As Jane was about to answer her, Myles appeared at Pamela's side.

'Steady with the vodka, old bean, got a long way to go yet. Jane, may I offer my sincere condolences? I hardly knew George, but he seemed a very honourable and decent man. May I introduce a friend and business partner, Mr Jack Blatchford? I apologise for bringing him to this very private family affair, but we are doing some business up the road at Long Moor House and it was an opportunity not to be missed. Also, I will have to leave early and Jack has kindly agreed to drive Pamela back to London for me.' He stood aside to let Jack take Jane's hand.

He is very handsome, thought Jane, and she smiled pleasantly at him. Jack greeted her with a warm and open smile.

'A pleasure to meet you, Mrs Lee. I am only sorry it is in such sad circumstances. Please accept my sincere condolences for your loss. Can I get you anything at all?'

'That is very kind of you. I think I would like a dry sherry, please. Are you from the West Country, by any chance? You have a lovely burr in your voice.'

'Oh yes, my lover, I be from Somerset originally – well

'spotted,' he joked gently. He went off in search of sherry and left Jane smiling to herself. But not for long as Pamela was soon back.

'Jane, dear, we really must start to keep in touch more. Life has been so hard since Sylvia died. Myles is even more impossible to live with, now his precious daughter is dead.'

'I am sure it is hard for both of you, Pam, and I do apologise for not ringing you at all. Life goes by so fast and the farm demands so much of George's time ... oh dear, what am I saying?' She stopped and her hand flew to her mouth to stem the words. She fumbled for a dry hanky in her handbag.

'Don't worry, dear, I know the feeling. You have to keep busy or you will end up an old soak like me. Speaking of which, would you excuse me? I need a refill.' And Pamela shot across the room.

Jane felt herself starting to panic. She drank the rest of the sherry, which seemed to have a calming effect, and looked around for one of her children. She spotted Meredith talking to that lovely Mr Blatchford and then she saw Frank coming towards her.

'How are you doing, Mum? Shall I get you another sherry?'

'Thank you, dear. Did you speak to the solicitor about the will yet?'

'Mum, don't worry about that. There will be plenty of time afterwards. Just try and get through today. Look, here comes Jenny with a plate of food for you.'

Over on the other side of the room, Meredith took a slurp of red wine and tried to stop staring at Jack. God, he was so dishy! He was telling her all about Long Moor House.

'So your friend Eva's family still live on the estate but I have bought the big house and want to turn it into a luxury hotel. Do you ever see her these days?' he asked.

'No, I haven't seen her for years,' Meredith said rather sadly. 'We grew apart, and when she left the flat we shared, she went to

America. How weird, seeing you again after all these years. Did you get married, by the way? You were about to, weren't you?'

A shadow crossed his face and there was a slight hesitation before he replied, 'Yes, I did. My wife died in an accident, three years ago. We have a son. Harry.'

Meredith wished she hadn't asked the question.

'How devastating for you. She must have been so young. It is terrible when people die young. It's just not right somehow, is it? Sorry, I am babbling. I am trying very hard to keep it all together today for my mum, you know?'

'Listen, you are doing a grand job, girl. Don't worry about me. Are you going back to London tonight? I could give you a lift as I am taking Pamela home as well.'

Meredith had been thinking about going back to her flat tonight because she wasn't sure she could cope with another night of trying to be cheerful for her mother. She had talked to Jenny about it, who had suggested that she and Frank would stay and clear up and make sure Jane took a sleeping pill and went to bed. Now the offer of a lift with a gorgeous man seemed too good to miss, even if she did have to share him with her aunt.

'Thank you very much.'

'OK. Well, let me know when you are ready to go. I was hoping to get away about four at the latest, so my nanny can have the night off.'

'Your nanny?' Meredith looked confused. 'Oh, you mean as in a child's nanny. Right. I thought you were talking about an old lady – nanny, you know? Oh dear, I am burbling again. Sorry, I think I need another drink. Come on.'

They walked across towards the drinks when Myles Harrison made a beeline for them.

'Jack, can I have a word? I need to leave in a minute and I just wanted to check a couple of things with you before I go. Would you excuse us, Meredith, my dear? You have done a first-rate job, by the way. I am sure your father would have been proud of you.' And with that he steered Jack away to the hall.

Meredith looked for Jane and saw her standing by the window with her glass of sherry talking to the vicar.

'Hi Mum, how are you doing? Hello, Mr Cox, thank you for a lovely service. It was lovely, wasn't it, Mum?'

'Yes, indeed. Thank you again for all your help.'

The vicar shook their hands and, smiling benignly, made his way to the front door, where he was accosted by Mary wanting to talk about Christmas services.

Jane looked out of the window and saw Myles and Pamela outside on the drive. Pamela was smoking and swaying like a reed in the wind. Myles seemed to be remonstrating with her. Jane had a flash of memory to that night in St John's Wood when she had heard the glass smash and voices raised. Her stomach turned over. She had managed to keep these emotions at bay so far. Seeing Myles had given her a jolt but she had managed to control the panic. It was like another life and, thank God, she would probably never have to see him again after this. She was sorry it had ruined her relationship with her sister. It seemed to her that Pamela could do with some friends. But Jane was too fragile now to even begin to contemplate her feelings for her sister.

'Oh dear, I think Aunt Pamela is two sheets to the wind,' she commented. 'Be a love, Meredith, go and bring her in and give her a coffee.'

While Meredith went to get Pamela, Mary came over to talk to Jane.

'I have brought you another glass of sherry,' said her mother, handing her the glass. 'Best way to deal with today, I think, don't you?' She smiled sadly and gave her daughter a kiss on the cheek. Over Jane's shoulder she could see Meredith join Myles and Pamela in the front garden, and she startled Jane by noting, 'There's a very strong family resemblance when you see them together, isn't there? I wonder if anyone else will notice. I do hope not. You must tell Meredith the truth one day – you know that, don't you? It's not right to keep it from her.'

Jane followed her gaze out of the window and saw Myles bend down to kiss Meredith on the cheek. A touching moment between father and daughter. *'No!'* Jane felt her legs buckle, and she grabbed Mary's arm. 'Mother, I don't feel well. Can you help me upstairs.' Her eyesight blurred and her legs gave way under her and then there was nothing but blackness.

Mary nearly went down with her as she was not as strong as she used to be, but she held onto the windowsill as Jane sank to the ground. Mary sent someone to find Meredith and sat down on a nearby chair.

Meredith came rushing up but was pushed aside by Myles, who was barking instructions to people to move back and give the woman some air.

'Meredith, fetch a glass of water. She will be fine. She has just fainted. Jane? Jane! Come along, try and sit up.' Myles leaned over to get his arm under her shoulders to help her up, at which point Jane came to, and seeing Myles so close to her, she started to scream uncontrollably. The more Myles tried to help, the more distressed she became.

'Leave me alone! You are a monster! Help me, someone. Please help me!'

The room had gone very quiet and no one quite knew what to do next. Myles finally stood up looking confused.

'I was only trying to help,' he said. 'What on earth is the matter with the woman?'

'It's the effect you have on women, Myles dear – sheer horror!' Pamela started to laugh tipsily and people moved away, embarrassed. Some went to get their coats. It was obviously time to leave. Meredith had come back with the water, followed by Jack, who tactfully suggested to Myles that he should get going or he would be late for his meeting.

'Don't worry about Pamela – I will get her back safely.' He steered Myles firmly to the front door.

Mary and Meredith had managed to calm Jane down.

'Get her upstairs and into bed,' said Mary. 'I will go and fetch Frank and Jenny and we will say the goodbyes.'

Meredith took her mother's arm and led her out of the room. Jane was whimpering softly. 'I am so sorry, please forgive me. Thank you all for coming. I am so very sorry.'

It was such a relief to Meredith to get her undressed and into bed. She gave her a sleeping pill, and plumped up her pillows, and tucked her in like a little girl. Her mother was trembling and looked so fragile. What on earth had brought this on? She took Jane's hand and rubbed it gently, trying to calm her.

Suddenly her mother opened her eyes and started to sit up.

'Mum, lie down. It's been a long day and you could do with some peace and quiet.'

'No. No, I have to talk to you, Meredith! I have left it too long, and it is really too late to make amends to you, but you must know the truth. Please let me talk and then you will see what an awful mother I have been. My poor, dear Meredith, I should have told you the truth a long time ago.'

Meredith had no choice but to sit down and listen to her mother as she unravelled her story. When she had told her all she had to tell, Jane Lee closed her eyes and fell asleep, still holding her daughter's hand.

Her confession, so many years in the coming, had left her daughter in shock. Meredith sat there trying to gather her thoughts. She just didn't know how to make sense of anything she had been told. All she wanted to do was to crawl away and hide. Her whole life was a lie! She had just buried the man she thought was her father. But that was a lie. Her father was a brutal rapist – and he was also her uncle, for Christ's sake! She looked down at her mother and was relieved to see that Jane was deeply asleep. Thank God, at least now she did not have to pretend. But her relief lasted only a minute, because just then, Pamela appeared at the bedroom door looking like the wreck of the *Hesperus*.

'Darling, are we nearly ready for the off? Oh good, Jane has gone to sleep, best thing for her. What a terrible time for her. I know only too well what it is like . . .' She hiccupped.

Meredith took her arm and wheeled her round and back out of the door, saying, 'Look, Aunt Pamela, I am not sure I will be coming back with you now. Mum really needs me here. I will just check with Frank. See you in a minute.'

Meredith hurried off to find Frank. What the hell was she going to do? She needed to get back to London because she had a production meeting first thing tomorrow for a commercial she was assisting on as the home economist. She had already missed one meeting because of the funeral, and she could not miss another as they would replace her very quickly. She would have to think about this other stuff later. Put it away in the drawer with everything else and get it out at another, more convenient time.

She saw Frank talking to Jack, and thought, Right – I can kill two birds with one stone.

'Frank? Excuse me interrupting, Jack. Can I ask you two for a little help and advice? Frank, I have to go back to London tonight because I have a production meeting first thing tomorrow morning. Will you and Jenny keep an eye on Mum? She is going to be in a bit of a state when she wakes up and will need you around.'

'No worries, Meredith. We will take good care of her.'

'And I can chauffeur you right to your door, ma'am,' added Jack with a mock bow.

'Thank you, that is very kind of you. I'll just get my bag and meet you outside, shall I? I know Pamela is ready to go as well.'

'Yep,' said Jack. 'See you at the front door in five.'

Meredith ran back upstairs to get her overnight bag. She went to the bathroom, and as she sat on the toilet, she started to shake. *Oh for goodness' sake, girl, pull yourself together. It's not the end of the world. Just get a grip*, she told herself fiercely.

On the way home, Pamela sat in the front of Jack's very lovely Jaguar and Meredith was more than happy to hide in the back. With any luck she could feign sleep and not have to make conversation. But Pamela had other ideas. She did not stop asking questions for the whole hour of the journey. First it was all about Meredith's career. Then she started on Jane. How would Jane manage without George? Would Frank run the farm? Would Frank inherit the farm? Would Meredith mind if she didn't have the farm? God, she did not stop.

Meredith was beginning to feel completely trapped, and Jack must have sensed her panic because he suddenly said, 'Pamela, enough with all the questions. Poor Meredith must be exhausted. Leave her be and tell me what you are planning for Christmas this year. Are you going to Bermuda again?'

Meredith caught his eye in the rear-view mirror and mouthed a thank you, and then laid her head down on the armrest and actually fell asleep. The next thing she knew, the car door was opened and Pamela was leaning in, wafting stale vodka all over her, saying, 'Goodbye, Meredith, dear. Please keep in touch. Families must stick together.' And she was gone, dropping that little nugget like a pile of poo in Meredith's lap. *Families must stick together.*

'Shall I get in the front now?' she said as Jack returned to the car.

'Be my guest. Where am I taking you?' he asked, slipping the car into gear.

'Oh, just drop me at the nearest tube,' she replied.

'No way. You have had a terrible day, and I am taking you to your door as I promised.' He smiled at her. 'Right or left?' he said as they came up round Swiss Cottage.

'Left, up Fitzjohn's Avenue please.' Meredith sat back and enjoyed the ride. They were outside her flat in no time.

'Would you like to come in and have a drink?' she said, before she had a chance to stop herself. The last thing she wanted to do now was to sit and make polite conversation after she had just buried her father, who was not her father because her father was a rapist. Great!

'Well, I would love a cup of tea actually, so yes I will, thank you.' Jack followed her up the path carrying her bag, and she unlocked the door and they went in.

Meredith walked straight into the kitchen and put the kettle on.

Jack went to the bathroom while Meredith picked up her mail and lit her fire in the lounge. It wasn't a real fire but it was a bloody good imitation and very comforting at times like these.

The phone rang, piercing the silence and making her jump. It was Oliver, ringing from France.

'Olly, can I ring you back? I have just walked in the door. All is well. No, I am fine. I have just had a bit of a shock but I will tell you all about it when I see you face to face. No, honestly, I am fine. I will ring you later. Love you lots.' She hung up as Jack came into the room.

'Your other half?' he asked.

'No, my best friend,' she replied. 'Please do sit down and I will get the tea.' Meredith went back to the kitchen and made a pot of tea and found some cake in a tin, put it all on a tray and carried it into the lounge.

'This is a lovely flat,' commented Jack. 'A very good conversion.' He laughed at the look on Meredith's face. 'Yeah, sorry, the builder in me can't help but notice these things.' He took the cup of tea she was offering him and sat back.

'Sorry, do you want sugar?' Meredith asked. 'It's in the kitchen. I don't take it, so I tend to forget about others' preferences.'

'Not for me thanks, but I will have a bit of that cake, it looks delicious. Did you make it?' Jack popped a piece of lemon drizzle cake in his mouth. 'Mmm, this is good,' he managed to say through the cake.

Meredith laughed. 'It is lovely to have an appreciative guest. Yes, I make all my own cakes, I find it very relaxing.' She watched Jack enjoying her cake while she enjoyed watching him. He really was very handsome and his eyes were still twinkly. She must be demented thinking about things like this now, just after her father's funeral.

Jack was asking her something. 'Have you lived here long?'

'Oh yes, a few years now. I love it here. I used to share a flat years ago with my best friend, Oliver Stanton, the man who just phoned, but then we decided we should both try and buy our own places, as an investment, you know.'

'I do, indeed.' Jack had finished his cake and was brushing the crumbs off his trousers. Meredith thought he looked like a little boy for a moment. A lost boy, there was such sadness in his eyes.

'I am so sorry you lost your wife – you must miss her terribly,' she said softly.

Jack didn't speak for a few moments and then he spoke very quietly and carefully as if he was trying to keep control of his emotions.

'D'you know, I think about her every day? It's over three years now but it seems like only yesterday. I cope because I have to for our son. He is adopted, as it happens. We tried for years to have kids but it didn't happen. Then a friend of ours told us about this baby and we adopted Harry. He changed our lives. We had everything to live for. I had the perfect life and I loved my wife very much and now I had the perfect family. Two years later, she was dead. She had nipped up to the village shop to get some nappies and was walking home on the side of the country road. Then this horse-box came round the corner too fast and the driver didn't see her in the dark until it was too late and caught her . . .' He stopped talking and just sat staring into the fire.

Meredith could physically sense the hurt emanating from him. It caught her off guard and she suddenly felt an overwhelming desire to cry. She tried pinching her nose but the tears began to fall. She then tried to distract herself with her tea, but all she could taste was the salt of her tears. She sniffed and Jack looked up.

'Hey, what's the matter? Hell, I am so sorry – I didn't mean to make you cry! You have done enough of that today. I guess that is the nature of the beast: funerals are very emotional. Your poor old mum got proper upset.'

Meredith smiled through her tears.

'What's funny?' Jack caught her expression. 'Oh, I know – my accent. Yeah, it does go a bit Zummerzet from time to time, especially under duress. Still, at least I stopped you crying. You all right now? Do you want something stronger than tea, maybe?'

'I would love a glass of wine. There is some white already open in the fridge. Do have a glass yourself if you would like one.'

'I'm driving so I'd better not. I might have another bit of cake instead.' He went off to get the wine and Meredith cut him another piece of cake, wondering how come Jack had such a lovely trim body if he had a penchant for cake. *Stop it*, she chided herself. *Stop thinking about this man like that, it is all wrong.*

Jack came back with a large glass of wine and put it down beside her. 'What happened to your mum today? Did something set her off, do you think?'

He devoured his cake and Meredith took a gulp of wine. She didn't really know how to answer. Here she was, talking to a perfect stranger – and let's face it, they didn't come any more perfect than Jack Blatchford! But she couldn't just blurt out the truth, could she?

'I found out today that my father was not who I thought he was.' Oh goodness, she could!

Jack regarded her carefully. 'How do you mean exactly?'

'I found out that my real father, my birth father, did not die of a heart attack. I did not bury him today. No, my real father is alive and well and raped my mother thirty-four years ago – and I am the result.' Meredith spoke the words slowly and precisely to somehow make them real for herself. This was the truth. 'My beloved daddy, George Lee, was not my father, but some monster of a man called Myles Harrison is.'

'Myles Harrison! Are you serious? Good grief! Myles is your natural father?' Jack sat forward in shock. 'How does that work?'

Meredith poured out the story, an edited version, but enough for Jack to understand the implications.

'So you see before you a woman on the edge, Jack. I have no idea why I have told you all this. I apologise if I have embarrassed you in any way, and please feel free to leave whenever you wish, but I thank you very much for being here so far and ...' Then Meredith burst into tears. It was no good – this would not go back in the drawer. It hurt too much.

Jack was by her side and took her into a big hug. He just held her and let her cry it out. Finally, she broke away and went and got some tissues and another glass of wine. That was the bottle killed.

'Are you sure you can't have one glass?' she asked him.

'Well, I am very tempted, but I have to get home soon as I promised my nanny some time off this evening, remember? Would you mind if I gave her a quick call?'

'Oh yes of course, I completely forgot. I am an idiot. Please go ahead. But let me at least give you something to eat. I think I had better have something to soak up the wine,' she added.

'That sounds fantastic. Where's the phone and I will ring her right now.'

Meredith indicated the phone in the bedroom across the way, so he could have some privacy. She went to the fridge to get out some cheese. She lit the grill and put slices of bread under to toast. She felt a bit drunk and a bit giddy, but mostly she felt excited at the prospect of spending more time with Jack.

By the time she had grilled the cheese on toast and laid it out on a tray with a bowl of salad, Jack was back.

'That's good. My nanny is quite happy to stay overnight because she's taking Harry on a school outing tomorrow, and would have had to come early to pick him up, so it suits her just fine. This looks delicious. I'm starving! All this emotion gets to you, doesn't it?' He gave her one of his radiant, stomach-lurching smiles. 'Not that I am lessening the importance of everything you have told me, Meredith. My heart goes out to you. What a story.'

They wolfed down the cheese on toast and Jack entertained her with stories of life as a single parent. He obviously lived for his son. Did he have anyone special in his life?

'Nah. That will take time, you know? I am quite happy building my empire. Myles has given me a tremendous boost to my company ... oh shoot, him again. Sorry, I didn't mean to remind you.' Jack paused a moment. 'Actually, Meredith, what are you going to do with this information? Don't answer that, it is none of my business.'

'I don't know, to be honest, Jack. I think I will have to let some time pass and let it really sink in. I just keep thinking about my poor mum. Do you know, when I was little I felt there was something sad about her. Oh, don't get me wrong, she and George were perfectly suited and they adored each other, but she was never overly demonstrative, certainly not with me. She was careful somehow, though with my brother Frank she was much warmer and less inhibited. Now I keep thinking what it must have been like for her to look at me every day and be reminded of a monster. I suppose I didn't mind her reserve with me because I was a daddy's girl. I had my lovely adorable dad. Oh dear, I am going to cry again. Pass the wine, quick.'

Jack filled her glass.

'Listen, it is quite late and I know you have a meeting or something tomorrow so I will leave you in peace.' He got up from the sofa and Meredith tried to get up with him but sat down again.

'Whoops!' She put her hand out and Jack took it and heaved her up. She was so relaxed she practically flew across the room – would have done so, had Jack not kept hold of her and steadied her. She bumped against him clumsily, falling into his chest, which felt so good that she looked up to tell him so and kissed him instead. It was the longest, most beautiful kiss she had ever had. It was as if their mouths just fitted each other. He slowed down, she slowed down, he kissed her hard and she kissed him right back, just as hard. They kissed forever. There was not a thought in her head but his mouth and tongue and taste and smell. She seemed to draw life from him and she wanted to feel alive. Death was not an option. She wanted to live forever, like this in Jack's arms. She wanted him inside her. More than anything in the world at that moment, she wanted Jack Blatchford to fuck her and take away the pain and to fill her up with himself.

She looked into his face. It was such a beautiful face and she could see his desire for her in his eyes.

'Please, Jack. I want you so badly. Please don't say no.'

His answer was to rip her shirt off and remove her bra, taking her nipples into his mouth until she cried out with desire. She tore at his shirt and the buckle of his belt, and dragged his trousers down, causing him to fall on the sofa. He tugged them off and grabbed her by the waist where she was standing and started to kiss her stomach. She struggled out of her skirt and lay down beside him. He lifted her round onto her back and caressed the inside of her thighs as he worked her pants down. Both of them were gasping now with desire and anticipation. Jack suddenly stopped just long enough to look at Meredith's face, as if to check that this was really what she wanted, and he could see the answer. He entered her fast and hard, it was a fierce coupling for both of them. An affirmation of being alive.

Afterwards they lay panting, letting their excitement subside and their breathing return to normal. Jack pulled himself up and kissed her tenderly on the lips.

'Let's go to bed,' he said. He lifted her up and carried her to the bedroom. They lay on the bed for a while without speaking, then almost as one, they turned and started to explore each other's bodies, very slowly and sensually, the way that lovers do. It was so easy and natural, as though they had been together for a hundred years. Each one held the other in their grasp. Every nerve-ending was an erotic zone. Meredith was trembling in every fibre of her body with a sexual need for this man.

They kissed again as Jack entered her and moved slowly inside her, achingly slowly so that the bitter-sweet pain of wanting him was exquisite. She could feel the smooth strength of his back and buttocks as he pushed into her. She held him fiercely between her legs, never wanting to let him go. She could feel her orgasm rising, and her muscles contracted around him, making him thrust deep and slow and hard, and she came with a cry of joy as he joined her in his climax, releasing his passion into her. It was his life energy and she took it greedily.

They lay next to each other holding hands until they fell asleep.

Meredith woke early and turned to see his beautiful face

next to her on the pillow. Then it dawned on her just what she had done. Before she could make a plan in her head, Jack opened his eyes and winked at her!

'Come here,' he said, and started to kiss her breast. They made glorious love and then she made coffee and toast. She packed her briefcase and they set off together. It was the most perfect and natural connubial morning she had spent with a man in her life. Oliver had been safe and comfortable, while this was exciting and dangerous, but still so easy.

It was only when they got to Hampstead station and Jack turned to her to say goodbye that it hit home.

'I would say a "when can I see you again?" – but that is not going to happen, is it, Meredith? I hope you can understand where I am coming from on this. I have to be honest with you because you are a special woman and you deserve my honesty. I have Harry to worry about for now. He is my life and there is no room for anything or anyone in my heart just now. You are a beautiful and remarkable woman, and I wish you a happy life. Let's just say we leave it for now, and I sincerely hope I see you around one day.' And he leaned across and kissed her on the cheek.

The shock was devastating. Meredith could think of nothing to say so she simply got out of the car and walked away. She just wanted to be sick.

And boy, was she sick! She was sick for three months. Meredith was expecting Jack Blatchford's baby.

Chapter Thirteen

How completely bizarre life was, thought Meredith. One minute she had been contemplating a solitary, childless life and now she was expecting a child. What on earth was she to do? Tell her mother? Since her father's funeral and Jane Lee's confession, Meredith understood her mother so much better. The reserve which she had misinterpreted as a coldness and lack of feeling had really been her painful guilty secret. However could she have kept that inside herself for all these years? Meredith was also beginning to understand how these secrets were born. What would she tell her child?

She thought of the night she had conceived. Jack Blatchford's face was still so clear to her. Maybe she should just call him up and confess, and explain that she did not expect anything from him; tell him she would bring up the child by herself. But she was thirty-four years old. How could she have been so irresponsible? Why on earth hadn't they taken precautions? Could she really involve this man she hardly knew in her life? The questions spun around in her head. Surely it was better he never knew. She had money and good family to support her. The baby would not suffer without a father. Better no father, than finding out like she had that her natural father was a rapist.

But Jack wasn't a rapist, was he? He was a decent bloke who had lost his wife tragically, and was now trying to look after a small boy on his own. There – that was it. Why complicate his life further by bringing another child into his life?

Maybe one day in the future, Meredith could meet him and tell him about his other child. She just didn't want him to pity her or, God forbid, to think she was a desperate woman trying to trap a man with the oldest trick in the book. No, she was not going to be a victim. Her mother had brought her up in unbelievable circumstances – except, of course, the wonderful George Lee had been there. Her dad. She started to cry. Her dad, but not her dad.

Oh, it was all such a mess. She was desperate to talk to her mother. She picked up the phone and dialled.

'Hello, Mum, how are you?' Meredith felt like a teenager. She tried to sound cheerful. 'I thought I might come and visit this weekend, if that was OK with you?'

'Of course. Are you all right? You sound a bit tearful.' Her mother was a witch, thought Meredith.

'No, I'm fine, really, just a bit tired. I'll tell you all when I see you. How's Gran?' she asked.

There was a silence on the other end of the line, then her mother responded.

'Not very well, I'm afraid. I was going to call you after I had talked to Doctor Riley this morning. She is with her now – I've moved her in upstairs. I didn't want to worry you until I had something definite to tell you.'

'Oh Mum, I am so sorry. I'll try and come down sooner if I can work something out at the office. Lots of love, bye.'

Meredith put the phone down and sat staring into space. How could she land her news on her mother now?

At work the next day, her fantastic PA, Alena, literally bundled her out of the office, saying, 'Everything will be fine here. Just go and look after your mum.'

Down on the farm, Jane seemed very calm and in control of the situation. The pair of them sat in the kitchen and Jane explained that Dr Riley had diagnosed cancer of the lymph glands. She had received the results of all the tests, and the cancer had spread pretty much everywhere. The prognosis was not good.

'Shall I go up and see Granny now?' asked Meredith, fighting back tears.

'Yes. Why don't you take her a cold drink?' Jane made a jug of cordial and put it on a little tray with a glass. 'Take this up and I will get us a bit of lunch.'

Meredith took the tray upstairs. Her mother had redecorated Frank's old room and it was bright and cheerful, despite now being a sickroom. Mary was propped up on pillows which looked huge framing her tiny, birdlike face with its big brown eyes staring out of the pale skin that was stretched across her cheeks. Meredith was shocked at the change in her grandmother.

The old lady reached out her hand as Meredith came close and gripped her wrist. The tray wobbled.

'Hang on, Gran, let me put this down. I have brought you a drink? Here you go.' She put her arm round the old lady's back to lift her up a bit. Mary was a bag of bones and light as a feather.

'Thank you, dear,' she said, and her voice was thin and rasping. She didn't sound like herself at all.

Biting back her tears, Meredith took the glass and returned it to the bedside table, before helping the sick woman to lie back once again. She picked up the tiny hand resting on the cover and held it gently, frightened it would snap it was so delicate.

'Better?'

Mary Hughes studied her granddaughter for a few minutes. 'Good to see you, dear, but what is troubling you? I can see it in your eyes. You can't hide anything from your old gran, you know.' She smiled and it lit up her stricken face for a moment. It was too much to bear, and Meredith let the whole story pour out. When she had finally finished she waited for a response from her grandmother but saw that her eyes were closed. It was alarming. Had she fallen asleep? Meredith felt guilty for burdening her with her troubles.

'I am not asleep, dear, just remembering,' came the frail voice, guessing her thoughts. 'Family secrets. What did I tell you? They all come out in the end. Now you have yours. Well, dear, at least you are upholding the family tradition.' She chuckled softly.

'What do you mean?' Meredith was baffled.

'Well, your mother told you her story, didn't she, at the funeral? And now I will tell you mine because it doesn't matter any longer. Alfred is long gone and I will be too, very soon. Oh, don't fret, my dear. I am quite content to die. That is one thing you can't change in life. Death.'

Mary sighed. 'I had a one-night stand, I suppose one would call it that these days. I had no idea, of course, at the time that it was only going to be one night, but that is what it turned out to be. And then I fell pregnant, just like you. Mind you, it was a lot more serious in those days than it is now.'

Mary told Meredith her story. It was a slow and painful process as she had to keep stopping to sit up for sips of the cordial, and once she had a coughing fit; Meredith was terrified she was going to pass away there and then. But gradually, the tale unfolded.

When she had told her story, Mary lay back and closed her eyes. Meredith thought she was done, but as she quietly got up to leave, Mary said with all the passion she could muster, 'I loved my baby. You will understand when your time comes, dear. What will be, will be – but you *must* love your baby.'

Meredith kissed her and went downstairs.

'You were a long time. Is she all right?' Jane asked anxiously. Then she saw Meredith's distraught face. 'Whatever is the matter? Here, sit down and talk to me.'

'Mum, I'm pregnant.' Meredith burst into tears.

Jane held her daughter until she could cry no more, then got her some hankies and made a pot of tea, just as her own mother had done for her back in 1944, and as Reginald had done for Mary, all those years ago. Setting the mug in front of Meredith, she sat down opposite her and said, 'Right, from the beginning, please.'

When Meredith had finished, Jane said, 'What a family we are, us Hughes girls. Hussies, the lot of us!'

Meredith burst out laughing despite herself. 'Oh Mum, you are priceless. That is the last thing I expected you to say.'

'Did you tell your grandmother – is that why you were such a long time upstairs? I suppose she told you her story as well.' And when Meredith nodded, she went on: 'So you see? I am right – we are all hussies. I am sorry, Meredith. I am not trying to make light of your predicament, but it is extraordinary that we have all fallen pregnant in unusual circumstances.'

Jane opened the biscuit tin, saying, 'Why can't you tell Jack Blatchford about the baby, my love? I am sure he would understand. He seemed such a pleasant young man.'

'Because I don't want it to look as if I am trying to trap him. I have got my pride, Mum.'

'And pride comes before a fall,' replied her mother. 'Still, it is your decision and I will help you in any way I can, you know that.'

Meredith spent the rest of the afternoon upstairs on her bed, trying to stop her brain going round in circles. She must have dropped off because the next thing she knew, she was being shaken awake and her mother's voice was saying, 'You'd better wake up now or you won't sleep tonight.'

Meredith's nap turned out to be a blessing in disguise because that night she was able to take over from Jane and keep an eye on Mary. The old lady woke up in the middle of the night, calling for Henry. Meredith soothed her until she fell asleep again. Now it was four in the morning and Meredith was reading to Mary from the Bible. It seemed to calm her.

Thinking she was finally asleep, Meredith had stopped reading and was just sitting, holding her grandmother's hand, listening to the ticking of the clock on the mantelpiece. It was a beautiful, ornate eighteenth-century clock with a delicate chime. Meredith had always loved it as a child in her grandparents' house. Whenever she had felt homesick or frightened, that clock had comforted her. She remembered Mary telling her that the tinkling chimes were fairy raindrops falling from the sky.

Now it chimed five and her grandmother stirred, as though she was trying to say something.

Meredith leaned forward. 'What is it, Gran?'

'Remember Jesus loves you ...' A flicker of a smile brushed her lips, and as they parted a tiny sigh escaped and floated up and hung in the air as the old lady died.

Meredith went to wake her mother and together they sat beside Mary in silence and shared the last remaining minutes of darkness. Dawn came deep pink and red, and painted over the night's passing. Jane shed no tears but said to Meredith, 'One life ends as another begins,' and patted her daughter's belly. 'Keep her safe,' she murmured.

'How do you know it will be a she?'

Her mother just smiled.

Meredith drove back to London and went straight to Notting Hill to see Oliver, who was having a day off. She was relieved to discover that Michael was away on business in Berlin. She did not relish telling her pathetic story in front of him. Time enough for him to find out later.

Oliver was thrilled. 'Merry, that is wonderful news!'

'No, it isn't, it's a disaster. The child doesn't have a father.'

'Be fair. It does really, you just don't want to tell him.'

'Yes, exactly. Do you think I am a complete idiot, wanting to keep this to myself?'

'A bit, yes. Why don't you at least find out where he is, and what his circumstances are?'

'But I know what his circumstances are: he is grieving for his late wife, and trying to bring up his adopted son. What's to know?' she retorted.

'But Merry, he might be more amenable when he knows you are pregnant.'

They talked round in circles for the next hour until Meredith had had enough.

'I'll give you a ring,' she flung over her shoulder as she left. She was tired and grumpy and pregnant. There was nothing more to be said.

Then she went home and had a nap. All this napping was a new phenomenon in her life. Was this deadly fatigue to do with the baby?

She decided to follow Oliver's suggestion and find out what Jack was up to. She looked up Harrison first, in the *Yellow Pages*, and found Myles's company, Harrison Construction Ltd. Then she tried Blatchford under *Builders* but found nothing, so she rang Harrison Construction.

'Harrison Construction, how may we help you?' answered a prissy female voice.

'Oh yes, hi, I wonder if you can help me. I am trying to find an old friend of mine called Jack Blatchford, and I believe he may have something to do with your company. Would you have information as to his whereabouts, by any chance?' Meredith held her breath.

'Why yes, of course, Mr Blatchford is a director of the company. Would you like me to put you through to his office?'

Hell no! thought Meredith. 'No, that is fine, I will call back later. Thank you for your time,' and she hung up quickly, her heart racing. What was she thinking?

She sat and waited until she had calmed down and got her

thoughts in order. What was she trying to achieve? Well, as Oliver had said, maybe things had changed in his life. *What, in three months?* sneered a voice in her head. *Don't be daft, woman!* OK, so maybe she should meet him and tell him the facts, and let him decide what to do. Her heart sank. She was back to square one. She didn't want his pity or his help. Deep down she wanted to have this baby on her own, didn't she? Getting right down to the nitty gritty here, she admitted to herself that she did not really trust Jack Blatchford. Her first instinct when she had met him with Eva at the Harrisons' dinner party was that he was a bit of a smoothie, and not to be trusted. Agreed, he had had a tragedy in his life and lost his wife, but maybe he deserved that. Maybe it was karma because he had been a bad husband and unfaithful, or something. And he was in partnership with Myles Harrison, for goodness' sake – and *he* certainly couldn't be trusted. Myles Harrison was a disgusting human being. *And your father,* came the voice once again. *No, please, let's not open that drawer just now.*

No, she was going to let sleeping dogs lie. Dogs being the operative word! She would get on and have this baby by herself, and trust that fate would take a hand, like it had with her mother and grandmother before her.

Fate did take a hand because when Meredith was back in the office, she had a meeting with a company who were thinking about promoting property through a documentary series for the TV. Property was very much on everyone's agenda these days as it was apparent, with rising prices, that it was a surefire way to make money. The series was commissioned, and lo and behold, Meredith soon received a call from Harrison Construction. The company had been asked to take part because they were one of the top organisations in London, and their ambitious redevelopment plans covered several areas of the capital.

Her PA took the call from a Mr Jack Blatchford!

'Do you want me to call him back for you?' she asked over the intercom. Just as well she could not see her boss's face, as Meredith had gone as white as a sheet.

'No, thank you, Alena. Just give me the number and I will do it later.'

Now what? What on earth was she going to say to him? She couldn't meet him as she was already showing and he was bound to ask her about it. Maybe she should just ignore the call. Get Alena to ring and apologise and say they already had a company they were using for the show. But what if she got found out? *Stay calm*, she advised herself. *Let's ring and find out what the situation is with the company.* She pressed the intercom.

'Alena, I have changed my mind about that property developer. Can you call him and find out what he wants, please?' Meredith sat back in her chair and waited nervously.

About half an hour later, Alena buzzed her. 'I have some info for you on Harrison Construction. Do you want me to bring it in to you?'

'Yes, please,' said Meredith, and got up to face the window. She looked out over Green Park. When Alena entered and placed the file on her desk, she didn't turn round in case she gave anything away, simply called out as she heard her leave, 'Thank you, Alena. You can take an early lunch.'

When the girl had gone, Meredith came back to her desk, sat down and opened the file. There was a transcript of the phone call Alena had had with Jack. As Meredith read it, she visibly relaxed. Oh thank God, this was wonderful news! It appeared that Mr Blatchford was going to the States as from next week, and then to Malaysia for six months. He regretted to inform the company that he would be unavailable to take part in the making of their documentary.

So fate had decided for her. Meredith would be a single mother.

PART THREE

Chapter Fourteen

Anna Lee was born in the Whittington Hospital, North London on 29 June 1980. Oliver had insisted he would be there for the birth, much to Meredith's dismay. Her understanding from her upbringing was that babies were very much left to the female department. She remembered her father saying, 'Don't worry, Meredith. When you have a baby, just ask for a bale of straw and some hot water and get on with it!' George had told her this while they were sitting in the barn with a ewe about to drop a lamb, and he had been showing Meredith how to ease the lamb's foot out of the womb at the time. Not quite the same as the birthing unit at the Whittington!

In the end, she had been grateful for Oliver's presence. He was completely beside himself with excitement and did all the breathing with her, all the stuff they had learned at the ante-natal classes. He took so many deep breaths he had to sit down at one point, because he was hyperventilating! He made Meredith laugh through several contractions, to the point where the midwife had to tell him to calm down and help his wife as she pushed. They had decided it was too complicated to explain their relationship, so Oliver became Mr Lee for the purposes of the birth. God, push! Meredith thought her eyes were going to pop out of her head. She loved the gas and air, and in the early stages of her labour, seriously thought women must make up all those horror stories about labour. Pain? She could feel no pain until suddenly it hit with a vengeance. She let out a yell and grabbed Oliver's hand.

'It fucking hurts!' she informed the room, and spent the next two hours screaming and swearing like a trooper.

Then suddenly the whole room seemed to hold its breath and then exhale as one, as a tiny cry was heard.

'It's a girl,' announced the midwife. 'Ten toes, ten fingers and weighing in at . . .' there was a pause while she placed the baby on the scales '. . . six pounds, nine ounces. Well done, Mum, here she is.' She placed the bundle in Meredith's arms and stood back. Oliver leaned in and kissed her.

'Congratulations, Merry, my angel. You did it, girl! Look at her – she is gorgeous. Hello, pretty baby.' He took a tiny hand and kissed it.

Meredith looked down at the wrinkled pink bundle and wanted to burst into tears. What could she possibly do with this baby? She wanted Jack; she yearned for him. She closed her eyes and all she could see was his beautiful face. She wanted his arms around her. All these months she had stopped herself thinking about him, and now the floodgates were opened. She did not want this baby, she wanted *him*.

The horror of the situation broke over her like a wave, and she could feel herself drowning. She tried to cry out but her throat was closed. She was coughing and spluttering, but she couldn't get any air into her lungs.

'What is it? What's the matter?' Oliver's voice was panicky. 'Nurse, please help her.'

'Come along now, dear, give me the baby, that's it. Now calm down. Everything is fine. Here, take a tissue and have a good blow. It's all right, it is perfectly normal to want to cry.'

Meredith was still sobbing, taking great gulps of air in with each sob. She just could not stop.

'I am so sorry, Oliver, I am so sorry,' she blubbed.

'It's OK, love, don't worry. God, I want to cry as well, but real men can't do that kind of thing. Hey, come on! Everything is fine. It's wonderful! You can have a big long sleep now, and when you wake up everything will be back to normal again.'

Except for the fact there is a baby in my life, thought Meredith. Oh God, don't let me wake up! Make this all a dream and send me back to life a year ago. Let me meet Jack and run away with him. I can't do this.

Meredith lay back on the pillows too exhausted to fight any more. Somewhere in the distance she listened to Oliver and the midwife discussing aftercare, and getting further and further away from her. She let herself float above a hazy corridor of dim lights and squeaking wheels, vaguely aware of a draught of air crossing her face like a whisper ... and then nothing.

Meredith was awoken by a nurse holding her wrist and taking her pulse.

'Hi there, how are you feeling?' she asked.

'Fine, thanks. Have I been asleep long?'

'About three hours. Would you like a cup of tea before we sort out your baby?'

'Baby? Oh yes, my baby.' Meredith closed her eyes and tried to will herself back to sleep. Baby!

'Tea then?' prompted the nurse.

'Oh, yes, that would be lovely. Thank you. Is Oliver around?'

'Your husband, is that? No, he said to tell you he will be back later with your mother.' She went, closing the curtains round the bed behind her. Meredith pulled herself up, and winced in pain as her stomach muscles complained. She also had a dull ache between her legs. God, she felt sore. Still, that was the least of her problems. She needed to pee, and managed to haul herself out of bed and find her way to the toilet.

The ward contained eight beds, all with mothers sat in them with babies, either in cots beside them or in their arms. Meredith shuffled down the centre with her head lowered, avoiding eye-contact with anyone.

'There we are, your gorgeous little girl. Isn't she a sweetie?' The nurse helped Meredith back into bed and put the baby in her arms before she could protest.

'Actually, could I have my cup of tea first, do you think?' Meredith said, longingly eyeing the cup and saucer on the top of her locker.

The nurse seemed rather taken aback. 'Oh, all right. Here, give me the baby. What are you going to call her?'

'Um ... Anna,' Meredith heard herself say. She and Oliver had discussed names, and he was desperate for the child to be called Anna after his mother. Meredith felt she should have her own mother or grandmother's name out of loyalty, so they had laughed at the time and agreed the baby would be called Anna Jane Mary Lee if it was a girl, and George Oliver Jack Lee if it was a boy. It had all seemed so unreal and removed from her at the time. Now here she was listening to this nurse wittering on, and Anna was lying in the cot beside her.

She drank her tea, which was cold by now and had sugar in it, but it tasted like nectar. Meredith watched the nurse as she held her baby. Her brain felt like cotton wool. Everything was fuzzy.

The nurse handed Meredith the baby. 'Now you take Anna, and let's see if we can't give this good little girl some milk.'

Meredith sat up rigidly as the nurse undid her nightie, took her breast and guided the child's mouth towards her nipple, gently tickling the tiny cheek to make her turn and root. All the while she was talking Meredith through the whole thing as if she were giving her a cookery lesson. First take one large engorged breast, locate the nipple and place it in the baby's mouth, adjusting the child's head in the crook of your elbow and keeping it firmly supported while placing your hand underneath its bottom. Take a glass of water with the other hand and sip frequently. Allow sucking to continue for ten minutes, then take out that nipple, burp the baby and switch her to the other one. This will result in a happy healthy baby full of natural nourishment.

'So there you go, Mrs Lee. I will leave you and Anna in peace. Just shout if you need me. Good luck!' and off she went down the ward as happy as a sand boy, her mission accomplished. Another bonding moment completed.

Meredith hardly dared move. Her bum had gone numb, and her stitches were tugging at her poor sore fanny, but she dared not interrupt the feeding frenzy that was taking place. Well, to be fair, not so much a frenzy as a contented gurgling and mewing, as her breast seemed to empty its contents into this tiny being in her arms. The baby responded with murmurings of pleasure, while its little fingers caressed her breast and the little toes wiggled with delight. She watched transfixed at this unbelievable phenomenon taking place in her lap. Perhaps things were not so bad, after all?

Once the feed was over, the nurse returned and showed Meredith how to change Anna's nappy and wash her. The baby was wrapped in her little pink blanket and laid in her cot, where she went straight off to sleep.

Meredith climbed back into bed and lay there thinking about her baby. OK, she wasn't a monster – she was rather sweet, in fact, and Meredith could not help but be taken by her. She was also a little bit of Jack, wasn't she? Well, half really. Would she ever be able to tell him he was the father? Would she ever even see him again? She might well do so – and bearing in mind that he worked with Myles Harrison . . . suddenly she was bang up against the real horror of it all. The whole turn of events that had led up to this moment. The birth of her daughter. Her natural father had raped her mother and Meredith had been born. She imagined Jane sitting in bed just like she was doing now. How on earth did her mother find the strength to look after her? Did she look down at the baby in her arms and see Myles Harrison's face staring back at her? Did she wonder how she would ever be able to love her daughter? Meredith's own lack of instinctive maternal love was tempered for her by the fact she had adored the father of her child. Her poor mother had had to learn to love Meredith, in spite of who the father had been.

She heard a whoop of delight and looked up to see Oliver dancing down the ward, with an enormous bouquet of flowers, followed by her mother carrying an overnight bag.

'Where are my two favourite girls?' He chucked the flowers on the bed and gave Meredith a huge hug, then completely ignored her for the rest of the visit, his attention captivated by the bundle in the cot.

'Hello, dear, how are you feeling?' Jane planted a kiss on Meredith's cheek and stood back and regarded her closely. 'Oliver told me you were very distressed last night.'

Meredith began to feel the tears welling up again and fought them back by taking a gulp of water.

'Oh I'm fine,' she said. ''Really I am – it was just the hormones kicking in. It is good to see you, Mum. Thank you for coming.'

'Don't be so daft. I wouldn't miss the chance to greet my granddaughter as soon as she arrived. Where is she? Come on, Oliver, budge out of the way and let me have a look.' Jane went round to the other side of the cot and leaned over. 'Oh, she is beautiful, Meredith, and she has your mouth. Look, Oliver, doesn't she have Meredith's mouth?'

'Let's hope she learns to keep it shut more than her mother does,' Oliver joked. Jane lifted her bag onto the bed and produced the perfect pair of knitted bootees and white knitted coat with pink ribbon ties threaded through the neck.

'Oh Mum, they are perfect! How did you know she was a girl?'

'I guessed. Do you remember that first morning you told me you were pregnant? But just in case I was wrong I took the precaution of knitting the jacket in white and buying two lots of ribbon to thread through, blue or pink.'

'How very ingenious!'

Jane sat by her bed and handed her daughter a card.

'It's from your old friend, Eva. Guess what! She has moved back to Burslet. She is married to a banker or something and has three children under the age of five. Can you imagine! She popped in to see me and give me her phone number, and to tell you to ring. I must say, she seems terribly happy. It is not at all what I would have imagined for her, but you just can't tell, can you? Now you get some rest while you can, my girl. You are going to need it. Come on, Oliver, stop drooling over the poor child and take me back so I can cook you a decent meal. None of that French rubbish.'

Meredith clung to her mother and whispered, 'I love you.' Jane searched her face then turned away.

'Bye, darling, see you tomorrow.' Oliver kissed her goodbye and followed Jane up the ward.

Being on the ward was like being on another planet. Meredith was acutely aware of every sound and smell around her. It was so hot in here. She could feel a drop of sweat trickle down her back. Her body was slow to respond and her legs felt heavy. One of her breasts was leaking milk through her nightgown. This was a world of nature and darkness and wombs. In fact, it felt like being inside a womb. The ward seemed to have a heartbeat: it was as though it was an organism in its own right, moving around and enveloping everything as it passed, the silence only broken from time to time by the cry of a baby, or the sound of sucking, or a soft snoring from an exhausted mother. The light from the nurses' station cast a yellow glow across the floor. It was like the eye of the womb. All-seeing. They were all wrapped in a cloak of fecundity. Meredith felt so small. A tiny figure in this huge canvas of life. It was awe-inspiring, mystical and frightening at the same time. It was also deeply touching. She picked up her tiny piece of this new life and held her close. She could feel Anna's little heart beating against her skin. She wanted them to touch skin to skin, life-affirming, the invisible thread between mother and child.

Over the next few months, however, and like every other important emotional crisis in her life, Meredith's bonding with her new baby had to be put on hold. There was just no time. At least Oliver was around most of the day. He had been made co-owner of Le Garcon Bleu and was therefore able to organise his day around Anna. Madame Broussard, who was thrilled about the baby, was very supportive. She did not ever ask about the question of parentage but carried on as if Oliver was the father.

Actually he might just as well have been, as he was more hands-on than most fathers. It was a nightmare schedule for them. Anna was quite good and slept from midnight to around 5 a.m. Meredith would get up and feed her and then gather the baby's stuff ready for the day. She had managed to wean Anna onto a bottle during the day, but they all had to be made up and left ready, plus nappies and a change of clothes or two. Meredith then had to haul herself through the daily routine of shower and shampoo. She took trouble about the way she looked and dressed, because at work she was surrounded by cool, trendy executives, and it was important that she looked as though she was a part of their world.

Babies and breast-feeding were not considered at all cool, and many times she had to nip into the ladies to wipe sick off her shoulder before entering the boss's office first thing in the morning. It was weird really, that these men seemed so oblivious to female physical reality; to them, women were simply fodder for their sexual appetites. They loved to screw them, but God forbid women showed any side of their reproductive nature other than their erogenous zones. Wives, if they had them, stayed at home, and certainly children lived in another space entirely in their world. For this was the world of 'Advertising' where everything was perfect. No clutter. No mess, no human detritus or any emotional upheavals. In this world, all women were gorgeous, sofas were white and stains did not exist except on the drawing board in a commercial. Life was a storyboard from someone's imagination.

The first three years of Anna's flew by! Meredith worked her socks off and loved every minute of it. A sauce campaign she had created was a great success, and lasted long after Meredith had moved on to her next assignment. She had learned a great deal from that campaign about how to make food look good under hot lights: little tricks like painting the roast chicken with varnish so it gleamed in the final shot and making sure that vegetables never looked soggy by keeping them raw. The poor actors would often make the mistake of popping a piece of cauliflower into their mouths, only to find it was cold and hard.

She would study the script for each commercial and talk to the director about the exact kind of people they were aiming their product at . . . how much money they had to spend in the home. It was no good advertisers giving the public a lifestyle they couldn't afford, but at the same time the nature of the beast demanded that life in an advert looked glossy and desirable. Lifestyle was becoming big business and the success of stores like Habitat and the famous Conran shops meant that certain products were now available. People started to learn to cook outside the normal English range of recipes. Oliver made an interesting point one night in his restaurant as he sat with some customers.

'It is extraordinary how things have changed since the sixties and seventies. A chef used to be regarded as the lowest in the pecking order within the catering industry. It was all about the front of house then, wasn't it? Remember all those trattorias in the sixties – those suave Italian managers giving you the chat? And those snooty maître d's looking down their noses at you in those plush French restaurants? But now suddenly it is the chef everyone is talking about. I shall have to look to my laurels if I want to keep on top. Not just what I cook, but how I present my food and even myself. In fact, I have been discussing with another customer, who is in television, the possibility of making a TV show about my cooking!'

It was true. At long last Meredith was working on a TV show for Oliver but also one for herself. She was fascinated by American television. Afternoon programming had really taken off across the Pond, and Meredith was determined to get ahead of the game here in the UK.

She did manage to find time to ring Eva eventually, and when Anna was about eighteen months old Meredith drove home to see her friend and visit her mother at the same time. She dumped everything at Jane's and then just took Anna in her buggy to visit Eva, who was living in a converted barn the other side of Burslet.

It was wonderful to see her again after all the years that had passed. As Meredith drove up, Eva came running out of the barn with a child swinging from one hip and another dragging a trike behind her. She looked amazing.

'Welcome to Chaos Hall,' she laughed. 'It is madness here. Oh, look at your gorgeous little girl! Come in, come in.' She led Meredith into a huge room with a vaulted ceiling of exposed beams. There were toys everywhere and a delicious smell of baking. 'I made a cake especially for you, although I am quite nervous as you are such an expert now. You even write books, Meredith.'

'Oh please, I have only just started. I have a lot to learn,' said Meredith, looking round for a suitable spot to park Anna's buggy.

'Put her over here by the window so she can look out at the birdfeeder. My lot love watching the birds fly in and out.'

Once the children were settled and the cake was produced and the tea poured out, Eva was able to pause for breath. Meredith could now fire at her all the questions she was longing to ask. Such as how on earth had Eva ended up here?

'You mean, how did a slapper like me turn into an earth mother?' Eva laughed gaily. 'Well, I met David and fell in love – hook, line and sinker – and that was that. We were in the States for five years, which is where I met him, but then we missed Europe, and because the whole school thing would soon become an issue, we came back. I wanted to be near Mum as my father died a while ago now. I think he lost heart when the Hall went and then the farm was too much for him. He sort of gave up.' Eva looked very sad for a moment. 'Anyway, Mummy lives in a little cottage in Redbourn and we found this fabulous place so here we are. It is upsetting, though, to drive past Long Moor House and remember all the lovely times I had as a child in that house. I believe it was bought by that guy we met years ago at your aunt and uncle's house, do you remember? I can't think of his name even though I recall he was very dishy, right?' She giggled. 'He fancied you, didn't he?'

Meredith sighed and took a sip of tea. Oh Lord, where to begin? She told Eva all about her dalliance with Mr Blatchford.

'Wow, that is some story,' her friend breathed. 'Are you going to contact him eventually?'

'I honestly don't know, Eva. I did try but he was abroad for six months and since then I have just put my head down and got on with everything. I realise I will have to deal with it one day, but you know what I'm like.'

'Oh yes, Merry – your famous drawer,' Eva grinned. 'But you will have to decide one day. He might be thrilled to hear from you. Have you got anyone in your life right now?'

'No,' Meredith said. 'And I don't expect to find anyone either.' She sighed. 'I just missed the boat, Eva. It is no big deal. I am quite happy on my own and there is always Oliver in the background for moral support. He came out of the closet, by the way, and is happily living with a literary agent called Michael.'

The friends chatted on through bath-time and the children's supper until Meredith realised she had better get back to her mother before Frank locked up for the night.

'Please come and stay one weekend,' said Eva. 'I would love you to meet David. I am sorry he couldn't get back tonight but he works late on Fridays, so he misses the weekend rush-hour tonight and then has Mondays off and goes back up on Tuesday mornings. It will be a lovely break for you. Anna can play with my three and somehow it is always easier feeding and bathing a few at once.'

'You should know!' laughed Meredith. 'I must say, you seem to have it all down to a fine art. I am so glad you are happy, Eva. Who would have thought it, eh?'

'I know, I was such a bitch.' She smiled ruefully. 'Belated apologies for screwing your uncle. What a horrible man! Sorry, but it's the truth.'

'Oh, believe me, I know exactly what he is capable of.' Meredith decided not to mention her relationship with Myles for her mother's sake. Jane did not need the locals hearing the family secrets.

Meredith gave her friend a hug and set off back to the farm. As she drove past the end of the driveway leading to Long Moor House she remembered about Jack Blatchford, and her guilty conscience tried to squeeze its way into her thoughts. 'Not now,' she whispered and cast a look at her daughter, who was fast asleep in the baby seat. 'But one day.'

The biggest problem for Meredith was childcare. Sometimes she had to work late into the night on a shoot and Oliver could not help because he was needed in the restaurant.

'Maybe we could get an au pair or something?' he suggested one day.

'But where would she live?' said Meredith.

'Let me talk to Lucette tonight at work and see if she has any ideas.'

Madame Broussard proved to be their saviour. She adored Oliver like a son and regarded Anna as practically her own child. So she put on her thinking cap and came up with a master-plan that very night. She had a sister in Bergerac in France, who had a daughter called Michelle who wanted to come to England to learn English. Her sister's husband was nervous about sending their daughter away on her own. Lucette Broussard had already told them that if they wanted to send the girl to London, she would be more than happy to have her live with her, so she could keep an eye on her. Perhaps this was the solution to everyone's problems. Michelle could work for Meredith as an au pair and live with her aunt. She would be working just enough hours to keep her out of trouble, but she would also have time to study. Madame Broussard rang her sister and the deal was done. *Voilà!*

It was great for Meredith to be able to go to work knowing everything was under control at home. She worked all hours and although she had help from Michelle, she always tried to be there at weekends and for Anna's bedtimes. Sometimes she would fall asleep reading to her daughter and wake up fully clothed the next morning in bed with Anna. Birthdays seemed to arrive so quickly, but they were always enormous fun for everyone, not least Anna. Jane took great pride in providing a different cake every year. On Anna's second birthday she had made a cake in the shape of a pink teddy, which had been the child's favourite cuddly toy. On that day, Anna blew out the candles with squeals of delight, but when Meredith poised the knife to cut the cake, the tiny toddler burst into tears, begging her mother not to cut her teddy.

'Don't worry, darling, it's not a real teddy, it's a cake. Yummy!' But Anna would not have it so the cake had to be left alone. When Anna went to sleep that night, the teddy cake had to be placed on the bedside table, with the real teddy tucked up beside her. They all laughed about it afterwards. Jane's cakes became a legend.

For Anna's third birthday, her grandmother had excelled herself and made a cake in the shape of a fairy with a wand. Anna had a fairy costume that she adored and she loved to wear it all day long. She put it on for her birthday and was delighted to see the same dress on the fairy cake. They had a lovely tea and then Michael and Oliver came round later and gave Anna her presents. After she had been bathed and put to bed, they all sat down to dinner. Jane helped Meredith clear up after the boys had left, and as they washed up, her mother broached the subject of Jack Blatchford.

'You are definitely a witch, Mother, dear,' said Meredith. 'I thought about him this morning for the first time in ages, maybe because it is Anna's birthday.'

'So what conclusions have you come to, if any?' asked Jane.

'I don't know. Should I ring him, do you think?'

Jane took a deep breath. 'As a matter of fact, I have some news about Mr Blatchford,' she announced. 'Not very good news for you, I'm afraid.'

'What on earth do you mean?' Meredith's curiosity was piqued.

'Do you remember that Harrison Construction was in negotiations to buy Long Moor House a few years ago and convert it into a luxury hotel? Myles and Jack were talking about it at Dad's funeral.'

'Yes, what of it?' Meredith was impatient for news.

'Well, Laura Hamlin was in the village shop the other day, you know her husband died, and she moved into a cottage in Redbourn?'

'Yes, yes, for goodness' sake get on with it, Mum. You are driving me mad!'

'Oh yes, well anyway, she was telling me that Jack Blatchford is engaged to a woman he met through them. She is the general manager of the hotel – quite a bit younger than him, I gather, and very pretty. But Laura thinks she is after his money.' Jane finished her story and sat down.

Meredith, however, had leaped to her feet, exclaiming, 'You see? I was right all along about him! First bit of skirt that comes along and shows him some attention, he falls for it. Stupid bloody man. Typical though, don't you think, Mother? They are all the same, these men. Just go for the sex every time.'

'To be perfectly fair, Meredith, you don't know that. There could be all sorts of reasons they are together. Maybe they are even in love,' suggested her mother optimistically.

'Oh, yeah – right. Anyway, that solves my problem. I am not telling Mr Blatchford anything. He seems quite busy enough, he doesn't need anything else in his life – and I certainly don't need him!' pronounced Meredith.

But that night in bed she let Jack into her thoughts. Was she just the tiniest bit envious of his latest squeeze? Surely not – it was all water under the bridge. So how come she could still remember his lips? How come she sometimes caught herself looking at Anna and seeing his face? It was bound to happen, she told herself. Inevitable that she would have these thoughts for the rest of her life. She would just have to live with it. Thank God for Oliver; he was the perfect father figure and Anna adored him.

Michelle went back to France after a year, but the family sent Michelle's Cousin Nicole instead. She was perfect and did all the fetching and carrying and bits in between. Thanks to her support and Olly's input, Meredith was going from strength to strength at the agency. After all this time, she had finally got a commission for Oliver to do a show on Sunday afternoon called *The Sunday Roast*. It was only half an hour, but it was a start. Oliver didn't let her down: he cooked up a storm and was suddenly being photographed all over the place. He revelled in the attention and Michael and Meredith had their work cut out to make sure he didn't get too big for his boots. They made sure of this by putting him on park duty, which entailed a good deal of running round after Anna on her trike, pushing swings for hours and feeding the ducks in the rain.

'I understand I must be more humble!' he screamed as he was shoved out of the car into the cold one day. 'Please may I be excused today? I am exhausted!'

'Very well,' said Michael. 'But if you even suggest to me for a minute that you are a star in any way, shape, or form, you will be back out there pushing the buggy before you can say "Toss a salad".'

As well as starting to put a show together for a new series, Meredith was also investigating the property world again. By the time Anna was ready to go to primary school, their lives had pretty much found the perfect routine.

Every now and then Meredith and Oliver would discuss the pros and cons of contacting Jack, but then they decided that as things had come this far, it was probably best to wait until Anna herself asked them about her parentage. For now, the little girl accepted her situation without any questions asked. She called Oliver 'Olly' and it didn't seem to bother her that she didn't have a daddy.

'Mind you, that may all change when she goes to big school,' said Oliver one day. They had been to visit the local primary school, met the Headmistress and explained the situation. The woman had suggested that they talk to Anna before she started school, but Meredith wasn't convinced.

Then one morning the phone rang – and her secret drawer, in which she stored all her secrets, unresolved problems and memories, good and bad – was well and truly opened.

Chapter Fifteen

'Meredith? It's me,' said Jane. 'I'm afraid I have got some bad news. I hate to do this by phone, but it's urgent. Your Aunt Pamela is very ill with cancer of the liver. She has asked to see me and I don't know what to do. The thought of going inside that house again and seeing that man again is just too much to bear. It was bad enough at your father's funeral. I really don't think I can do it.' And Jane started to cry.

'Mum, don't get all upset. Of course you can't go there. Is she not in a hospital?' Meredith asked.

'Apparently not, she is being nursed at home. Myles rang here, and fortunately I was out so Jenny took the message. What on earth shall I do?'

'Nothing – I will go and see her. I will sort it out, Mum, so please calm down and stop worrying. Give me the number, and I'll ring Myles Harrison and find out what is going on.' Jane gave her the number and Meredith continued: 'Now just forget all about it for the time being, and I will phone back when I have found out what is going on.'

Well, this is going to be tricky, Meredith thought. She sat and tried to work out what she should do. She didn't want to see Myles any more than her mother did; the thought of being in the same room with him made her feel quite sick. So maybe she could arrange to see her aunt at a time when he was not around. That would be the best solution. Steeling herself, she rang the number.

'The Harrison residence, how may I help you?' It was a woman's voice, sounding very efficient.

'May I speak to Myles Harrison, please.' Meredith guessed he would not be there at this time in the morning.

'I am sorry, he is not here at present. May I take your name and number and he will get back to you.'

'Well, actually, I am his niece, Meredith Lee, and I am ringing on behalf of my mother Jane, who is Mrs Harrison's sister. We understand that Aunt Pamela is very unwell and wishes to see Jane. Unfortunately, my mother is unable to visit at the moment so I was going to come in her stead. Is that possible, do you think? Who am I speaking to, by the way?' Meredith wondered if it was a secretary or a nurse, maybe.

'I am the nurse,' the woman said. 'As a matter of fact, I am not sure what to suggest. Mrs Harrison is really very weak, but of course, if she has asked to see her sister I am sure that would be fine. Mr Harrison is away until tomorrow. He had to go to a meeting in Switzerland yesterday.' Immediately, Meredith asked if she could come that morning.

'I daresay that would be fine. Would you be able to get here by eleven? I give Mrs Harrison her lunch at noon and her medication, and then she sleeps for a couple of hours, so before that would be best.'

'That is perfect,' said Meredith. 'I will be there. Thank you very much, Nurse . . . ?'

'Oh yes, sorry, Nurse Delaware. I look forward to meeting you, Miss Lee. Goodbye.'

The line went dead and Meredith breathed a sigh of relief. This was going to be interesting. She left a message for Oliver to call her later, letting him know that she would be able to pick Anna up from school on her way back from St John's Wood.

It had been twenty-odd years since Meredith had come to this imposing house for that dinner party with Eva. She rang the bell and waited, going over different conversations in her head. What would Pamela want to talk about, she wondered.

The door opened and a uniformed woman greeted her. 'Good morning – Miss Lee, isn't it? I am delighted to make your acquaintance. I am Nurse Delaware, but please call me Joan. Follow me.' She shut the door and indicated for Meredith to go upstairs. She remembered the tiled hallway with its chandelier and the huge staircase from her last visit. Nothing seemed to have changed much over the past two decades.

As they went upstairs Nurse Delaware said, 'Mrs Harrison is gravely ill. I regret to say that we do not expect her to live long. I am sure you are aware, Miss Lee, that a disease like cancer takes its toll on a patient. How long ago is it since you last saw your aunt?'

'Oh, quite some time ago – several years at least.'

'I see,' replied the nurse, and she stopped at the top of the stairs and turned to face Meredith. 'In that case, you must prepare yourself for a shock. Your aunt has lost a considerable amount of weight and is very feeble. I hope you can cope with this visit and will be able to stay calm. Mrs Harrison is weak but she is very alert to everything around her. She was adamant that she must speak to your mother, and I have explained that it is not possible. Do you understand?'

'Yes, of course,' said Meredith. 'I will make sure I do not register my shock at seeing her and try not to upset her in any way.' Did she really need this condescending little lecture from the nurse? How bad could her aunt look, for goodness' sake! The answer hit her like a slap as she walked into the bedroom. Aunt Pamela was skeletal. Meredith could have counted every bone in her body. She was wraithlike, but out of this excruciating collection of bones shone two black orbs. Her eyes were as bright as new buttons, and they took Meredith in with a practised sweep from head to toe.

'Sit down, dear. How lovely to see you.' Her voice was a thin rasp on a breath of air. 'I am only sad my sister could not come. Could not or would not?'

Her question took Meredith by surprise and she hesitated before answering. 'No, she ... well ...'

Pamela held up a tiny finger. 'Please don't bother to lie. I know everything, you see. Come closer, can you?'

Meredith sat next to the bed and leaned towards the dying woman. There was an odour she could not quite capture, but it was very unpleasant. It was all she could do to remain there and not recoil.

'Meredith, I want to give you a present,' came the whisper. 'Nurse, bring me that box from the dressing table and then you may leave us.'

The nurse fetched a small box and placed it next to her patient's hand. 'If you need anything, ring the bell. I will be just outside,' she said and left.

Pamela fumbled for the box and grasped it in her claw-like hand. 'This is by way of an apology to you and your mother,' she managed to say.

Meredith tried to protest but Pamela carried on, desperately trying to get what she needed to say off her chest before it was too late.

'No, please let me speak. For many years I was in denial about the kind of man I had married. Myles is cold and cruel and heartless, and I would have left him long ago but I had nowhere to go. When your mother came to stay in 1944 just after poor Sylvia was born, I knew then that I had made a terrible mistake. I talked to Jane about it, in fact. Tried to explain what an animal Myles was even then, but I could see she had no idea what I was talking about. A good and kind woman herself, she could not comprehend the wiles of human nature. She was such a loving sister to me, and I abused that love. Our father always paid me more attention and spoiled me rotten, but I was envious of Jane because she had our mother's affection. I knew from a very early age that there was something different about Jane, but I could not understand what it was and I still can't to this day. What I do know is that Jane did not deserve what happened to her, and I hold myself to blame for the terrible wrong that was done to her.'

She paused and coughed and the effort wracked her frail body. Meredith took the glass of water from the bedside table and held it to her lips as she drank. She took this opportunity to say, 'Pamela, did you know that Myles raped my mother?'

Pamela nodded and swallowed hard; she could hardly speak. 'Not at the time but later. When Jane left in such a hurry I suspected something was wrong, but I did nothing about it and tried to wipe the thought from my mind. I didn't hear from my sister again until the death of her husband. When we came to George's funeral and I saw you, I realised the dreadful truth.' The dying woman's eyes fixed on Meredith. 'I am sorry to say you have a strong resemblance to my husband. When Jane collapsed I knew it was from the trauma of seeing Myles again. I wanted so much to talk to her, to reassure her and make amends – but there was never an opportunity to talk to her alone. And I was always drinking; I wasn't sober for years on end. I am so very sorry, my dear.' A huge tear rolled down her cheekbone.

'Please, Aunt, try not to get upset,' Meredith said gently. 'It is all a long time ago now. Jane is fine. I am sure she knows you meant her no harm. I now want to tell you something that will help you understand your childhood better. Jane was not Alfred's natural daughter. He married Mary, your mother, knowing that the baby she was expecting was not his. Then she gave birth to you a couple of years later, and he was over the moon. That is why he favoured you, and he used to use Jane as a reminder to your mother that she was in eternal debt to him. So Jane knew all about cruelty long before Myles came along. You couldn't have known about this – you were only an innocent child – and you shouldn't feel so bad. Please try to let bygones be bygones.'

Meredith gave Pamela another sip of water and then sat down again and took her tiny hand in hers. It was ice cold. Pamela tried to squeeze Meredith's hand.

'Thank you for that. It does help a little. But here, take this box.' She picked it up and pushed it into Meredith's other hand. 'It is a gift from me to you, to say sorry anyway. I want you to have it. I miss my daughter every minute I am alive. When she died, I believed God was punishing me for my weaknesses. Myles deserved to be punished, but I felt it was too great a sacrifice for me. I drank to numb the pain.' Pamela gave a painful sigh. Then: 'Does Myles know you are his daughter?' she asked.

'No, I don't think so,' replied Meredith. 'I have wondered whether to confront him, but the time has never been right, and somehow I don't think my mother would want me to.'

Pamela stiffened and her grasp on Meredith's hand hurt because her nails were sinking into her.

'Please do tell him one day. I want him to suffer, to know he not only lost one daughter but now he has lost another. I want him to die a lonely old man. He deserves to suffer like the people around him have suffered. Yes, he was devastated when Sylvia died, but he recovered soon enough. Ask his secretary how he grieved; she was always on hand to take away his suffering. Please, promise me you will tell him!'

Meredith could feel the hatred emanating from her aunt. It was as if the cancer was the manifestation of all her years of pent-up rage and frustration. It was very uncomfortable to be near this bitterness and grief, and Meredith resisted the urge to get up and run as far away from this room of darkness as possible.

'Pamela, I cannot promise anything. I understand how you feel, but you must also understand my point of view. I have a young child to bring up and I want to be as positive for her as possible. Does it really help matters to continue to bring up the past?'

Pamela seemed to shrink back into the pillows.

'What you say is true, dear. No good ever came of revenge. I am sorry – I should have taken my disgust to my grave. So be it. I have at least been able to make some kind of restitution to you and Jane. What is your daughter's name?'

'Anna,' said Meredith, desperately trying to think of a way to leave graciously. 'I have to pick her up from nursery shortly.'

'Do you have a husband?' Pamela asked.

'No I don't, but Anna has a lovely family around her.' Meredith did not want Anna to be included in Pamela's web of hate.

'So the little girl is Myles's granddaughter then. How bizarre life is, don't you think? He has no idea of the trail of destruction he has left in his wake.'

'My daughter is not part of any destruction,' Meredith said firmly. 'She is a beautiful child with a wonderful life ahead of her. She will not have been touched by any of this.' She tried not to sound too irritated. The woman was dying, after all.

'You are quite right to correct me. Please God she will remain untouched by my husband's evil influence. Of course, I have kept you long enough. Please send my love to your mother. Goodbye, my dear – and have a happy life.'

Pamela closed her eyes and let out a deep sigh. For a moment Meredith thought she had gone, but then she could see the tiny chest moving up and down beneath the pale pink satin nightdress, the last vestige of the glamorous woman that Meredith remembered. She rose as quietly as possible, holding the box in her hand unopened, and tiptoed out of the room. Nurse Delaware was sitting outside on the landing reading a paper.

'Everything all right?' she asked.

'Yes, fine, thank you, Joan. She is resting now, I think. Thank you for letting me visit. I would appreciate it if you could call me – you know, when she dies. I am sure Mr Harrison will invite us to the funeral but I would like to know when she goes.'

Meredith passed a card to Nurse Delaware, who took it and said, 'Of course I will. No problem at all. Can you see yourself out? I need to go and give Mrs Harrison her medication. Goodbye.' She shook Meredith's hand and turned and went into the bedroom.

Meredith hurried down the stairs and left. It was a relief to get out into the crisp November air. She drove home wondering how much a woman could take of a man as cruel as Myles. No wonder she drank herself to death. Meredith recalled that dinner party when Pamela had been on such good form. Mind you, she drank then, but she had already had years of living with a man who constantly put her down and threw his infidelities in her face. She had been so beautiful. Meredith remembered how she had compared Pamela to her own mother. Chalk and cheese, of course. Once you knew the secret, it was all so obvious. Pamela had said she looked like Myles. No wonder Jane looked at her coldly sometimes. No wonder she had found it easier to show her brother Frank affection.

Meredith suddenly felt very sad and defeated by life and all the lies and secrets – including her own. She was as bad as her mother and grandmother. All of them had kept a secret. She made a promise to herself that she would talk to Anna as soon as she was old enough to understand.

Parked near the gates, Meredith had a few minutes to wait

before the children were ready to be collected. She looked at the little box on the seat beside her, opened it and gasped. Inside was a huge diamond ring.

Meredith took it out of the box and slipped it on her finger. God, it was so beautiful! Somewhere in the back of her mind she had a memory of seeing a ring like this … why, yes, of course – the dinner party. It all came flooding back. Meredith had been transfixed at one point that evening by her aunt's ring. This was that very ring.

Two days later Meredith received a phone call from Nurse Delaware regretfully informing her that Pamela Harrison had died that morning. Meredith had already spoken to her mother about her visit and the ring, and Jane had expressed great sadness. Now, when Meredith rang to tell her that it was all over, she said, 'We must gird up our loins and face the funeral. Myles must not stop us paying our respects to my sister. She suffered a good deal over the years, I fear. I am so sorry we did not reconcile before she died. You will help me with this, won't you, my dear?' She sounded so forlorn.

'Of course I will, Mum, it goes without saying. It is you and me, against the evil wizard. Lots of love and I will pick you up from St Pancras on Sunday evening.'

The funeral was Monday at 2 p.m. and Meredith and her mother spent the morning deciding what to wear. In fact, Meredith was deciding for both of them. It was partly therapy to make her mother feel secure and to take her mind off the coming ordeal. Meredith had made meringues, a ritual between them in times of stress, ever since she was a child, and they sat by the fire and ate them with vast amounts of clotted cream.

They arrived at Hendon Cemetery and finally found somewhere to park after driving around for fifteen minutes. It made Meredith so mad because it was one of those times in your life when the last thing you should be worrying about was where to park. It was all stress, and somehow she felt that the powers that be, whoever they were, should take these things into account and provide parking facilities. She was ranting on about this to Jane as they drove round and round looking for a space. It was her way of dealing with her nerves. Jane, on the other hand, had gone very quiet and withdrawn.

They got out of the car and Meredith took her mother firmly by the arm and steered her towards the crematorium. Myles Harrison was at the door greeting everyone. He came forward to meet them and took Meredith's hand as she had managed to put herself between him and Jane.

'Meredith, how good of you to come. Thank you. Jane, I hope you are well. I am sorry we meet again at such a sad time.'

Myles moved in to Jane but Meredith whisked her out from under his nose, saying, 'We are so sorry for your loss, Myles. We will see you after the service. Excuse us.' And they were gone.

Meredith was just congratulating herself on her manoeuvre when she heard her mother saying, 'Mr Blatchford, how nice to see you again. You remember my daughter Meredith?' Jane turned to introduce Meredith, who was caught trying to escape.

'Of course I remember her. How lovely to see you again.' Jack was beaming at her, and holding out his hand. 'You look blooming, if I may say so. May I introduce a friend of mine, Denise Gregg.' He stepped aside to reveal a very glamorous blonde. So this was the gold digger.

Meredith wanted the earth to open up. A nearby grave would have been perfect!

'Lovely to meet you, Denise, and to see you again, Jack. Come along, Mum, we need to get seated.' She dragged Jane towards the front of the chapel, calling back over her shoulder, 'I am sure we will see you at the reception.'

Her mother cast Meredith a sideways look. 'So that is the young bird. Bit common, isn't she?'

241

'Mother, please, what are you saying! Now is not the time. Sit down and let's just get through this.'

Meredith spent the whole service trying to calm down. She was trembling from head to foot and had to will her hands to keep still as she held her hymn book. Why had it not occurred to her that *he* would be here? Being close to Myles, of course he would. Oh God – and with some awful blonde slapper! She had been so busy worrying about her mother and Myles Harrison she had completely forgotten about her own indiscretions. Well, she would have to blag it. If she could get through today she would never have to see any of them again, ever!

The service finally came to an end, and the congregation filed out into the grey afternoon. As they stood round the grave Meredith cast a sneaky look at Myles. He stood erect and rigid, holding a red rose. His face was drawn and haggard and made him look older than his sixty-eight years. Meredith tried to see herself in him. It was impossible – and foolish too. Why would she want to associate herself in any way with this man? *Because he is your father,* said a voice in her head. What had made him like he was? Why was he so cold and hard? She knew so little about him. She felt that she needed to learn why he had raped her mother. She needed that closure. She decided to try and talk to him when they got back to the house.

Her eye caught a movement nearby and she stiffened as she saw Jack lean across and whisper in Myles's ear. Jack Blatchford, she thought, how could you work with this man, knowing what he did to my mother? Well, business is business, what did Jack care about her emotions? He really knew nothing about her, including the fact that he was the father of her child. *Oh God, here we go again!* For the second time in a fortnight her secret threatened to erupt. She pushed it back inside the drawer – hard. If only that drawer had a key! She'd lock it up for ever.

She quickly lowered her eyes as Jack looked across towards

her. *Please let this be over soon,* she prayed. Finally, the last rose had been thrown into the grave and the mourners started to wend their way back to their cars. It was beginning to rain, and a number of black umbrellas were sprouting up like weird plants from Outer Space. Meredith and her mother hastened their steps before the rain could soak them too badly. It was such a relief to get in the car, away from everyone. For a moment Meredith just sat and took deep breaths.

'I know this must be very hard for you, my dear. Lord, Myles looks so old.' Jane let out a heavy sigh and reached across and held her daughter's hand. 'It is such a long time ago now.'

'Yes, but you can't forget, can you, Mum? I watched you during the service.'

'True. In a way, I am sad I did not try and reconcile myself with Pam. It was not her fault, any of it. Not the circumstances of my birth, not her marriage to that man. She was a victim, wasn't she, whereas we have managed to push them all away from us – all the bad, negative things. We are so lucky, you know. We have had a happy life.'

'Yes, you are right, but I still have a father who is evil. What do I do about that?'

They drove through the rain to the reception, each wrestling with their own thoughts. Meredith saw her mother playing with her handbag strap and earnestly watching everything out of the window – and suddenly realised how selfish she was being. It was not her but Jane who had lost first her husband and then her sister, and who now had to deal with Myles, and all the memories that must still be so painful. How dare she indulge her own insecurities and problems? She was a grown-up woman and could deal with this later. Right now, her mother needed her to be strong.

Taking hold of Jane's hand, Meredith squeezed it and said, 'I know that going to the house will be hard for you. Just let me

243

know if you can't cope at any point, and we'll hit the road, all right?'

The front door of the house was open when they arrived and they followed the other guests through the hall into the dining room. Meredith remembered that this was where they had had dinner that night. They were ushered on through to the drawing room where they were greeted by a waiter holding a tray of drinks. Meredith took a glass of sherry for her mother and a glass of white wine for herself, and moved over to the window seat where there was a beautiful armchair facing the garden.

'You sit here, Mum, and I will plant myself on the window seat.' Meredith handed her mother the sherry. 'A bit of fortification,' she grinned.

Her mother smiled wanly. 'Better make sure we don't fortify ourselves too much!' She took a sip and looked around. 'Nothing has changed much in this room really since the war. No blackout drapes, of course. And such a beautiful garden. I used to love to sit out there and write my letters to George, when I had time, that is.'

'Here, Mum, have a sandwich.' Meredith was grateful for the interruption to her mother's reminiscences as a waitress appeared with a tray of perfect little sandwiches. The woman gave Jane and Meredith a plate and napkin each, and proffered the tray.

'Thank you,' said Jane. 'Salmon is my favourite.' The waitress smiled and moved away and Jane tucked in.

'Oh, this is delicious. Do try one, dear. I didn't realise how hungry I was until I saw that plate.'

Just as Meredith had popped a sandwich into her mouth a voice said, 'So tell me, how are things with you these days? I hear you have a little daughter?' Jack was standing at her side. She swallowed the sandwich whole and took a large gulp of wine.

'Um, sorry, got a sandwich in my mouth. I am fine, thanks. Yes, I have a daughter called Anna. How is your son – Harry, wasn't it?' she asked, managing to stop herself from choking on smoked salmon and emotions.

'Well remembered,' Jack nodded. 'He is great, thank you for asking. He is ten already and a little devil. How is your pal Oliver?'

'Fine, he has done really well. He has a Michelin star now.'

'Oh, I know, I watch his TV show.' Jack gave a beaming smile and Meredith gritted her teeth. *Please go away*, she prayed silently.

Fortunately her mother interrupted. 'Mr Blatchford, are you still in property development?'

'Please call me Jack,' he replied. 'Yes, I am still in business with Myles a good deal of the time, but I also have a couple of my own projects that I am dealing with at the moment. Can I get you another drink, by the way? Meredith, how about you?' He took their glasses and went in search of the waiter with the tray.

Jane smiled at her reassuringly and said, 'You are doing very well. Keep it up.'

'Mother, if you are OK for a moment I am going to find the loo.'

'Of course, dear, I am very happy to have Jack all to myself!' She winked at Meredith, who scowled back and said, 'Mum, please, this is no joke.'

She made her way through the guests towards the hall and across to the other side where she recalled there was a cloak-room. As she passed an open door on her right, she heard Myles call, 'Meredith, would you come in here a minute?'

Christ, thought Meredith. Now what?

Chapter Sixteen

She pushed open the door and entered a wood-panelled study with a huge desk in the corner and books lining the shelves. It was a very masculine room with an odour of whisky and cigars and leather. Myles was sitting behind the desk, and he indicated one of two large winged chairs in front of it for Meredith. She sat on the edge and waited as Myles took a sip of cognac from an enormous balloon glass. He swirled the golden liquid around several times, savouring the aroma. He studied her for what seemed an age. Oh God, thought Meredith, does he recognise me?

His voice seemed to come from nowhere. 'So my wife gave you a ring, I understand.' He fixed her with a cold hard stare. 'It is very valuable, you know. Do you appreciate just how valuable?'

Meredith held his gaze as she replied steadily, 'Yes, I do. It is beautiful, and it was incredibly generous of Aunt Pamela to give it to me.'

Suddenly, Meredith realised that this was the moment of truth. He was going to know who she was, and he was going to understand the full implications of his actions.

'I must say it was a shock to me. You see, it was a present from me to her for our Silver Wedding anniversary. Did she give you any explanation as to why she wanted *you* to have it?' He rose and came round to the front of the desk.

Meredith looked at him standing there, intimidating, imperious, awaiting a response. This was a man who was used to being obeyed. Well, he was in for a shock now. Two could play at this game. She held his gaze until he dropped his eyes first. He shifted his weight and leaned against the front of the desk.

Here we go, thought Meredith. It is now or never.

'Oh yes, Myles, she did, and it was a very tragic story she told me. Although to be perfectly honest I already knew most of the story because my mother had told me. In fact, ironically, she told me on the day of another funeral – that of my father, George Lee. The sad truth is, it turns out he was not my father. Not my *natural* father.' Meredith paused. She wanted Myles to suffer through every moment of this revelation.

'You are!' Her voice rang out. 'You raped my mother in 1944. Do you remember that, Myles? That seems a good enough reason why Pamela wanted to give me her diamond ring. Of course, it can never make amends for what you did, but for your wife it was a way of apologising for keeping quiet. You have never had that guilt, obviously. Do you even remember performing that atrocity on a vulnerable woman who was a guest in your house, not to mention your sister-in-law? I want to hear your explanation for how a man can do that and live with it for the rest of his life. Please tell me, Myles. I need to know what kind of monster you are. You, *my father*.'

Meredith was shaking with anger. Her eyes were bright and there were pink spots on her cheeks. Myles looked at her for a long time. He seemed to be taking her in, in every detail. Then he finally turned away and poured himself another drink. There was not a sound in the room except the clink of glass as he put the stopper back into the decanter. He began his swirling ritual again and slowly turned to face her.

247

'You want an explanation? Very well, I will try to give you one. That is the least you deserve. I am not sure how satisfactory the answer will be, but I can only try. Meredith, I am a man. A difficult man, who has had to fight a great deal in life in order to succeed. Unfortunately, I have seen a good deal of the worst side of humanity and have had to adjust my attitudes accordingly. I offer no excuse for my attitude to women. I can only say that all men are animals to a certain extent, but some are able to tame their baser instincts while others cannot. I did love Pamela, believe it or not, at the beginning of our marriage. She had a lot going for her in those days. She was a beautiful young woman with a hunger for life and a willingness to learn. I enjoyed teaching her things. I liked the way she grabbed life by the neck and shook it. She was a fast learner and we made a good team. I needed a wife who would know how to entertain my business associates. Know how to make those men feel good and receptive to my demands. Pamela was a genius at this. I am sorry if this offends you, but she was sexy and luscious, and instinctively knew how to make a man feel good about himself.

'We had a fantastic time early on. I had so many plans for us, travelling abroad together and taking on the world. The war was not going to stop *me*! But unfortunately the birth of Sylvia changed Pamela. It wasn't just that she hated being pregnant or had a tough delivery, it was more fundamental than that. She hated the fact that her body had changed. I still wanted her, but she pushed me away. She would not get out of bed. I tried to win her round but she wouldn't let me touch her. I thought it was just one of those things that happen after a woman has given birth, and let her be. But I felt alienated, alone and unwanted. Then your mother arrived to help out. She seemed very pleasant and capable, but I hardly noticed her at first. Then she started to have dinner with me, and it was a very enjoyable interlude each night. Jane was intelligent and

248

interested and seemed to enjoy my company. I relaxed and started to look forward to our meals together. She was the antithesis of her sister, unassuming, gentle and not at all predatory. But she had a quality about her that was very attractive to me. I suppose, if I am really honest, it made me want to conquer her. Corrupt her, even. I am not proud of my intentions, Meredith, and they were certainly less than honourable. However, I had never seriously considered acting on these thoughts, until that night.

'I had had a terrible row with Pamela: she had rejected me yet again and called me an animal. The truth always hurts, doesn't it?' Myles sighed. 'Later on, Jane came into my study and announced that she would not be joining me for dinner as she was off to do good works somewhere. I felt rejected again! Ridiculous, I know, but I thought, Bloody hell, this woman would rather go out and attend to worthy causes than spend an evening with me. It rankled. I decided to go to my club. I spent the evening there getting drunk and exchanging crude jokes with an assortment of men who, like me, should all have been at home with their wives, not in a club in the middle of an air raid. The dreadful thing about the war, Meredith, and I don't expect you to understand this, is it made you very aware of life. There was death all around one, all the time. Every night when the sirens went off, it was a reminder that death was just around the corner. It gave everything one did a sharpness around the edges. It heightened emotions, rather like alcohol. So the mixture was dangerous sometimes.

'When I got back to the house that night I was high with drink and fear and frustration. Yes, frustration! This is a male reaction sometimes in heightened emotional crises. Do you have any understanding of what I am talking about? You must do, because young women today are liberated, I am told. They are allowed to indulge their sexuality in ways my generation

249

never could. But you see, however liberated a woman is, she is never going to have this reaction, because she doesn't have a cock. Do I shock you? Well, I want to shock you because you should know these things about men. *Women* should know these things about men. We do see things differently, react differently. When a woman cries, it can be in anger or frustration. She can release herself through crying. Not so a man. Sometimes he needs a greater physical release, and it can manifest itself through his fists, for example, or more often than not through his sexual desire.'

Myles stared at Meredith, daring her to interrupt. 'That night, I needed a fuck! I was so strung out that by the time your mother appeared at the door I was ready to burst. Jane was in a terrible state because she had been through a traumatic incident in which a pregnant woman and her baby died in the underground. She was wet and cold and shaking, and when I held her to comfort her, all I could feel was her energy and her body, and her cold skin against my hot face. I translated her need for comfort into my need for sex. I just could not control myself. I couldn't hear her sobs or pleadings to stop. I just had to assuage this thirst in me. Cure the pain of wanting to release myself. It was primal. I cannot excuse it but I have tried to explain it.'

During this tirade, Myles seemed almost possessed. The words poured out of him as if he was purging himself. Meredith sat completely still, afraid to break the spell. Now he had stopped suddenly, and his entire demeanour shrank before her eyes. The man who had ranted about his sexual hunger and male dominance was a shrunken old man. His eyes were dull and stared into nothingness as he sank down into the armchair opposite her, in a crumpled heap.

Silence hung in the air, joining the whisky and cigar smoke. Meredith felt a bit sick. She didn't know what to say or do and the two of them sat for ages waiting for the moment to end.

Meredith finally got up and said, 'I have to go. I appreciate your honesty – it helps me to close this chapter of my life. Your wife was deeply wounded by your actions and wanted you to be punished. It is not my place to do that. The tragedy is, you lost your daughter Sylvia and you lost me, and you will never know your granddaughter. Yes, my daughter is four now. You are a lonely man, Myles, and you deserve to be, but at least we have had this conversation. And although there is no way I can forgive you for what you did to my mother, I respect your honesty here today in this room. I wish you could have the opportunity to apologise to my mother, but that will probably never happen. Our paths will never cross again. Goodbye.'

She walked to the door and looked back at the old man. He was holding onto the arms of the chair as if his life depended on it and did not look at her. Meredith closed the door and walked away.

She found her mother talking to Jack and the blonde, Denise.

'Where on earth have you been, dear?' asked her mother. 'I thought you had deserted me for good. Poor Jack and Denise have had to look after me.' She got up. 'Are we ready to go?' There was a pleading note in her voice.

'Of course, Mum, ready when you are. Thank you for looking after my mother for me.' She turned to Jack and tried to smile as if she hadn't a care in the world. 'Hope to see you again sometime. Bye, Denise, nice to have met you.'

Meredith took Jane's arm as much to steady herself as her mother, and moved away. It seemed an endless walk to the door but they made it. Out into the driveway and straight to the car. Meredith helped her mother in and shut the door. Got in the driver's seat, started the engine and put her foot down. Neither of them spoke until they were halfway home.

'Dear God, I thought we would never make it out of there

without a hitch,' Jane sighed. 'Well done, but why did you take so long to come back from the loo?'

'I bumped into Myles, Mother, and we had it out.' Meredith glanced briefly across at Jane. 'I asked him why he raped you.'

'And what did he say?' Jane's voice was cold. 'What excuse could he possibly have given you?'

'Oh, there were no excuses. He just tried to explain why he was in such a rage that night and why, when you came back to the house, you reaped the result. He was rather pathetic, to be honest. He just looked old and alone and defeated. So I really think we should put him out of our minds forever, don't you? Let's move forward and make a new life. You are brilliant, Mum, and I want you to spend the rest of your life having fun.'

Jane stared straight ahead. 'I miss George so much, you know. I hope he knew how much I loved him.' Her voice trembled.

'Of course he did, Mum. He loved you to bits. You deserve to enjoy your life now. Look, it's Frank and Jenny and you and me and Anna now. We are the team!'

'Yes, dear. We are the team. Onwards and upwards!'

Chapter Seventeen

'Ladies and gentlemen, Primetime Television is proud to present the award-winning daytime show *Meredith Lee at Three*! Please give a warm welcome to the star of the show ... Meredith Lee!'

The studio audience whooped and hollered like demented baboons as Meredith Lee walked the walk down the shiny black staircase to take up her seat in the mock lounge created in the studio. Everything was bright and cosy and warm and comforting. This was afternoon TV, designed to make the audience at home feel good. Safe and sound.

Meredith was very aware that her TV days were numbered. She was still attractive and well groomed, and looked younger than her years. Having a teenage daughter meant she had always been aware of what was around fashion-wise, and having to earn a living for herself meant she had had to keep fit and re-invent herself. Many of her contemporaries were succumbing to the knife to maintain their youth. Life on TV was cruel and relentless, but Meredith had managed to survive so far without resorting to procedures of any kind, and represented to many of her viewers the real face of a woman in middle age. She was sassy and outspoken, and her shows were often very lively and controversial. Although they were, in fact, recorded, they were done like a live show, with as little interruption as possible. This gave it an edge and made for some interesting viewing.

Meredith had come a long way since her days as the Head of Catering at Tubbs, Steele & Lane.

She paused at the bottom of the staircase and turned into the camera with one of her famous smiles.

'Hello, and welcome everyone to *Meredith Lee at Three*. I'm Meredith Lee and today I am going to be talking about teenage pregnancy. The UK has the highest figures of teenage pregnancy in Europe. It is a huge problem and something has to be done. I will be speaking to a teenage mum and her mother, and also to the Education Secretary Marjorie Johns and the Bishop of London, John Ridder.

'We will also be taking a trip down Memory Lane with our cookery expert Jean. She will be showing us the delights of a typical 1960s dinner party. In our fashion slot we will be looking at leggings. Love them or hate them, they seem to be here to stay. But first, the overwhelming figures on teenage pregnancy and what can be done.'

Meredith walked across the studio and sat in a large armchair. Opposite her was a sofa on which were perched the Education Secretary and the Bishop of London.

'I am going to ask you first, Marjorie Johns, to give us your thoughts on this problem.'

'Cut to camera one, please.' The director, in the box above the studio floor, barked out the camera shots to the team.

Sitting in the viewing box behind the director was Meredith's daughter Anna and her friend Millie. They had just finished their GCSE exams and were off to France in July. Anna had had a steady boyfriend for the last year, and it had been a bone of contention between her and her mother. To be fair to Anna, she hadn't let the romance interfere with her schoolwork and her predicted grades were very high. The school was pleased with her. For Meredith though, it was a diversion she could do without. She wanted so much for her daughter. She had tried to support the girl through her life so far, to the point where it could be seen as controlling, but she would never admit that. She just wanted the best for Anna. It had been a long struggle for Meredith to keep herself and her daughter together emotionally and financially.

The Bishop of London was now giving a rather stilted view of teenage pregnancies and advocating more religious instruction in schools.

Meredith cut in to suggest that what was needed was more practical help, surely?

'We cannot be seen to encourage underage sex! Making it easier by offering contraception and condoning this kind of behaviour will only make things worse.' The Bishop had taken to his high horse with a vengeance.

Meredith turned to the camera and said, 'I would like to introduce Jade and her mother Kath at this point. Please give them a warm welcome.' The camera panned to the staircase and a mother and daughter came gingerly down the stairs. The daughter was wraith-thin and her eyes wide, like a rabbit in headlights. The mother, a big woman, appeared determined and defensive in equal measures.

'Welcome to you both.' Meredith smiled warmly at the mother and turned to the daughter. 'Hi Jade, how old are you?' she asked the tiny figure sitting on the sofa, her legs dangling like a small child's.

'Fourteen and three quarters – nearly fifteen really.' She said it proudly.

'I see. And how old is your baby?'

The audience gasped.

'Three months old. He's doing well. Mum helps me look

after him.' The girl gestured to her mother, who now looked merely tired and defeated.

'How will you manage though when you have to work, Kath, and you have to go to school, Jade?' Meredith needed to move the interview forward: time was always against them.

'Well, I work part-time as a cleaner at the school and so we can arrange feeding and things during the breaks.' The mother offered this with a resigned look at the audience, as if she was almost waiting for the abuse to start.

But Meredith was in control and the audience did what she wanted. Keeping quiet was a given.

'Jade, what about your schoolwork? How will you cope with all the homework?'

'I will do my best, but to be honest I don't really like school much anyways and I want to get a job as soon as I can. I'm not after hand-outs, you know.'

Anna and Millie were watching this in the box open-mouthed.

'Can you believe that girl has had a baby?' Millie breathed. 'Can you imagine being pregnant now, let alone giving birth? Oh my God, how gross is that!'

Had Millie not been so appalled by the idea of giving birth, she might have noticed that her friend Anna had gone very pale. In fact, she excused herself and went to the toilet, where she was violently sick.

When Anna got back to the viewing room, the interview with the girl was over and the screen was filled with Black Forest Gateau. Oh God – another reason to feel sick! She managed to perk up, however, and she and Millie spent the rest of the show giggling at various assistants who came and went, and eating peanuts from the hospitality table. They had been tipped off that in the next studio was a band they really liked, doing a pre-record. One of the assistants offered to take them to meet the boys. So they escaped Studio One and disappeared into Studio Two . . .

Meredith closed the show with her usual panache and spent a few minutes signing autographs for the studio audience. She didn't have a problem being pleasant to them. They were her bread and butter and she was very grateful to them. She moved off to the make-up room and wiped off most of the studio make-up, just leaving her eye-shadow and mascara on. There was nothing worse than seeing an older woman with too much slap on, especially when the powder settled in the lines on one's face. Oh God, how depressing was getting old! She patted on a bit of fresh foundation, thanked her make-up girl as usual for her magic touch, and went off to the Green Room where she was to meet her daughter. On the way there, the producer cornered her in the corridor with a couple of ideas for the next show and Meredith took a new script from her; she was then stopped by the PR lady wanting a slot from her to do an interview for the *Sunday Times* magazine. Meredith told her to ring later when she was behind her desk at home.

Surprised to find the Green Room empty, she stopped a runner and asked where the girls had gone.

'Oh sorry, Ms Lee, I think they are in the next studio watching The Computers.'

'What computers are you talking about?' she asked, baffled. 'They know nothing about IT.'

The runner laughed. 'Oh, very good, Ms Lee. Nice one. It's the band – you must know them.'

'Course I do,' she murmured. 'Computers?'

As she opened the door, she was greeted by a pounding bass guitar and an ear-splitting lead singer. Ah, so these were The Computers, she realised, as she pushed her way through several people who had no business being there at all. She could make out her gorgeous daughter's blonde hair at the front, shaking wildly in time to the music. Meredith tapped her on the shoulder and tried to make herself heard above the racket.

'Come on, you two, time to go.' Anna made a face and put her hands together in a pleading prayer, to no avail. Meredith had work to do; she didn't have time to hang about the studio while her daughter chased pop singers. Anna grabbed Millie's arm and they followed Meredith out into the corridor.

'Oh Mum, you are such a party pooper,' moaned Anna.

'Sorry, Meredith, did we keep you waiting?' Millie was apologetic.

'No, don't worry, Millie, but we can't stay because I must get home and finish an article I am writing for a magazine. Come on, Anna, let's go. Did you enjoy the show today? What about that poor young girl having to cope with a baby at her age, for heaven's sake.'

They climbed into the waiting studio car and drove off.

Meredith lived with her daughter in a Georgian cottage in Hampstead. Meredith had bought it with the proceeds from the sale of Pamela's magnificent diamond ring. The house was in a quiet leafy road close to the Heath. The views were spectacular, and Meredith loved the feeling of being on top of the world, looking across to Canary Wharf and beyond. You really could see for miles and miles, like that old song. It was a good compromise for a woman like Meredith, who had been brought up on a farm. She was only twenty minutes from the centre of London, but enjoyed the trees and parks around her home.

There was a village quality about Hampstead with its individual shops and quaint alleyways. Anna went to a wonderful school in Highgate up the road, and though it cost the earth, it was worth it in Meredith's opinion. She thought it was vital that her daughter had the best education and start in life. She herself had gone to a grammar school in St Albans, and it had been a fantastic opportunity to get on and make her way in the world. Things had not turned out quite how she had wanted, of course, but that was life. One had to seize the moment and make the best of what was on offer.

Meredith unlocked the door and let the three of them into the house, then immediately went into Mother Mode. She opened the French doors into the garden as it was a lovely afternoon in late June, put the kettle on for a cup of tea and got out a loaf of homemade bread to make some cucumber sandwiches. Well, why not? She always felt her spirits rise in summer.

'Girls, you have ten minutes to do whatever you need to do then tea will be ready outside.'

As well as sandwiches she had some homemade meringues, a tribute to her mother and still her favourite, and there was a carton of fresh double cream waiting to be whipped. Meredith made up a tray and carried the teapot and cups and saucers out into the garden. Anna made fun of her mother for insisting that tea be drunk from china cups, but it was one of Meredith's little foibles – and it was these foibles that had made her such a success. She had written several books in the last few years on cooking and how to make a perfect home. She was a complete A–Z of Living in the 1990s.

Ridiculous really, bearing in mind she was a single mother with a terrible record in the marriage stakes; namely no marriages at all!

The girls joined Meredith and they ate in contented silence for a bit. Then talk turned to the summer and what they were going to do.

'Mmm, delicious, though I say it myself,' said Meredith, licking a dollop of cream from the side of her mouth.

'Mum, you are terrible,' giggled Anna. 'You are like a little girl when you eat meringues.'

259

'Blame your grandmother – she was the one who got me hooked and they are so bad for my figure,' replied her mother.

Millie leaned across and popped a strawberry into her mouth. 'I am so looking forward to France,' she said. 'Mum has rented a villa as usual near Bordeaux for the whole of August, and it has got a pool and everything. So it should be fabulous. I'm so glad that Anna will be coming – and Tom, of course.'

'Oh yes, of course, Anna doesn't go anywhere without Tom.' Meredith could not disguise the sarcasm. It wasn't that she didn't like Tom. The boy was pleasant enough and actually a very talented artist, but he and Anna were inseparable and this was not a good thing for Anna's future, in her mother's opinion.

'Oh Mum, don't be mean,' Anna implored. 'You know how much I care about Tom.'

'Yes I do, and it is not good news for either you or him. You should be out there enjoying life. Meeting lots of new people and experiencing new things. You are both too wrapped up in each other and far too young for a serious relationship.' Meredith got up and started to clear away the tea things. The happy mood was broken.

'At least I have got a relationship, unlike some people we know.' Anna grabbed Millie's arm. 'Come on, Millie, let's go upstairs.'

Her words hit Meredith in the gut like a punch. How cruel her daughter could be to her at times! She knew it was not meant to hurt as much as it did, but boy, did it hurt. Meredith had struggled for the last sixteen years on her own. There had been lovely Oliver, of course, and her darling Mum to help from time to time, but in reality she had been on her own.

She dumped the tea things in the kitchen and went into her office. It was a beautiful light airy room with a huge window looking out into the garden. Although she loved London, Meredith could never be far from greenery, a reminder of her childhood on the farm. She was not much of a gardener herself but she admired and respected anyone who was. Thanks to George Lee, planting seeds and watching them grow was one of life's wonders to her. She missed her father on an almost daily basis . . .

Her musings were interrupted by a noise from upstairs, that thumping bass again. Could it be The Computers? She looked at her watch and decided she had better put a stop to this right now before they settled in for the evening as there was school tomorrow, albeit the last days of term. Not work as such but they still had to go in, and she herself had a big production meeting scheduled for tomorrow to discuss how her show was going to move on in the future. Was this TV speak for 'we think it is time *we* moved on and *you* retired?'

Well, she was ready for 'em. She had spent the last ten years consolidating everything. While she was still at Tubbs, Steele & Lane she had formed her own property company and by now had a healthy portfolio. In addition, she had her publishing deals, and for the last year her own production company. She was also looking into spas. The whole spa thing was starting to take off, and recently Meredith had been to stay in a beautiful country-house spa down in Wiltshire. It was like staying in a luxury hotel, but instead of cream teas and too many glasses of wine, she had had hot water and lemon and sitz baths!

There was a lot going on in her life, and although she hated the idea of losing her TV profile, she was excited about becoming a woman of means and property.

Meredith made her way upstairs, following the rhythm of the music and bracing herself for abuse. That was the trouble with being a single parent: you had to be the bad guy and the good guy, and somehow her daughter only remembered her as the bad guy.

261

She knocked on the door. 'Can I come in, please?' she shouted, but nothing happened. 'Anna, please open the door. You have school tomorrow, so I think Millie should go home now. Sorry to be a pain.'

She banged on the door again, which suddenly opened and there was Millie looking terrified and all ready to go. Mumbling a goodbye, she brushed past Meredith and sped off down the stairs and out of the front door.

'What the hell was that all about? Have you two had a row? Anna, what . . . ?' Meredith stopped and took in her daughter's tear-stained face. Anna was sitting cross-legged on the floor, surrounded by all the usual rubbish that a girl her age deems necessary, chocolate wrappers and CDs and magazines, but it was what she was holding in her hands that Meredith zeroed in on. The room seemed to shrink and everything went into black and white – except for the bright blue marker-pen Anna was holding in her hand.

Meredith looked from the marker to her daughter. Anna was speaking but Meredith could not hear the words, did not want to hear the words. *No, please not this. Please God NO!*

'Mum, I am so sorry. I am pregnant.' Anna burst into tears.

Meredith knew she should respond here. Try to comfort her or something. But she was rooted to the spot. Could not take it in. She felt bile rise to her throat. Everything she had worked for and done for Anna was about making her life wonderful, wanting her precious daughter to have freedom of choice. She had tried so hard to give her a stable background, against all the odds. She had been the constant in her daughter's life. In the months after she was born, Meredith had struggled to bond with her baby. But that had passed and as time went on, they had become a team. She had had to rely on Oliver and au pairs and the like, but at the end of the day, Meredith had always been there for her.

Certainly, in the last couple of years there had been arguments, but that was normal surely? Anna had told her that all her friends had fights with their mothers. Meredith had taught Anna to be independent and they had discussed sex and relationships very recently, but Anna had given no indication at all that she was sleeping with Tom. What would Meredith have done if she had? Suggested the Pill? God Almighty, how did it get to this? Anna was sixteen, for God's sake, only a child herself!

Meredith suddenly saw that young girl from the show today, the terror in her eyes, her mother broken by what had happened. Was this to be her and Anna? How could her daughter have been so stupid?

She could feel the anger starting to rise, and Tom became its target. It had to be all his bloody fault! He must have forced himself on her. Had Anna been underage? She would sort this out. That bloody little toe-rag was not going to ruin her daughter's life!

'Mum, I am so sorry—'

'It's Tom, isn't it? He made you do it. Did he rape you?' Meredith took Anna's shoulders and held her in front of her.

'Oh for goodness' sake, Mum, don't be ridiculous. Of course he didn't rape me. We have been going together for a year. I love him.'

'Don't be so bloody stupid. You must have been underage, for goodness' sake! It was illegal for you to have sex, Anna. How could you? What do you know about love?' she snapped. Then Meredith bit her lip and stepped away from the girl, realising she needed time to think, to cool down. She didn't want to say anything she would regret.

'I am sorry I shouted,' she said breathlessly. 'I am just upset, that's all. Get some sleep and we will talk about it in the morning.' She started down the stairs.

'Oh, Mum, that is so typical of you,' Anna shouted after her. '"Don't think about it, shove it away until tomorrow". I am pregnant, Mum! What am I going to do?' Then she turned away and slammed her bedroom door. Five minutes later, she came downstairs and said, 'I am going round to Tom's. You obviously can't help me with this. Maybe he will give me some sensible advice.' And with that she was gone.

Meredith went to her study and tried to finish her correspondence. She had a deadline on this article for the *Sunday Times* magazine but she just couldn't concentrate. She managed to hold back on ringing Tom's home until about eight o'clock, but by then she was beside herself. She dialled the number and then hung up. She needed a glass of wine first.

She went to the kitchen, opened a bottle of Montepulciano and took down a huge glass from the shelf. The glasses were from the Conran shop, and one glass must have held half a bottle of wine. She had joked with Anna that she only ever had 'just the one glass of wine, Doctor.' Where was the harm in that! Well, she needed it now. She took a sip and savoured the warmth of an Italian summer in her mouth and thought about times gone by. Happy times with her little girl. How had it come to this? It was in moments like this that she wished she still smoked. Still, better to drink than smoke.

Heaving a sigh, she went back to the phone and dialled Tom's number again. Someone answered on the third ring.

'Hi, we can't take your call right now. Please leave a message and one of the clan will get back to you.'

Meredith took a breath and spoke to the dreaded answer-machine. 'Hello this is Meredith Lee. I was hoping to talk to Tom or my daughter. Could they ring me back, please?'

Meredith shivered, and realised that the French windows were still open. It had become quite chilly. She closed them and turned on the kitchen light. Somewhere along the way, it had got dark. She looked at her reflection in the window, this woman with a large glass of wine in her hand staring into the darkness, and felt overwhelmingly tired and sad. She turned off the light and made her way towards the stairs and bed. Sleep was always her escape. When she was a girl, whenever things went wrong, her mother would always tell her to go to bed and sleep, and wake up to a new day when things would never look quite so bad.

The ring of the phone cut through her thoughts. It sounded so loud in the silence of the house. She went back to the kitchen and picked up as the light from the hall fell across the phone.

'Hello?'

'Meredith, this is Estelle, Tom's mother. Can we talk?'

'Yes, of course, but would you mind if we did it tomorrow? Is my daughter there with you? Is she OK?'

'Yes, she is fine. Well, a little upset, obviously. They both are really. It is quite a blow, isn't it? My husband and I are in shock, I think. You must be also. I am so sorry. Well, let's talk tomorrow then, shall we? Do you want to come here in the morning? Coffee-time maybe? Whatever suits you.'

'Yes, that's fine, about eleven then. Please give my love to Anna.' Meredith put down the phone and let out a sob. She just felt so lonely. She virtually staggered to her bed, toppled on to it, fell asleep and dreamed of Jack Blatchford.

Meredith woke up the next day with a start. She sat up and found she was still fully dressed on top of the covers. Then she remembered and lay back on the pillow, her heart sinking. She thought about her dream and about Jack. Anna was his daughter, after all, and now he was going to be a grandfather, and he still didn't even know he was a father. Should she tell Anna the whole story? It had always been something she had kept

265

putting off. Her mother had encouraged her to tell Anna from the beginning because Jane hated the idea of family secrets. Looking back, Meredith could see why. But telling Anna who her real father was didn't really help her present predicament. Meredith needed to make a plan, and find a practical solution to the problem. But what on earth might that be?

She got up, showered and did her hair and make-up, and decided to dress like a grown-up. It always made her feel in control of things, even if she was not at her best. Tom's parents were ex-hippies from the 1960s. They were the smokers, not the drinkers. Meredith had only met them a couple of times but they made her feel very unworthy and rather superficial. She was part of the consumer society. They were artists and very spiritual. This was the bloody trouble with Tom, she thought savagely, he had not been taught to take responsibility for himself. She stopped herself right there. She could not go round to meet them in an emotional state. Nothing would get solved. She must be calm and detached. Mature about the whole thing.

She made some coffee, but couldn't eat anything, although her stomach had a gnawing sensation going on. After ringing her production office to tell them she would be in meetings for most of the day and they could contact her later, she grabbed her bag and car keys and set off. The traffic was fairly light until she got to Whitestone Pond. There was always a bit of a queue here. She fiddled with the radio and then found her thoughts going back to Jack. What would he have made of it all? The trouble was, she would never know – and indeed, she had never got to know him well enough to make a guess. God, if only things had been different. Would they have managed to make a go of it? Why was she thinking about him, for God's sake? It was Anna she should be worrying about.

Tom's parents Estelle and Robert Neil lived in a big mansion flat at the top of Fitzjohn's Avenue, a gloriously wide, tree-lined road. She pressed the doorbell and leaned into the intercom to state her name. The buzzer beeped and the door sprang open. It was dark in the hallway and she waited for the clanky old lift in the gloom, like a child visiting the dentist. She wished she was visiting the dentist. She struggled with the lift doors and got them shut, and the lift screeched its way up towards the fifth floor. She felt sick and her hands were sweaty. Christ, she thought, she was over fifty, not twenty, and it wasn't she who was pregnant!

Estelle was waiting at the door and gave Meredith a hug. Why did this irritate her? Why did she feel instinctively as if it was them against her? She tried to brush Polly Paranoia off her shoulder. Estelle led her into a huge living room with very high ceilings and lots of light. The room was full of everything, from wall-hangings to paintings to sculptures, and in the middle was a huge grand piano. Tom and Anna were sitting engulfed in an enormous, rather tatty sofa. Tom's father, Robert, came forward and shook her hand. Thank God he didn't feel the need to give her a hug. Meredith wanted to run and scoop Anna up and hold her close like she used to when she was little, but that did not seem to be the right thing to do at this particular moment.

'Coffee?' Estelle pointed to a cafetière on the table.

'Yes, please. White, no sugar, thank you.'

Robert indicated for her to sit in an armchair as vast as the sofa. Meredith sank back into it and immediately forced herself forward to sit on the edge. She took the coffee from Estelle and waited for someone to speak. No one did, and then everyone did at the same time. They all laughed. It was Tom who finally broke the silence.

'Look, I know this must be a shock for all of you, and it is for me and Anna, but to be honest, guys, it is not the end of the world. Anna and I are completely committed to each other. We are in love, and although this baby has come a bit too soon, in the great scheme of things it doesn't really matter.'

Meredith practically dropped her mug. 'Yes, it does matter!' she said hotly. 'It is a disaster for Anna. Her whole life is ruined. She won't be able to do her A-levels, which means she won't be able to go to university. What kind of life is she going to have? You can't look after her. But anyway, she shouldn't be in a long-standing relationship. She is sixteen, for God's sake. She is still a child.'

'Oh Mum, please try and be reasonable. I am not a child and I am nearly seventeen, as you well know. I love Tom and I want to be with him. I want to have the baby and get on with my life.'

'What life?' Meredith could feel her control slipping away. This was a nightmare. She turned to Estelle. 'How do you feel about this? Do you want to see your son tied to a baby at his age? Who is going to support them? How will they live?'

Estelle crossed to her husband and took his arm. Together they faced Meredith, and never had she been made so acutely aware of how alone she was until this moment.

'Robert and I feel that we must support these young people in whatever they decide to do. It will be hard for them and they know this, but we think they are both very strong and will make a go of it.'

'I can't believe this! Anna, you can't have this baby! Please think about this. If you want to be with Tom, OK we can work around that, but if you have the baby, your life is changed for ever. I have worked so hard all these years for you to have choices, to make something of your life, and now you are just throwing it all back in my face. Why?' Meredith could feel the tears welling up and knew she had to get out of there. She mumbled her apologies and fled down the five flights of stairs and out into the street.

She started towards the car, then felt a hand on her arm. She turned and looked into her daughter's eyes. They were calm and focused.

'Mum,' Anna said, 'I am going to have this baby whether you like it or not. I also need you to know that I have been to see my real father. I am sorry to have to tell you like this, but you always make it so difficult to discuss things.'

Meredith grabbed her arm. 'Wait! Wait a minute, Anna, please. Slow down. You have been to see Jack Blatchford? How did you . . . ? Please, just sit with me for a minute. We can't discuss this in the street.'

Anna took Meredith's arm and they walked up to a little square where there was a vacant wooden bench; they sat down and Meredith tried to focus.

'Who told you about your father?' She could scarcely say the words.

'Oliver. Mum, please don't be angry with him. It's not his fault. I went on and on at him.'

'But he had no right to tell you,' whispered Meredith. 'It is my secret, my secret to tell, not his. How dare he?'

'Mum, stop for goodness' sake. There you go again. It is just as much about Oliver. He brought me up for ten years. He was my father, as far as I was concerned. OK, I knew he wasn't really, but he is still very important to me and he has always been there for me. Then as I got older I started to think about who my real father was, and what he was like. Then, when I met Tom it made me think about him even more.'

'But why? You had me,' Meredith cried out. 'Why did you need to find your father? He has nothing to do with us. He doesn't know you. What can he possibly do for you that I can't?' Meredith felt as if she was hitting her head against a wall. Where had all this come from? How could she have missed all the signs? How bad a mother was she? Here she was, a media personality famous for asking the questions and having all the right answers. She told people how to run their lives, decorate their homes, cook their dinners – yet she couldn't see that her own daughter needed help?

Anna's voice cut through her thoughts. 'Mum, please try and understand. I didn't do it to cause you grief. I needed to know for myself, and now I am pregnant it makes even more sense to me. Oliver told me you and my father were not able to be together, but that you really loved him—'

'Stop! Stop, for fuck's sake! Oliver has no idea what I felt about Jack. No fucking idea. And you have no fucking right to talk about me behind my back like this. I can't believe this is happening to me.'

'Oh, for crying out loud, Mother, it is always about you in the end, isn't it? *You* are depressed. *Your* life is a mess. How many times have I had to listen to your worries and woes? It is me who is pregnant, remember? Me who has to find a way to survive – and here we are discussing your bloody mistakes again. Well, don't worry, I will not be around, so that is one less problem. I am going to stay with Tom until we find a place to live. Then I am going to work for Tom's dad in his gallery and Tom is applying for teacher's training college so he can teach and paint. See? We can manage without you.'

And she was gone. Meredith sat on the bench trying to hold herself together. It started to rain and she ran to the car. Saw the penalty notice under the wiper and tore it away, threw it into the gutter. She drove back to the house trying to see through the tears and raindrops, as the wipers whined and wiped at her life.

Back at the house, Meredith hurried inside. She was soaked from the rain and ran upstairs to change, taking an old kaftan off the hook on her bathroom door and grabbing a towel to dry her hair as she made her way downstairs again into the kitchen. The bottle of wine from last night was still there and she poured the remains into a glass and went and sat on the sofa to think.

She felt betrayed. Why the hell did Anna need to speak to Jack? What the fuck was Oliver doing, telling her who her natural father was? God, what a mess! Last night she had dreamed about Jack Blatchford. It was so long ago and now it had all come back to haunt her.

Meredith tried to work out what she was going to tell Anna. That she had had a one-night stand because she had found out her real father was a rapist. 'Oh, and by the way, your grandfather happens to be your great-uncle, Myles Harrison.' Meredith had always been honest with her daughter about her birth, in the sense that she had explained to Anna when she was little that her real father was not around, but that Oliver loved her so much, *he* wanted to be her father. The little girl had been completely happy with that. Like many important issues in her life, Meredith had then filed it all away in her special drawer, to be taken out tomorrow – always tomorrow, never today. But now someone else had forced open the drawer.

She thought about ringing Oliver. After all, he was a part of this whole thing. Why had he opened his big mouth? He answered on the second ring.

'Oliver? It's Meredith.'

'Hello, babes, how are you? My little TV star—'

'Oliver, shut up. We have a crisis. Anna is pregnant.'

There was a long pause. Then: 'Oh, shit a brick – whatever next!'

'Well, that's not quite how I'd put it. Oh Olly, I have been hopeless. I reacted really badly – I mean, I just fell apart and started shouting, and now she has gone off to bloody Tom's house and left me on my own.'

'Wait, hold on, dear. Don't get your frilly knickers in a twist.

271

Start at the beginning. Better yet, why don't you get over here, and Uncle Oliver will sort it.'

'Oliver, this is not a joke. She has been talking to her real father. Thanks for nothing, by the way. What gave you the right to tell her all about Jack?'

'I am sorry, Meredith, but I warned you a long time ago that you had to deal with the issue, and yet you just ignored it and hoped it would go away, like you always do. The girl has a right to know. And she certainly does now, if she is going to have a baby. Family ties and links and genes and stuff are very important.'

'Oh God, I have just about had enough of all that, with a cupboard full of family skeletons.'

'Exactly, my little fruitcake. God knows, the stories in your family read like *Grimm's Fairy Tales*. Mind you, Anna will be doing nothing that the rest of you haven't done already. Have you told her about Great-Granny Mary's faux pas? Look, seriously, come over tonight and let's see what we can sort out. I will ring Anna and try to persuade her to come as well. Keep your pecker up, old girl.'

'Enough with the old – see you later.' Meredith felt better already. Oliver always did that for her; she made a note to call him more often. She missed him.

The phone rang and she rushed to pick it up, thinking it might be Anna. No such luck. Instead, it was her producer Marcus.

'Hi darling, just wondering if you will be able to get in today. We do have to get this meeting sorted, sweetie. The Network is becoming impatient. Schedules to fill – you know how it is.'

Oh yes, she knew exactly how it was. 'Yes, of course, Marcus. I was actually about to come in right now. Do you want to call everyone for two thirty?'

'Fab. OK darling, catch you later,' and he hung up.

Damn and blast and bollocks! This was all she needed right now. Why did everything always happen at once?

The phone rang again and she picked it up impatiently. 'Yes?' she snarled.

'Mum? Is that you?'

'Oh God, I am sorry, Anna, I thought it was the studio nagging me. Did you speak to Oliver, by any chance?'

'Yes, that's why I am ringing. I will come and meet you both tonight, if that's what you want, but can Tom come too?'

Bloody Tom! 'Well, I suppose so, but I don't really want to wash my dirty linen in public. I was hoping to talk about your father and so on, in private. Could it not just be the three of us tonight?'

There was a pause, then Anna said, 'All right, I suppose so – see you later then. Is Oliver cooking? I hope so, it is always so yummy. Bye, Mum.'

She sounds like a little girl, thought Meredith. She *is* a little girl, for God's sake! Oh, what a mess. Still, she couldn't think about that now. She had to go and fight a battle with TV executives who wanted to give her the boot.

Meredith rushed upstairs and changed into something chic and business-like. It was always good to dress well under pressure, and hide behind the charade. She took more time than usual with her make-up, and did the best she could with her hair. At the end she looked more Catherine Cookson than Catherine Deneuve, but it would have to do. She helped herself to a banana on the way out and prepared to do battle.

Chapter Eighteen

Meredith loved driving in London. It was a real challenge, and she prided herself on her knowledge of the rat-runs and back routes learned over the years from black-cab drivers. She never went in a straight line! Now she wended her way down through Hampstead and round the back of Kentish Town, through Russell Square and down to Waterloo Bridge, then across the river to the London Television Centre. Once there, she waved her way through security, parked in her reserved spot – one of the perks of having your own show – took the lift to the twenty-fifth floor and strode into the office on the dot of 2.30 p.m. Stick that in your pipe and smoke it, guys!

Marcus came sashaying over to meet her, wearing something lovely by Armani Creation.

'Hi, sweetie, what timing! Tea? Coffee or champagne?'

'Champagne? Are we celebrating something?' Meredith threw her tote bag on the seat by her desk.

'Well, no.' He looked confused.

'Just tea for me, please. Where is everyone?'

'They are in the conference room, ready and waiting.'

'Then let's go.' And Meredith set off down the corridor to the far end. Seated round the conference-room table were Sheila

Jones, Head of Daytime Television, Jamie Mackintosh, Head of Programming, and Keith Edwards, Commissioning Editor and arsehole extraordinaire. Meredith and Marcus took their seats. Let the Games begin!

'Welcome, Meredith. Thank you for coming in.' Sheila Jones had her posh voice on today. She was anything but posh really, but she was OK, just a bit dull. 'We have been looking at ratings for the afternoon slots and there seems to be a bit of a dip around three through until five.'

'Well, it is summertime,' chipped in Marcus, tossing his fringe carelessly.

'Of course, I agree the figures cannot be taken at face value,' Sheila went on, ignoring the interruption, 'but it has given us cause to think about where we might go in the autumn. I don't know if you have caught any of Casey Brown's new show on cable, have you, Meredith? She presents a really aggressive, fast-talking, edgy programme, with the general public as the stars. The public showing their less than pleasant side, you might say.'

'No, I haven't seen it but I know the one you mean.' Meredith was trying to gauge what was going on here. Casey Brown was American. Were they thinking of importing the show or making their own version, and if so, where did that leave her?

'Well, the Network loves the idea of a British version, and there is that lovely girl who does the weather at the moment on the six o'clock show who would be rather good as the anchor, don't you think?'

Why are you asking me? thought Meredith. Tracey, the weather girl in question, could hardly find Cornwall on a map of Great Britain without help, so how could she possibly solve someone's marital problems?

'I am not quite sure why my opinion should matter, Sheila. I am more concerned about how to make my own show better.

I have some ideas to suggest for next season which I have out-lined in these dossiers, if you would like to pass them round, Marcus.'

Marcus hopped up, took the pile of files and whipped them round the table with a flourish.

They all made a huge point of reading them intently. After about five minutes Jamie Mackintosh looked up and asked, 'Where exactly are you aiming for with this, Meredith? Are we still talking three o'clock or earlier or where?'

'Now here's the thing, Jamie. I believe it's time you looked at Breakfast. It is a no-man's land at the moment and needs a real overhaul, don't you think? So I am suggesting I front it and then we add on all sorts of strands over and above the big news and interviews. It could be right across the morning, almost. Not me all the time, of course – maybe the weather girl could have a strand about weather? But I really think that Breakfast TV needs a new look.'

Keith (arsehole) reared his ugly head. 'Meredith, we are already in discussions with Jonathan Blake about fronting a new breakfast-time show. Jonathan, and that lovely anchor woman – well, girl – Carole Connolly.'

'Carole Connolly? She was a page three girl, for God's sake! That is hardly the face of TV news journalism, Keith.'

'But things are changing, Meredith,' he replied coldly. 'Or perhaps you haven't noticed?'

Now she could see which way this was going, and it was no surprise to Meredith. Rather than bother to play the game or be humiliated, she decided to cut straight to the chase.

'OK folks, so what are we trying to say here? Does *Meredith Lee at Three* stay or go? Have we decided to go for the young and trendy ratings, or will there be a place for good old Middle England?'

There was a pregnant pause. *Oh please, not that word again today.* A vision of her daughter flashed across Meredith's mind. Stop it. Not now. It was a bit like her life flashing before her eyes as she drowned in the sea of TV ratings. But she was not going to drown – she was going to rise up from the depths and strike a blow for older women and mothers of pregnant daughters everywhere. *Stop it!*

'Well, to be honest,' Posh Sheila Jones again, 'I think we need both, and I would hope that you will stay with the Team, Meredith, and possibly come up with a remit that encapsulates the spirit of *Meredith Lee at Three* with a view to a younger market to please our advertisers.'

Phew, what a load of bullshit. The same but different. How original!

Meredith had expected no less and was prepared. What she had offered them today, but they had chosen to ignore, was an idea for a series about property. When she had had the idea to buy some kind of stately home and turn it into a spa, she had also realised that it would make a great TV show. The viewers loved Before and After programmes. So she had written a treatment for a series involving the general public buying their dream property and renovating it. Her new production company had done a budget for it and she had already sent it to another station who were extremely interested and about to make her an offer. So frankly, 'the Team' could go and take a running jump or join her in making innovative television for a reasonably intelligent audience.

'Why don't you take away the ideas I am offering there and let me know your thoughts.' Meredith smiled warmly round the table. 'I must tell you I have had a great deal of interest in *An Englishman's Home* and there is an offer on the table. So I will await your decision with interest.'

She rose and left without a backward glance.

She sailed down the corridor waving to right and left, and as luck would have it, the lift arrived as she pressed the button. Straight in she went, and as the lift doors closed she presented a smile. If there had been a soundtrack, she would have said 'Ta Dah' at the end of 'I Will Survive'.

Driving home, Meredith was on a high. She always rose to the challenge. It was a shame her private life was so different. No control there at all. She stopped at the patisserie in Hampstead High Street and bought some gorgeously over-the-top cakes for dessert at Oliver's, and arrived home in remarkably good spirits considering. There was a message on the answerphone from her mother. God, she should ring her really and tell her the news. Or maybe not. Jane had remarkable stamina and had coped with so much in recent years, but this might be a step too far.

Meredith went upstairs and ran a therapeutic bath. It had been a very tense couple of days, one way and another. She always loved to take a bath and soak the bones. As she lay drowsily in the steaming tub she tried to form a plan of action for tonight with Anna. Abortion was out of the question. What about adoption or fostering? Meredith did a good deal of charity work, and one of her chosen charities was Barnardo's. Maybe she could talk to someone there about the options available for Anna. What if Anna really was going to keep the child and live with Tom? What a nightmare that would be! They would want her to pursue granny duties. Well tough luck: she was not babysitting for them, she had a career to pursue. This was the age of the older woman. She hadn't got time to sit at home and knit bootees.

Listen to yourself, scolded a tiny voice in her head. *You can't go and see your daughter in this frame of mind. This is her life you are dealing with. Her life, a baby's life – your own life, for God's sake!*

Suddenly feeling depressed and anxious again, she got out of

278

the bath and dried herself vigorously, trying to pummel away all the negative vibes she was putting out. She dressed and went downstairs and made a To Do list for the next day. It was Saturday tomorrow and she and Anna usually did a shop, then had a coffee together somewhere and discussed the week's gossip before going home to do the homework/housework. Meredith allowed herself the luxury of a cleaner these days, but she loved pottering on Saturday afternoons, maybe doing a bit of baking or writing. She had a new cookery book she had to work on that could fill up the hours if she was going to be on her own tomorrow. Everything was going to change. And with that sobering thought, she collected her cakes from the fridge and set off for Notting Hill.

As she got closer to Oliver's incredibly desirable residence in Pembridge Gardens, she found she was becoming more and more nervous. This was ridiculous, considering she had wiped the floor with TV executives this afternoon and thought nothing of it, yet the prospect of trying to talk sense into her daughter was reducing her to a quivering wreck. It was a glorious evening again, and everybody was out on the pavements drinking and laughing and having fun. When did she last have fun? Meredith had spent all her time getting on with the job. There had been the odd affair but nothing serious because it was all so difficult trying to conduct a romantic liaison between school pick-up times and after-school classes. Men did not find it sexy or enticing making love to a woman who spent the post-coital hour sewing nametags. Her TV image as the woman who had it all could not be further from the truth. It seemed to take every hour of her day merely to keep on top of it all.

Meredith had very few real friends any more. Those she made through Anna's school were subject to the ebb and flow of the relationships between their daughters. However, there was one woman called Penny who was terrific fun and made all the school 'Do's' bearable for Meredith. Parents' Evening was the nadir of the social calendar, as far as she was concerned. Meredith always felt it was her career that was before the Head Teacher for discussion. She hated herself for feeling so meek, and for sitting up straight in the tutorial, nodding with feigned interest at the school project that year. Dental hygiene? The school had long ago stopped asking her to open a fete or a Sports Day, but were blatant in their courting of her in order to get some really famous person to come to the school. Didn't she know Dame Judi Dench? She only lived up the road – surely Meredith could do them a favour and call her?

Penny Wilson proved to be her saviour. At school Sports Day they had each filled a flask with white wine and sat on a rug under a tree and got pissed as the other mothers fronted each other up in the sack race.

'Please come and do the race, Mummy,' begged Anna, and Penny's daughter Millie was tugging at her arm. 'Yes, please, come on, Mum, we need you.'

The two women were helpless with laughter, most likely from too much white wine.

'Girls, we can't – look at us! We don't want to embarrass you both. Go on, we promise we will next year.'

Next year had come and gone. In fact, Meredith had sent Oliver who was brilliant at games and proved a worthy winner of the Dads' Race. She had expressed concern that Anna might be psychologically damaged if her parents or loved ones showed no interest in her school activities.

'She will be a hell of a lot more damaged if you do turn up to a Mothers' Race!' snorted Oliver. 'It's bad enough that you are on the telly, never mind physically challenged in every way.'

Meredith smiled to herself as she manoeuvred the car into a tiny space. The parking boded well. Whenever she went for a job interview or important meeting and found a parking space, she got the job. Maybe tonight would be OK, after all.

She ran up the perfect white steps and stood between the equally perfect box trees at the front door and rang the bell. There were footsteps, and the door opened to her daughter red-eyed and in tears. Meredith followed her through the elegant hallway, past the huge floor-to-ceiling mirror in an ornate wooden frame, past the stairs winding upwards in the thickest cream carpet, past a David Hockney . . . and downstairs to the basement kitchen from which the most delicious smells were emanating. Anna had not said a word nor given Meredith a hug or a kiss.

As they arrived at the bottom of the stairs, Oliver was there to meet her, wooden spoon in his hand.

'How are you, Merry?' He gave her a huge kiss on the lips. 'You look divine. Have you lost a little weight? It suits you. Come and sit. Anna, give your darling mother a glass of Montrachet, if you please.'

Oliver was a big man these days, tall and broad-shouldered with a fine head of dark hair. He had gained a few pounds over the years, but this only added to his persona as a chef. He was like a culinary opera star – the Pavarotti of the kitchen. He practically pushed Meredith into a chair and swept off to the other end of the enormous kitchen to stir and taste.

'Michael sends his apologies,' he called over his shoulder, 'but he has some party to sort out tonight for a client. He will be back for pudding.' He came back to the table. 'Are those for us?' He pointed to her box of cakes. 'How yummy, give them to me. I have made a little zabaglione, but we can have both and really pig out, eh, Anna?'

Anna almost jumped at her name. She turned to them both and Meredith thought she looked haunted.

'Yes, lovely, Oliver. Here you are, Mum.' She handed a large glass of white wine across to Meredith.

'Anyway, it is probably just as well Michael is not here, if you and I are going to talk about our colourful past, don't you think?' Olly went back to his sauce. 'We are having vichyssoise followed by veal tournedos and salad. Does that suit.' He stated rather than asked this. When Oliver cooked, you ate what he told you to eat. Even in his restaurant there had been the odd complaint from a customer who tried to choose something that Oliver disapproved of, or ate something in the wrong order or selected the wrong side dish. It was part of his personality. People loved it and flocked to the restaurant, half-hoping to be bullied by him. But the quality of his food made up for everything. Meredith was so proud of him. He had always worked so hard, from the very first day she met him. He had had a vision and in fact, had changed the face of cooking in Britain.

Meredith tried to grab Anna's attention. The girl was pretending to read a cookery book in the corner.

'How do you feel, love?' she asked.

'Fine,' Anna mumbled. 'Is dinner ready yet? I'm starving.' She got up and went to stand by Oliver as if for support. Meredith felt very isolated. When had she stopped communicating with her daughter?

'Please come and sit down beside me,' she said. 'I won't bite. I need you to understand why I am so upset. This is a disaster – for you, for me, for Tom, and especially for the baby.'

'Why is it? Why is it such a disaster? Here you go again, giving your opinions. It's always about you, Mother. Tom and I don't mind that I am pregnant. We are happy to be having a baby.' Anna glared at Meredith defiantly.

'But that is ridiculous. You have no idea what you are talking about. For God's sake, Anna, you are a child!' Meredith could feel her control going and turned to Oliver.

'OK, girls, time out! Here, Anna, pass this bowl of soup to your mother. Let's eat first and talk later. Meredith, stuff some bread in that gob of yours and shut up. *Bon appétit*!' Anna giggled and Meredith pretended to look hurt and stuffed a roll into her mouth. The tension was broken, and the three of them managed to enjoy their delicious dinner while Oliver regaled them with stories of his pre-college days as a young waiter.

'I remember one time, a woman who was an absolute bitch, and who had spent the whole evening complaining about everything, finally called me over and demanded a "very, very, very dry martini". "So you want an empty glass?" I asked. She threw a complete wobbly and flounced out of the restaurant. The owner made me pay her bill out of my wages, the bastard!' Oliver shook his head. 'Another time when I was a waiter in this really posh restaurant, I had had enough of the owner who was a complete prat. He was so pretentious and thought he knew everything about food, but in fact he knew fuck all! Sorry, Anna, slip of the tongue. Anyway, he had this little yappy dog that he absolutely adored and used to carry in his arms everywhere. He even used to come into our kitchen and stand over us, telling us what to do with this bloody rat under his arm. It was unhygienic and we told him so many times. Well, one day he and I were yelling at each other and the dog was yelping so I flicked it round the head and tried to shut it up. Somehow it escaped from the owner's arms and ran away. We searched high and low but we couldn't find the dog. By the end of the night the guy was in bits. We all thought it was hilarious. Someone shouted to him as he left that I had boiled it in the broth. Bugger me – sorry, Anna – if he didn't come in the next day and accuse me of cooking his dog! I told him to get stuffed and quit!'

Meredith looked at Oliver and smiled fondly, remembering the fun times. She would always be eternally grateful to him for sticking by her, and being so fantastic with Anna as she was growing up. He might not have been Anna's natural father, but he was anything but second-best. He had loved that baby from the moment she arrived. And now they were expecting another baby.

At that moment, the door burst open and Michael swept in with, 'Honey I'm home!' Then he stopped and looked at them all sitting there with long faces. 'Goodness, has someone died?' He kissed Oliver and went to the fridge to get some white wine. 'So come on, spill the beans. Tell Uncle Michael all your troubles.'

'Michael, Anna is with child and wants to keep her baby and give up going to college, and live with Tom. We are pondering the conundrum,' said Oliver.

'Oh dear,' replied Michael.

'See? It's impossible – you are all against me!' Anna jumped up and went to leave the room.

'Sit down this minute!' commanded Oliver, and she obeyed. 'Behaving like a spoiled brat is not going to help. If you think you are mature enough to have a child, then try and behave like an adult. We have to get through this and preferably together.' Oliver was relishing the drama.

Meredith was beginning to feel a bit drunk and tired and emotional. She really didn't think they were going to get anywhere tonight. Talking about the past had made her very melancholy and aware that she had made a cock-up of her own life. She was in no position to lecture Anna. Except that she did know how hard it was to bring up a child.

'Let's have some pudding and cheer ourselves up,' Oliver said. 'Anna, clear away the dishes, Meredith, put the coffee on, and Michael, put out these amazing buns her ladyship brought us. I will get the zabaglione out of the fridge.' Oliver handed Michael the box of cakes and went to the fridge to fetch the desserts. Everyone performed their tasks in silence, each with their own thoughts before they all sat down again and attacked the delicious sweets in front of them.

'How was the party?' Oliver asked Michael through a mouthful of chocolate éclair.

'You really shouldn't eat with your mouth full, dear,' joked Michael. 'It is so unseemly. As a matter of fact it all went rather well, and I think we have signed up Robbie Williams to do his autobiography.'

'Oh wow, that's amazing,' said Anna, perking up. 'Would I be able to meet him?'

'I will make sure you get an invitation to the launch party,' Michael promised her.

'That's if you can find a baby-sitter,' retorted Meredith, and then immediately regretted it. Now who was being childish? 'Sorry, I didn't mean to say that.'

There was silence again and then Oliver once more took control.

'Right – enough with the sniping. Let's get down to business. Anna, you tell us why you should be allowed to have this child.'

Anna finished her last spoonful of dessert and wiped her mouth on her napkin. She looked at the table and took a deep breath.

'Well, because I love Tom and he loves me and I don't believe in abortion.'

'Neither do I!' butted in Meredith. 'There are other options I would like to suggest to you.'

'Meredith, be quiet. Let Anna finish,' said Oliver.

'I know it means I will have to put my college stuff on hold for a while, but does it matter?' Anna continued. 'People go back to college all the time. I will be more mature and better able to take my studies seriously. How many times do you hear about students not using their time properly at uni? Too many parties and having a good time? Well, I will be beyond all that.'

'But you will have a child, for God's sake.' Meredith could

not keep quiet. 'What are you going to do with it at uni? Shut it in your rooms? They don't have crèches at Oxford, Anna.'

'Please let Anna finish her justification, Meredith. You will have a chance to respond in a minute.' Oliver placed a hand on Meredith's arm and squeezed it.

'Sorry,' she mumbled. 'Carry on.'

Anna tried to pick up the thread but had lost her impetus. 'Oh never mind,' she said angrily. 'What's the point? Mum is impossible to talk to about this. Let's just forget it. I will go and live with Tom or my father and she can stew away in peace.'

'Well, that is very mature, Anna,' said Meredith. 'Can I just ask what the hell any of this has to do with your father? Natural father, by the way. Not this man here, who has loved you and watched over you from day one. He is the real father in all this, not a man you hardly know. And what on earth makes you think he would let you stay with him?'

'And whose fault is that, Mother dear?' Anna was quick to turn on Meredith. 'Why did I not know who my real father was from the beginning? I love Oliver, of course I do, it goes without saying, but why didn't you explain to me what had happened to my real father?'

'Because it did not seem to be important when you were born; things just went along. I know I should have told you at some point, but the time never seemed to be right. Oh, why did you tell her, Oliver?' She turned on him.

'I have already explained, Merry, now please everybody calm down. The trouble is there are several issues here. Anna needed to know who her father was, and I assumed, wrongly, she at least knew his name. After all these years I assumed, wrongly again, that you had discussed some of what went on. It was only as we started to talk that I realised she had no idea about any of it, by which time I had already spilled the beans, as it were.'

Oliver turned to Michael for support but Michael had diplomatically gone into the other room.

'Why didn't you come to me?' Meredith asked her daughter. 'I would have told you all you wanted to know.'

'Because you never have time to sit and talk, and actually I hadn't gone to talk to Oliver specifically about that; it just came up one day because we were talking about genetics due to a project I was doing at school,' replied Anna. 'And now that I am pregnant, the issue does become rather important. I want to know my origins. It is only natural.'

God, I wish I didn't know my origins, thought Meredith but she answered, 'Yes, I accept that. So now you know, why do you have to pursue the matter any further? Why did you go and see Jack Blatchford?'

'Because she is a woman and she was curious,' Oliver chimed in. 'Can you blame her?'

'No, I don't blame her. I blame you, as a matter of fact. Why didn't you come and talk to me first about all this? Why let her go off at half-cock? What did Jack say, for God's sake? Did you ring him first? What on earth did you say? "Hi, Dad, I am your long-lost daughter"?' Meredith took a large swig of wine.

'Oh please shut up, Mother! As usual you are managing to turn this into a whole drama about you.'

'Well, I am involved, aren't I? It takes two, you know, to reproduce. Don't my genetics count?'

'Now, now, Merry.' Oliver took her hand. 'Palms up and breathe.'

'And you can shut up – you're not helping things at all,' she snapped at him.

'Well, pardon me for living. I will go and sit with Michael, who loves me.'

'No, please don't go, Oliver,' begged Anna. 'We will never get anywhere on our own. Please stay.'

Oliver sat down and sighed: 'Listen, never mind who said what to whom, the problem now is where do we go from here? Meredith, I think you have to accept that Anna is serious about having this baby, and you have to decide to be with her or against her.'

'I don't want to be against her,' said Meredith, who was nearly crying, 'but can't you both understand I am trying to help Anna, to stop her making the biggest mistake of her life!' She tried hard to keep her voice steady as she asked desperately, 'Will you at least talk to someone I know at Barnardo's about adoption and fostering? If you have the child fostered you could keep in contact with it, and then maybe later on when you are more settled, and you have finished your education, you can have it back. By the way, just one other thing about Jack: does he know you are pregnant?'

'No, not yet. I went to see him a couple of weeks ago, and I didn't know I was pregnant then.'

'So why do you think he will help you now? What makes you think he will welcome you with open arms? Doesn't he have a life? A wife and children of his own?' As she asked this, Meredith could hear a tiny voice in the back of her head whispering, *Maybe he is alone. Maybe there is no wife. That's what you want to hear, isn't it? Be honest.*

'He lives alone – well, with his son Harry. I don't know about any wives or girlfriends. He was so kind and interested in me though. He asked about you and how you were, et cetera. When I left he said to call him anytime if I had a problem or needed help. He also said he would be happy to meet up with you if it helped. I told him that I had kept the meeting a secret from you and he said that was OK.'

'So why didn't you keep it a secret!' exclaimed Meredith.

'Because then all this happened. Mum, please don't keep shouting at me,' and Anna burst into tears.

Meredith got up from the table and went to fetch some kitchen roll which she handed to Anna. She knew she should comfort her daughter, but her gut was telling her that if she showed any emotion she would break down – and that was certainly not going to help anyone at this point.

Oliver had his arm round Anna and was murmuring, 'Come on now, don't cry, sweetheart. It is all going to be fine. Your mum is upset, that's all. It's been a·shock. You have got raging hormones and we are all tired. Let's leave it for tonight and talk again tomorrow. Meredith, do you want me to get you a cab? You can't drive, you've had too much to drink.'

'Oh for goodness' sake, Oliver, I will be fine. I need the car tomorrow to get everything done for the weekend. Are you coming home with me, darling?' Meredith asked Anna.

There was a pause then Anna said, 'Actually, I don't think that is a good idea, Mum. We'll only row. Tom's parents have said I can stay with them for as long as I like. Well, while we are sorting everything out. They have accepted that Tom and I want to have the baby, and are happy to plan with us how we can best go about it all.'

'Well, how fucking lovely of them!' Meredith was losing it and she knew it, but she just couldn't stop herself. 'How very liberal and understanding and just fucking lovely! Well, you carry on then, darling. You and Jack Blatchford and the whole fucking caboodle. It is just one big love-fest. Whoopee doo! I will keep out of your way. I can be the wicked Fairy Godmother and tip up at the christening with a big wand and send you all to sleep for a hundred years. That is about the size of it, isn't it, really? Fucking Fairyland!'

She got up and grabbed her bag and keys and made for the door, where she was stopped in her tracks by Michael.

'Hold up, madam, and hand over your keys. I will drive you home. You are not fit to drive.'

'I am obviously not fit for very much of anything, it would seem,' she said, and ploughed on past him out to the car.

'I won't be long. Keep the home fires burning.' Michael blew a kiss and hurried off.

Oliver hugged Anna and said, 'Don't pay any attention to your mum, she will calm down. It has been a big shock, you know.'

'Yes, I do know, and I am so sorry, Oliver. And please don't think I don't love you and appreciate everything you have done for me.' She blew her nose.

'I know, darling, and I love you. Now come on, get to bed. Do you want a hot chocolate?' he asked. Anna had her own room here with Oliver and Michael and would often stay overnight. She started for the door.

'Yes, I would love a hot chocolate. Thank you.'

'I will bring it up to you. We could read *Sleeping Beauty* and remind ourselves of what your mother would be like as the Wicked Fairy!' They both laughed naughtily and Anna pottered off to bed as Oliver put on some milk to heat.

Meanwhile, Michael was driving a fuming Meredith through North London.

'I mean, how does she think I feel, going behind my back to find Jack? He must think I am a complete idiot! It is so embarrassing, having to deal with him after all these years,' she moaned.

Michael stole a glance at her and said, 'Please tell me to mind my own business if you want to, but aren't you just a little too concerned about Jack? Are we thinking of Anna or Meredith here? Do I detect an opening of old wounds here between you and Mr Blatchford?'

'What on earth are you getting at, Michael?' she replied. 'I haven't seen Jack Blatchford for a hundred years. It was actually when I went to Pamela's funeral and had that disastrous meeting with Myles. I saw Jack there with his latest squeeze, some blonde woman with huge tits, as I recall. I have had no real contact with him at all, and I certainly never intended him to know he was Anna's father.'

'But surely it must have occurred to you that it would all come out one day? As you said tonight, you had every intention of telling Anna who her real father was eventually.'

'Yes of course, but I am very bad at confronting things. You have probably noticed.'

Michael smiled and nodded. 'Well yes, I had, and Oliver warned me ages ago about your "drawer". He used to say where most women have a knicker drawer, you have a problem drawer.'

They both laughed.

'Yes, I am hopeless and many times my drawer has been full to bursting! But I didn't want to ever have to get the Jack problem out again.' Meredith paused. 'But I guess that is going to be impossible now. Oh Christ, what am I going to do?' She caught her breath.

'About Anna's pregnancy, or your feelings for Jack?' Michael looked at her as she turned to him.

'I don't know,' she whispered.

They had arrived at her gate so she was saved from having to elaborate any further. She leaned across and kissed Michael on the cheek. 'Thank you so much for this, and a big thank you for being my friend and loving Oliver. He is the best, isn't he?'

'I think so.' Michael got out and locked the car, then came round and gave her the keys. 'Hopefully, a car will arrive any minute now and whisk me back to Notting Hill away from these pagan highlands of North London.' As he spoke, a car pulled up and the driver spoke through the open window: 'Car for Mr Lyons?'

'That's me,' said Michael. He gave Meredith a quick hug and was gone.

Meredith let herself in and dropped the keys on the hall table. She noticed the light flashing on the answer-machine and switched it on. It was her mum.

'Hello, dear, just a quick call to see how you are. You have been rather quiet the last couple of weeks. Not that I am complaining, just wanted to check everything was all right. Give me a call when you can. Goodnight.'

Her mother definitely had sixth sense, thought Meredith. Jane always knew when something was wrong, God bless her. It was too late to ring her back now, and anyway, Meredith couldn't trust herself not to spill the beans. She had become very close to her mother in the last few years, ever since Jane Lee had revealed her secret to her daughter. Anna knew nothing about her grandmother's past, nor how Meredith was conceived. Ripples in a pool, travelling outwards. Meredith remembered sitting in her mother's kitchen and bursting into tears when she told Jane Lee she was pregnant. It would never have occurred to Meredith to give up her baby – so why was she being so adamant that Anna should give up hers? *This is different*, she told herself. *Anna is still a child, I was thirty-four. Yes, and should have known better.*

Meredith groaned inwardly and climbed the stairs to bed. She was too tired to deal with it now and she had had far too much wine.

Chapter Nineteen

Meredith woke up at five the next morning with a splitting headache, once more fully clothed on top of her bed. She went down to the kitchen and drank several glasses of water and then climbed the stairs again. She started to undress and then realised there was no point in going back to bed as the dawn was already breaking, and the birds were giving their all in glorious stereo. So she had a long hot shower instead, washed her hair, and decided to brazen out any hint of a hangover and get some work done. She wanted to finish the rough draft of the cookery book ready for her publisher on Monday, and she also wanted to tighten up the script for the pilot of the property show. She had a good feeling about it and wished to be ready should the Network pick it up.

She set to work with a large cup of coffee and a bacon sandwich, and by nine thirty she had nearly finished the book. The telephone interrupted her sprint to the end and she was reluctant to answer it, but figured the way things were going in her life it was better to get any bad news quickly.

'Hello, Meredith speaking.' She walked into the kitchen to put the kettle on.

'Hi, Meredith, I hope I am not disturbing you. It's Jack Blatchford here.'

'Oh, hello Jack, no, you are not disturbing me at all. I'm just pottering about – you know, Saturday morning.' *Shut up and stop wittering, woman. Why do you always witter when you talk to this man?* 'How can I help you?' God, was he going to talk about Anna? Oh my lord, she wasn't ready for this!

'I am afraid I am the bearer of bad news. Myles Harrison died last night in his sleep. I am sure you will have very mixed feelings about the news, but please accept my condolences. I have been asked by his lawyers to contact you as you are a beneficiary of his will.'

'Myles is dead? Oh my goodness, I don't know what to say.' Meredith felt as if she had been kicked in the gut. She tried to understand what she was feeling. Shock, disbelief or relief? 'I am a beneficiary? No, there must be a mistake. I can't be, I haven't seen him for over ten years. In fact, the last time I saw him was at Pamela's funeral, do you remember?'

'Yes, but there is no mistake, Meredith. Myles asked me before he died to contact you and make sure you received a letter, which I have to give you, plus another letter for your mother, and an undertaking from you to act as instructed by his lawyers. Are you free on Monday to come and meet them?' Jack sounded very business-like and distant. Meredith was completely thrown.

'Very well. Do you want to give me the address? I have a pencil so go ahead.'

'Harcourt House, number 121 Lincoln's Inn. I can meet you there at ten on Monday.' He reeled off the phone number, then added, 'I don't suppose you are around today for a quick drink, are you? Only I shall be up your end of town later, and I wondered if you wanted to have a chat about ...' there was a pause '... our daughter.'

'Um, yes, I suppose I could be free. What time did you have in mind?' Meredith was gripping the phone.

'What about midday? The Royal Oak pub in Highgate?' He sounded so casual and normal now, as if they did this all the time.

'OK fine – see you then. Bye.' Meredith hung up and stood rooted to the spot. What was happening to her life? It was spiralling out of control. Everything was happening so fast. She went and got a glass of water and checked her head. Was she hung-over? Hallucinating? No, she was fine. The shock had driven any thought of a headache from her mind. Right, she could do this. Whatever life was chucking at her, she would clasp it to her breast. Embrace it.

What was she going to wear for lunch? She rushed upstairs and surveyed her wardrobe. It was a gorgeous summer's day, which helped. The hair would work better. So – smart casual? Casual? Smart? What hid her fat bits the best was more to the point. A dress with sleeves or a jacket? Her jeans because she still had quite a good bum for her age. Yes, that was it, her jeans and a lovely white cotton sweater she had bought recently from Nicole Farhi, and loafers, and her big white tote bag. She re-dried her hair and applied her make-up with great care. Thank God for her wonderful make-up girl Pattie who had taught her all the tricks of the trade. She looked pretty good by the time she had finished, even though she did say so herself.

She hadn't rung her mother. Would she be able to talk to her without giving anything away? Probably not, so she would ring tonight. She decided she was not going to drive up to Hertfordshire tomorrow after all, as Jane would be up the following weekend anyway for Anna's seventeenth-birthday lunch.

It was only 11.15, so she'd be too early if she set off now. That would not be good. Well, she could park up and get groceries in Highgate first. Good plan. She liked a plan. She suddenly realised how excited she felt. It was as if she was going on a date with him again. Again? She had never been on a date with Jack! She had just slept with him for one night only and then had his baby! That was more than seventeen years ago. It was an awfully long time between a one-night stand and the next date. Oh dear, this was going to be so scary. She was over fifty, for goodness' sake, nearly a pensioner! OK, maybe not quite that old, but nevertheless too old to be coping with this level of romantic stress. Tough. It had to be done. The drawer was well and truly open now, and the contents were strewn across her life. It was time to take stock and start picking them up.

She arrived in Highgate at 11.30 and found a parking space straight away. She then strolled down the hill to Tesco, and spent the next twenty minutes buying her weekend groceries. It was strange, not buying food for masses of people. She usually cooked for Anna and her friends on an ongoing basis at weekends. She chugged back up the hill again and put the shopping in the boot. She checked her watch: it was 11.55.

Right, she would walk to the pub the long way round. God, this was tedious. She suddenly saw one of the mothers from Anna's school across the road and quickly ducked out of sight. She really didn't want to see anyone she knew at this moment. She hovered behind a tree and then felt rather foolish as a young couple who were coming up the road gave her a very odd look. Don't worry about me, she thought. I am just the local bag lady taking my morning constitutional. She smiled and said, 'Good morning,' and they looked away and hurried past.

She was approaching the pub now and scanned the gardens at the front for any sign of Jack. There was none. Oh goodness, that meant she would have to walk in and look around. She hated having to do that. She always felt so self-conscious and never seemed to be able to recognise faces she knew. She usually just walked through hoping someone would call out to her.

Well, here goes! It was like holding your nose and jumping into the water and praying you would come up for air.

'Meredith, over here.' She heard Jack's voice but couldn't see him. Panic! Please make him come to her. She turned a full circle and bumped straight into him.

'Oh sorry, how stupid I am. Here you are.' She stepped back and bumped into someone behind her. 'Sorry,' she said, flustered. 'Sorry – excuse me.' She was like Mr Magoo.

'This is Harry, my son,' said Jack, indicating the young man whose toe she had just trodden on.

'Oh hello, I am so sorry about your foot.' She shook a firm hand and looked into a handsome, open face.

'No problem. Pleased to meet you. I am just dropping Dad off, actually. I'm not stopping.' He gave her a radiant smile and she felt herself simpering.

'Please don't leave on my account. Your father and I can talk another time. I mean . . .' *Here we go again, Meredith, witter, witter. Like father like son as far as you are concerned.*

Jack interrupted: 'No, he is off to football at Highbury. Arsenal supporter and all that. You don't have that problem, I take it? With Anna being a girl, football is not high on her list, is it?'

'Oh no, that's right. Saturdays are meant for shopping in our house.' Meredith was in desperate need of a seat as her legs were about to give way under her. Two Blatchford men were too much to cope with at the same time.

'Shall we sit down?' Jack suggested as if he had read her thoughts. 'Go on, Harry, buy us a drink before you go. What would you like, Meredith?'

'White wine, please. A Pinot Grigio, if they have one. Here, take my purse.'

She fumbled in her bag but Jack put a hand on her arm and said, 'No, don't worry. Harry is more than capable of buying us a drink, aren't you, my lover?'

297

'Oh yes, my lover,' replied Harry and they both laughed.

Meredith smiled. 'Not lost the Somerset brogue then?' she said.

'Oh no, I don't think I will ever lose it now – I'm too long in the tooth.' Jack steered her towards a table in the corner and they sat down. 'Well, here we are then.' He looked at her long and hard. Meredith busied herself getting settled, trying to think where to start. She couldn't help chuckling.

'What's the matter?' Jack asked. 'What's so funny?'

'Well, this really,' she replied. 'Did you ever imagine in a million years that you would be having a conversation with a fiftyish-something woman, about her having had your baby?'

Jack smiled wryly. 'Put like that, no, I never did . . . Oh lovely, stick 'em down here. That's great.' He moved out of the way as Harry put the drinks down on the table.

'So shall I come and pick you up later after the match?' asked Harry.

'No, I'll make my own way back. Have a good time. Good luck with the game.'

Harry turned to Meredith. 'Cheers, Meredith, lovely to meet you. See you again.'

'Goodbye, Harry, lovely to meet you too. Take care.'

Harry loped off and Jack said to Meredith, 'He's a great lad, has been no trouble at all. I have been really lucky. No drugs, nothing. The odd drunken night, but nothing too serious.' He said this with great pride.

'Well, that is lucky these days, I must say, especially with boys. They usually seem to be the trouble but—' She stopped suddenly and realised exactly where this was going. Her child was a problem. Her child was a girl. Her child was . . . She suddenly wanted to cry. Why her daughter? Their daughter. Dear little Anna who had always been so loving and good and bright and carefree. She took a big gulp of wine.

'It is tough for you, I guess,' said Jack softly.

Please don't be nice to me, thought Meredith. I can't stand it. I will just burst into tears in a minute. She pinched her leg under the table to stop the tears. 'Have you spoken to Anna at all since she came to see you?' Meredith cautiously pressed to find out if Jack did know about the baby.

He sighed and leaned forward over the table. 'She rang me first thing this morning, which is why I rang you straight away. I had to tell you about Myles, obviously, but Anna's news came as a complete shock.'

'Yes, it has not been the best week of my life. She has never been any trouble either. Not like some of her friends, who have been taking drugs or going out and drinking themselves into a stupor. But then she had Tom. Have you met the boyfriend?'

Jack nodded. 'Yes, I met him the other day when he dropped Anna off at my house. He seemed like a good kid, pity he wasn't a bit more responsible though. Christ, Meredith they are so young.'

'He is a good kid. I am just being grumpy because I wish they had not got involved so soon. Why, Jack? She has everything going for her. She has predicted Grade As and Bs for her A-levels, and until she started going out with Tom she was always talking about trying to get into Oxford to read History of Art. Now that is all out the window. God knows, I have spent a fortune on her education. OK, I know it's not about the money as such, but it is a bit disheartening, don't you agree?'

Jack drank his pint slowly. He put the glass down and sat for a minute. She watched him, thinking how incredibly handsome he still was, even though his hair had gone grey at the temples and he had fine lines round his eyes. It just seemed to make him more attractive. I wonder how I look to him? she thought. Do I look more attractive with my fine lines? I doubt it somehow. It did not seem to work quite like that for women. She looked up.

'Sorry, what did you say?' she asked.

'I said it is very hard, but Anna is a lovely girl. You have done a good job, Meredith. Have you been on your own a long time?' He asked this casually.

'Yes, years. No one wants a fairy when she's forty!' Meredith laughed at the joke she and Anna had shared when she was younger and they were still reading fairy stories. Anna had asked her one day why no one loved her like other mummies who had daddies, and Meredith had remembered that line from an old music-hall song. It had stuck ever since. She told the story now to Jack, who looked bemused.

'That's a bit harsh, isn't it? You are a very attractive woman. There must have been lots of offers?' He gave her a look that made her blush.

'Actually no, to be honest, it has been a bit of a desert. But I couldn't have coped with Anna and a bloke in my life. It is relentless, this parenting business, didn't you find?'

'Is that why you decided to leave me out of the equation?' Jack was suddenly serious. 'Don't you think it was a rather childish reaction to just leave me in the dark?'

'Well, we were hardly close, were we, and you made it very clear when you dropped me off that day that you were not interested in a relationship,' retorted Meredith. How dare he criticise her! What right did he have to tell her what to do?

'Yes, I did, and for exactly the same reasons that you have just given me for being on your own. I couldn't cope with a child and a relationship. However, it's a bit different from discovering I have fathered a child. I had a right to know, Meredith, and to make a decision of my own about how to deal with it.' Jack had raised his voice and the couple on the next table had stopped talking.

'Keep your voice down, please,' said Meredith. 'I don't want the whole world to know my business.'

'You don't seem to ever want anyone to know your business, not even the father of your baby,' hissed Jack.

'Look, I didn't come here today to be lectured,' said Meredith. 'I have got enough on my plate. I apologise for not telling you, but may I point out it was many years ago and life has moved on. You have a very different life now, I am sure, and how would I have been able to know if your life could have accommodated a child. I did what I thought was best at the time.' She was beginning to feel tearful.

'And what about later?' Jack was not going to let up. 'Did you not think you could have mentioned it when you saw me at Pamela's funeral?'

Meredith scoffed. 'Oh please, come on. That was hardly the time or the place, was it? Do you remember what it was like for me and my mother that day, having to cope with Myles Harrison?'

Jack had the grace to look apologetic. 'Oh yes – right, sorry. I had forgotten about all that shit,' he said.

'"Shit" is right. I also noted that you had a young lady with you at the time, and rumour had it you were going to marry her so I hardly thought you would want a child involved in your new life.'

Jack started to chuckle.

'What's so funny?' demanded Meredith.

'Gossip. I remember everyone thinking I was too stupid to understand that Denise was chasing the money. Believe me, I knew exactly what was going on. She was a good laugh and her ample bosom was a comfort to me, but as I had taken great pains to explain to you previously, I was not in the marriage stakes. I had had my one-time chance and I lost her. Harry was my number one priority after that, and always has been.'

'And I am sorry, Jack. It must have been a terrible time, but surely you can sympathise with me in that case. I made Anna *my* number one commitment.' She finished her wine and stood

301

up. Jack just sat there and Meredith was unsure whether to go or stay, so to fill the silence she offered Jack another drink.

'Thanks, a pint of Special, please.'

She took his glass and made her way to the bar. It was still quite early in the day and she did not have to queue for many minutes. The boy behind the bar gave her a cheery greeting.

'Hi, Miss Lee, how you doing?' Meredith looked at him, and then it dawned.

'Hello, Tim, how are you? How long have you been working here?' she asked. Tim was one of the gang that Anna went around with. He was a lovely boy who had been two years ahead of Anna all through school, ever since primary days.

'Only started a couple of days ago. I am hoping to make enough money to go travelling. Large Pinot Grigio and a pint of Special, was it? Coming up!'

Meredith looked round the bar to see if there was anyone else she knew. News spread fast and she didn't want to be part of the village gossip – or worse still, if someone from school inadvertently let on to the press that she had a date with a man in a pub. One of the mothers at school had been a gossip colum-nist, and was always trying to sneak information out of Anna about what Meredith was up to. So far, she had been unlucky since Meredith led such a boring life.

Tim came back with her drinks, saying, 'There you go.' Meredith only had twenties so she gave him a twenty-pound note and said, 'Keep the change.'

'Wow, thanks, Ms Lee – are you sure?'

'Yes. It can go towards your holiday. Take care.' She took the drinks and went back to the table to find Jack reading the local estate agent's magazine, which someone must have left on the table.

'Still looking for bargains?' Meredith asked. 'Are there still any bargains to be had?'

302

'Oh God yes,' came the reply. 'I always manage to find something.' He took his glass and drank thirstily.

'Good job you are not driving,' remarked Meredith. 'You would soon have reached the limit at this rate.'

'Why do you think I got my son to bring me? Anyway, back to the business in hand, our daughter.' He stopped and studied Meredith. 'I am not very happy about the whole thing, to be honest, Meredith.'

'And you think I am? Look, I am so sorry that our moment of passion has turned into a lifetime's commitment. What was I supposed to do? You didn't contact me so I naturally assumed you were not interested.'

Meredith knew this was a pretty lame excuse but there was nothing else to hand. Jack let out a sigh of exasperation. 'Oh, for goodness' sake, woman! I thought you weren't interested in a relationship! You had your career all mapped out. You really seemed to know what you wanted.'

'Well, I believed I did until I—' Meredith stopped. Did she want to admit to Jack just how smitten she had been by him? It was a bit late now to start confessing one's deepest desires. If only they had been able to see each other back then. If only she had not got pregnant straight away. If only . . .

'Meredith, are you listening to a word I have said?' Jack broke into her daydream. 'You should have told me. I had a right to know.'

'"Right to know"? Would you really have been able to deal with a pregnant woman you hardly knew?' Meredith challenged him.

'Well, I think I had a right to at least know about the situation, in order to make that decision. Don't you?'

Meredith twiddled her glass. 'Yes, you did,' she whispered. 'And for the life of me I really don't know why I didn't tell you, except I had so much going on in my head about my father and

Myles, and my mother being raped and giving birth to me. Looking back, I wonder if I thought that somehow I had to be like my mother and deal with my pregnancy alone. But the ridiculous thing about that argument is that my poor mother had no choice. There she was, pregnant from a man she despised, who had raped her, whereas I was pregnant because I had slept with a man I found totally irresistible and could have made a completely different choice about what to do with my life.' Meredith paused; she was feeling incredibly emotional.

'Jack, I don't know what to say,' she went on. 'The trouble is, one makes a decision in a vacuum, without ever understanding the consequences. Look at all the lives involved in my selfish choices. You and Anna, Oliver ... Everyone's lives are inextricably entwined. Don't you see, that is why Anna must not have this baby? It will be another set of lives ruined along the way. Oh God, it is such a mess.'

Meredith looked for something to wipe her nose with as it was starting to run, and Jack produced a silk hanky.

'Here, blow into this. Go on, that's what it's for, you numpty!' Meredith smiled and took it gratefully.

Jack waited until she had finished blowing her nose and then said, 'Meredith, why do you feel so adamantly that Anna's baby is a disaster? Yes, she and Tom are very young, but it has been known to work, you know. I was only twenty-one when I married Carole. Admittedly she died, so we can never know if it would have lasted, but what I can say is that I knew exactly what was involved in that relationship, and I wanted the responsibility. Tom seems like a very grounded guy. He knows what he wants to do with his life. He wants to paint. Now that is a difficult choice on any level. He will always have to find an alternative way of earning a living to fund the painting. Being in a committed relationship does not affect his career choice.

304

Anna has to give up going on to further education, and that is a setback in a way, but in reality it is only a temporary thing.'

Jack took a swig of his pint but he was far from finished. 'You know very well that the baby thing lasts no time at all,' he said. 'Three years and she can pick up where she left off. She is already going to be in a creative environment where she can read and learn all day long. She might decide not to bother with university to get ahead in the art world. What about the University of Life? It is not an unreasonable assumption, is it? At least she is with the father of her child. At least they want to make a go of it. Let's give them our blessing and help them as much as we can.'

He finished the rest of his pint and held up his glass. 'Do you want another wine?'

Meredith shook her head. 'No, thanks, I had better not. I have got the car here. Can you get me a sparkling water and a bag of crisps, please?'

While he was gone Meredith tried to digest everything that Jack had just told her. It was true she had jumped on the negative aspects straight away, and in a sense she was being selfish. She was seeing it from her point of view. She had wanted Anna to go to university and have a career. To travel the world and have lots of different experiences in life, because that is what she would have loved to have done. Deep down, Meredith knew that she had never been brave enough to follow her instincts. College had been a way to leave home, not an opening to another world. She had met Oliver and followed in his wake really. He was the ambitious one. The one with a dream of owning his own restaurant; she had simply fitted in.

She had never really had a clear view of what she wanted in her life. As a woman growing up in the sixties, Meredith had appreciated that society was changing and that women were becoming a very different species, but somehow she never

quite escaped her own upbringing to benefit from that independence of spirit. Having said that, she had had a baby with no
husband and gone on to earn her own living and bring up her
child as a single mother. She was successful in her field and had
never relied on a man for money. So in essence, she was very
much a product of her time.

Unfortunately though, there was the other part of her that she
had learned from her mother – and that part wanted a husband
and family. She had grown up watching her mother run a home
and support her man. Jane had created a safe and cherished environment for her family, from which they could go out into the
world with some sense of self. She had turned a tragedy into a
positive story and proved the importance of human relationships.
George and Jane Lee had discovered each other through their
lives together and against all the odds. George was the ultimate
in male understanding and strength of character. He had been
able to accept another man's child as his own and love that child
unconditionally. He had given Jane Lee back her self-respect and
she, in turn, had given him a loving family and a beautiful home.
Deep in her heart, Meredith craved that kind of stability.

She looked up and saw Jack coming back with the drinks.
Right, enough of these musings, she thought, it was time to
make a plan.

'Thank you, Jack,' she said. 'You are right – I am jumping to
conclusions. What do you think we should do next?'

'Well, personally, I think it's a done deal. They are going to
have the baby whatever we say, so in a sense we have to provide
damage limitation. I am fine with the whole thing, but then I
am very much standing on the edge of this, whereas you are
going to have to deal with a daughter whom you have nurtured
and cherished for the last seventeen years leaving the nest to
make one of her own. If you are not careful, Meredith, you are
going to be left out in the cold.'

'Very succinctly put, if not very subtle,' she said. 'You certainly know how to make a girl feel good!'

'I am sorry if I am being too blunt, but that's me. Let's face it, my lover, it is your choice. It doesn't have to be a bad thing. I want you to know that the reason I am sitting here today is because, although it is a bit late in the day, I want to help. I want to accept the responsibility of being Anna's father, and to show you that you are not alone.'

He stopped and took a breath and looked away, gathering himself together. Meredith felt such a wave of longing to hold him. It was as if the last seventeen years had never been. She felt as if she knew this man through and through. He was part of her and always had been since that night they had made love. Not just because she had carried his child and given birth to Anna, but because he had touched her so deeply that night. She wanted to tell him this but it was all too late. Maybe if they managed to get through this, they could start at the beginning again ... Meredith suddenly became aware that Jack was talking.

'I have discussed it with my lady and she is happy to support me in this. Obviously it is a shock and it affects her life too ... Meredith, are you listening to me?'

She was drowning. She could hear the words, but they were like bubbles floating away from her. There was a pounding in her ears. She tried to hold on to the meaning of what he was saying to her. Lady? What lady?

'I have been seeing her for the last couple of years. As you know, I am not a man to commit, but she accepts that and we have fun and it works for us. We don't live together and she has two grown-up children so we have separate lives and meet sometimes in the middle.'

He had finished. Thank God he had finished. The cotton-wool effect in her ears started to dissolve and she leaned against the seat and managed to lift her head and look him in the eyes.

'Oh, you have a partner then.' Her voice came out as if in slow motion and Jack was swaying in front of her.

'Are you OK?' he asked. 'You have gone very pale all of a sudden.'

'Yes, I am fine. I haven't eaten for a few hours – I think I just need some food.' She managed to pull her mouth into shape. It was as if she was out of sync with everything. She must get away quickly.

Hauling herself up, she said, 'Thank you for seeing me today, I really appreciate it, and hopefully we can move forward and—'

Jack grabbed her hand. 'Whoa, steady on! We haven't finished yet, my lover. We have to discuss Myles Harrison's will.' He pulled Meredith back down into her seat. 'What's the hurry? Shall we have some lunch? I am starving. Come on, what else have you got to do this Saturday afternoon?'

'I don't know,' said Meredith dully. 'I mean, what's to talk about? I am sorry Myles is dead. Actually that is a lie. I am not particularly sorry, even though he was my natural father. But what I mean is why would he remember me in his will? My aunt did give me this incredible diamond ring, you know, just before she died. It was nine carats! I sold it and used the money to buy my house.'

'Just shut up a minute,' said Jack, 'and listen to what I have to tell you. After Pamela's funeral Myles decided he wanted to change his will and he asked me to be an executor. I wasn't very keen as it happens, because although I did a lot of business with the man, I didn't socialise with him, nor did I like many of his views on life, especially his attitude to women. I also knew the story behind your mother, don't forget, and I could see what he had done to Pamela over the years. She didn't help herself with the drinking, but I felt sorry for the woman, stuck in that marriage with a man who screwed anything that moved. Excuse my bluntness but that's the truth. So anyway, I didn't really want to be involved but eventually he persuaded me, and I am here to fulfil my promise.'

Jack cleared his throat and said, 'I don't know how you stand financially, but Myles has left you most of his estate. We are talking several million pounds.'

Meredith stared at him. 'Millions of pounds? You mean he has left me several million pounds? Me, personally?'

'Yes, and there's a letter for you, and one for your mother. Without being too nosy I suspect it has something to do with what you told me that night.'

Meredith just could not take it in. This wealth would change her life forever. But did she want that? How could she control this? What would she do? She could feel the panic rising.

'Jack, I am not sure I can cope with all this. I cannot comprehend that kind of money.'

'Believe me, my lover, you will learn,' he joked. 'The lawyers will help you. I can help you, if you want. Mind you, I will have to be careful that you don't think I am after your money.'

Meredith looked up, startled. 'What do you mean?'

'Well, just that I wouldn't want you to think I was only interested in you and Anna because of the money. I have quite sufficient funds of my own, thank you very much. But you can see how this might change your thoughts about Anna's future. Not that I am suggesting you just throw money at her, but it would mean you could help her and Tom buy a home maybe?'

Meredith was plunged back into shock again. 'Oh my goodness, this is a ridiculous conversation! I can't believe this is real, Jack. Please stop now. I need to eat something before I pass out. You can take me through it all again over lunch, step by step.'

'OK, lunch it is – but you are paying!'

They both laughed and moved into the restaurant where

Meredith proceeded to order fish and chips. There was nothing like a plate of carbs in a crisis.

By the time they had eaten lunch Meredith was back in control. She had learned that Jack's lady was called Mo; she was fifty-two and she was an accountant. *So there you go, Meredith, another dream down the tubes!* She managed to make reasonable conversation, and even talk about her new projects; in fact, it helped to block out the voice screaming at the back of her mind, *'He's gone, he's not available. You lose again. Get over yourself, Meredith Lee!'*

'The thing is,' she told Jack, 'I have put in a treatment for a TV series about buying and developing property. You know the kind of thing: someone has a dream to live in a castle or something, and we find them one that is all run down and we help them restore it, et cetera. The working title is *An Englishman's Home*. I got the idea because I want to open a spa hotel or a health farm that is like a really luxurious country-house hotel. I have been looking for the right property. Which reminds me, you turned Long Moor House into a hotel, didn't you?'

'What a memory you have,' Jack said with admiration. 'As a matter of fact, I did buy it and turned it into a hotel and leased it off. Bizarrely, it has recently come back into my sights because the people who lease it want out. They are not managing to make it pay. How weird that you should bring this up now.'

Meredith felt a flutter of excitement. 'Jack, please look into it. It could be exactly what I am after, and now I have the money to pay for it. The trouble with my project for TV was that whatever I found to develop was going to be too expensive for a private production company to fund, and what would be the point of me putting everything into the show and ending up with no property for myself at the end of it? I have so many fantastic ideas for the series, I can't tell you.'

'Hang on, slow down. One thing at a time, Meredith. Go home and put your feet up and absorb today's news. That is enough for anyone to cope with. When we meet at Harcourt House for our appointment with the lawyer on Monday I will have found out the SP on Long Moor House for you and we can have a chat. More importantly though, are you happy with the whole Anna and Tom scenario now? What is the plan?'

Meredith stopped and turned to him. 'Jack, I truly do not know how to thank you. You have helped me see everything clearly and put things into perspective – and you're right: I think Anna should go ahead with whatever she has in mind. I will ring her when I get home and arrange to see her and listen to what she has to say. I must confess I haven't given her a chance to talk to me properly. I have been too busy ranting and raving. Did you know it's her birthday next Sunday? I had been planning a birthday lunch. I don't know if it is too soon for us all to get together, but I will ask her, and maybe you and Harry would like to come – and Mo, of course,' she added.

'Let's see how you get on this week. Talk to Anna first and let's take things slowly. We all have our separate lives. I have to talk to Harry about all this as well. It will affect him in many ways.'

As they left the Royal Oak, Jack took her keys and opened the car for her. Meredith suddenly felt incredibly shy. She covered the moment with a laugh, then took a deep breath and quickly kissed Jack on the cheek. She practically threw herself into the car. He held the door a moment longer, looking at her. She started the car and promptly stalled. How embarrassing was that! He was laughing at her. She waved him off but he remained standing there until she had finally got the car in gear again and pulled away. She waved again and he turned and started to walk away. She gripped the steering wheel and gritted her teeth, and willed herself home. This was a day she would never ever forget. Not because she was suddenly a millionaire, but because she had found Jack Blatchford again and it was too late. Or was it?

By the time Meredith got home she was in a complete state of panic. For a woman who had managed to survive quite adequately for the last fifty-odd years, she was now a complete wreck. Jack had lulled her into a sense of security. This was a ridiculous premise, bearing in mind she hardly knew the man. He could be a complete bastard and a useless businessman. Maybe he really was an opportunist who had landed this gift of executing Myles Harrison's will and decided she was an easy target. Win the old bird over and take all the money. There you go, the perfect scenario!

She actually managed to make herself laugh out loud at her vivid imaginings. She looked at the clock. It was six, she should call her mother and apologise for not getting back to her yesterday. Or should she ring Anna first and make a plan? Anna first probably, as her daughter would be wondering what was going on. Had she known that Jack was going to see her today? Meredith dialled the Neil house and waited.

'Hello, Robert Neil here,' the voice said at the other end of the phone.

Meredith jumped. 'Oh hi, Robert, how are you? It's Meredith here. Is my wayward daughter around?'

'Sorry, Meredith, she and Tom went out about an hour ago and I have no idea when they are expected back. May I take a message?'

'No, that's OK. I will catch up with them later, I expect. Have a lovely weekend. Bye.' Meredith hung up before Robert could respond; she was in no mood to make small talk. She dialled her mother's number then went into the living room, sat on the sofa and put her feet up.

'Hi Mum, how are you?' she asked as the phone was picked up.

'Well hello, stranger. I thought you had deserted me.' Jane pretended outrage. 'How are you, dear?'

'I'm really sorry I didn't ring you back yesterday, Mum, but I had a hell of a day, and I was so tired by the time I got home I just went to bed. Rather a lot has happened this week and I am not sure where to begin. Are you busy or can you talk?' Meredith was trying to remember her mother's routine on a Saturday night.

'No, I have just had some tea with Jenny and Frank and their two, then I was going to settle down and watch some TV,' Jane informed her daughter. 'So, come on then, tell me what has been going on up there.'

'First things first.' Meredith cleared her throat. 'There's no easy way to tell you this, Mum. Anna is pregnant.'

There was a sharp intake of breath. 'Dear Lord, how is she, bless her heart?'

'She's absolutely fine. She and Tom, do you remember him? Well, they are determined to have the baby and live happily ever after.'

'I take it from your tone that you don't approve?' Her mother never missed a trick.

'Um, that was my initial reaction I must confess, but since then I have had time to consider all the options and I am coming round to accepting that there are pros and cons to this situation. Of course, I am desperately disappointed that her schoolwork is going to suffer and she won't be going to university any time soon, but then again ...'

'Maybe she is happy?' her mother interjected. 'You know, Meredith, we are all different and we all need different things in life.'

'Yes, but Mum, this is not what she chose, is it? This is one of those things that happen and we find our lives changing overnight. God knows, you and I have both been faced with that dilemma. Do you not think it is an unfortunate recurrence in our family? Sorry, but it must occur to you that this is the fourth generation of unwanted pregnancy.' Meredith had not meant to go down this route but it was too late now.

Her mother replied softly, 'Though in this case, it may be a surprise to Anna, but it seems this baby is not unwanted, nor is Anna in the position of having to face her situation alone. This time we have a young woman who seems to be in love with the father of her child, and he with her.'

Touché, thought Meredith. 'Point taken and beautifully made, Mother,' she said aloud.

'Have you talked to her about other options like adoption?' asked Jane.

'A bit, but to be honest I reacted rather badly and she has gone to stay with Tom and his parents.' Meredith felt slightly foolish admitting this to her mother.

'Oh Meredith dear, you must learn to think before you open your mouth. So what is the situation now then? Are you speaking to each other or not?'

'Well, I just tried to ring her but she is out. The thing is, Mum, I have another confession to make. I am not sure I should be doing this over the telephone but you need to know everything before you come up next weekend. You are still coming, aren't you?'

'Of course, if it is still on,' said Jane. 'Goodness knows what might have happened before next weekend at this rate! Come on, spill the beans. What else is there?'

'I got a call from Jack Blatchford.' Meredith paused, expecting her mother to react but there was silence at the other end of the line. 'Are you still there?' she asked.

'Yes. I am waiting for you to continue,' Jane replied.

'Oh right. Well, it's bizarre, but ...' Meredith poured out her news in a stream of incomprehensible babble.

'Stop! For goodness' sake, calm down,' Jane implored. 'What are you trying to tell me? Myles has left you some money?'

'Not just some money, millions of money, I mean pounds! Mum, we are rich!'

'Meredith, please calm down. I can't take this all in. Are you sure? Who arranged this?'

'Jack Blatchford was appointed Myles's executor. He didn't want to be, but Myles eventually wore him down. I have got to go to the lawyer's offices on Monday to sign the papers. There is also a letter for you. It is unbelievable, Mum. He has left the bulk of his estate to me. Jack has offered to help me buy some property, but that is another issue. We also have the matter of Anna's parentage. Unbeknownst to me, she managed to persuade Oliver to tell her who her real father was; she then found out where he lived and presented herself to him.' Meredith ran a hand through her hair. 'It has been an unbelievable two days, Mum. I don't know where or how to begin to sort it all out.'

'Well, Anna is the most important issue,' said her mother. 'Your daughter's happiness and welfare are all that counts.'

'Yes, of course, Mum. I know that, and I will sit down with her and talk it all through.'

'Good. Well, try not to make any hasty decisions. Life is precious, Meredith, and there are lots of lives that will be affected here. You need to discuss matters with everyone concerned. I am sure you will eventually reach the right decisions. I love you, dear, and look forward to seeing you at the weekend.'

Meredith smiled to herself and put the phone down. Just then, she heard a key in the door and turned to see Anna and Tom appear.

'Oh hello, Mum. I thought you might be out.' Anna looked sheepish.

'So you thought you would pop round and avoid seeing me, is that it? No, don't bother to answer that. Listen, I have been trying to call you to apologise. I am so sorry I over-reacted to everything, Anna. But it was such a shock. Please come in and don't worry, we are not going to row about it any more. Hello Tom.'

Meredith went to him and gave him a hug. He looked taken aback and just stood there. Anna rushed to her mum and hugged her.

'Oh Mum, I am so pleased you understand. I hate it when we have an argument. I know it is hard for you and everything, but we will be responsible and cope with this, I promise.'

Pity you were not more responsible sooner and had taken precautions, thought Meredith. She said, 'Well, we just have to make the best of it. So what are you two up to tonight then?'

'We are going to see a friend of Tom's at the King's Head in Islington in a new play. Do you want to come with us? It won't be a problem,' Anna said.

Meredith shook her head. 'No, thanks. It is very sweet of you to ask, but I am whacked out with all the excitement in this family and I have a great deal of work to do. Will you be coming back here tonight?'

'Well, we had planned to stay at Tom's because you were a bit, well, you know.' Anna stopped.

'I know, don't worry. Anna, I think you should have a check-up, don't you? I will make an appointment for us to see Doctor Silverman early next week. You have to be sensible now, my girl. You are going to be a mother.' Meredith forced herself to smile reassuringly at her daughter though she felt anything but reassured herself. She was terrified. 'We were going to the pub tomorrow for lunch to meet up with Penny and Griff and Millie to make holiday plans. Do you still want to do that, or shall we leave it for a bit until we know all is well in the baby department?'

'OK, let's leave it. I'll call Millie and cancel. She will understand – she has been so worried about me.' Once more, Anna looked sheepish.

Meredith smiled. 'I am sure she has. Millie is your oldest friend, after all.'

'It all feels so weird, Mum.' Anna came and put her arms round Meredith.

'I know, it is all a bit overwhelming.' Meredith saw Tom looking uncomfortable in the doorway. 'Come on, Tom, come and have a group hug. You must be feeling pretty weird yourself.'

After a moment, Meredith gently moved away so that Anna and Tom were left in an embrace together. As she made her way into the kitchen she called over her shoulder, 'When in doubt, put the kettle on. I will see you guys later.'

She stood in the middle of the kitchen and listened for the sound of the front door closing and then let out a long sigh and sank onto a chair. She was so tired all of a sudden. After a few minutes, she got up and made herself a cup of tea and sat at the kitchen table. Picking up the newspaper and skimming the front page, a small column caught her eye.

This week at the London Clinic in St John's Wood, multi-millionaire Myles Harrison died in his sleep, aged 81. He was a well-known figure in the City, with companies including Harrison Estates Ltd and Overseas Property Consultants Ltd. It is expected that his long-time business associate Jack Blatchford will continue running the companies, already owning a 50 per cent share and possibly taking over the remains of the business. Myles Harrison had no immediate family as his wife Pamela died in 1984 of cancer and his only daughter died of a heroin overdose.

The article went on to give a brief history of how Myles had made his fortune.

Meredith raised her eyebrows. Well, that answered any doubts as to whether Jack was after her money. He seemed to have plenty of his own, as he had suggested. And now so did she! It was beyond comprehension. She was a millionaire!

Her Grandmother Mary's voice wafted through her consciousness: *Jesus loves you* . . .

Chapter Twenty

Monday morning found Meredith sitting in the reception of Hanson & Hill Solicitors. It was a very impressive building with a huge glass atrium. The two girls on the front desk were like racehorse fillies, they were so well bred. Probably belonged to some of the partners, thought Meredith; keep it in the family. She was feeling incredibly nervous and inadequate for some reason. In fact, she felt like a fraud!

When Jack appeared through the huge revolving doors, she breathed a sigh of relief. There was a quality in Jack that was so positive it was infectious. He made her feel that she could do anything.

He kissed her on the cheek and said, 'Morning, Ms Lee, how are you doing?'

'I feel ridiculously nervous for some reason, as if I shouldn't be here, and that I am going to be found out,' she confessed.

'Found out for what? Don't be daft, you are on the receiving end today. This is your big day, girl. Enjoy!'

He left her and went across to 'les girls' and gave them some instructions. They fluttered and twittered like sparrows, and next thing, he and Meredith were in a glass lift rising up through the atrium at an unnerving speed.

'It's like being in *Star Wars*,' Meredith giggled.

The lift doors purred open and they walked across to another reception desk. The lady behind this was definitely the mother of all thoroughbreds, thought Meredith.

'Good morning, Mr Blatchford. Mr Hanson is expecting you, please follow me.' She went over to an enormous door, knocked and entered. Holding the door open, she announced, 'Mr Blatchford and Ms Lee to see you, Mr Hanson.' She ushered them through and swirled out with a whiff of Chanel No. 5.

Mr Hanson was a tiny little man in a pinstriped suit, with huge black-framed glasses that made him look like an owl. Meredith had been expecting someone big and imposing to match the surroundings!

'Good morning, Jack, Ms Lee – a pleasure to meet you. Please have a seat.' He indicated two leather armchairs either side of a coffee table on which stood a silver tray with coffee and tea, and china cups and saucers. 'Please help yourselves to tea and coffee.'

Meredith did the honours then sat down. It was like sitting in front of a Headmaster, she thought, stifling a giggle as an image came into her head of tiny Mr Hanson being chased round his desk by the very tall secretary outside. Spanking extra! She bit her lip and concentrated on her coffee.

'I believe Mr Blatchford has already informed you that you are the major beneficiary of Myles Harrison's last will and testament. Is that the case, Ms Lee?' The little man peered at Meredith through his glasses, which made his eyes look huge.

'Oh yes. Yes, he has told me,' she stammered.

'I should inform you that there are also two letters he wished us to give to you and your mother, Mrs Jane Lee – is that correct?'

'Yes,' Meredith replied, quietly now.

'In addition, there are several items of jewellery and some artworks that are listed specifically, which are to go to you and your mother and daughter, Anna Lee; the rest are to be divided amongst the household staff. In the matter of all his business assets and corporate finance, Mr Harrison has bequeathed the total sum to his business partner, Mr Blatchford. There is an apartment in Paris to be left in perpetuity to a Mademoiselle Lamarr.' Mr Hanson paused here for effect. 'I have no doubt you will deal with this matter privately.'

Meredith interrupted, 'Who is Mademoiselle Lamarr?'

'A friend of Mr Harrison's – an intimate friend, you might say.' Mr Hanson was actually smirking. Dirty little man, thought Meredith. God, the old boys' club, eh? They were all at it. Poor Aunt Pamela.

'Please go on,' she said coolly, and had the satisfaction of seeing the man adjust his face into a more appropriate expression for reading a will.

'There are various other properties listed here, as well as the financial assets, and stocks and shares. In the matter of inheritance tax, should you be concerned, this has all been dealt with accordingly. We have taken the liberty of liaising with Mr Harrison's accountants, Lowe & Sons, who will be providing you with a detailed audit of the accounts for your attention, so it only remains for me to ask for your signature on the final paperwork – and then you may go.'

Mr Hanson stood up and turned a leather pad round to face Meredith on the desk. He then passed her an impossibly expensive Mont Blanc fountain pen with which to sign the papers. She felt the weight of the gold pen in her hand, and it was like a reminder of how different life would be in the land of money.

She signed and passed the pen back across the desk to Mr Hanson, who took it to write his signature alongside her own. His writing, she noted, was tiny and precise.

'Well, that's it, then,' said Jack. 'Thank you very much, Richard. I look forward to our next encounter, which should be to secure the Malaysian project. I am hoping to go out there in the next few weeks. It is such a pity that Myles did not live to see that come to fruition. He was so proud of the project.'

'Yes indeed, such a pity. Well, thank you, Ms Lee, for coming in, and if Hanson and Hill can be of any further assistance, please do not hesitate to get in touch. Here is my card.' He handed Meredith a business card with gold embossed lettering on it.

Meredith took the card and shook his hand, saying, 'Thank you so much Mr Hanson. Goodbye.' She couldn't wait to get out of the place.

Jack followed her to the lift, muttering under his breath, 'Slow down, you are not in a race!'

She got in the lift, and as the doors shut, let out a huge sigh of relief. 'God, that was something else, Jack! I mean, there he was, handing me these millions without a word. The only time he registered any expression was when he mentioned Mademoiselle Lamarr, and I assumed from his sly expression that she was Myles's mistress. Nasty little man.'

They were outside now in the sunshine and Meredith was already feeling much better.

'God, I don't know what to do, laugh or cry,' she said.

'I think most people would be laughing, my lover,' said Jack. 'Come on, let's go and celebrate with a glass of wine at the Ritz.' He hailed a cab and bundled Meredith inside.

Later, as they toasted her good fortune, Meredith was brought back to earth with a bump when Jack said, 'So, what are we going to do about Anna and Tom?'

'Well, I can buy them a flat now,' she replied.

'Now hold on a minute. That is exactly what I was worried about. Meredith, can I offer you some advice?' Jack looked serious.

'Go on,' she said.

'Well firstly, it is not a great idea to tell everyone about your inheritance.'

322

'Anna is not everyone, and she needs a flat,' said Meredith.

'But does she really? She is on the cusp of seventeen, Meredith. She should be at home with you, at least until she has had the baby and everything is sorted out. What about Tom and his parents? What would they think if you steam in, all guns blazing, buying flats and telling them all how to live their lives? Just stop and think. You need to really take stock of where you want to go with all this. Look, I'm aware you don't know me very well but I do know a bit about property, and stocks and shares, and what I don't know, a good lawyer and accountant will do. Why not just keep it all under your hat for the time being until you have talked it through with an accountant. There's no hurry, for goodness' sake.'

Meredith knew he was right, but she said, 'That's all very well, but I've told my mum already. I couldn't keep something like that from her, and my brother needs to know because I want to help him. He has been going through a really hard time this last year. They are broke, basically. I can help them now.'

'Well fine, help your brother by all means, but you don't have to tell them just how much you have inherited. Just explain that Myles has left you money and the letters.'

'Oh yes, the letters. I had forgotten about them.' Meredith got them out of her bag. She took the one addressed to her, tore it open and read out loud:

Dear Meredith,

When you read this I will be dead. 'Good riddance' I hear you say. Well, that's as maybe. When we had our discussion at Pamela's funeral you made quite an impression on me. Apart from the fact that you brought me devastating news about yourself and your daughter, I was forced to face things about

323

myself that might never have come to the fore, but for you. It is not easy for anyone to accept their faults, especially when they are as serious as mine. Words will never be enough to compensate for my actions in the past, but I can try to make some recompense for the future, for you and my granddaughter.

I am consumed with regret that I shall never know the joy of watching Anna grow up. I lost Sylvia first and thought my heart would break. Yes, believe it or not, I have a heart! Maybe not a romantic one, but certainly my paternal instincts were all intact. I think they were numbed by my daughter's untimely death, and were obviously never going to be brought to life again, even with the knowledge that I had another daughter. I suppose I deserve this punishment for other things I have done in my life.

But enough, I am not a sentimental man: it does not go with the territory. I leave you my wealth because you are my sole heir. What you do with it is your business. I had hoped you might rekindle your friendship with Jack Blatchford, whom I regard as a son. He is a man of complete honesty and integrity, and he would be able to guide you through the pitfalls of handling a fortune. However, I would ask that you make sure that Anna is taken care of in the future. Perhaps you could set up a trust? I apologise for trying to rule from the grave. It is my nature to control.

Please do not be shocked by the mention of my mistress Mademoiselle Lamarr. A leopard will never change its spots even at my ripe old age. She has brought me a great deal of pleasure and should enjoy some security until she dies. Kindly respect my wishes in this instance and leave her in peace in the Place de l'Opera in Paris.

Thank you for reading this, and thank you for listening to me that day at the funeral. I have a feeling you are quite a

remarkable woman, Meredith, and I would like to think there
is a small chip off the old block in there somewhere.
    I wish you a long and a happy life, and will do my best to
watch over you and Anna. Be it from heaven or hell.

Myles Harrison

Meredith folded the letter and slipped it back into the envelope.

'Well, that is quite a letter,' said Jack quietly. 'I know you think he was a monster but it's hard for me, because I did work with him for many years, and he was quite a formidable character. He taught me so much about business. But I guess that is not enough, is it?'

Meredith looked at him and smiled sadly. 'No, it is not enough. All the money in the world does not make it right to dismiss other human beings, to have so little respect for them that you violate their very souls. I understand what you are saying, Jack, but God forbid if you had an ounce of admiration for Myles the husband and father, rather than Myles the property magnate, we would not be sitting here together.'

'I understand,' said Jack, holding her gaze. 'Let's drink up and forget Myles. He has done his stuff, now it's your turn, and with the kind of money you have got, you can change the world, my lover.' He threw back the last of the champagne and called for the bill.

'Where are you off to now?' asked Meredith.

'Didn't you tell me earlier you had to go and face some TV executives?' he said.

'Oh blimey, yes of course, what am I thinking? Look at the time! I am late already. I need a cab now.' She was grabbing her bag and stumbling to the door of the Ritz as she spoke.

Jack called after her, 'Ring me when you have finished with them. Maybe we can have dinner?'

But Meredith had gone. Out she went, through the revolving doors, and into Piccadilly, arms flailing as she tried to hail a cab. Meredith Lee, millionairess.

Meredith sat in the cab trying to get her thoughts together. Never mind Myles and his millions, she had to secure this bloody deal. It meant a lot to her, that she did this on her own merit. OK, she would never have to work again, but that was not the issue. She wanted this deal to go through to prove a point to the powers-that-be at the Network. She was a woman and she was over fifty. Two things that did not work in her favour, but she was going to win this battle.

With that thought in her head, she stormed into the studio. She reached the top floor of the twenty-six-storey building and bumped straight into Marcus, who was flapping.

'Oh, thank heavens you are here!' he squeaked. 'I thought you weren't coming, after all. Meredith, you will be the death of me, you really will. Has something happened? You look a bit flushed.'

'Marcus, stop panicking – I am fine. Where are we meeting, in the boss's office or the boardroom?'

'They are all in his office at the moment, but I—' He was left in mid-sentence as Meredith made a beeline for the MD's office. She knocked on the door but did not wait for a response.

'Good morning,' Meredith said breezily. 'I am so sorry I am late, the traffic was terrible. Shall we get down to business? I don't want to hold you up before you go to lunch.' She sat down and proceeded to get out her portfolio.

David Gilbraith, the head of the Network, was a smooth operator. He was young for the job, in his mid-forties, and had worked his way up from the studio floor, literally, as he had started life as a floor manager. He was handsome in a bland sort of way, clean cut and well-dressed, but not too trendy. He never appeared without a shirt and tie.

326

'Good morning, Meredith – or should I say good afternoon?' He glanced at his watch. 'It is always a pleasure to see you. You know Sheila, of course, and Keith. So yes, let's get on then. As you are aware, the Network is concerned about the ratings for all afternoon programming, not just *Meredith Lee at Three*. However, we have been looking at a couple of alternatives for your slot and we do feel it is time for a change. So we are going to introduce a new programme called *Girl Time* directed at our younger mums – the stay-at-home mums with small babies – you know the kind of thing?' He paused and waited for any comments. Meredith could think of nothing she would want to say that was not a swearword so she kept quiet.

David was forced to continue. 'So, sadly, Meredith, it is with great regret that I have to inform you that we will not be renewing your present contract. However, we are very keen to pursue your treatment for a series called *An Englishman's Home*. This really is a very exciting concept and we would like to commission a series of six to be made in-house, with a view to airing them on a weekday at two p.m.' He seemed very pleased with himself and looked round the table for affirmation of his beneficence. There was a good deal of nodding from his minions.

Meredith allowed the room to settle and then delivered her bombshell.

'Thank you, David, I appreciate the offer. However, I do not appreciate the thoughts behind taking my show off the air. The ratings are not down for my show, as well you know. It caters to a demographic that is vital to television because it will only grow in numbers as the years go on. Did you know that by the year 2012, half the population of the UK will be over fifty? That is a hell of a lot of people watching afternoon television, don't you think? Why on earth do you want to cater for young mums who are usually out in the afternoons collecting their older children from school?'

Meredith took a breath, but no one interrupted her as she continued: 'Is it not the truth, that you are foolishly listening to your advertising and marketing mentors who want you to chase young money? I say again: who has the money these days? It is not the twenty-somethings any more, it is the baby-boomers – my generation. We are the ones who are going to be footing the bills. Believe me, I have statistics here to show you, although I don't have time right now because I have programmes to make. Though not for you, it would appear.'

Meredith stared round at them all. 'I have decided to go to Channel Seven, who have offered me a five-year plan to make three major series for them, one being a twelve-part series of *An Englishman's Home*, to be shown at seven thirty p.m. on Sunday nights starting in the autumn, so as you can imagine, I am keen to get started. Thank you for the last six years, it has been a lot of fun. Goodbye, and good luck – and do give Tracey the weather girl a kiss from me!'

Meredith waved a farewell as she left a room full of TV executives catching flies.

She took the lift to the ground floor and hastened across to the make-up room to find Pattie. She had a show to do today, and the rest of the week to get through, before she could finally leave this place. She found Pattie ready and waiting

'Well, look who just flew in!' Pattie announced. 'How are you, Meredith, my little diva? I thought you had fallen by the wayside over the weekend, and had decided to desert us. Not that you would, you are far too professional. But you look positively blooming. What gives?' she asked as she put a make-up gown round Meredith's shoulders.

'I have been given the elbow, Pattie. We have been made redundant.'

'Well, fuck a duck!' said Pattie. 'Why? When?'

'Just now,' Meredith told her. 'They will not be renewing my contract, so when we finish this season on Friday, that is it, girl, we are gone!'

'I can't believe it,' said Pattie.

'Believe it, dear.' Marcus made his entrance into the make-up room. 'The end is nigh. I cannot believe you, Meredith. You might at least have warned me. When did you plan all this, you witch?' he whined.

Meredith laughed. 'I am truly sorry, Marcus, I just did not have time. Channel Seven only came back to me first thing this morning. I mean, obviously we have been in negotiations for a while, but I couldn't say anything to you until I knew for sure, and then I got so mad with them all on Friday when we met that when Channel Seven rang and gave me the green light this morning, I am afraid it all came out just now. David Gilbraith was just looking so smug!' she said crossly.

'But how did you know about Tracey?' he screamed in delight.

'Who is Tracey?' asked Pattie, looking confused.

'Tracey Field, that weather girl in the mornings? Well, she is going to front this new show that is replacing *Meredith Lee at Three* called *Girl Time*, but it hasn't been announced yet. No one knows. How did you do it, Meredith?' Marcus was beside himself with glee.

'Just an educated guess,' she beamed. 'That's showbiz! Now let's look at today's script and get things moving. We are going to make the shows this week the best ever, OK? I am really sorry I didn't keep you in the loop, but I knew you would be all right, and as for you, Pattie, well I hope you will come with me? I will get you more money.'

'You know me, Meredith honey. Where there's wedge, there's a way!'

After the show Meredith went to her dressing room and worked with Marcus on the rest of the week's scripts. There were various themes that they chose between them, and then they discussed guests. If they wanted a particular actor or writer, or whatever, the celebrity booker would check their availability and come back to them with a Yes or No. Meredith preferred to have someone from the general public with something of interest to say than some pop star who was as thick as two short planks, and she would always go for a good discussion about a human interest story, rather than idle gossip. This was obviously not a popular concept these days, she realised now, but she was not going to sacrifice her integrity for a section of the public who didn't know any better.

She discussed the final show with Marcus in detail, and they decided she would go out with a bang, and announce it on air. Marcus had told her that the bosses did not want any big deal made about her leaving because they were worried about the press. Meredith was very popular with the media; they had respect for her because she didn't bullshit and she always tried to work with them. Well, this was a great story and Meredith wanted to get the most out of it. Although Marcus would still be working for the Network he loved a drama and was all for it. So they swore each other to secrecy and parted company.

Meredith then took a cab to her agent's office to meet her new employers. She knew exactly what she was going to do for the next five years. She had a writer working on a new cookery show with Oliver. Then there was *An Englishman's Home*, and finally she had commissioned a new chat-show format for herself in which she interviewed stars about their favourite charity, finding out why they supported it. The programme would show the charity during the first half, and talk to various people involved with it, and the second half would feature the well-known person being interviewed. She hoped it would help charities raise their profile, and also give a fresh slant to celebrity interviews and get the stars to open up more about themselves, because it would not just be gossipy stuff, or flog-ging their latest book or film or whatever.

She had formed her new production company, called Fifty Plus, last year and was very proud of the fact that they had achieved all this in a year. God knows what could be done now she had her own finance.

Meredith literally floated up the steps to her agent's office and rang the bell. She must savour these moments forever, as she knew it might never be as good as this again.

Chapter Twenty-One

The next few days before the party were crammed with activity. Poor Anna was having terrible morning sickness. Meredith would leave the house every morning to the dulcet tones of her daughter puking in the toilet. She could only give her a hug and assure her that it would pass. Meredith was full on with the final week of her show, and didn't have much time for anything else, but one development had stopped her in her tracks. Jack had suggested she go with him and Mo to Malaysia, to research an amazing spa resort out there which had just opened.

'You will be able to see first-hand just how to do it,' he said. 'This place is the dog's bollocks!' Meredith had laughed at his quaint turn of phrase and said she would think about it – meaning No. She didn't want to be a gooseberry, thank you very much!

'Well, hurry up about it,' he warned her, 'because I need to get out there soon, to sort this deal that Myles and I have set up.'

She could do with a break, Meredith thought. The show would be finished – and what better way to get over the end of six years of her life than to take off to foreign climes? She mentioned it to Anna, who gave her a very funny look and said, 'Mum, is there something you want to tell me?'

'No, don't be so ridiculous. Jack and I are friends, that's all, as well as being your father. He is taking his woman, for goodness' sake! But he is trying to help me with this programme I shall be making. Don't keep looking at me like that, you little minx. Go and be sick!' Meredith had laughed it off, but actually she was trying very hard not to think too much about her motives or his, for that matter. She had shoved all such thoughts into the drawer.

The most difficult conversation she had had to deal with was the one with her mother about the money – and the letter. She decided it was better to discuss it before Jane arrived at the weekend for Anna's birthday, so she rang her again as soon as she could after her meeting with Mr Hanson. Her mother still seemed to be in shock about the whole thing.

'Oh dear, why has he done this? Will we never be free of him?' she said bitterly. 'I just wish you didn't have to take the money, Meredith. Do you have to do so?'

Meredith hadn't told her mother exactly how much money was involved, just that it was a quite substantial inheritance.

'I do understand how you must feel, but I would be mad not to take it,' she told her gently. 'Think about Anna's future. What Myles did to you can never be forgiven, Mum, nothing can ever make that right, but at least we can use the money to help us for the future. I can help Frank for one thing,' she added.

'Goodness! Frank is much too proud to take anything from you, Meredith. You know what he is like,' Jane said.

'True, but between you and me, Jack is helping me with a project involving Frank and Jenny that will be so good, and make so much sense to Frank, he will have to agree. Trust me,' Meredith replied.

When she had spoken on the phone to Jack and mentioned that she wanted to help her brother, he had reminded her of what he had said to her at the very beginning, about not telling too many people about her money. They had agreed she would tell her mother about the inheritance, but not how much, but that she would say nothing to Anna for the time being. It was too delicate a situation with Tom and his parents. The couple were, indeed, very young; better to leave things as they were until after the baby was born. Frank posed a more complicated problem, because the family farm was in need of some serious dough being spent on it, and there was no way he would accept a hand-out from his sister, even if she had inherited millions! Jack had suggested that maybe Frank would sell the farm and he could be the anonymous buyer, but Meredith told him there was absolutely no way Frank would sell Malthouse Farm, even if he was on his death-bed.

'That's a No then, I take it,' Jack chuckled. 'OK, leave it with me. I am going up to Hertfordshire at the end of this week to look at some property, so I will see what's around and have a think. By the by, I could pick up your mum from Burslet and bring her here for the party. Would that help?'

'Oh Jack, that would be fantastic! Thank you so much.' She was delighted that Jack had agreed to come to the party on Sunday and that he would only bring Harry. He had thought it best to leave Mo out of the equation for the time being. Meredith thought that was sensible. The situation was so new to all of them, and Mo wasn't really part of the family.

It would be quite a celebration in their household. Anna was seventeen, and a mum-to-be. Meredith and Jack had met again after nearly thirteen years, and would be in the same room as their daughter for the very first time! And Meredith was a secret millionaire. She had mild feelings of unease about yet another secret in the drawer, but Jack had assured her it was for the best all round. Life was complicated enough at the moment. For once he approved of the drawer!

In between appearing every afternoon on her show and trying to put a team together for the new series, Meredith had hardly had a moment to discuss anything with Oliver, who was in charge of the catering for the party, including supplying the birthday cake. He rang Meredith one morning at the crack of dawn.

'Why so early, you mad man?' croaked Meredith, who was awake but not quite compos mentis.

'Because it is the only way I know I will get you. Honestly, you flounce off into the night, full of wine with my other half, and I don't hear from you again. What is going on?' He feigned annoyance.

'Olly, precious, I am so sorry but you have no idea what has gone on this week. I promise I will sit down and tell you all, but first things first: Anna's party. Are you all sorted?'

'Well, yes, I am, but are we going to be all right on the night? Are you on speaking terms with your offspring?'

'Oh yes! Everything has been agreed. I have apologised, swallowed my pride and admitted defeat. Jack made me see the error of my ways and—'

'Jack? Did you say Jack, as in Blatchford Jack, father of your child?' Oliver demanded.

'Um, yes.' Meredith was suddenly uncertain as to how this would go down with Oliver. 'We met and talked and agreed it was better all round if Anna and Tom could be allowed to get on with their lives, while we would support them as much as we could. As I say, I have been made to see the error of my ways. I am really sorry I have not had a chance to discuss everything with you.'

There was a pause then Oliver said, 'Listen, Meredith, I am just happy that you and Anna have made it up. A girl needs her mother. Well done. So it will be Happy Families on Sunday then. How many are we going to be again?'

'Eleven – say twelve to be on the safe side. Is that OK?'

'*Naturellement.* I am going to cook a whole salmon with new potatoes and lots of salads and garlic bread and homemade mayonnaise. Then we will have fresh strawberries to go with the cake, which is a kind of chocolate mousse thing. It is very rich and a new creation of mine. Will you order in the drink? Lots of pink champagne for me, please! OK, so Michael and I will be round about ten in the morning. Have you picked up the present yet, by the way?' They were giving Anna a mobile phone from all of them.

'Oh Christ no, I haven't! Don't worry, I will do it on my way home this afternoon. They did ring and say it was in the store.'

'Lovely. Good luck for today, by the way, Merry. It's your last show, isn't it?' he said.

'How did you know that? It is supposed to be a secret,' she wailed.

'Secret? It's the end of the season, is it not?'

'Oh yes, I see what you mean. Actually, Olly, it is the end-end. *Finito. Kaput!* I was fired, can you believe it? But before you swallow your apron, it is all good because I have a whole new career starting at Channel Seven. I haven't got time to tell you all the goss now, but believe me it is all good.'

'What about my series?' he butted in. 'You promised you would make me a star!'

'And you will be, it has all been agreed. The offer will be winging its way to you pronto. A star is born! Twinkle fucking twinkle! See you on Sunday!' Meredith put down the phone and lay back on the pillows. Just another five minutes to let the face settle and she would be ready to go!

Pattie was waiting for her when she got to the studio.

'I thought we might do false eyelashes today as it is your last appearance,' she said, holding said lashes between her thumb and forefinger like big spiders. 'How are you feeling, Diva dear?' she asked.

'Nervous,' replied Meredith. She had hardly slept a wink, there was so much going round in her head. She closed her eyes and let Pattie work her magic while she went through the script for today. They had a very well-known celebrity coming on who had written her first novel. 'Written'? That was a joke, as all the woman had done was speak into a tape-recorder; some poor ghost-writer had done all the hard work. Talk about trade descriptions! Meredith had plans to bring this up. It was about time the public understood some of the cons that went on in this business.

They also had a strand about hormone replacement therapy which Meredith was particularly interested in, considering the moment was fast approaching when she would be requiring some help in the hot flush department. She had been to the doctor recently, and when he had asked her about panic attacks and feeling nervy and unable to cope, she had burst out laughing. Well, that was the norm in Meredith's life!

She and Marcus had decided to finish the show with a live rendition of a Peggy Lee song 'I'm a Woman' sung in the studio by the latest hot property, Toni Braxton. They thought that Meredith should come off the back of that and make her farewells. Goodnight, sweetheart!

Pattie was finished and sent her packing, and Marcus joined her in her dressing room to put the final touches to the show. They were like naughty school children plotting her exit.

'I can't wait to see their reaction,' snickered Marcus. 'Can you imagine Keith's face? Smacked arse is not in it!'

'Sheila will look like she is sucking a lemon or two,' Meredith giggled. 'Oh Marcus, I will miss you. Promise me if you decide to leave, you will let me know. We will always find you a place with us.'

She gave him a hug, and then shooed him out, so she could change. Six years was a long time and she would definitely miss the buzz. Still, I could be on a slow boat to China next week, she thought to herself. Well, Malaysia anyway. She was having an early dinner with Jack because he wanted to tell her his plan for her brother Frank. He was due back this afternoon and was dropping her mother off at the house, where Anna had promised to look after her and get her some tea.

Right, she was ready to go. She walked into the studio and stood at the side listening to the audience chatting. The sound man came and fixed her microphone and she gave him a hug too and thanked him. She had had silver pens engraved for everyone in the crew, and all the production team, and they had all come up at some point to say a fond farewell. At this rate she wouldn't last the show without bursting into tears, and she did not want to do that. The warm-up man was telling his usual terrible jokes and whipping the audience into a frenzy of indifference! She smiled to herself and walked to the back to make her entrance.

'Five seconds studio,' the voice of the director sounded in her ear. 'Three two one, go music go titles go Meredith, and good luck, babes.' Dear Jo, her director, was a good friend as well as a colleague.

'Ladies and gentlemen, please welcome your hostess with the mostess – Meredith Lee!' And she was down the steps and smiling to camera one.

'Hello and welcome everyone to *Meredith Lee at Three*. Today's show is the last of the series . . .'

'Aah . . .' the audience performed perfectly with their group sigh.

'. . . but before we go, we have a packed show for you today.'

The next hour went like clockwork and Meredith performed effortlessly. The MD David Gilbraith had the show on in his office high above on the twenty-sixth floor. There was no doubt that Meredith Lee knew her stuff. Pity they had to let her go, but no doubt in a couple of years she would be back doing a strand on feeling fab at fifty. Suddenly, he leaned forward in his leather chair and turned the sound up.

What the hell was happening?

'So, ladies and gentlemen, I am sorry to say that I will not be coming back next season. I have been replaced by a younger model – but that's showbiz. I wish you all a happy summer, and remember, ladies, like it says in the song, 'I'm a WOMAN'. Take it away, Toni Braxton! Goodbye and thank you to everyone who has worked with me on the show for the last six years. Goodbye!'

The camera cut swiftly to Toni Braxton who was trying to sing above the noise of a booing studio audience. The control room was buzzing: no one could believe what they had just seen.

Meredith ran from the studio, picked up her bag and left through the back entrance of the studio car park. She was not ready to face the press just yet. Let things die down over the weekend, and come Monday she would put out a statement. She got in the waiting car and set off for the Ivy, where Niko the superb maître d' would be waiting for her with a glass of champagne. She felt sad yet exhilarated. It was the end of an era in more ways than one. And the best was yet to come, she just knew it.

She walked into the Ivy and Niko greeted her with his film star smile.

'Good evening, Meredith. Been causing a bit of a stir this afternoon, I see. You were superb, a real Pro – we were all cheering for you.'

Meredith took the proffered glass of bubbly and hugged him. 'Thank you, Niko. Is Mr Blatchford here yet?' She looked around the bar as Niko took her arm and escorted her through into the restaurant.

'He is already waiting for you at table four as requested.'

Meredith loved table four because she could watch everyone in the room without them seeing her looking.

Jack stood up as she approached the table and delivered a mock bow. 'Your Majesty, Queen of Daytime TV, always a pleasure.' He kissed her hand with a flourish and sat her down. She was laughing out loud. He made her laugh so much, it was a fantastic feeling.

'Oh shut up, you numpty!' She was even using his expressions now.

'Well, that's it, girl, you are done for good with three o'clock. How do you feel?' he asked.

'Good.' She looked him in the eye. 'No, really, I feel fine. Thank you, Jack.'

'Don't thank me, what have I done?'

'Made me feel invincible. And it has nothing to do with the money either. Did you pick up my mum?' She deftly changed the subject to something a little less emotional.

'I did indeed, and we had a very pleasant hour or so, with a pit stop for a cup of tea and a pee. She is a lovely woman, is Jane, and very bright,' said Jack, his eyes twinkling naughtily.

'What did she say?' Meredith was immediately on her guard.

'Oh, just this and that. She told me what you were like as a little girl – you know, all those embarrassing things that mothers talk about.' He chuckled. 'Oh, don't look so worried, Meredith. She didn't give away any trade secrets.' He then produced a brochure which he handed to her. 'Now take a look at this, my lover. This could be the answer to your prayers. It's that big house and estate bordering your farm. Do you remember it from your childhood?'

'Yes, of course – Marsh Hall. It belonged to the village squire. We always had the village fete in the grounds every year. It's a beautiful house, and there is a lake as well. I think the estate is about two thousand acres. What about it, anyway?'

'The owner has died and the relatives can't afford to run it – they're not interested. So it is going to auction. I had a tip-off that it might be coming on the market. Obviously it is just the sort of thing I am usually interested in, so I was pleased when an old mate of mine rang to see if I was up for it. However, it struck me that this could be exactly what you want for your country-house spa or health farm and hotel, or whatever you call it. But,' Jack took no notice of Meredith's attempt to interrupt, 'the real reason I think you will be interested is because it bor-ders your family's farm – and if you put the two together, you would have a sizeable amount of land for your brother to really make a go of things. He could have the farming side of the busi-ness and stay in his home, and you could develop the house and some of grounds into a very handsome spa, with treatment rooms and staff accommodation, possibly a swimming pool. There is a fantastic orangerie with orange and lemon trees. It really could be the dream location. You get your film crew down there, toot sweet, and away you go, my lover. Job done.' He sat back and waited for the response.

'Jack, you astound me! This is fantastic.' Meredith was leaf-ing excitedly through the brochure which had glossy photos of all the important features. 'But can I afford it?' she said, look-ing crestfallen.

Jack stared at her as if she was stark raving bonkers. 'Afford it? *Hello?* How much money have you got?' He poured them both another glass of champagne.

'Oh yes, silly me.' Meredith smiled ruefully. 'Sorry, I forgot. It is a huge thing to take in, you know.'

'Listen, you are doing great. So what do you think about this? Is it not perfect?' He was so obviously pleased with himself and Meredith could not think of a single reason to disagree with him.

'So that's sorted then,' he said happily. 'Now, what about Malaysia?'

341

Meredith didn't answer straight away because their starters arrived and she was rather glad of the diversion. She was desperate to go on this trip with Jack, but had no idea of the practicalities. Could she cope with being the odd one out? Was it going to be all business and no pleasure? She just didn't know how to broach the subject. Then as she was tucking into her smoked duck, she suddenly had a brainwave.

'Should I be bringing a camera crew with us?' she asked. 'Only it could be deemed as a recce for the show, and that way it is tax deductible.'

Jack stopped eating, his fork in mid-air. 'Well, I have heard of three being a crowd, but an entire camera crew? Actually though, that is another thing I wanted to mention. Mo can't come now. One of her sons is moving to America and she doesn't want to be away when he leaves. She might join us for the last week, but it is unlikely. I just thought you ought to know. It doesn't make any difference to my plans, and Mo had already told me that she would be quite happy to go off and leave us to work out all our business stuff.'

'Oh yes, yes of course,' Meredith stammered. She stuck some duck in her mouth and chewed in silence, trying to hide her excitement. At one point she looked up and caught Jack's eye. He was watching her with a smile on his face and it was very disconcerting.

'How's the duck?' he asked.

'Lovely, thank you.'

'So shall I get my secretary to book the flights then? I thought we would fly next Monday to Kuala Lumpur. Malaysian Airways have a fantastic first class.'

'First class! That will cost a bloody fortune—' Meredith stopped and looked at Jack, who had an eyebrow raised.

'Yes – and? Here you go again. For God's sake, woman, you are rich beyond your wildest dreams. This is what money is for, so you do not have to travel steerage. You will arrive fresh and rested and ready for business.' Jack raised his glass. 'Here's to travelling first class all the way! When we get to Kuala Lumpur we can spend a couple of days getting acclimatised and I will get my business out of the way, and then we will drive to the island of Pangkor Laut where we will spend a fabulous week being pampered in one of the world's finest spa resorts. You will pay attention to all the finer details and ask intelligent questions, while I sit in a Japanese bathhouse and get my back scrubbed by fifty Balinese virgins. Well no, maybe not – that is my own particular fantasy!' They both laughed.

'It sounds absolutely amazing. I can't wait. Did you really say you could organise the tickets?'

'Of course, not a problem,' said Jack.

'Right, so next on the agenda is this weekend and Anna's party. Have you asked Harry if he would like to come?' Meredith had suddenly remembered that they had forgotten poor Harry in all the excitement.

'He is looking forward to it, and we will be giving Anna a course of driving lessons as her birthday present – if that is OK?' Jack suddenly looked worried.

'That is more than OK, it is extremely generous of you,' said Meredith. 'How can poor Harry afford it?'

'Ah well, the deal is I pay for the lessons and he buys the card!' Jack nodded to the waiter to bring the bill.

'I am absolutely knackered,' he went on. 'It must be all that country air – and I am sure you must be exhausted after all your exertions in the studio. Shall we call it a day, my lover?' He paid the bill and they walked to the door.

Niko came towards them and said, 'Your car is ready for you, Mr Blatchford, and there is a car waiting for you, Ms Lee.'

Jack took her arm and explained: 'I took the liberty of ordering you a car because, to be honest, I am too tired to drop you

Chapter Twenty-Two

Meredith woke up on Saturday morning, and just as she was about to relax and enjoy the day off, she remembered just how much she had to do. Not only did she have to finish all preparations for the party, but she had to pack for Malaysia. And what about her roots?

She hurled herself from the bed to the shower and on down to the coffee pot, by which time it was a reasonable hour to ring Andrea who did her hair colour. With any luck it was the Saturday in the month when she worked. It was a bit like oysters with Andrea and her working days – never with an 'R' in the month type of thing – only with her it was never on Saturdays except the first one of the month or something. Oh well, fingers crossed. She dialled the number.

The phone was picked up and a voice said, 'I will only listen if you talk dirty!' Andrea was at home.

'Andrea, it's Meredith. Please, please tell me you can do my roots this morning because I am off to Malaysia on Monday and it could be life-changing,'

'Is this a man I see before me? Out, out, damned grey.' Andrea laughed. 'Well, something like that – apologies to Shakespeare. Of course I will do your hair. Can you come right now though, because I am having lunch with Tony today, otherwise he complains he never sees me outside of work.'

'I am there already!' Meredith slammed down the phone, picked up her keys and bag and was out of the door.

Andrea and Tony worked from their house in North London so it was only a hop and a skip for Meredith. She made a quick detour to the phone shop to pick up Anna's birthday present, which she had forgotten to do yesterday. She had also completely forgotten that her mother was in the house. Well, Jane should be fine for a couple of hours, but Meredith made a mental note to get something nice for lunch. She also needed to go to Boots and purchase holiday stuff and – shit! What about injections! By this time she had arrived at Andrea's.

Tony opened the door and she greeted him with: 'Tony, you have got to help me. How do I get injected for Malaysia today?'

'Good morning, Meredith, how lovely to see you. "Hello, Tony, how are you?" Whatever are you babbling on about, girl?'

'I just realised I have to have injections to go to Malaysia. Will I get malaria, do you think? Tony, help me! What do I do?' she wailed.

Tony placed a gown round her shoulders and sat her in front of the mirror.

'Calm down. I will ring the Royal Free. They have a travel clinic. You will have to pay, mind you.'

'Tony, you are a star. Thank you so much.'

'All part of the service.' He started for the door, where he bumped into his wife.

'Who are you servicing now?' Andrea quipped.

'Ha, very amusing,' he replied, and retired to make the coffee.

'Your husband is a saint and you know it,' said Meredith. 'He just organised me some injections for Malaysia where I will be going on Monday morning, God willing.'

Andrea started to mix her colour. 'Was I right in assuming there is a man involved?' she asked.

'Yes, but not in the way you think. It's complicated,' Meredith told her.

'Isn't everything in your life, Ms Lee?' Andrea beamed.

'Well now, that's not very fair. My life was quite calm – dull, even – until last week. Andrea, it has been a roller-coaster. Basically my daughter is pregnant and this has caused ripples dating back to when she was born because she went to look for her natural father and found him, and now he has found me, and we are talking, obviously because of Anna ... well, something like that anyway.' Meredith looked up into the mirror at Andrea who had stopped mixing to take all this in.

'That is quite a week's worth for anybody to deal with. I am sorry to be thick, but Malaysia fits in where?'

'Jack, that's Anna's father, has to go there on Monday for a project, and he suggested I go with him because I'm producing a series about property development and buying a hotel to convert into a spa.'

Andrea burst out laughing. 'Enough already, I'm confused. So this trip could be romance?' She gave Meredith a long look in the mirror.

'No, Andrea, no romance, because he has a relationship sort of, and if *you're* confused, think how I am feeling. But let's just say that whatever happens, I don't want any grey roots to complicate matters.'

An hour and a half later, Meredith emerged from the house like the proverbial butterfly. She took off to the hospital and miraculously found a meter. Good sign. The nurse was wonderful and took her through the gamut of possibilities for health hazards in the jungle.

'Actually,' suggested Meredith, 'I think I will only be going as far as the steam room at the spa, but thank you anyway. It is good to know I am covered for all eventualities.' She finished with the nurse and then nipped into a chemist on Haverstock Hill and found holiday 'stuff' like mosquito spray and sun cream and shampoo and body lotion. She was trying to run through the things she would need. The trouble was, Meredith had hardly been anywhere apart from France in the last sixteen years, because she was so busy trying to earn a living and bring up Anna.

People often assumed that because she was on TV she lived a very glamorous life, travelling the world first class. Nothing could have been further from the truth. So she did not have a vast wardrobe of floaty, hot-weather kind of gear. She was trying to think if she even had a swimming costume. The answer flashed like a neon sign. NO. She had a bikini she wore on holiday in France, but only in private. She had to buy a costume now! Glancing anxiously at her watch, she decided to go home and sort out her mother first.

'Meredith, where have you been?' Jane opened the door to her daughter, who had her arms full of bags, having done some food shopping on the way home.

'I am so sorry, Mum, but I had to go and have my hair done. Make me a coffee while I unpack this lot and I will tell you all.'

Jane made coffee and they took it outside in the sunshine. Meredith also brought out a pad and pencil to write a list. She told her mother everything that had happened to date, only leaving out how much money was involved in Myles Harrison's estate. Jane was still very wary about accepting the money, but when she heard the plans for Frank to take over Marsh House, she was beaming.

'Oh Meredith, what a fantastic suggestion. I know Frank would make it work. And that was Jack's idea, was it? How very kind of him to take so much trouble.' She looked at Meredith with a knowing smile. 'He must think a lot of you, dear. And now he's taking you to Malaysia!'

348

'Now, Mother, don't start, I have got enough on my plate. I am going to Malaysia because it is a wonderful opportunity. I need a holiday and I can do some research for my project. End of story.'

'Oh absolutely, dear, I quite understand. But will Anna be all right? Do you want me to stay on for a bit?'

'No, it's fine, thanks, Mum,' replied Meredith. 'She and Tom are off to France next weekend with the Wilsons for the usual summer of fun. I will probably join them for a week then come back to London to start my new series. Obviously, if Jack can get this sale going with Marsh House, Frank could be in by September and you will all have rather a lot to be getting on with, Mother dear. Now I need to write my list and start packing. Are you OK on your own for a bit?' Meredith looked at her mother.

'Oh yes, of course. I heard Anna come in last night; shall I take her a cup of tea, do you think? Mind you, I am not sure if she is alone. It is difficult these days, isn't it, not quite knowing what the form is with people sleeping together and suchlike. I am not so sure it is helpful really. Anna is still so young, and to be having a child . . .' Jane looked sad for a moment. 'Oh well, times change. Thank God she is healthy and has a good family to look after her. That is the main thing.'

As she stood up to go into the kitchen, her granddaughter appeared.

'Hello, Granny!' Anna gave Jane a big hug and looked so pleased to see her. 'Granny, what a lovely dress. Come on, come and tell me all your news.' Before Jane could answer, Anna suddenly turned very pale. 'Oh excuse me!' and she rushed out of the room.

Meredith couldn't help laughing. 'Poor Anna, she is really suffering. Give her the benefit of your advice, Mum. Got any good tips to stop morning sickness?'

'Leave her with me,' said Jane, and went to put the kettle on.

Meredith checked her list. A hat, a swimming costume and some kind of kaftan thing to sit about in just about covered it, plus a couple of dresses for the evening, and some linen trousers. She didn't want Jack to think she was trying too hard, but at the same time she needed to know she had a choice should the chance arrive to amaze him with her beauty. She went up to her bedroom to check out her summer wardrobe. It was not very inspiring at all. Maybe she could take Anna and her mother into the West End for an hour and she could raid Harvey Nichols. That was a plan. She gathered the clan, who were more than happy to do a bit of shopping with the promise of lunch as well, and set off.

Central London was packed unfortunately, and it was hot and sweaty. Jane and Anna decided to leave Meredith to shop on her own, which made life a lot easier. Meredith was a woman on a mission. She found a lovely hat straight away – a cream Panama, which was way too much money, but looked fab and was totally uncrushable. Then she went to the swimwear department and got very depressed. She was not in bad shape for her age but she didn't think she could wear a bikini any more. To have to stand in front of those mirrors in the changing room was torture. How could she possibly take her clothes off in front of Jack, unless it was seriously soft lighting? Preferably dark! Most of the one-piece costumes looked like she was entering a Miss World competition circa 1954.

A very sweet Japanese assistant, who was probably a size two, dared to make a suggestion: 'Please, madam, perhaps you visit Rigby and Peller. Do you know this shop? It is behind Harrods. They have wonderful swimwear and underwear. It is very good.'

'Thank you, I will.' Meredith knew exactly where the shop was, and had always passed it by because it was famous for being the shop which supplied the Queen with her undies. Somehow,

Meredith had never thought she could have a great deal in common with Her Majesty. But how wrong could she be!

Rigby & Peller was an Aladdin's cave of sumptuous silks and satins. The swimwear was fantastic. So sexy, and cleverly made to hold you in, in the places that rarely saw the light of day. Meredith bought three costumes and several beautiful wraps to disguise the thigh area, and then moved on to the underwear. She had never been measured in her life for a bra, but that was just about to change.

A very lovely lady, with quite a large bosom herself, explained to her that women just did not understand the importance of a correctly fitted bra. A bad bra could affect your posture, which in turn could lead to back pain, and if your breasts were not correctly uplifted, you could find you did not hold in your stomach muscles, which in turn made you look fatter. It was a whole catalogue of information to change your life.

Meredith learned she was a bra size larger than she thought, and could not get over how much better she looked when her boobs were encased firmly in the correct cup. She had a waist, for a start. She found two fantastic kaftan-type outfits in which to sit on the balcony in the spa in the evening; a pair of cream silk pyjamas in case she was entertaining(!); and two sets of bras and thongs. Yes, thongs, which were so soft she hardly knew she had them on. Meredith stared at herself in the changing-room mirror. Not bad for an old bird!

She glanced at her watch again. Phew – just in time to meet up with Anna and Jane round the corner in a lovely Italian restaurant that Meredith had been going to for years. They all had huge plates of pasta and a bottle of Chianti.

Anna scolded Meredith. 'Mum, you'll get fat. What about your holiday? You need to be careful in your costume.'

'Hah – listen to this!' Meredith regaled them with her new-found knowledge of underwear, explaining that with her new

Rigby & Peller swimming cossies, a plate of pasta could be cunningly disguised. The Queen probably ate loads of the stuff.

By the time they got home to Hampstead, it was late afternoon and Meredith was absolutely pooped. She and her mother had a cup of tea and fell asleep on the sofa, while Anna went to meet Millie to discuss what they were going to wear for the lunch-party tomorrow. Refreshed after her nap, Meredith laid out her clothes to pack later and spent the rest of the evening getting everything ready for the party. She and Jane moved tables and wiped glasses and cutlery and picked flowers from the garden.

By ten o'clock, Meredith said, 'No more, Mother. We have done enough. How do you fancy some cheese on toast and a cup of cocoa?'

'Lovely. Just the job. I will go and put my nightie on, if I may, while you do that.' And Jane went off upstairs to change into her comfy nightclothes.

Meredith set two trays, and by the time Jane came back down, the supper was ready.

'This is just like when you were little,' Jane said happily. 'Do you remember how we used to sit in the snug in our dressing-gowns in front of the fire? It was madness in the winter because we got completely toasted all down the front but our backs were exposed to all the draughts and we were freezing. But it was so cosy, wasn't it? Do you remember your dad roasting chestnuts – and every time one exploded, you got frightened and burst into tears!'

Meredith gazed at her mother now and marvelled at how young she could look sometimes. She had fantastic skin with hardly a wrinkle, and when she smiled her whole face lit up like a child's, as it did now as she remembered happy times. Life was so precious, she thought, and so was the gift of living long enough to understand how it went round in circles. A sudden thought occurred to her.

'Mum, did you open the letter from Myles?'

Jane looked away, her smile gone.

'What did it say? Don't you want to tell me?' Meredith could see that her mother was struggling with her emotions.

'It's not that I don't want to tell you, but the letter made me realise something quite profound and I'm not sure I can explain it to you properly. But I will try.' Jane put her hand into her dressing-gown pocket and brought out the letter. She unfolded it slowly and passed it to Meredith, saying, 'Myles Harrison was a complicated man. Aren't they all?' She sighed. 'But this letter gave me a small inkling into his soul, and for that honesty, he deserves some credit. I will never forgive him, but I do understand him better now.' She sat with her hands in her lap, waiting for Meredith to read the letter.

Dear Jane,

It has taken too many years for me to write this letter. I do not expect forgiveness but rather understanding. When I spoke to Meredith at Pamela's funeral I knew what I had to do, and I have done it: I have made our daughter my sole heir. This in turn will ensure the future of my only granddaughter. It is not about money, you will say, and I agree. No amount can compensate for the destruction of another human being. But I did not destroy you in the end, did I? Your goodness shone through and it was that goodness which first made me want to hurt you. I could make excuses for my behaviour that night, and say I was drunk and that I didn't know what I was doing, that I misunderstood the situation. But I did understand, and I knew exactly what I was doing.

When you came to our house you were like a light in the darkness. Pamela and I were poles apart and Sylvia, my baby daughter, was the only hope for us. Me, at any rate. That little girl had shown me what it was to love something more than myself. It was a chance to redeem myself. But Pamela could not see that. She thought I was an animal, that I was only interested in desire. She rejected me and cut me off. Then there you were, a glowing beacon of warmth and humanity sitting at my table every evening, talking to me, and listening to me talk in turn, about my boring life. You made me feel interesting but you did not want me as a man. There was not a hint of sexual desire for me.

I, on the other hand, became overwhelmed by a desire to have you, and to take that life energy from you and feed myself, to taint you and use your innocence and humanity to my own ends. When you came back that night, cold and wet and frightened and in need of comfort, I saw my chance. As I put my arms around you, it was to trap you, not to comfort you. I could feel your fear, and translated it into my own sexual desire for you. It drove me on and made me mad to have you.

Nothing can atone for what I have done, but Jane, I know you rose above my evil because I can see you in our daughter. You must have had huge reserves of good to bring up a child who every day must have reminded you of a monster. My respect and admiration are boundless. I have lived a successful life and enjoyed the games and the rewards and the conquests. But I never found the contentment or the love I know you have had in your life.

I will die a lonely, empty man and I accept my fate. I only ask that you read this, and know that I bow to you and yours.

I am truly sorry.

Myles

Meredith folded the letter and handed it back to her mother.

'Do you understand what he is saying?' she asked gently.

Jane looked up and took Meredith's hand. 'Yes, I think I do – and this is what I have been thinking so much about today. Being here with you and Anna, and looking back at my sister Pamela and then our mother, I see a kind of pattern – perhaps more a jigsaw of our lives as women, and the men who have played a part in our development. When I listen to the women of today talking about equality and liberation, I cannot quite see it from the same perspective, because it seems to me that they are confusing the issues. A woman can be equal to a man but she can never be *the same as* a man. To me, a woman cannot live without love, an emotional connection of some kind, whereas a man cannot live without desire, a physical connection. A woman can marry for duty, for example, like my mother did, but she was lost without any real love. Alfred wanted his physical desires to be satisfied in their relationship, and at first he took it regardless, making my mother and me unhappy. But then Pamela was born and Alfred found love. Not from his wife, but she was able to benefit, because his love for his daughter made him softer, which in turn made it easier for my mother to do her duty by him.

'Unfortunately,' Jane paused, choosing her words carefully, 'my mother had loved Henry when she gave herself to him, whereas he obviously only felt lust. I suspect that many men and women have this misunderstanding and yet still get married. Pamela blossomed in our family because of our father's love for her, but she misunderstood this love when it came to the men in her life. She knew all about men's sexual desires and gave them what they wanted, but was disappointed when this did not translate into her idea of love. The birth of her baby showed her how to love, but I think Myles was jealous of this love, and came between her and her daughter, and turned his

355

love towards the child. Here was someone he could love without feeling vulnerable. Myles was stunted in his emotional growth – for whatever reason, we will never know – but he did try to show his wife love in the only way he knew how – physically. And when she pushed him away, because she didn't understand that he could only express his love through desire, he in turn rejected her.'

Jane sighed and got up. She went to the window and looked out. Meredith could see her reflection in the glass.

'I am trying hard to make myself clear,' she said in a low voice, 'but it is so difficult because I feel so much a part of this confusion. Myles writes about tainting me, and that is exactly what he tried to do. I had no experience of sex in those days, not even with George. But as I had tried to explain to Pamela, when she said all men were animals, I knew, in my heart, that it was just not true.'

Jane turned to face her daughter. 'George and I had a wonderful, powerful physical sense of each other, but it was touched with emotion. Love. You must have both things to have a complete union. When I told George what had happened, and he still wanted to marry me, I knew I could survive whatever Myles had tried to do. It was a long slow process, because at first I could not bear to be touched. I was also pregnant so my whole body was changing. My greatest regret is that George was never once able to make love to me as I was before nature and rape changed me. My body was never my own again. That is what happens to most women though. Not the rape, of course, but childbirth. So many women lose their sense of self, and then cannot understand how their husbands still want them physically, even though they have become a feeding machine and birth canal. It sounds crude, but nature is very raw, and if women could accept that rawness more, but temper it with their loving emotions, it would help men to feel more from their

356

hearts, and the balance between love and desire might even out more.'

Jane sat down and took Meredith's hands in hers and stroked them as she continued, 'When you meet a man who has that balance it is explosive, Meredith. George showed me so much love that I learned to give him fantastic sex. Does it shock you to hear your old mother say these things? Well, it's the truth. There is nothing new in life, you know, though every generation thinks it is the first to discover sex. It is one of the most powerful energies in all of humanity. Life, death and reproduction.

'You are the product of two very strong personalities, and much as it pains me to admit it, you have a good deal of your father in you. But this is tempered by my genes, and though I say so myself, I have very strong positive genes to counteract any negative energy that might come down through Myles's line. Goodness, this sounds like a biology lesson!' She laughed and went on, 'What I am trying to say is that you, dear girl, seem to have a balanced view of yourself and your place in society as a woman. Sadly, however, you have yet to meet a man of similar strength and qualities. But you will do so very soon, I know it, and when you do, the jigsaw will nearly be complete, because the final pieces will come from your daughter Anna and her union with Tom. They have a very innocent, untainted love, and it must be allowed to grow uninterrupted, unlike the rest of us women in this chain. So you see, I and you and your grandmother Mary and Pamela and Anna, we are all connected. Not just by blood, but by our heritage as females of the species. We are continually adapting as society demands more from us. But we must never lose sight of our differences with the male. Yes, of course we are equal – but we can never, ever, be the same.'

Jane shook her head. 'Oh dear, here endeth the lesson. I am

so sorry for heaping that on you, Meredith, but it has been going round and round in my head all day. I wanted to understand so I could finally let Myles go in peace. Now come on, let's go in peace ourselves and get to bed. You will be exhausted by tomorrow.'

Meredith gave her a hand up and they made their way upstairs.

'Have you got everything you need?' asked Meredith fondly on the landing.

'Yes, thank you, I have got all I need. Lots of love to you, dear Meredith. Don't worry, things will all work out in their own good time.' Jane kissed her daughter on the cheek and gave her a hug, then went into her room and closed the door.

Meredith felt safe and warm, just as she had as a child when her mother had shown her affection. It was good to know that Jane had come through all the pain and was now able to open herself to her daughter completely. She was imparting her strength to Meredith, so she in turn could pass it on to Anna. Continuity. Life goes on.

With this comforting thought, Meredith got into bed and fell deeply asleep.

Chapter Twenty-Three

Sunday morning was a gorgeous start to a brilliant day. Meredith was up and out in the garden picking some more flowers for the tables by eight o'clock. She was so ahead of herself she was even able to read a Sunday paper, eat a croissant and drink two cups of coffee before her mother came down.

'Goodness, you must have got up as soon as it was light,' remarked Jane. 'Mind you, it's usually me who is up so early but I have to say I slept like a log. I must have needed it. Shall I help myself to breakfast?'

'Please do. Mum, would you be able to set the table while I get the wine sorted out?'

'Yes, of course I will.' Jane sat down to eat her croissant before starting her chores just as the doorbell went.

'I'll get it.' Meredith was already halfway to the front door. She flung it open with a loud, 'Hurrah! It's the magic chef and his little helper!' She threw her arms around Oliver's neck, causing havoc amongst the carrier bags.

'Put me down! I know where I have been and it is fishy! Help Michael, he is carrying cake,' Oliver ordered, and Meredith quickly went to relieve Michael of several boxes.

'Careful, that is raspberries and that is the cake,' cautioned Michael. 'Hello, Mrs Lee, how are you today?'

Jane came over and took a bag from him. 'I'm in the pink, thank you, Michael. Now – shall I put these potatoes in the sink and wash them for you?'

'Oh, that would be fantastic. Thank you,' said Michael.

Oliver had taken up his position as head chef by the cooker and was already giving orders.

'Meredith, we need coffee and serving plates, please.' He turned to Michael. 'You may take five minutes to have coffee and then I need you to wash salad and fruit in that order. Where is the Birthday Girl?'

'Still asleep,' said Meredith. 'I will take her a cup of hot water and lemon and ginger in a while. Poor girl spends the first waking hour being sick, so be kind to her, boys.'

'When are we ever not kind?' said Oliver, as he started to chop chives for his mayonnaise.

'Do I get a job?' asked Meredith.

'Of course. In a minute I need you to pick me some mint from your garden. How are we doing with the wine? What have you chosen for me today?' Oliver asked.

'I have chosen a lovely light Frascati or a slightly posher Chablis for you, and for the pink champagne I have gone with Vintage Louis Roederer Rose and then I got a few bottles of Fleurie.' Fortunately Meredith had two fridges, so there was no problem keeping everything cool. She had set up a bar in one corner of the kitchen for the drinks and started to put out some extra glasses.

'Mum, is the table nearly finished?' she called out.

'Yes, all done,' came the reply as Jane walked in from the garden. 'Have you wrapped Anna's present, by the way?'

'Oh no, stupid me. Oliver, do you and Michael want to take a look at it quickly, then Mum can wrap it before Anna comes down?' Meredith went into her office and came back with the phone.

'Marvellous, isn't it?' said Michael. 'They get smaller by the minute. I saw a programme the other day that said in the next five years, people will be able to do everything on their phones. They will be like a mini-computer. Here you are, Jane.' He passed the box to Jane, who went off to Meredith's office to wrap it up.

Meredith was chopping parsley and mint for Oliver, who was now giving his full attention to the salmon. 'Isn't this the most beautiful fish you have ever seen?' he murmured, rubbing it with sea salt and laying it on a bed of dill and coriander leaves. 'Mmm ... smell those herbs.'

Meredith laughed. 'Olly, you sound as if you are rehearsing for the new telly programme. You are such a natural.'

'Oh no – he will soon become unbearable again,' said Michael. 'We will all have to keep an eye on him to make sure he doesn't get too big for his boots.' He flicked some cold water at Oliver. 'Calm down, you star!'

By noon everything was just about ready. The boys were sitting in the garden, having already cracked open a bottle of bubbly, Jane was upstairs changing, and Anna and Meredith were finishing off putting garlic butter into sticks of French bread.

'God, we are going to be so smelly,' giggled Anna.

'Rub your hands with a lemon,' advised Meredith. 'That will do the trick. Then when you are ready and Mum comes down, we can open your cards and prezzies.'

'OK, I'll just go and do that.' Anna hurried off, and Meredith wiped her hands on her apron, collected a glass and went to join the lads.

'Here's to us!' She raised her glass. 'Thank you, guys, for everything – and I don't just mean the culinary skills you have either. You are two of life's specials.'

'So you are off to Malaysia tomorrow, Anna tells me,' said Oliver. 'What can we deduce from this, Miss Marple?'

'Absolutely nothing, Professor Moriarty, it is business before pleasure all the way,' Meredith replied.

'But what about *after* the business?' Michael prodded. 'You can't hide from us, dear girl.' He beamed at her.

'There is nothing to hide. It is all above board,' she said, sounding more positive than she felt. She didn't want to have this kind of conversation today, and especially not within earshot of Jack. 'So please can we not mention it again today?'

Oliver and Michael exchanged a look, then both of them put their fingers across their lips and made a zipping motion.

'Our lips are sealed,' mimed Oliver.

Anna and Jane came into the kitchen and Meredith went to get the presents and produce all the cards that had come through the letter box that week and which she had hidden from her daughter.

Anna opened each card and showed them round, saving her presents until last. The first one she opened was from her Uncle Frank and Auntie Jenny. It was a box of soaps, all handmade.

'Oh, these are beautiful, aren't they, Mum?' She passed them to Meredith, who had a sniff and then passed them on to Michael.

'They got them from a lovely new market near St Albans that has all handmade things and embroidery and suchlike,' said Jane. 'It's nice to see the old-fashioned crafts have not been forgotten.'

Then Anna had a present from her grandmother.

'If you don't like them I shan't mind if you want to change them,' said Jane, ever practical.

'Oh, but I love them, Gran. They are beautiful!' The girl had opened a small box which contained some exquisite mother-of-pearl and garnet earrings. They were so delicate and would really suit Anna. She had had her ears pierced when she was quite young, even though Meredith had not approved at the time. However, now she was relieved that her daughter's ears seemed to be the only part of her body that Anna had wanted to pierce.

'Gran, they are really lovely. You are clever to find such a perfect present.' Anna squeezed her grandmother's hand.

Finally, Anna opened her phone. She had had an inkling that this was what she was going to get, because they had talked about mobile phones a while back, but she had not been sure. She was over the moon and let out a yell.

'Yeah! Thank you, guys, this is fantastic! Thank you so much.' And she ran around kissing them all. 'I am going to call Tom straight away. Oh no, I can't, silly me – the battery has got to charge. Oh well, never mind, I will ring him on the landline and tell him the good news.' And she raced off to phone Tom.

Meredith went to change her dress and put some make-up on, while Oliver and Michael polished off the bottle of champagne and started to take out the salads and put the potatoes on to cook.

The doorbell went and Anna opened it to find her new father standing there with her new brother. She was suddenly a little shy, but Jack swept her up in his arms and gave her a kiss, saying, 'Happy Birthday, Princess, say hello to your brother, Harry.' He put her down and stepped out of the way so Harry could greet her.

'Hello Anna, Happy Birthday. This is for you.' He handed her an envelope.

'Wow, thank you very much. Come in and meet Oliver, he is my—' She stopped, not sure what to call Oliver, but he was ready and stepped in with, 'I am her other dad: we can alternate according to the days of the month!' He shook hands with Jack and Harry, and joked, 'I said to Anna, it is always good to have a spare. Oliver Stanton, pleased to meet you. This is my partner, Michael Lyons,' he added.

'Pleased to meet you,' said Jack, shaking his hand. 'This is my son Harry. Hello again, Jane, you look very lovely, if I may say so.' He went across and sat next to her.

Anna got a bottle of fizz out of the fridge. 'Oliver, would you do the honours? I'm always scared of the cork popping. Is champagne OK for you guys?' she asked.

'Great for me,' Harry said immediately.

'Could I have a white wine instead?' asked Jack.

'Of course. There is Frascati or Chablis.' Anna showed him the bottles. 'Take your pick.'

'Chablis would be lovely.' Jack looked round. 'Where's Meredith?'

'Here I am,' she announced, coming down the stairs. 'Just washing off the garlic butter. Lovely to see you, Jack, and hello again, Harry.' She gave them both a kiss on the cheek and went across to stand by Oliver. 'Well, chef, do you need me at all?' she asked. 'I await my instructions,' and she put her hands on her hips and made everyone laugh.

'You may laugh,' retorted Oliver, 'but believe me, folks, that is about all the use she is to me. You just can't get the staff these days!' The ice was broken and everyone relaxed.

Suddenly Anna let out a yell of delight. 'Oh my God! Driving lessons! Thank you so much. I can't believe it.' She ran over to Jack and threw her arms round his neck.

'Hey, they are from Harry, as well,' said Jack.

'Thank you, Harry.' Anna gave him a shy kiss on the cheek. 'Now I have everything I could possibly want,' she told them. 'What a great family I have – thank you, everyone. Now come on, let's get this party started.' And she bounced off to put some music on.

The Wilsons arrived next and finally the Neils. It was the

first time Meredith had seen Tom's parents since her outburst at their house, and she was aware that she needed to set the record straight. Taking Estelle aside, she said, 'I want to apologise for my behaviour the other day. It was very childish of me, and I am truly sorry.'

'Please, Meredith, we quite understood. It has been a difficult time for us all. I am just so glad that you and Anna are not fighting any more. She is such a lovely girl and a real credit to you. I can't imagine how I would react if my only daughter got pregnant. Believe me though, Tom is an old soul. He loves Anna and will do his utmost to look after her and the baby. I know they are very young but let's hope and pray they can make it work.' She gave Meredith a hug and the women went back and joined the group. Meredith was not quite so convinced that the young couple had a future together, but she would reserve judgement.

Lunch was a joyous affair. Oliver and Michael were on fine form and treated the whole thing like a sort of 'happening'. They were a fabulous double-act. Millie Wilson was entranced by Harry, who was the perfect gent and attended to her every whim, and he also managed to bond with Adam, Millie's brother, which Meredith thought was very clever. Harry had an easy and natural charm about him. Just like his dad! Jack, of course, was just brilliant. Many men might have been thrown by the high level of camp dished out by Oliver and Michael, but he took it all in his stride and gave as good as he got. Meredith thought he was even flirting with Michael at one point.

Anna looked so happy and so in love with Tom, who never left her side. Her mother blossomed and was given special treatment by all the men, and Millie's brother enchanted her by sitting next to her at lunch and telling her rude jokes. Penny Wilson was lovely as ever, and at one point followed Meredith into the kitchen and whispered, 'Who is this dish you have kept hidden away?' Meredith had been wondering quite how she was going to break the news to everyone about Jack without creating too much of a big deal about it. So she said, 'Penny, it is a long story and one day I will tell you the whole thing, but for now can I ask you to keep this in the family? Jack is Anna's natural father and we have not seen each other for nearly eighteen years. Anna is pregnant and wanted to find her real father. So here we are. It has been fantastic that we all seem to get along, but it is early days and I don't want Oliver to feel left out, because let's face it, he has been so supportive and like a father to Anna over the years. If you can tell your lot at a later date, then it would put my mind at rest. Is that OK?'

'Of course it is. Bless your heart, Meredith, you are amazing, the way you take things in your stride. We are here for you. But back to my original observation, what a dish! I will watch with interest, my dear friend.'

She left Meredith in the kitchen pondering the problem of how best to clear the air with everyone today. She had discussed it with her daughter, who had told her that Tom's parents were up to speed with the whole thing, so the only people she hadn't really talked to about it all were Jack and Harry. It had completely slipped her mind. As she stood in the kitchen trying to decide on the best way to approach it, her thoughts were interrupted by the man himself.

'Fantastic party, Meredith, well done. Our daughter seems so happy, doesn't she? Are you going to make a speech or anything?'

'Well, here's the thing. I was actually just trying to decide what we should do about that. Everyone sort of knows now what is going on. They know who you are, and about Anna and Tom, but do we have to make a big statement about it? The trouble is, it could be a bit awkward for Oliver if you lay claim to Anna at this point, and people are not quite sure where you and I stand.'

She caught him looking at her strangely. 'What's the matter? Why are you looking at me like that?' she asked.

'No reason really, except I agree: where do you and I stand exactly?'

'Well, I don't know. I mean, what do you want me to say? I just think it is for us to work these things out over time, don't you? People are always so quick to put things in boxes and label them. It is nobody's business except ours. It is lovely that Anna has found you and Harry, and now has a new family. It is strange for Oliver, obviously, because he has been around Anna all her life, and he loves her very much; and for me it is strange because, well, you are Anna's father but I don't really know you that well. So it will take time, won't it, for things to settle down? I think we should just wish Anna a very Happy Birthday and leave it at that for now, don't you?' She was feeling very unsure of her ground all of a sudden and Jack was too close for comfort.

'Stick it all in your drawer, you mean?' He was laughing at her.

'Well yes, I suppose so, just for now,' she mumbled, blushing.

'Meredith, it's OK. I won't embarrass you or upset Oliver. I want Anna to have a lovely birthday as well. You are quite right, we should just let things be for a while. Now come on, let's go and cut the cake. We will have lots of time to get to know each other properly on that twelve-hour flight to Malaysia.' He put his arm around her and took her outside to the table.

Oliver was gearing up for his moment of glory. Michael was out of sight with the cake, ready to go with the candle lighting. Meredith took a fork and tapped her wine glass.

'Ladies and gentlemen, pray silence for the chef, Monsieur Oliver Stanton.' She started the applause and sat down as Oliver rose to take his bow.

'It gives me great pleasure to start the communal hymn this afternoon: Happy Birthday to you . . .'

They all joined in and while they were singing, Michael appeared, carrying the gorgeous chocolate confection that Oliver had created, covered in seventeen candles. Anna clapped her hands in delight.

After the noise had died down, Meredith gave her a knife and prompted, 'Cut the cake and make a wish, darling.' Anna cut and they all cheered, then she closed her eyes and stood very still, making her wish. Meredith held her breath and wished with her, then caught Jack looking at her and quickly lowered her eyes. Anna then blew out the candles to raucous applause.

Michael popped a champagne cork and poured everyone a glass of bubbly, then got a ten-pence piece, cut the top of the champagne cork and slipped the coin in the top. He handed it to Anna, saying, 'For good luck, babes. Happy Birthday.'

Jane was cutting the cake up and putting a slice on each plate. Meredith handed them round and then sat down at the end of the table. She looked round at everyone, taking in the scene. It was such a happy tableau. None of us can ever know how our lives will pan out, she thought. Never in a million years could she have imagined that she would be sitting here with a daughter of seventeen, never mind one who was going to have a baby, and never mind with her father, who had been absent for all those years, and a surrogate dad who was gay. She looked at all the smiling faces and took a mental snapshot to be taken out later and revisited.

'Hey, come on, everyone say cheese!' It was Harry taking a photo. Probably more reliable than my mental photo, thought Meredith, and smiled for the camera.

By seven o'clock that evening, there were just the hard-core partygoers left. Oliver and Michael and Meredith and Jane were in the kitchen, clearing up. Oliver was pissed and breaking glasses rather than drying them.

'Come on you, time to go,' said Meredith. 'I would like to have some china left. You have done a brilliant job, but you can go now. Take him home, Michael.'

'Will do. Come on, Toots, let's bugger off. Pardon my French, Jane.'

'Oh, don't mind me. It was lovely to see you as always, and the food was just perfect.' Jane took over the wiping up.

Meredith had packed up all their bits and pieces and helped them to the car.

'Thank you again, it was a huge success.' She hugged Oliver. 'You have been a fantastic spare daddy.'

'I know, and you don't have to worry any more, Meredith. We all know our place. I want you to be happy and I hope that maybe you will find your place while in Malaysia, know what I mean? Nod nod, wink wink.' He swayed in front of her.

'Yes, thank you very much. Enough of that, now go away! Good night, Michael, lots of love and I will ring you from the airport.' She kissed him goodnight and waved them off. Back in the kitchen, she sighed and said, 'Goodness me, Mum, we have got so much to clear up. I will have to stay up all night.' She got the rubbish bin and started to fill it.

'Now listen to me, Meredith,' said Jane. 'I am very happy to clear all this away tomorrow. Anna can help me, and I know your cleaner comes tomorrow, so please leave it now, and let me deal with it. I am not going home until Tuesday, am I?'

Meredith had arranged for Penny to come in the next evening to collect her mum and take her to the Wilsons' place for supper, and then Anna was going to take her to the station in a cab on Tuesday morning. Meredith was very tempted to accept her mother's offer. She felt absolutely whacked and would have to be up at seven to get ready to leave for the airport.

'Well I must say that sounds like a wonderful plan, Mum. Are you sure?'

'Of course I am. Now go and get packed and I will make us a cup of tea. Off you go.' Jane hustled her out and Meredith gratefully went upstairs.

She chose her travelling outfit carefully, bearing in mind she was going first class this time, and got her passport and everything ready. She then went back downstairs and sat and drank her tea with Jane, and they made plans for when Meredith got back.

'I will let you know about the sale of Marsh Hall as soon as I hear anything,' promised Meredith.

'It will be so exciting,' said her mother. 'I'll have a job keeping it all to myself,' and she giggled like a schoolgirl.

'Well, make sure you do, Mum. Can't let the cat out of the bag until it is all signed, sealed and delivered.'

'I won't, I promise. Meredith, I do hope you have a wonderful trip. Keep strong and remember . . .'

Meredith finished the sentence: '. . . always think good thoughts. I will try, Mum. Thank you for everything. I love you.'

'I love you too, my dear. God bless you. Goodnight.' Jane kissed her daughter and both women parted with a little of the other in her soul.

Chapter Twenty-Four

The flight to Malaysia was lengthy, and Meredith was dreading it. When she got to Heathrow she insisted on buying at least four paperbacks to keep her going. Jack had to order her not to buy hardbacks because of the weight. Meredith had never travelled long-haul first class, so it was a revelation when she turned left instead of right into the Boeing of Malaysia Air Lines flight MH 3 to Kuala Lumpur. The mood was hushed and reverential. The air was fresh and light and the soft leather seats lay beckoning to her. The hostess was incredibly beautiful and floated rather than walked up the aisle. Meredith took the proffered glass of champagne and sat down.

'How is this for you, Miss Lee?' enquired Jack. 'Bit different from the old charter flight, isn't it?'

'Yes, it's amazing,' replied Meredith, checking out the seat pocket and finding a bag of 'in flight' goodies. She felt like a little girl at Christmas as she opened her leather bag of toiletries. Jack was watching her and smiling broadly.

'Stop looking at me!' she blushed. 'Just because you are a seasoned traveller.'

The stewardess brought them menus for lunch, and newspapers, and Meredith discovered it was surprisingly easy to adapt to first-class living. By the time they were flying over France, she had fallen asleep and had to be woken up for her lunch.

'Sorry,' she said sleepily. 'I hope I didn't snore too loudly.' She prayed she had not snored at all.

'No, don't worry,' said Jack. 'You only dribbled.' Meredith shot him a look of horror. 'Nah, I am winding you up, you numpty,' he chuckled.

'Oh, very funny.' She would have been mortified if she had dribbled. How on earth was she going to keep control for the rest of the flight?

Lunch was superb – a mixture of Asian and Western cuisine – and there was a choice of wonderful wines and champagne. By the end of the meal, Meredith was a bit tipsy and starting to flirt.

'So then, Mr Blatchford, I hope you have arranged lots of massages for me at this spa. I need to know all about the different techniques,' then she added naughtily, 'I bet you are an expert on massage, aren't you?'

'Not really,' he replied. 'I don't usually have time for all that malarkey. I will leave that to you to arrange when you are in situ.'

Meredith had planned to spend a good deal of the flight catching up on Jack's past. The last couple of weeks had been so jam-packed there had never really been any time to fill in the missing years. However, the combination of too much wine and feeling tired and emotional, made her pass out completely for the next two hours. By the time she woke up, everybody else was going to sleep, including Jack; the lights had been dimmed and she was abandoned to her own thoughts. Being awake in a plane when everybody else is asleep is like being the last man left on earth. There is an eerie sense of one's aloneness and vulnerability.

Meredith tried to assess what had happened to her in the last three weeks. She was to become a grandmother, well that was scary enough, but then she had had to come face to face with her own past and meet Jack. That was something else altogether. This whole trip could end in disaster. She had no idea what Jack expected from her. He had said it was just a road trip between old friends. A chance for them to catch up, to see if they could put up a friendly show of support for their daughter, Anna. Meredith wasn't sure she could do that, though. Deep in her heart she wanted more than a friendly front. Well, she would just have to wait and see. At least if the romantic element disappointed, she could concentrate on the research for the series.

Meredith was excited about her career move. It was something that she had been planning for the last year, but like all these things it took the right moment to decide when to make the move. In this case, it had all been taken out of her hands. She welcomed the challenge. Work had always been her salvation.

With that thought she fell asleep and dreamed of water flowing over rocks and the smell of rose petals . . .

'Wakey, wakey, Sleeping Beauty.' Jack's voice broke through the peaceful sound of running water. 'It's breakfast-time. Well, teatime in old money, but you know what I mean. Here, take a hot towel.' He handed her a towel that smelled of rose petals and reminded her of her dream.

'How long did I sleep?' she yawned.

'I couldn't tell you because I only woke up a little while ago. We are a right pair of old fogeys, aren't we? Back in the day I would have been awake the whole twelve hours, watching movies and drinking champagne.' Jack sighed. 'Perhaps you should make a series about nursing homes!'

Meredith laughed and gathered up her washbag. 'I need the toilet,' she said, and pottered off. She examined her face in the mirror and did a few necessary repairs then cleaned her teeth and felt more human. Waking up next to Jack had brought back a memory of the night they had spent together. They had been so natural together the next morning. She had just wanted to stay with him. If only she had . . .

By the time she had sat down again they were serving breakfast. She was ravenous and ate everything that was put in front of her. They talked a bit about Anna and Tom and what they would do after the baby was born.

'I know you want to buy them a place, Meredith, and now you can afford it, but what about Tom's parents? They might want to do something.'

'I happen to know they don't have any spare cash,' said Meredith. 'Anna was telling me they were hoping to downsize next year.'

'Fine. If they need your help that is different, but you will have to wait for them to bring it up. Don't barge in and start organising everybody.'

'I don't organise everybody,' she retorted, hurt. 'You have no idea what I am like, anyway. You hardly know me.'

'True,' he said. 'I apologise, but I bet I am not wrong. Come on, be honest.' Jack waited for a response to his challenge.

'Maybe I am a bit bossy,' Meredith confessed, 'but only because I like to help.'

The captain interrupted their conversation by switching on the seatbelt sign. They were starting their descent. Meredith peered out of the window and could see nothing but jungle. It seemed to take forever, and by the time they actually touched down, Meredith felt sick. Her hastily gorged breakfast threatened to return. She went very quiet and tried to calm down. She felt like a child, hardly the image of the sophisticated career woman that she was trying to maintain.

'What's up?' Jack looked at her white face. 'Do you feel sick?'

'No, I am fine – really, just tired,' she lied, gritting her teeth.

They were through the airport remarkably swiftly. It was incredibly quiet and seemed really empty after the chaos of Heathrow. No queue at all at immigration, and suddenly they found themselves out on the concourse in tremendous heat.

'Oh, what a fantastic feeling!' said Meredith. 'That heat hits you like a sauna.' And she stopped and breathed in the wonderful smells of flowers and spices that assailed her nostrils. Now she really felt as if she had landed in another world.

A smartly dressed gentleman was coming towards them with a big smile on his face.

'Mr Jack and Miss Meredith? Welcome to Malaysia. Please to follow me to the car. Give me your bags, please.' He took Meredith's suitcase and tried to take Jack's as well, but Jack waved him away, saying, 'Don't worry, I have it.'

They followed him to a waiting 4 x 4 and climbed in. After the heat outside it was like a fridge, but they soon adapted and sat back to enjoy the ride.

'We will be four hours in the car. I hope this will be OK for you?' said their driver.

'Not a problem. What is your name?' asked Jack.

'VJ,' he said. 'I am happy to drive you,' and he moved off through the lines of parked cars onto the highway.

Meredith watched the city pass in a flurry of highrise blocks and palm trees. Then the houses gradually became shabbier and more rundown. Many of them were built on stilts in the old-fashioned style. It was a coast road most of the way to Pangkor Laut, and there were tantalising glimpses of the Indian Ocean through the trees. There were miles and miles of coconut plantations, the tall trees creating an oppressive cover of green over the road. It was a relief to come out the other side and be able to see into the distance again, to the hills beckoning them from afar.

Jack asked VJ about the building projects going on everywhere.

'Oh yes, sir, we have many new office blocks and apartments being built. There is lots of development in Malaysia,' he said.

Jack turned to Meredith. 'You see, this was where Myles was so clever. He could spot an opportunity long before other people. He was out here ten years ago, looking at prospective deals.'

'How did he originally make his money?' asked Meredith.

'Well, there are various stories about him. Some truer than others, I suspect, but I do know that he actually started with a project importing birdseed from America during the war. Believe it or not, it was impossible to get seed and the price rose ridiculously. People still wanted to keep their budgies, Hitler or no Hitler, and Myles found he could buy it in the USA then ship it back to the UK and sell it at a handsome profit. He was in the Merchant Navy for years, you see, and had lots of contacts. There were rumours that he then moved on to diamonds, but he never talked to me about things like that. Then, of course, his biggest coup was buying property cheap when war broke out. All those beautiful houses in Harley Street and blocks of flats in Knightsbridge? He bought them cheap because people were frightened they would be bombed and there would be no insurance, so they wanted out. Myles had all the building contacts, so even if they did get bombed he could rebuild. He also made a lot of money from government contracts for rebuilding works. His luck was that most of those expensive properties did not get bombed, so by the end of the war he was a very wealthy man. All he had to do was rent them out and sit on them. You could live off the rent from the houses alone, Meredith, and still be worth a fortune.'

Meredith stared out of the window, thinking about Myles and his millions. It was immoral that anyone should make so much profit during a time of war when so many thousands of his fellow countrymen had lost everything.

'You must be pretty rich yourself then?' she ventured.

'Yes, I have done very well, but I was doing very well before Myles took me into the business. When I first met you in 1965 I was only twenty-one but I had already got my own building business, and ran my own team. I did a conversion job for Myles and he was impressed enough to take me on and use me for more and more of his contracts. I was very grateful to him and I still am, to be honest. It was a very successful partnership for both of us.'

Meredith looked at him. 'It must have been terrible to lose your wife so suddenly,' she said gently, not wanting to upset him.

'Yes, it was a bad time. I didn't even have a mum and dad to fall back on because my mother died in childbirth when my sister Julie was born, and my dad died of cancer when I was six, so my sister and I were brought up by foster parents. I left school when I was sixteen and came to London; started working as a labourer on building sites and later set up my own firm. Julie came and joined me after Carole was killed, to help me look after Harry. He was only two then, and my wife's parents chipped in a bit, but they had never been happy about me and Carole getting married in the first place. They reckoned I wasn't good enough for her. They were probably right.' He smiled ruefully and shrugged. 'Still, we were determined to make a go of it. I had put down a deposit on a house in Southgate in North London. We set up home and were as happy as Larry, except as the years went by Carole couldn't fall pregnant. It nearly destroyed her, until these friends of ours told us about Harry. He was only a month old when we adopted him. We were over the moon.'

Meredith took his hand and they sat in silence, both deep in their own thoughts.

The journey finally came to an end at a jetty. Ahead of them was a jade sea sparkling in the sunshine. A beautiful Malaysian girl came to greet them and lead them into an ice-cool reception area where she proceeded to take down their details and register them.

'So that is two sea-view rooms for one week: is that correct, Mr Jack?' She gave him a dazzling smile.

'Yes, that is correct, thank you,' he said. 'Come on, Meredith, let's get on the boat.' And he was off towards the waiting motor-launch.

The journey took fifteen minutes and then they were stepping onto a wooden walkway being led towards paradise. All around them was turquoise water and deep green foliage. Huge palm trees soared towards the sky on the hills around the resort. As they walked into the reception they passed a peacock strutting his stuff, and the sound of birds and crickets was overwhelming. A porter took off with their luggage while a young man gave them each a glass of fruit juice.

'Please be seated and we will brief you on the details of the resort,' he said.

They sat down on enormous cream and walnut couches and leaned against plump silk and brocade cushions. Everything screamed luxury and good taste. The young man explained that there were different restaurants scattered around the island, with a wide range of cuisine. On the other side of the island was Emerald Cove, where they had arranged for Mr Jack to have a private dinner on the last night. At the spa, Miss Meredith was invited to enjoy a complimentary bath experience and massage – and perhaps they would like a Couple's Bath one day?

Meredith shifted uncomfortably on the sofa and quickly changed the subject. 'Can one swim in the sea?' she asked.

'Not this side of the island, no. We don't recommend it because of the jelly fish,' said the young man. 'But you can certainly do so on the other side at Emerald Cove. You should also try the jungle trek across the island and see the wildlife, such as the monkeys and Monitor Lizards.'

They finished their drink and the young man showed them the way to their rooms along a slatted walkway over the impossibly blue sea below. He pointed out the dreaded jelly fish which were happily floating in the clear water. It took at least ten minutes to walk to the houses on stilts that Meredith could see in the distance, but what a joy to stroll in this unbelievably beautiful environment! They stopped and watched a Monitor Lizard waddle along the shore. There were rocks covered in crabs, and fruit bats hanging from the trees above.

Their guide stopped finally and opened a door into a huge room flooded with light from all the windows which looked out over the ocean. The bed was inset into the wall, with a brocade bolster across the top and a perfect walnut chaise at the foot. Crisp, blindingly white sheets and masses of pillows beckoned to Meredith. Bliss! Double doors opened to reveal a bathroom with an enormous bath like a small swimming pool; its windows overlooked the ocean again. More doors led out onto a deck above the sea, completely private and not overlooked by any of the other bedrooms. Meredith looked down through the crystal-clear water and could see hundreds of little fish ducking and diving as one in a shoal.

'I hope this is to your liking?' enquired the young man.

'It is perfection. Thank you,' said Meredith.

'Mr Jack, I will take you to your room now, which is next door. This way, please.' And he left the room.

Jack turned and said, 'Right then, Miss Meredith, shall we meet at seven for dinner? I will come and pick you up.'

'Lovely, see you then.' Meredith closed the door and threw herself on the bed. It was so comfortable and the sheets were cool against her cheek. She sighed: this was heaven.

She unpacked and checked out the fridge and the mini-bar and then put on her old bikini and went and lay down on the deck. The sun was boiling even though it was already four o'clock by now. She smothered herself in sun cream and lay there soaking up the rays feeling the heat seeping into her bones. God, it felt good. She wanted to fall asleep again but thought that was maybe not a good idea as she would never sleep later, so she found the book on the spa treatments and studied it from cover to cover, noting which treatments she would like to have. Her eye caught a photo of a couple in a bath covered in rose petals: beneath it was a description of the Couple's Bath experience. It sounded amazing, and lasted three hours! Hardly suitable for her and Jack though, considering they had not touched each other for years. Best avoid that, she thought.

She had a long hot shower with the windows open so she could look out and see the sun go down. Tiny fishing boats were now dotting the horizon as it got dark. She dried her hair and put on a plain white linen shift then decided she hated seeing her pale white arms. Old lady arms! How depressing it was to get old. Once she had a bit of a suntan she wouldn't feel so bad. It was like one's fat bits – they always looked better when they were brown, and middle-aged arms looked more toned with a suntan. She changed into a long-sleeved loose-fitting kaftan and flip-flops, and went to sit on the deck with a glass of white wine, waiting for Jack to pick her up. He arrived on the dot of seven.

'This is the life, isn't it?' he said, and joined her with a glass of white wine. 'I must say, it is even better than I imagined.' He leaned on the railing and watched the fishing boats. 'They catch anchovies here apparently, the guy was telling me. Sunrise and sunset. Split shifts – now that is hard work. Come on then, let's go and sample the goods. What do you fancy eating tonight?'

'I don't mind,' said Meredith. 'You be leader.'

'Very well then, the Chinese is the closest, let's go there.'

He led her along the walkway. It was lit with hanging lights, and as Meredith gazed towards the land, there were more lights angled up into the trees, casting dramatic shadows. It really was like Fairyland. The Chinese restaurant was actually perched on top of a huge rock, jutting out over the sea. A huge tree grew up through it, and the roof had been cleverly built around it. It was like a Robinson Crusoe house and reminded her of the pictures in her book as a child.

The dinner was superb. The chef was called Master Ken, a strange name for a native Chinese. He was the longest-serving member of the resort, a venerable gentleman who still went to the local market every day and chose the produce that would be presented on the menu. The customers ate what he told them to eat, which included the fresh catch of the day, huge butterfly prawns and succulent duck. After their dinner, Meredith and Jack walked along to the next restaurant, which was a bar also. Here they had a coffee and a brandy, by which time Meredith was ready for bed.

They strolled back, enjoying the starry tropical night. Meredith, who was obsessed with mosquitoes, had covered herself with repellent, which felt sticky on her skin.

'Just forget about them,' said Jack.

'No, I hate them, they can ruin a holiday. Who wants to be covered in bloody great lumps?' she complained, swatting the darkness.

Fortunately, her room was cool and the maid had left a big mosquito-repelling dish to keep the pesky critters away.

Meredith bade Jack goodnight and fell into bed. Nothing would have woken her that night. In fact, she slept until eight o'clock and could not believe the sun streaming through her windows. She opened the doors and went out on the deck, where it was already very hot. The phone rang and she picked it up.

'Morning, Miss Meredith, are you ready for breakfast? I waited for you, and I thought this was a reasonable time to wake you up.' Jack sounded bright and bushy-tailed.

'Yes, absolutely. Give me five minutes and I will see you out the front.' She jumped in the shower and was in and out in a jiffy, not bothering to dry her hair; she whipped a pair of linen trousers on and a T-shirt and was outside her door as Jack was locking his door.

'I can't believe it but I am starving again,' she giggled, following Jack as he strode down the path.

'Me too,' he called over his shoulder.

Breakfast was a veritable feast. There was every conceivable kind of food, from Coco Pops to fish curry. It was a global kitchen, laid out for all to come and help themselves. There were chefs at various stations cooking eggs or waffles, even slicing sushi. Meredith didn't know where to start and ended up returning to her table with toast and marmalade.

'How mundane is that?' said Jack. 'Christ, Meredith, you had better get a bit more adventurous than that, my girl.'

'OK, Mr Flash "I have travelled the world" Blatchford, give us a chance,' she retorted. 'All in good time.'

'So what is the plan today then?' asked Jack. 'I'm going to make some calls from the library and send some emails, so shall we meet for lunch?'

'Yes, fine,' said Meredith. 'I shall check out the spa after breakfast and arrange my appointments. Do you want me to book anything for you?'

'No, don't worry, I will sort myself out later. Right, let's meet at twelve thirty at the sushi bar. Have a nice morning.' He was up and gone.

Meredith walked along the beach and checked out the huge Infinity pool near the main reception and then she had a quick look round the shop, which sold lots of yummy things like wraps and the kind of dresses that only ever look good in the sun and are always left in the back of the wardrobe at home. She made her way back to the spa, which also had a pool, and went into the reception area; it was like a temple, with a pond and a fountain and pots of incredibly sweet-smelling flowers everywhere.

Another exquisite young girl came and asked her, 'What can we get you, Miss Meredith?' It was just so incredible that all the staff somehow knew one's name. It was obviously a very clever marketing ploy, but it worked a treat!

'I would like to book some treatments, please,' said Meredith.

The girl led her to a couch by the fountain and gave her the book of treatments.

'Please choose and I will bring you a cold drink,' she said. She was back in a moment with a cold towel and a glass of fresh juice. Meredith made a time for her complimentary massage and also booked a facial. She had no idea what to expect so thought it best to start slowly.

'If you would like to come back in one hour we can start your bathing experience.'

'Bathing experience?' Meredith repeated.

'Oh, yes, you are bathed before all your treatments whatever they may be.' The girl smiled and continued, 'Then we give you your massage. This will take two hours. So you will be finished by twelve o'clock. Is this convenient for you?'

'Sounds perfect,' smiled Meredith.

An hour later, she returned and was greeted by the same girl, who took Meredith to a changing room and asked her to remove all her clothes. The girl then gave her a soft wrap to wear; she helped to tie it round Meredith's waist and fastened it with a safety pin with a tiny Chinese clog attached to it, on which was the number of her locker. Meredith was gently led to a seat next to a bowl on the floor full of water and petals. The girl washed Meredith's feet, dried them and then took a wooden stick and beat the soles quite hard until they tingled.

'This is because in China, small feet were considered beautiful and young women had to bind their feet so they became numb,' the girl explained. 'This beating helps the circulation and flow of blood to the feet.' She put a pair of flip-flops on Meredith's feet and led her to the bathhouse.

'First you have Malay Bath Experience,' she said brightly, and escorted Meredith to the edge of a well. 'Please to take a coin and make a wish.'

Meredith wished with all her heart for happiness for Anna and the family. She threw the coin into the well and then followed the girl to a pool. There was a waterfall and steps leading down into the water.

'Please enter,' said her helper. It was freezing cold and Meredith let out a yell which made the young girl laugh.

'Stay five minutes – it is good for circulation,' she said. 'Stand under the fountains and relieve your tension.'

There were three huge pots with spouts in them from which the water was gushing out like a big shower. Once she was used to the cold it was very refreshing; Meredith went and stood under one of the spouts and sure enough, the pressure was strong enough for her to feel it pummelling her shoulders. It was exhilarating.

After five minutes the girl appeared at the other end of the pool and directed Meredith up to a verandah where three pots stood in a row. Each pot had a plaque attached to it, describing its contents. Number one was cinnamon and turmeric, for passion. Number two was grapefruit and lemon, for cleansing, and number three was geranium for energy. The girl told her to inhale from one of the pots. Meredith decided the cleansing pot might be the safest and took a big snort.

Now it was onto the Japanese Bathing Experience. For this, Meredith had to sit on a stool in front of a tap with a rough flannel and soap, washing herself, and then finishing with ladles of water poured over her head. From here Meredith was taken outside – to a wonderful pool surrounded by gardens.

She lay in the warm scented water looking up at the blue sky through the overhanging trees. It was magical. But there was more to come. Her girl returned five minutes later and led her into a room where she had to lie face down on a table. The girl scrubbed her all over and then rinsed her with bowls of water. After Meredith had dried herself, she was given a clean sarong and was shown to an open room with beds and couches to sit on, looking out over the pool to the sea beyond. Her helper brought a pot of ginger tea, and left her to relax for a few minutes before someone else came to take her for her massage. By this time she was floating!

The massage table was ready for her to lie on in a beautifully cool room. The tiny slip of a masseuse held the sarong so Meredith could lie down on her stomach, and then arranged the sarong over her. Then the massage began. Meredith could not believe the next hour. Every muscle in her body was kneaded and teased into submission. The scent of the oils transported her to some distant land. Slowly she drifted into a semi-conscious state of complete pleasure. It was so sensuous she was aware of every nerve-ending tingling and her body relaxed into the caresses of the girl. She found herself thinking of Jack, of making love to him and what it would be like. She felt beautiful and sexy and her skin was alive.

By the time the young masseuse had finished, Meredith felt as if her body would melt if she lay there much longer. She went back to the changing room and had to sit for a minute to bring herself back to earth. She felt amazing – but so horny! How on earth was she going to explain this on the TV when she was extolling the virtues of massage and herbal treatments? Somehow, she managed to pull herself together, got dressed and went to find Jack in the sushi bar.

'How was it?' he asked, looking her up and down, and taking a sip from a tall glass of chilled beer.

'Unbelievable,' Meredith said softly. 'Jack, if you do nothing else this week, you must take the bathing experience and have a massage. It is indescribably wonderful.' The waiter brought the menu and Meredith concentrated on the food to take her mind off sex and how gorgeous Jack looked in his linen trousers and shirt.

'Right, well, that's me told. I will book it straight away after we have had lunch. I must say, you do look very chilled.'

After lunch, Jack went off to book a massage and Meredith went to lie by the pool. She read her book and fell asleep and was awoken by Jack with a tray of drinks.

'Here you go, light refreshments before we change for dinner. They have arranged our sunset dinner for tonight, I'm afraid, so we will have to get ready by six thirty to go to the other side of the island.'

'Oh right, what time is it now?' she asked dreamily.

'Five o'clock, so there's plenty of time. I have booked a course of four treatments,' Jack went on. 'I go every day starting tomorrow and have special oils to help me de-stress. So look out, I will be so laid back you won't recognise me. And I checked out the Couple's Bathing Experience: we don't have to get naked or anything, just have our massages together and then we end up in a scented bath – but we can wear a costume. I think we should do it for a laugh.' Jack was looking at her, eyes twinkling. 'Come on, Ms Lee, you can do it!'

Meredith looked at him sitting in front of her and wanted to kiss him so badly. Well, maybe tonight after the sunset supper and a few glasses of wine, she could test the water?

'We will see. Right, after this drink I shall go off to get ready for dinner. I take it we are going in the shuttle car rather than trekking across the island on foot?'

'Absolutely, my lover.' He grinned at her.

They clinked glasses and made a toast: 'To the Couple's Bathing Experience' – and burst out laughing.

Chapter Twenty-Five

Meredith went to a great deal of trouble with her hair and make-up that evening, and chose a long dress with a split up the leg. She had a few swigs of wine for Dutch courage and by the time six o'clock came she was raring to go. She slipped her arm through Jack's and they set off to the pick-up point. Jack was on great form and made her laugh all night. It felt like a date and both of them were aware of how beautiful the surroundings were and how everything was geared up for romance.

The food was sexy – starting with prawns heated in a dish on an open fire. The chef cooked them in seawater so they were salted naturally and the whole dish smelled of the sea. There were scallops tossed in butter, their soft shiny flesh dissolving on the tongue. They were served lobster which they ate with their fingers, dipping the pink morsels into bowls of melted butter which ran down their chin. Several times Jack leaned across and wiped Meredith's mouth with his napkin. She was aware of his fingertips on her cheek and felt a shock of electricity as his elbow brushed her breast. She felt her nipple harden and knew he had noticed because he paused ever so slightly and held her gaze. His eyes were so bright in the firelight.

They finished with watermelon and went and stood in the sea to clean their hands. Jack splashed her and she splashed him back and suddenly they were in the water and he was holding her against him and laughing, and then they both tripped and fell in the waves and choked on the seawater.

'Look at my dress – it's ruined!' Meredith cried.

'Take it off,' said Jack.

'Oh yes, very funny,' she replied. 'Just what the staff need to be seeing.' She dragged herself back up the beach where the waiter was standing with a huge towel.

'Please, Miss Meredith, take towel. Here is sarong – you go over there to hut and change.' He pointed to a wooden changing room which Meredith hadn't noticed before, hidden in the trees.

'Oh, perfect. Thank you so much.' She took the towel and set off for the hut.

'Watch out for the snakes,' called Jack as he took another towel and followed Meredith up the beach.

She stopped dead in her tracks. 'Are there snakes here? I am terrified of them. You have to go first and check for me. Please, Jack, I am serious,' she said.

'There aren't any snakes, I was only joking,' he said, but one look at her face and he knew nothing would convince her unless he did his snake duty. 'OK, OK, I will check.'

He disappeared into the hut and a few moments later he called to Meredith: 'This is a five-star hut! There is even air-con in here.'

Meredith walked in and leaped ten feet into the air as Jack jumped out from behind the door and grabbed her.

'You bastard, you absolute bastard. I hate you,' she spluttered, but then Jack kissed her hard and pulled her to him. She kissed him back, her tongue seeking his, tasting seawater and aftershave. She wanted to wrap herself around him but her wet dress got in the way. She tugged at it.

'Wait – don't, you'll tear it,' gasped Jack. He tried to get it over her head but it kept sticking to her. She half-wriggled out of her pants as he fumbled with her bra, attempting to get his trousers off at the same time, but they were soaking and like Meredith's dress, they clung to him. Seeing the funny side, they both burst out laughing and sat down on the bench in the hut.

'Stop it, this is daft. Let's go back to that beautiful bedroom, please. I am too old for all this,' said Jack.

'I am so glad you mentioned the "old" word before me,' Meredith giggled. She slid off her dress, started to dry herself and wrapped the sarong around her body.

'Aren't you going to put your knickers back on?' Jack asked cheekily.

'There doesn't seem much point if you are going to take them off again later,' responded Meredith, picking up all the wet things off the floor.

Jack held her by the shoulders and looked at her. 'Is it really what you want, Meredith? You mustn't think you have to do anything because I brought you here and I joke about having baths and stuff. God knows, I don't want to spoil any friendship we might have, but I have to tell you, Meredith, I want you so badly and I have wanted you from the first moment I saw you again.' He leaned in and kissed her deeply and passionately until she couldn't breathe any longer. She pulled back.

'Oh Jack, me too. I have dreamed of this moment.' She took his hand and they went back and asked the attendant to call the shuttle. They drove back in absolute silence, holding hands in the back of the car, hardly daring to move in case they broke the spell. They found their way along the walkway still holding hands, carrying their wet clothes, and stopped at Meredith's room. Her hand was shaking as she unlocked the door. Suddenly she felt so shy and nervous.

Jack shut the door and they both stood in the middle of the

room not quite knowing what to do next, then Jack said, 'Shall we wash the saltwater off?'

Meredith went into the bathroom and let out a yelp. 'Jack, come and look at this!' He rushed in expecting at the very least a spider in the bath, if not a snake, but was stopped in his tracks by the sight of the bath full to the brim with water and rose petals floating on it, and lighted candles all around.

'What the hell is this all about?' he said.

Meredith started to laugh. 'I bet that this is all part of the Sunset Dinner Experience. Couples go out, have dinner and come back and find this. Well, all I can say is, why not? Let's do it, Mr Jack.' And she pulled off her sarong and stepped into the warm luxurious water smelling of roses.

'I agree wholeheartedly, Miss Meredith,' said Jack and joined her. 'Well, we won't need the Couple's Bathing Experience after this, will we?'

Meredith slid her leg across him under the water and whispered, 'Oh, I think you'll find we will, Mr Jack,' and took him in her hand and guided him into her as she kissed him deeply.

The next morning, they ordered breakfast in bed and every morning after that. Meredith lived in a continuous state of euphoria. It was ridiculous to be this happy at this late stage in her life. She lay naked on the deck and drank champagne and ate watermelon, and let Jack have his wicked every-which way with her. She couldn't believe she could be so uninhibited about her body. Even when she was young and not bad-looking, she had been shy and had never felt pretty. Jack made her feel gorgeous. He was a fantastic lover and also he made her laugh. They laughed all day long. The week flew by in a haze of sunsets and flowers and sex.

On the last evening, Jack seemed moody and withdrawn on their way back to his room from the beach and Meredith began to feel uneasy. The dream was coming to an end. What would happen to them when they got home? Jack hadn't mentioned Mo at all, and Meredith had deliberately not asked about her. But she knew they would soon be back to reality. She couldn't contemplate a future without him, could not accept that this was all there was going to be between them. Was Jack Blatchford the same old schmoozer? Had he seduced her like before, and now she would be dumped again?

'What about Mo?' The words were out of her mouth before she could stop them.

Jack didn't bother to pretend. 'I don't know,' he said quietly. 'She is a good woman. She doesn't deserve this.' He got up and walked across to the edge of the decking.

'So what are you going to do then?' asked Meredith, trying to keep the panic out of her voice.

'I honestly don't know.' And Meredith was shocked to see how tormented he looked. 'I had no idea I was going to feel like this about you, I really didn't. Yes, I knew there was a bit of a spark between us, and I guess I thought, What the hell, when we made love the other night. It was a kind of for old times' sake thing, you know? But it has caught me by surprise. I do care about you, but there is so much to deal with here. It is not just you and Mo, it is Anna and her baby. Suddenly I have a whole load of new stuff to take on board, and it's a shock. To tell you the truth, I have enough trouble at the moment coping with Harry and all his shit, little sod. I honestly don't know what to do. I don't want to hurt anybody, but I guess that is inevitable in the end. But please, can you give me some time to work through how I feel?'

Meredith felt numb. 'Of course,' came a tiny voice out of nowhere. 'Do what you have to do, Jack. We are not teenagers. We have baggage in our lives and people around us who need us. Of course I understand. I just hope . . .' She ground to a halt as she fought to keep the tears at bay. *Don't cry. Don't you dare cry. Just get out of this room now!*

She turned and left. Back in her room, she collapsed on the bed. She let out a sob and then shoved her fist into her mouth. She must not cry. She had to keep herself together. Her instincts told her that the way she handled the next twenty-four hours would affect the rest of her life. She had to back off and let Jack work things out for himself. Did he care about her enough? She could not be sure, but she had to trust it would turn out all right. She had come this far in her life, and if she had to walk away from him – so be it.

She must have fallen asleep because suddenly there was a knocking on the door and when she opened her eyes it was dark.

'Who is it?' she called out.

'Room service. You want your bed turned down, Miss Meredith?'

'Oh no, don't worry, I'm fine, thank you,' answered Meredith. She wondered where Jack had got to and rang his room. He picked up on the second ring.

'I fell asleep,' said Meredith. 'Have you had dinner?'

'I wasn't very hungry, to be honest. Do you want to walk over and get a snack now? It's not too late.'

'Yes, OK. See you outside.' Meredith went to the bathroom and splashed cold water on her face. Thank God she had staved off the tears otherwise she would not have been able to show her face. She could never cry prettily; everything swelled up. She put on some more mascara and a bit of lipstick, and changed into a long dress. It was very warm tonight. Strangely, she was feeling completely calm now. Her mind was empty of any thoughts and she was operating on autopilot. She would deal with everything when she got home, she had decided. Make this last evening a lovely memory, not an unhappy ending.

Jack was waiting on the walkway and they strolled to the restaurant in silence. They ordered a Thai curry and went and sat in the corner.

'Are you all right, Meredith?' Jack asked. 'I have fucked this up, haven't I?'

Meredith looked at his lovely face and saw how sad and haunted his eyes were.

'No, you haven't, Jack. I am as much to blame. I knew you were in a relationship but I suppose I just didn't want to think about it.' She smiled at him wistfully. 'I don't regret the last few days, though,' she added.

'Neither do I. I will work it out, Meredith, I promise.' He picked up his glass. 'I want to propose a toast. '"To your drawers, Miss Lee. As one drawer closes, another one falls open!"'

'What the hell does that mean!' exclaimed Meredith.

'I have no idea, but it sounds profound, don't you think? Come on, let's get drunk.' He tossed back his cocktail and ordered a bottle of champagne, even though he said it gave him indigestion.

They did get very drunk and fell into bed. They did not speak as they undressed, and as they kissed their way to the ultimate conclusion of their last night, Meredith held a silent scream in her throat.

They made love slowly and intensely, and Meredith pulled Jack into her and tried to keep him there. She wanted every last bit of him inside her forever.

Chapter Twenty-Six

Stepping into her house was like returning from Outer Space. Meredith felt light-headed and mildly hysterical. She wanted Jack! She wanted to hold him and kiss him and feel him inside her. Jesus, she was hysterical. Maybe the first order of the day was a visit to the GP to get some Valium to calm her down. Or maybe she should get straight onto the HRT, to make sure she didn't fall apart now. Just dive into the menopause and forget Jack Blatchford.

She was stopped in her reverie by the pile of mail stacked on her desk. Where to start? She decided to call France first and check that all was well with Anna. She put the kettle on while she waited to connect.

'Hello, who is calling?' It was Penny Wilson.

'Penny, it's Meredith. *Bonjour! Ca va?*' She chuckled as Penny screamed into the phone.

'*Ca va* very bloody well, my dear. Are you back? How was it?'

'It was great, but before you go off on one and interrogate me, can I speak to my daughter first?'

'Of course. I will go and get Anna – she is by the pool sunning her little bump. It's so cute! Will you talk to me when you have finished with her, please?'

'Yes, of course, you idiot.' Meredith smiled at her friend's inability to hide her curiosity.

'Hi Mum, welcome home. Did you have a great time?' Anna sounded so young on the phone.

'Hello, darling. Yes, it was wonderful. How are you feeling? How's Tom?'

'I am fine – no more sickness, thank goodness, and Tom is great. He is really looking after me. It's fantastic weather here – are you going to come out soon?'

'Well, yes. I was thinking of coming at the weekend and—'

'Oh, that would be great. Will Jack be coming with you?'

'I am not sure, dear. He has a lot on his plate at the moment. Let's wait and see. Now put Penny back on so I can arrange flights, et cetera. Lots of love, darling.' Meredith took a deep breath as tears pricked at the back of her eyes.

'So, was there any romance?' Penny demanded.

'Now hang on a minute, give us a chance: we hardly know each other.' Meredith tried to make light of a potentially disastrous conversation. Her friend knew her too well not to pick up the vibes.

'Um excuse me, but do you not have a daughter together?' asked Penny.

'Well yes, but that is different. I mean, we don't actually know each other. Anyway, enough already. I will explain all when I see you at the weekend. If I take a flight on Friday night, I will get down to you around midnight and then we have got all weekend. I shall have to come back on Monday because I start this new series then. Do you want me to bring anything?'

'All the latest mags would be great, and tea bags, as we've nearly run out. How delicious it will be to see you and give you a hug. Bye.' Penny hung up.

Congratulating herself on her control, Meredith made a pot of tea and got down to opening the mail.

Two hours later, she had a pile of To Do's, and a stack of bills to be paid. Leaving them on the desk, she lugged her cases upstairs and decided to take a short nap. She closed her eyes and could see Jack's face. The next thing she knew, it was evening, and she was awakened by the phone.

'Hello? It's Mum,' Jane said. 'Just wanted to know how it all went.'

Meredith's heart sank. She had really wanted to avoid this conversation until she was feeling stronger. Her mother's radar would be twitching the moment she heard Meredith's voice.

'Hi Mum, it was fine but not what I hoped, and now I am going to be a pain and burst into tears.' Meredith was true to her word.

'Oh dearest heart, I am so sorry. Don't cry. What happened?'

'We made fantastic love and I fell head over heels in love, and Jack was scared off basically. Mum, he has got a woman he obviously adores, well, he cares about her anyway, and the relationship suits him. He doesn't want any complications.' She sniffed and blew her nose on a tissue.

'I see. Are you sure about that? What are you going to do about Anna? Is he still going to be around for her?' Jane asked carefully.

'Yes, we will be "friends", Mother. We will behave like reasonable grown-up human beings, I suppose. Damn it!' She shed some more tears. 'Oh Mum, it's such a mess. But I will get over it. I will have to, for Anna's sake. I am just so sick of being on my own, and we get on so well, and he makes me laugh and he is fantastic in bed . . . and he belongs to someone else!' she wailed.

'Now come on, dear, it's not all bad. You can find a way to move forward – and never say never. He may change his mind as time goes on.' Jane tried hard to give her daughter a positive take on the situation. 'Now go to sleep, and remember: things always look better in the morning. What are you doing tomorrow, by the way?'

'Going to see the Accountants and find out how much my inheritance is going to be,' replied Meredith.

'Well, that's something to look forward to, at any rate,' Jane said bracingly. 'You will be lovelorn but rich, dear! Now go to sleep and lots of love.' She put down the receiver.

Meredith suddenly realised she was starving. She made some beans on toast and took it to bed with her. As she always said, there was nothing like carbs in a crisis . . . and Meredith fell asleep with a ring of Heinz tomato sauce around her mouth.

'Sixty-five million, eight hundred and thirty pounds to be precise,' announced Mr Lowe, of Lowe & Sons Chartered Accountants.

'Oh my God,' whispered Meredith. 'This is insane.' She turned to Jack and took his hand, and said, 'What on earth do I do with sixty-five million pounds?'

'Don't stress too much, Meredith, because it is all being taken care of, as I am sure Jeffrey here will explain,' he said. This was the cue for Mr Lowe to step forward importantly and proceed to list exactly where all the monies were invested, and deposited, and collected and retained. He droned on and on and Meredith just tuned out. She couldn't believe that any one person had this much money: it was immoral. She interrupted Mr Lowe to ask, 'Can I give some away to charity, please?'

'Yes, of course you can, but I should point out that Mr Harrison had already made provision for several charities by way of a contribution of ten per cent of his annual global profits. That is quite a considerable sum, as you can imagine.'

So Myles was not all bad then, thought Meredith. 'Yes, well, I have several charities of my own that I would also like to benefit from this money,' she told him.

'Of course, Ms Lee. If you would like to give us a list and tell us how much you wish to donate, we will set up a payment annually. Now, with regard to all the rented properties, would you like to leave things as they are for the time being?'

Meredith looked at Jack, who nodded and said, 'Yes, I think Ms Lee would like time to adjust to her new position as head of the company before she makes any decisions.'

'Very well then, we can talk sometime soon and we will await your instructions. As I have already said, all the tax has been taken care of, and of course if you are happy with our service, we will continue to monitor all payments and investments on your behalf.'

When Meredith said, 'Yes, that's fine. Thank you very much, Mr Lowe,' the man looked relieved that he was still in a job. Meredith then asked: 'Re. the purchase of the Marsh Hall estate, how long do you think it will be before that is finalised?' She was so excited for Frank and Jenny and was desperate to tell them the good news.

'Oh, any day now, I should think. We have had all the searches back and the survey has already been done through Mr Blatchford's company; and being a cash deal, we should be able to exchange next week.'

'That is great news. Well, thank you, Mr Lowe, for all your hard work. I will no doubt be in touch very soon.' Meredith shook hands with the accountant and turned to Jack. 'Are we ready then?'

'Absolutely. Thank you, Jeffrey, always a joy doing business with you.' The men shook hands and then Jack and Meredith were out of the door and down the stairs.

Meredith was in a daze. She took Jack's arm and let him

guide her down the Strand towards the Savoy where they had decided to have lunch.

It was only once they were seated in the Grill Room with a large vodka martini each that she was able to put her thoughts into some kind of order.

'This is ridiculous, Jack!' she burst out. 'I don't need all this money. I really don't want to know, honestly.'

'Steady on, girl, as I've tried to explain before, you don't have to deal with any of it if you don't want to. It all works perfectly well by itself. All you do is carry on and live your life as usual, but somewhere in the back of that drawer of yours, you will know that you never ever have to worry about money again. Forget it! Come on, drink up and let's eat. I am starving and we have important things to discuss later.'

'Like what?' she asked.

'How you are going to get this TV show up and running. We need to see the property and get a crew down there asap.'

'Christ, I had completely forgotten about that!' cried Meredith, flustered. 'How the bloody hell am I going to set this all up in time?'

'Oh, you'll do it. We will go to Marsh Hall on Wednesday morning very early with a cameraman and your director and do a recce. Then we can go and break the news to Frank, and take him and the family out for lunch. After that, we can sign the solicitor's stuff at their office down there and be home by teatime.' He beamed at her.

Meredith laughed. 'I am exhausted already.'

But that is exactly what they did. Meredith got the cameraman and Jo her director to come with them, and they did a full tour of the estate. It had been empty for a few months now so although it was not exactly derelict, it needed some tender loving care and money spent on it. Meredith had left her plans with the architect before she went away, and he had returned a set of drawings as a rough guide. It helped having Jack with her because he could point out all sorts of things she had no idea about, like drains and electricity cables and structural work that would have to be done.

They tried to cost it approximately so that they could work on a script for the first episode of the show. Meredith had agreed with Channel Seven that this particular project was incredibly expensive and that she would have to foot a good deal of the costs. However, she was quite happy to do this because they could create a fantastic opening episode for the show. It would be a real one-off and would hopefully hook their audience straight away. The rest of the series would be rather more modest properties that anyone with a vision and a good bank manager, or mortgage company, could develop. She already had a couple in Scotland who had found a castle they wanted to restore, and a young lawyer who wanted to turn a former vicarage into a boutique B&B, and a young artist who had found a barn to convert into a studio.

The Marsh Hall estate was a fantastic challenge. The house itself was built in the eighteenth century. It had fourteen double bedrooms, all big enough to build in bathrooms en suite. There were five or six smaller bedrooms, which would have been the servants' quarters; these were still classed as double rooms, and a couple of them could convert into further en suite bathrooms. The ground floor had an impressive entrance hall with a huge stone fireplace set to the side, in front of which were two heavy brocaded armchairs. On the left was an arch leading through into a large reception room. Meredith and Jack thought it could be turned into an office and front reception area, incorporating the foyer. The office part could be disguised by panelling or some-such in the style of the period of the house.

A long corridor stretched either way at the back of the foyer, off which were three huge reception rooms, all with floor-to-ceiling double doors leading out onto the patio, which ran along the rear of the house. A graceful flight of stone steps led down to sweeping lawns, which in turn led down to the lake. The garden was incredibly beautiful and owed its elegance to Capability Brown, the renowned landscape gardener. One reception room would be the dining room, one the drawing room and the other a library. Although Marsh Hall was destined to become a health farm, Meredith's vision was that the guests would experience the life of a lord or his lady in these magnificent surroundings. The furniture and other items would be antiques, chosen to fit with the style and period of the house. Jack had managed to secure the property before it went to auction, but the contents were still going under the hammer, and Meredith intended to make sure she was first in line on the day, to secure as many of the original treasures as possible.

The orangerie needed serious restoration, but even in its present shabby state one could see the potential. The fruit trees were mature and full of oranges and lemons. The smell was fantastic. To the side was the perfect spot to build a swimming pool.

In the basement, Meredith discovered a warren of rooms and a massive wine cellar. The stone vaults could be converted into treatment rooms.

'My goodness, this really is a vision and a half you have here,' said Jo, her director. She sounded awestruck. 'How will we shoot it?'

'Well, obviously it's going to take longer than the whole series, so I am proposing we film as we go along, and each week we come back to it,' Meredith said. 'We can get lots of footage from now on, of all the big building stuff going on.'

Outside, there were loads of barns and stables, all of which would become treatment rooms and staff quarters. From the top of the hill across from the main house the crew all looked down over a rolling field to one side of the lake, and in the distance, Meredith could see her old childhood home.

'There it is, see?' she said, pointing at the cluster of buildings. 'That's the Malthouse Farm, where my brother Frank lives. So what we will have is a working farm right next door, which will provide all the organic produce for us and keep my brother gainfully employed for the rest of his life.'

They had finished up walking round the estate and then agreed to let Jo, and Bill the cameraman, go to the pub while Jack and Meredith went to visit her mother. It was a few months since Meredith had been up to the farm and she was shocked at how dilapidated it all looked. Frank and Jenny and her mother were all there to greet them and take them into the big farmhouse kitchen, which held so many memories for Meredith.

Jane had told Meredith in advance that they wouldn't hear of her and Jack going to the pub to eat. They would all eat together at home.

Frank was so chuffed to see his sister. He gave her a big hug and said, 'Right then, what'll it be to drink? Homemade cider or that rubbish from a bottle you like so much?'

Meredith couldn't stomach the homemade stuff any more, it was way too strong for her, so she chose the bottled cider. Jack, however, was quick to answer: 'Oh, now you are talking, my lover. Give me a drop of the hard stuff, please. There's nothing like a pint of Scrumpy to put hairs on your chest!'

They all laughed and Meredith relaxed as she watched her brother showing Jack his array of homemade ciders and elderflower wine. She gave her sister-in-law a hug. 'Jenny, you look wonderful. How are your two terrible teenagers?'

'Terrible,' grinned Jenny. 'A real handful. Well, Sam is not as bad as Mary, to be honest, though he hates school. He wants to be with his dad on the farm. I think that when he finishes his GCSEs next year, that will be it for your nephew. He will leave school and come and work here.'

'Nothing wrong with that,' said Meredith. 'It's exactly what Frank did, isn't it, Mum?'

'I know, but I just hope there is enough for him to do – you know, with the farm as it is and all.' Jenny went quiet and looked to Jane for help.

'Come on, sit down, lunch is ready,' said Jane, changing the subject. 'We know you haven't got much time so let's get on. Frank, come on now, wash your hands and let Jack sit down. Jenny, you dish up the vegetables.' They all sat down round the huge kitchen table and tucked into juicy steak and kidney pie, topped with soft buttery pastry, creamy mashed potatoes and beans from the garden. It was perfect. For dessert they had fresh strawberries and huge jugs of thick Jersey cream from Frank's cows.

'This is heaven,' said Jack. 'It brings back my childhood in Somerset. Sitting here, I realise how much I miss the country-side.' He looked across at Meredith and smiled.

Trying not to think about how wonderful it would be to live with Jack in a beautiful house in the country, she turned to Frank and, taking a deep breath, decided the moment had come to make her announcement.

'Speaking of buying property, I want to put something to you, little brother. You may remember I always had this dream to buy somewhere and do it up and turn it into a luxury hotel or spa or something. Well, I have found the perfect place, and because I am doing this TV series about property and develop-ing, they are willing to help me with the project and we will film it as part of the programme. Jack has agreed to go into partner-ship with me and take on all the building side, so I can concentrate on the design and marketing. As regards funding the whole thing …' she swallowed. 'Well, I have inherited some money which will go towards it, and it looks like we have a deal.'

Meredith paused and looked round the table. Frank and Jenny were listening politely and her mother's eyes were shining brightly. Well, here goes, she thought. 'The thing is, the property I have bought is the Marsh Hall estate, and what I am hoping is that you will agree to combine forces with me, and look after the whole caboodle. I would like you, Frank and Jenny, to manage the estate; this will be a salaried position, but you will have a special interest in farming your land to service the Hotel and Spa. That way, we would be able to be completely self-sufficient, you see.'

Meredith took advantage of the stunned silence to hurry on with: 'I wondered if you would mind if we did a bit of renovating on this place as well, while we have everyone on site. We could renew the roof and maybe put in a new kitchen while we're about it. The costs would be swallowed up by the scale of the other works. I don't want to interfere, and it is absolutely your decision, you two, but it would be brilliant if we could turn this around and make a big family business out of the whole thing. Please!' She crossed her fingers under the table.

Frank went and stood with his back to them at the Aga. One of the collies went up to him and licked his hand as if to check he was all right. He stroked the dog's head absentmindedly and then he turned with a huge grin on his face and said, 'Well, that sounds like a plan. I'm up for it if you are too, Jenny.' And when Jenny nodded excitedly, her face pink with emotion, Meredith sprang up from the table and flung her arms around them both.

'I knew you would see sense. Frank, it is going to be wonderful, I promise you. Jenny, are you really OK with this?'

Jenny had tears in her eyes. 'I don't know how to thank you. This is the answer to all my prayers.' She gave Meredith another hug.

Meredith left them and went to put her arms round her mother, saying, 'See, Mum? I told you it would be OK.'

'No, dear,' replied Jane. '*I* told *you* it would be OK.' And she smiled at her daughter and held out her hand to Jack. 'Thank you for all your help.'

After they had all recovered themselves, Meredith and Jack bade everyone farewell and went into St Albans to see the solicitors and exchange contracts. They picked up Jo and Bill on the way, and then drove back to London. After dropping the others off, Jack made for Hampstead.

'What did I tell you?' he bragged, pulling up outside Meredith's house. 'Home by teatime.'

'God, it must be a terrible burden, being right all the time,' teased Meredith.

Jack opened the car door and leaned across to give her a kiss on the cheek. He paused and looked into her eyes. 'I hope we can have a chat sometime soon about everything.'

He moved back into his seat and Meredith waited for him to explain. Nothing was forthcoming, however, so she gathered her things up and said gently, 'I am fine, Jack. I understand it is hard for you. I am just so grateful for everything you have done for me and the family. Goodnight.'

She got out of the car and walked up to her front door, not turning round to wave goodbye because she couldn't trust herself to keep up the calm front. The thought occurred to her that maybe Jack had done all this in order to appease his guilt for sleeping with her. If that were the case, at least there had been a positive side to her holiday romance. But it was no consolation at all.

Meredith worked all day Thursday and Friday on the scripts for the show and managed to put a schedule together to start shooting the week after she got back from France the following Monday.

She had a meeting with Oliver about the format for his cookery show, and promised she would have a team sorted to start shooting in October. She then had a meeting with the boss at Channel Seven and it was decided that the chat show would have to wait until after Christmas, which was fine by Meredith, who was up to her neck.

When she finally left London to join the others on holiday, Meredith sat on the plane to Nice, tired but happy. All the plans were in place. It was going to be a busy few months. Good job, because she wouldn't have time to think about Jack too much. That's a joke, she thought. I will be seeing him all the time on the project. She looked out of the window as the plane began its descent. She would cope for Anna's sake. Her heart filled with love at the thought of her gorgeous girl, and she promised herself that no matter how busy she was, she would enjoy time with her daughter and help give her strength for the coming birth. If her mother could do it for her, and Jane's mother had done it for her daughter, Meredith could certainly carry the flag.

Walking out of the airport feeling the warm Mediterranean breeze on her cheek and inhaling the perfume of bougainvillaea, Meredith's spirits lifted. Maybe there was a dishy vineyard-owner living next door to the Wilsons' villa. *Vive la France!*

Chapter Twenty-Seven

Summer gradually came to an end, and Meredith had never worked so hard.

By the end of September, Frank and Jenny were camping out in the barn while the farmhouse was being given a new roof and kitchen; when that was done, it would be redecorated throughout. Jane was in her element, helping Jenny to choose fabrics, making cushion covers and knitting for Anna's baby. Frank was spending hour after hour with local providers of stock. He had decided to start a rare pig herd as well as his herd of Jerseys, and with some help from Meredith, who took no notice of any protest he tried to make, he increased the numbers. This was the only way to make farming pay these days.

Marsh Hall estate was mostly arable: 1,000 acres of wheat and 1,000 acres of rapeseed, which was the new thing. But then he and Meredith, with input from Jane and Jenny and the kids, had to plan the vegetable gardens for the health farm, and the greenhouses for the tomatoes and salad products. It was going to be a massive enterprise. The building works on the main house were just about to commence, and Jack kept a close eye on this, even though he was busy elsewhere with a block of offices in the City, as well as the Malaysian project. He just seemed to thrive on stress and challenges.

By the beginning of December, Meredith was working on her plans for Christmas. It was going to be difficult because of space. She didn't have enough room at her house for everybody to stay. She discussed it with Jack, who suggested they all go to the Caribbean.

'Well, that is just ridiculous,' Meredith scoffed. 'Think of the cost!'

'Oh, don't start that again,' he grumbled. 'How many times do I have to remind you that you are rich?'

'I know that, but how do you think I can justify or explain that kind of money to Anna or Frank?' she replied. 'It has to be something reasonable. Maybe we can all go to a hotel some- where? That would be lovely and no one has to do any cooking. Mind you, that is very impersonal. I love Christmas so much: it has to be like I remember them when I was young. A real Christmas tree and log fires and chestnuts and all that.' She sighed, the memories flooding back.

'Why don't you rent a house?' Jack said. 'Then you can dec- orate how you want and cook and do everything.'

'Yes, perfect. Mr Clever Clogs has done it again!'

Meredith found an amazing house in Wiltshire, which was not too far for everyone to get to. The plan was to travel down the day before Christmas Eve and stay until 27 December. Everyone could then go off and do their own thing for New Year. Jack had suggested he and Harry could come for Christmas Eve and leave the day after Boxing Day. Apparently, Mo had her family coming on Christmas Day but wanted to spend New Year with Jack. Meredith had no choice but to agree. She had been so busy the last few months that she hadn't had time to fret over her situation with Jack, but she was dread- ing the holidays for this very reason.

There would be Meredith and Jack and Harry and Anna and Tom and Jane and Frank and Jenny and their two, Sam and Mary, the Wilsons and the Neils. The latter would come for Boxing Day and then take Tom and Anna back to London on 27 December. Oliver and Michael would also drive down for Boxing Day. The house had ten bedrooms in the main building and four bedrooms in the barn-annexe at the side, which had its own bathroom and even a kitchen. Harry, Adam, Millie, Tom and Anna, and Sam and Mary could sleep there, and the adults could all be in the main house.

Meredith was in her element. She hired a catering company to do Christmas Eve and Boxing Day, and she would cook Christmas Day. Jack thought she was crazy, but she wanted the most important day to be just family. She ordered a twenty-foot tree for the front garden and a fifteen-foot tree to go in the hall. All the kids had trees in their rooms. There were fairy lights everywhere. Way beyond good taste! When Anna was little, Meredith would never let the poor child decorate the tree because like all small children she wanted to hang too much on it. So she was banned from touching the big tree, but Meredith always got her a little tree of her very own in her bedroom to decorate as she wanted, and sure enough the little tree would bend under the weight of so many baubles and trinkets and a huge angel teetering on the top.

Everyone was informed that they had to buy a present for Secret Santa. This involved drawing a name from a hat which was a secret to everyone except the person who drew the name. Then that person had to buy a present for said recipient, and it would be whatever they could afford. The presents would be given out on Boxing Day when everyone was there.

The whole venture turned out to be a big success, and Christmas Day especially was one of the happiest Meredith could remember. She spent Christmas Eve night in a state of exhausted excitement, waiting for everyone to go to sleep so she could creep round the teenagers' rooms with her sack of goodies. Jack tried to watch TV in between Meredith coming into the room to report another successful deposit in a stocking. By 3 a.m. she fell into bed, her mission accomplished, and when the alarm went off at 7 a.m. on Christmas morning, she was almost too tired to speak. But the excitement of the day took over and a glass of Buck's Fizz kept her eyes open enough to get the turkey in the oven. Actually it was Jack and Griff Wilson who did the honours, as it was bloody heavy and almost as big as a small pony! Meanwhile, Penny and Meredith and Jane peeled potatoes and sprouts and parsnips and drank too much.

By noon Meredith was in serious trouble of being drunk and disorderly. Jack suggested she lay down for half an hour and escorted her to bed where she tried to seduce him through fits of giggles. He gave her a hug and said, 'Don't be naughty, Ms Lee. It is very tempting.'

'Obviously not quite tempting enough though,' said Meredith grumpily, the drink making her bold. 'Have you still got nothing to tell me? How is dear Mo?' She stopped herself and had the grace to look ashamed. 'Sorry, but it still hurts, believe it or not. Please go downstairs. I need to change for lunch.' She dismissed Jack with as much good grace as she could muster and spent the next half-hour trying to make herself look ravishing.

'Well, you look refreshed,' said Penny snidely, giving her a sidelong glance. 'Amazing what a little nap can do, eh, Jane?'

Her mother was folding napkins with enormous concentration. 'Yes, dear,' came her reply.

Meredith threw Penny a dirty look and went to her mother's side. 'Mum, sit down and have a rest. I'll do that – give it here.' Taking the napkins, she tried to repeat her mother's impressive

411

folding but soon gave up and stuck them at the side of the plates. All the teenagers were watching some terrible American comedy DVD; the men were dozing in front of *The Sound of Music*. The perfect Christmas Day, thought Meredith, and went to make the bread sauce.

Everything went without a hitch – and by six o'clock it was all over bar the odd cracker. It was then that Harry suddenly appeared from the annexe and said, 'Dad, would it be OK if a friend of mine came to stay tonight? Her grandparents only live a few minutes down the road, as it happens. Her parents have come down to visit, but are going back to London first thing in the morning and she doesn't want to go with them as she'll be all alone in her flat in Finsbury Park.'

'Do I know this girl?' asked Jack.

'No, I don't think you have met her but she has been sort of going around with us lately. She is really nice.' Harry was look-ing awkward.

'I am sure that would be fine, wouldn't it, Jack?' Meredith said. 'We have got lots of space. She could share with Millie. Is that OK with you, Penny?'

'Doesn't bother me – I'm not the one who is going to be shar-ing with her,' joked Penny. 'No, I'm sure Millie won't mind.'

'OK then,' said Jack. 'Go ahead and call her. Can she get her-self here though, because we have all been drinking.'

'Yeah, that's cool; she said her parents would drop her off on the way back to London. Thanks, Meredith, thanks, Dad.' And he disappeared off to phone her.

'Girlfriend?' asked Meredith.

'Nothing special, I wouldn't think. Harry always seems to have several on the go.' Jack laughed. 'God knows what we are letting ourselves in for tonight.'

An hour later, Meredith could see exactly what was afoot. Carla was a siren. Five foot ten with long blonde hair, three pairs of false eyelashes and nails that belonged on the Wicked Queen in *Snow White*. She had not dressed in quite the spirit of Christmas that was appropriate for a family gathering, thought Meredith. A red mini-dress with white ermine trim and thigh boots took the biscuit. Even Harry had the grace to look gob-smacked.

Carla swanned in the front door with a cry of delight. 'Ooh, what a fab house, Harry! What a cool pad, babes. This is the business. Where's my room?' She handed Jack her overnight case. 'Hi, you must be Harry's dad. Lovely to meet you, I'm Carla.' She kissed him on the cheek. Then her gaze rested on Meredith. 'Ooh, you're that woman off the telly, aren't you? *Mary Lee at Three* or something. Lovely to meet you. I want to be on TV one day.' She waltzed towards the drawing room calling to Harry to come over quick and get her a glass of fizz.

Meredith and Jack exchanged looks.

'Don't say it!' said Jack. 'You said she could come as well as me. I only said yes because you said yes.'

'How dare you blame me!' exclaimed Meredith. 'God, can you imagine Oliver talking to that tomorrow over the canapés? What can we do?' she asked.

'Pray,' he replied.

Supper was hysterical as the whole household grew quieter and quieter as Carla grew chattier and chattier. Meredith noted that poor Millie was practically in tears. She had a bit of a thing about Harry and had been enjoying the fact that he was there giving them all such fun and being very flirty with her. She wasn't best pleased to hear she had to share her room with Carla, and Penny had to take her outside and have a word. Meredith felt for her – but what could she do?

After supper, Meredith suggested they all play a round of Scrabble.

'Scrabble – is that like Sardines? Are we all going to hide in

413

the dark? Mmm, lovely Harry, we like a scrabble in the dark, don't we, babes?' And she giggled inanely, finishing with a snort like a Shetland pony.

Adam and Tom were having a fit of the giggles and Anna and Millie sighed theatrically and went off to the annexe to listen to music. Jack looked at Harry and said very pointedly, 'Why don't you take Carla out to the club room and play some snooker or something?'

'Oh right, OK – sorry. Come on, Carla.' He took her hand and pulled her out of the room.

There was a brief moment of complete silence then everyone burst out laughing at once.

'Christ, where did he find her?' chuckled Tom.

'Come on, mate, let's go and watch her boobs jump up and down while she dances,' said Adam.

'Adam, that is disgusting. Don't talk like that,' said Penny. 'You should show some respect.'

'For what, Mother? A total scrubber like that.'

'Meredith, I am so sorry about my son. Please accept my apology on his behalf,' Penny sighed.

'Oh don't worry about it,' said Meredith. 'I am inclined to agree with him. Anyway, I am going to bed. Goodnight, everyone.'

'I'll lock up,' said Jack. They all decided to go to bed and left the tree shining and twinkling in the hall.

Before locking up, Jack took Carla's case across to the annexe. There was music playing loudly and lots of laughter so everyone was happy then. He left her case in the hall then went up and knocked on Millie's door. 'Come in.' Millie and Anna were sitting on the floor playing cards.

'Hi, Dad, everything all right? We are hiding from Carla; obviously the boys have a different perspective! Sorry, but what a slapper. Whatever is Harry thinking of?' Anna said.

His dick, thought Jack, but said instead, 'I don't know. Let's hope she gets bored and goes home tomorrow with her parents. I will personally run her home if necessary.'

'Good,' murmured Millie under her breath.

'Goodnight, girls. See you tomorrow. The front door key is hanging on the hook outside in the little room by the garage if you need to get into the main house, but don't tell the lads or they will be in after the booze.' He shut the door and made his way down the stairs. As he passed the big club room, he popped his head round the door and said, 'Goodnight.' Carla was dancing in the middle of the room and all the boys were gawping. Nothing changes, thought Jack. He went back into the lounge of the main house to watch a bit of TV and unwind – and fell fast asleep.

'Jack, Jack, wake up, wake up!' Meredith was leaning over him, shaking him violently.

'What is it? What's the matter?'

'It's Carla and Harry and Adam – they are causing havoc. Please, you have got to go and stop them.'

Jack dragged himself up off the sofa. 'Where are they? What are they doing?'

'I don't know, but Millie went to get Anna, and Anna has come and woken me up. Just get down there and see what is happening. Quick!'

Jack went out into the hall to find the front door wide open. He followed the noise into the club room and found Harry and Adam naked and Carla in a bra and pants sitting in front of the coffee table snorting cocaine with a rolled twenty-pound note off the top of a very expensive book on art and design.

'What the fuck do you think you are doing? Get out of my house now.' Jack got hold of Carla and was hoisting her to her feet. Harry stepped in and grabbed his father's arm.

'Leave her alone, Dad – what do you think you are doing? You're hurting her, let go.' And he tried to help Carla to get free.

'You can shut the fuck up as well, my boy. Get out of here. Adam, go to your room at once, do you hear me?'

Adam, who could hear nothing but buzzing in his ears, suddenly went as white as a sheet and threw up, fortunately in the fireplace and not on the carpet. Carla by this time was screaming at the top of her voice.

'Jesus, Harry, make her get dressed. Have you had any of this shit?' He took one hard look at his son and could see the answer. Harry was feeling no pain. 'For fuck's sake, how could you do this, you stupid twat! Get out of my way, you disgust me.' Jack stormed off to find Meredith, who was in the kitchen next door making coffee.

'I am taking that bitch Carla home right now,' he raged. 'She is doing coke in there with my son and Adam. What has got into him? I will just get my coat. Keep an eye on them, will you?' He ran off upstairs and Meredith and Anna went to find Harry. He and Carla were outside smoking cigarettes. Harry had got his clothes back on but Carla was still in her underwear.

'I think you had better get dressed as quickly as possible, Carla, Mr Blatchford will take you home. Harry, put that fag out and go with Anna and get some coffee. Come along, Carla. Hurry up, please.' Meredith went to take her arm, but Carla was having none of it.

'Get your fucking mitts off me, you old cow! Just 'cos you're on TV doesn't give you the right to tell me what to do.'

'Ah, but when you are in my house breaking the law I have got every right, lady.' Meredith hauled her back to the club room, grabbed her clothes and her case and her boots, and a blanket as an afterthought, and followed Jack as he came out of the door and got into the car.

'Here you go, dear – in there, that's right.' Meredith shoved the girl into the front passenger seat. 'Now fuck off back to where you came from, and a Happy Christmas to you and yours!' She then stood back and dusted her hands off.

'Way to go, girl,' cheered Jack, as he leaned across and strapped Carla in the seat. 'See you later, tiger,' he called and put his foot down.

Meredith and Anna put Harry to bed, and then checked on Adam, who was sound asleep on top of his bed. They cleaned up the fireplace and generally put everything straight for the morning, which was fast approaching.

'Get to bed, love. Are you feeling all right?' Meredith gently rubbed Anna's bump.

'Yes, I am fine – just got a bit of indigestion. What an awful way to finish Christmas Day. Poor Harry! I have never seen Jack lose his temper,' she said, shivering.

'No, me neither. Not a pretty sight. Oh well, as Granny would say, "It will all look better in the morning." Thank goodness she didn't wake up. Or the Wilsons, for that matter. Oh God – what are we going to tell them?'

'Let's worry about that tomorrow. Goodnight, Mum. I'd better go and find Tom. He was out for the count,' she giggled. 'He'll be sorry he missed all the fun. Thank you for a lovely day.' Anna hugged her mother and went off to bed.

Meredith poked the fire into life, put another log on and drank her coffee and waited for Jack to come home. She fell fast asleep and was awoken by Jack carrying her upstairs.

'Are you Father Christmas?' she mumbled.

'In your dreams. I only come once a year and you missed it, so go to sleep.' She giggled as he tucked her into bed.

Boxing Day dawned and it seemed most appropriately named as Jack prepared to face Harry.

'He is going to be on a plane to Kuala Lumpur tomorrow, and

417

that is that!' he fumed, pacing the kitchen while jabbing at the air with his fork. 'He won't know what's hit him!'

Meredith wasn't quite sure how much to get involved in this. She understood that Jack was angry because he was upset and concerned for Harry, but she had never seen him like this before.

'Maybe you should calm down a bit before you talk to him,' she suggested. 'I am sure he doesn't take drugs all the time, Jack. It was probably just that girl encouraging him.'

'No, Meredith, this has been going on for some time, believe me. I had a feeling something wasn't right but I just couldn't put my finger on it. My son is not going down that route. He has had it too easy up until now, and he has got to learn. He will be fine in KL. I have got this great site manager there called Malcolm Turner. Malc will sort him out and keep an eye on him. Harry won't have time for cocaine out there, believe me, he will be working so hard. I am going to suggest he does a carpentry apprenticeship for the next three years.'

'But what if he doesn't want to be a carpenter?' asked Meredith.

'Tough. He has blown any chance of deciding for himself. If he doesn't like it, at least after three years he will have a profession he can always fall back on. Anyway – enough: I am going to wake him up.'

Jack went stomping off and Meredith made some coffee. She was beginning to dread today's special lunch with Olly and Michael and the Neils. The atmosphere was going to be far from pleasant or festive.

Anna and Tom were in the kitchen already, having cereal at the table.

'Morning, Mum. What happened last night? Did Jack get back OK?' asked Anna.

'Yes, don't worry. How are you feeling?' Meredith kissed her daughter on the top of her head as she was sitting eating her breakfast.

'I am fine, but my ankles are all swollen,' replied Anna, showing Meredith her ankles encased in bedsocks.

'Well, sit down and stick them above your head,' suggested Meredith. 'Oh dear, I think there are going to be fireworks this morning. Jack is livid with Harry.'

Just as she said this, there were footsteps thumping down the stairs and Harry appeared in the doorway, shouting, 'No way, Dad, I am not going to fucking Kuala Lumpur. You must be joking! It was one lousy time and I didn't get the stuff – Carla brought it with her, for Christ's sake.'

'Don't give me that bullshit,' snarled Jack. 'You wanted her to come here last night exactly because you knew she would bring the gear. I knew there was something going on, but I just couldn't believe my son would be so stupid as to take drugs. You have got everything you want in life and this is what you do? Well, it stops here and now. You will be on a flight tomorrow morning and that is that.'

'You can't make me go,' challenged Harry.

'Oh believe me, I can,' replied Jack. 'If you do not get on that plane, you will collect your things from home and be gone for good. If you try to come back, you will find the locks changed. Is that clear enough for you?' He strode off to get his laptop.

Meredith felt so sorry for Harry, who looked like he was going to burst into tears. She went over and put her arms round him, murmuring, 'Come on, he will calm down. Have some breakfast.' She pulled a chair back and Harry sat down and put his head in his hands.

'He won't change his mind though,' he groaned. 'Oh shit, this is terrible. I don't want to go.'

'Look, maybe if you go for a bit, he will change his mind

419

later,' said Meredith, wondering if she should have a word. She gave Harry a cup of coffee and went to find Jack.

He was in the drawing room, tapping away on the laptop.

'Right, there is a flight tomorrow at noon and he will be on it. I will drive him back tonight and he can pack his stuff,' he said grimly.

'Maybe you are being a bit harsh, Jack. Harry is young. We all do stupid things at his age. Perhaps you should at least give him a chance.' Meredith sat down and put her hand on his arm. 'Come on, it's Christmas,' she smiled at him.

Jack turned to face her and she was shocked by the hardness in his eyes.

'Don't interfere, Meredith. I know what I am doing. Harry has had a fantastic education and I give him a generous allowance. He doesn't seem interested in going to university, or doing anything remotely stimulating or worthwhile, and he's done nothing but piss around for the last few years. I am not prepared to fund him and his drug habit while he "finds himself". I have seen too many friends watch their children go down the tubes being kind and understanding. Trust me, this is the best way. I am sorry to spoil the day, but this is the end of the line.'

Jack turned back to his laptop and Meredith was duly dismissed. So she went back into the kitchen to find Harry sitting on his own.

'Where have Anna and Tom gone?' she asked.

'Back to bed, I think,' said Harry. He looked at Meredith. 'I take it my dad is not going to change his mind?'

Meredith shook her head. 'I am so sorry, Harry.' She went to take his hand but before she could do so, he scraped back the chair and stood up.

'Oh don't worry about it. I'll manage. I've got no fucking choice!' Like his father, he shrugged her off and went across to the annexe.

Well, this is going to be a fun day, thought Meredith and went to find her mother. Jane was in her room writing a letter.

'I was just finishing this and then I was coming down to help you prepare the lunch,' she said, then seeing the look on Meredith's face, she stopped her letter-writing. 'Whatever's the matter?'

'Jack and Harry have had a huge row and Jack is banishing Harry to Kuala Lumpur.' Meredith related the events of the night before.

'I feel so sorry for Harry,' she ended. 'It seems very harsh to send him away.'

'Possibly, but you cannot come between them. It would be different if Harry were your son, but then you probably wouldn't win this one anyway. Sometimes we mums are too soft. Boys need a firm hand. Don't worry – they will sort it out. Jack may be tough, but he is always fair.'

The rest of the morning passed uneventfully and everyone did their own thing until Oliver and Michael arrived full of Christmas cheer and armfuls of goodies. They burst into the house like a benign tornado. Oliver dropped everything to sweep Meredith off her feet, moving on to give Anna a much gentler embrace.

'Happy Christmas HO HO HO!' he chanted. 'Look at this wonderful kitchen. Meredith, dear, you have surpassed yourself. Now show me where everything is and we can get on. Michael, open the champagne, darling. Anna, put the Secret Santa presents under the tree and Tom, go to the front door because your parents were arriving just behind us. Jane, you look gorgeous – now get those spuds in the pan.'

Everyone jumped to attention and after Meredith had gone through the menu with Oliver she went to welcome Estelle and Robert. Tom had taken their things and shown them into the drawing room.

'Hello, you two, Happy Christmas. How was your drive down?' Meredith started to make up the fire.

'Oh fine, thank you. Here, let me help,' said Robert.

'No, please, it won't take a minute. We are a bit behind with the chores. Can I get you some coffee? Come on, we will fight for a corner of the kitchen as Oliver has taken over.' They followed Meredith across the hall and into the kitchen, which was a hive of activity.

'Coffee, please, for our guests!' shouted Meredith. 'Anna, put the kettle on.' Robert and Estelle watched with a bemused expression on their faces as the team worked away. Penny Wilson appeared then Frank and Jenny, and suddenly the kitchen was very crowded.

'Come on, everyone,' said Meredith, 'we need to get out of here. Let's all go to the pub. Follow me.' She led them out to the front of the house like the Pied Piper. 'Now it is a fine morning and the pub is literally just round the corner so I suggest you get jackets and coats and we walk there. By the time we have imbibed a few eggnogs and mulled wines, lunch will be ready.' Everyone went off to get their coats and Jack appeared beside her.

'Where's Harry?' he asked.

'Over in the annexe, I think,' said Meredith. 'Are you coming to the pub?'

'I'll join you later. I just need to go through a couple of things with my son. Don't worry, I won't shout any more. I know you think I am hard, Meredith, but sometimes it is necessary.' He kissed her and went off in search of his son.

Meredith got her coat and headed off down the lane followed by an assorted band of happy folk.

By the time they tumbled into the house, a little the worse for wear, Oliver and Michael had worked a miracle. The caterers had been instructed by them from day one, so all supplies

422

had been delivered beforehand and it was really only a matter of organising everybody and setting the table. Meredith had insisted that Oliver should not have the total responsibility for this lunch as he would not enjoy the day himself. He confessed to her later that what he had really enjoyed about the day in the end was bossing everyone about.

Jack and Harry appeared, and although Harry did not look happy exactly he seemed resigned to his fate, and Jack gave Meredith a big wink.

Secret Santa came with his sack. Michael was a natural for the job and had excelled this year on the costume and beard. He looked like one of those wonderful rosy Father Christmases on Victorian Christmas cards, with incredibly white beards and twinkling eyes. He had even managed to find black boots that were so shiny you could see your reflection in them.

'Just think, Anna, this time next year you will have a little person to share this with.' Meredith gave her daughter a cuddle.

'Oh Mum, can you imagine how much a child would love this?' She was bright-eyed and rosy-cheeked herself tonight.

Everyone agreed it was the best Boxing Day they had ever had, and as the adults retired to their rooms the teenagers decided to watch Michael Jackson's *Thriller* in the annexe. Meredith went to find Harry, who was outside having a cigarette.

'How are you doing?' she said, putting her arm through his. 'I am glad you are not going off tomorrow. Better to get back and sort yourself out.'

Jack had at least relented and agreed to Meredith's suggestion that Harry go a day later so they could all travel back together from Wiltshire. It gave him time to sort out his stuff and ring a couple of friends.

'Yes, thanks for that, Meredith. I appreciate the support. I am so fucked off about it, you have no idea.' He swallowed hard and sniffed. 'I'm sorry.'

'Harry, don't worry. You know what? You will be fine. Malcolm is a lovely bloke apparently; he will look after you, and Malaysia is absolutely beautiful. You will probably get some time off to travel around a bit. Your dad loves you very much, you know that, and he gets angry because he is worried sick about you.' She yawned. 'Oh dear, pardon me. Come on, let's get to bed and get some sleep. We are up at the crack of dawn tomorrow.'

Meredith went back inside and found Oliver and Michael packing Christmas decorations away.

'Time for Bedfordshire, you two. Chop, chop.' She hustled them off to their room.

Everyone else had gone already. Frank and Jenny and the children would leave the same time as Meredith and the others left for London. The house would be cleaned and everything packed and sorted after they had left. Thank God she had splashed out and got it all catered. She was exhausted. She looked for Jack downstairs and couldn't find him so turned off all the lights and made her way upstairs. She found him in his bedroom on the laptop.

'Come on, enough now. Stop!' she said.

'I just have to send this email to Malcolm so he has all the flight details. He is sorting a flat for Harry with one of the other Brits there, so that is good. There, all done.' He sighed and shut down the computer, then got up and went downstairs.

Meredith went to her room and sat on the edge of her bed, fighting back a small flutter of panic. Why was she feeling like this? It was as if every time things were going well in her life, something cropped up to remind her not to get too complacent. Lord knows she never took anything for granted. She thanked God every day for each moment of happiness. So why was she feeling wobbly now?

She got ready for bed, then put her dressing-gown on and

went downstairs to say goodnight to Jack. She longed for him to take her in his arms and wish her a Happy Christmas. Then her life would be perfect.

'What's up?' he said, on seeing her. 'Feeling a bit down in the dumps, are we?'

'Oh, I don't know. I just get like this sometimes. I am tired, that's all. I just want everyone to be safe and happy.' She could feel a tear very close.

'I know you do, and that's why we all love you. Don't fret about Harry, he is going to be fine. He knows it is for the best, and once he gets over there and sees all those gorgeous girls, he will soon forget his troubles.'

'I know I am just being silly. I hope Anna will be OK. She will, won't she? She hasn't got long now, you know.'

Jack put his arms around her and searched her face. 'Stop worrying. Everything is going to be just fine and dandy. You have given everyone a fantastic Christmas. You are a remarkable woman, Meredith, and I hope one day you find the happiness you deserve.' He kissed her gently on the lips and then pulled back.

'Please, Jack,' whispered Meredith. 'Stay with me tonight. I need a friend.'

Jack held her close. He sighed deeply and muttered, 'I am sorry, but I can't give you any more at the moment. I am here for you in my way.'

Meredith trudged back upstairs and got into bed. She felt so alone. Fortunately she was too tired to ponder her fate for long and was asleep as soon as her head hit the pillow.

Chapter Twenty-Eight

The next morning the household packed themselves into the various cars, bade each other farewell, and drove away into the frosty morning. Meredith, Jack and Harry got back to London in record time and Jack dropped Meredith off then went back with Harry to sort out his trip.

Meredith looked around the house. She always hated those days between Christmas and New Year, when the decorations seem to lose their sparkle, yet cannot be taken down until Twelfth Night. The holiday seems to drag on and there is a sense of melancholy about it all ... Dear me, she was being a right little party-pooper, she chided herself. Her thoughts were interrupted by the phone.

'Is that Ms Lee? Meredith Lee?' asked a woman's voice.

'Yes, who is this?' Meredith could feel her legs begin to give and she sat down next to the phone table.

'My name is Sister McDonald in the Neo-Natal Unit at the Whittington Hospital in Archway. We have your daughter here, Anna Lee, and her boyfriend Tom Neil. She was admitted an hour ago with suspected high blood pressure and complications. Would you be able to get here as soon as possible?'

'Yes, yes, of course, I know where it is, I shall set off

immediately.' Meredith slammed the phone down. She then rang Jack but he didn't answer so she left a message explaining where she was and telling him to get to the hospital as quickly as he could.

She drove like a maniac, not daring to give herself time to think. Just get there! The receptionist pointed her in the direction of the Neo-Natal Unit and Meredith remembered how she had supported a campaign to raise money for this same Unit a few years ago. She saw Tom sitting in the corridor further down and ran towards him.

'Tom, what is it?' she panted. 'What happened?'

Tom was trying not to cry, but when he saw Meredith he let out a sob.

'She just collapsed. We were in the car and I had just dropped stuff off at Mum and Dad's and we were coming to your house. She passed out and seemed to have a kind of fit. I just drove straight here.' He was sobbing now in great gulps, and Meredith made him sit down and went and got him a paper cup of water from a stand.

'It's all right, come on, calm down. She will be fine.' Meredith could hear no conviction in her voice whatsoever. 'Let me go and find someone to talk to, OK?'

She went across to a nurses' station and asked the nurse who was standing there making notes: 'Could you tell me what is happening to Anna Lee? She was brought in about an hour ago.' She tried not to sound impatient but the woman was taking her time putting down her notes and looking at another list.

The woman traced her finger down the page with exasperating slowness.

'Oh yes, here she is, she is in Room Two. I will go and check. Stay here, please.' She went off down the corridor and Meredith followed, paying no heed to her instructions. They arrived at

427

Room Two and the nurse was about to open the door when she became aware that Meredith was right behind her.

'Please stay here, no one is allowed in.'

Meredith heard an agonising scream and pushed past the nurse into the room. She took in a doctor and another nurse and Anna writhing on the bed, her face grey and her hair plastered to her head with sweat.

'Anna!' She rushed to the bed, but was stopped by the doctor, who grabbed her by both arms and twisted her away from the bed.

'Please leave us to deal with this,' he said firmly. 'You are not helping – time is precious. Now go with the nurse and we will let you know when you can see your daughter.' The nurse steered her out of the door.

'I am sorry, but that's my daughter,' Meredith said in a shaking voice. 'What is the matter with her? Is she going to lose the baby?' The nurse did not reply, but simply escorted her back to where Tom was waiting, his face white with fear.

Meredith sat down next to Tom and tried to make sense of what was happening. She could feel the panic rising in her. Something was horribly wrong. She looked at Tom who was watching her now with such a look of terror that she took his hand and said, 'It's all right, love, I am sorry if I scared you. Don't worry, I am fine now, I won't do anything stupid. You and I have got to be brave for Anna. Come on, mate, we can do this.'

They sat side by side holding hands, rigid like statues.

Meredith had no idea how long they sat there, but suddenly the doctor came towards them with the nurse.

'Would you follow me, please?' said the doctor, and showed them into a side room.

'Please sit down,' he said. Then: 'There is no easy way to tell you this, Ms Lee. I am so sorry but Anna has lost her baby.'

428

Meredith couldn't get her breath; when she tried to speak, nothing came out. She felt the back of her throat contract and all the air disappear. She choked and coughed.

'Would you like a glass of water?' The doctor opened the door and called to the nurse for some water.

Tom was crying now, softly whimpering like a wounded animal. Meredith wanted to say his name but still nothing would come out. She tried to take a breath again and heard a croak – and the sound caught the back of her throat. The doctor handed her the water. She drank some but it trickled from her mouth onto her lap. She went to wipe it away and felt a wave of nausea rise up through her stomach, and was sick all over the floor. The nurse came and cleaned her up, but she was shaking now, unable to control herself. Yet she must control herself; she must see Anna, she must help her daughter.

'Can I see my daughter, please?' she managed to ask. 'I am fine now. I am sorry for making all that mess, but I must see my daughter now.'

'Yes, of course, but let me at least explain to you both what has happened so you can understand and help Anna to understand. She is sedated at the moment so she is calm. Ms Lee, Tom, Anna was suffering from eclampsia – a condition brought on by high blood pressure. It is extremely rare and we really do not know what causes it. Unfortunately, it causes death in the foetus, which then has to be removed.' He cleared his throat. 'We have made Anna as comfortable as possible. She has no physical injuries and no damage has been done as far as her being able to bear more children is concerned.'

The doctor looked sympathetically at Tom, and then he turned to Meredith. 'However, the psychological effects are something quite different. She will need a lot of love and support, but I don't need to tell you that. We have a Bereavement Nurse here at the Whittington who will be very happy to help you, should you feel the need. I am so very sorry.' The doctor then quietly left the room.

Meredith and Tom sat opposite each other wrapped in their shock and grief. Meredith pushed down the tears and the panic, and willed herself to a state of quiet control. She had to do this for Anna. She had to go to her daughter with strength. She had nothing left to give poor Tom, who had crumpled in the corner. She touched his arm and said, 'Tom, why don't you call your parents. I will go and see Anna.' She got up and went out into the corridor and beckoned to the nurse.

'May I see my daughter? Please?' she said, and the nurse led her back to Room Two. Meredith went through the door and paused a moment, to get her balance. Then she walked over to the bed and took Anna's hand. It was cold and clammy. There was a drip in her arm.

Meredith leaned in and whispered, 'Anna, it's Mummy. I am here. Can you hear me?' Anna did not move and Meredith could not see her properly as her face was turned away into the pillow. Meredith squeezed her hand gently. 'Everything will be all right, darling, just get better.' Meredith wanted to grab her child and hold her tight; she wanted to scream at the top of her voice that it *wasn't* all right, it was fucking not all right ... but she bit her tongue, literally, and tasted blood in her mouth. She swallowed hard several times. *Please God make Anna OK.* She stroked the girl's hair from her forehead and bent to kiss her cheek.

Anna half-turned towards her. Meredith watched a tear escape from her daughter's eye and roll down her cheek, and she thought her heart would break.

'He's dead, Mum,' she whispered. 'My baby is dead.' A cry escaped from her lips – a cry that grew into a primal scream of pain, and left the young girl gasping as she lay back on the pillows. Meredith could only sit and hold her hand, willing every ounce of love she had for this beautiful young girl into her. Gradually Anna's moans subsided and she fell asleep. Meredith dared not move in case she broke the connection and all her life force would disappear into thin air. The nurse came back.

'Ms Lee, you should leave her now. She will sleep for a good few hours as she is heavily sedated. Why don't you come and get a cup of tea with the young man? Oh, and your husband is here,' she added.

'My husband? But I haven't got a— Oh yes, Jack, of course. Sorry, but he is not my husband.' She got up and followed the nurse out into the corridor to find Tom and Jack and Estelle Neil standing there.

Jack took her in his arms and held her tight. She refused to cry. She must not break down until all this was sorted. *Anna needs me to be strong.* She heard her voice and realised she had said the words out loud.

'Of course she does, and you will be, my lover.' Jack's voice was gruff with emotion. 'Come on, let's go and get a cup of tea. Tom, would you like us to bring you one back?'

Estelle answered for her son. 'That would lovely, Jack, thank you very much. We will try and just pop in to Anna and send our love, and then I may take Tom away for a bit. He can do nothing here.'

Tom blurted out, 'But it's my baby too, you know! I don't want to leave her, Mum. I want to stay here.' He burst into tears again and collapsed onto the seat. Estelle looked lost and out of her depth.

'Look, don't worry,' said Meredith. 'Let Tom stay here with us, Estelle. We will keep an eye on him.' She somehow managed to smile.

'Well, all right, if you think so. I need to get back and talk to Robert. If you are sure then, thank you very much. We will talk

431

later. Bye, Tom darling.' She kissed him then hurried off down the corridor.

Meredith turned to Jack and said, 'Would you mind going on your own to get the teas? Tom and I will sit in that side room and wait for you.' Jack nodded and went off, and Meredith grabbed Tom by his arms and hauled him up. 'Come on, my love, let's go and sit in here where it is a bit more private.'

They stayed in that room most of the rest of the day. Jack went back to Meredith's house and got her some clean clothes, and later on he went to see Harry and sort out his pick-up in the morning for the airport. He also rang Jane Lee and arranged to collect her from St Pancras station the next afternoon, once he had said goodbye to Harry.

Meredith had a meeting with the Bereavement Nurse who gave her all the necessary information about registering the baby's death; this had to be done by law as he was over twenty-four weeks old. Meredith had no idea what arrangements they would make for a funeral or anything, but the nurse was fantastic and said the hospital could organise it all if she wanted, but that it was important for Anna's recovery that she decided what she wanted to do.

'But we can't expect her to go through all that!' Meredith objected. 'How will she cope if she has to talk about funeral arrangements?'

'You will be surprised at how much we can take as human beings, you know,' said the nurse kindly. 'Everyone is different, of course, but in my experience nearly every mother I have helped through the death of a child finds comfort in a burial ceremony. Did she and the father have a name for the baby, by the way? It is important that they give the infant a name.'

'Yes, they did.' Meredith recalled Tom and Anna sitting in her kitchen, excitedly explaining to her that if it was a boy they would call him Alfie, and if it was a girl she would be called Millie.

'That's good. I will be on call when Anna comes round, so I will see you later.'

Anna woke up briefly that evening and Tom spent a few minutes with her, but when he came out of the room he was drained of all colour, and trembling all over.

'She-she doesn't want to t-talk to me,' he stammered, looking completely desolate. 'Does she think it's my fault?'

'No, of course she doesn't, Tom,' Meredith said compassionately. 'You have to understand, Anna is very fragile at this moment. She will hit out at all of us, but she will blame herself mostly and we will have to keep telling her it was not her fault. This was a terrible tragedy for you both, with no rhyme nor reason for it. That is what is so hard for us to comprehend. You must not take it personally. Just try to be there for her. Now I suggest we ring your mum and dad to come and get you. You go home and get something to eat and some sleep, and then you will have the strength to fight another day.'

Meredith went to talk to the nurse about staying the night. Wild horses would not drag her away. She was going to get her daughter through this if it was the last thing she ever did. She then rang the Neils and they agreed to come and fetch Tom. Next, she rang Jack to tell him she would be staying at the hospital and that he could leave her for tonight and come back tomorrow after he had dropped Harry at the airport. He agreed but added, 'Harry wants to talk to you. Here.' Meredith heard Harry take the phone.

'Meredith? I am so sorry about Anna. I wanted to come but Dad says there is no point as she is sleeping. But you know I would come, don't you? I love Anna: my sister is the best. She doesn't deserve this shit. Sorry, didn't mean to swear.'

Meredith swallowed hard; hearing Harry's voice and his concern for Anna was very moving.

'Swearing is allowed today,' she said. 'Bless your heart, you

433

are a lovely boy and I will tell Anna you send your love. Good luck, Harry, please be careful and don't do anything stupid. We love you very much and I look forward to seeing you soon.' Meredith held it together and waited as she heard Harry pass the phone back to Jack.

'Are you there, darling?' said Jack. 'Harry was a bit choked. See, he has got a heart really.' He laughed huskily. 'Meredith, do you want me to come to the hospital?'

'No, don't be daft, I am fine. You get on – I am going back to check on Anna. See you tomorrow,' she said, and put the phone down quickly before she could lose control. She walked back, stopping at the ladies' toilet to wash her face with cold water. She looked at herself in the mirror and said aloud: 'It is going to be a long night, Meredith Lee, but you will do it. Love is everything.'

Her vigil that night was long and lonely. People always say that when they encounter situations of great danger or near-death, their lives flash before their eyes. Well, that night, Meredith's life paraded itself before her. Every memory of her childhood was clear and sharp. Watching Anna's sleeping face, she recalled her as a baby. Remembered the night in the maternity ward watching Anna suckle and trying to understand the emotions that were swirling around in her head. The idea that she didn't really want the baby made her gasp now, in this moment when that baby had just lost her baby. Where did the years go? How many lives are touched by each of us as we go through life? How do we manage to survive?

Anna stirred and called out, but Meredith could not catch what she was saying. She went to the bed and wiped a cold flannel over her daughter's forehead, and the girl seemed more peaceful now. God only knew what it would be like for her to wake up and have to cope with the pain that consciousness would bring.

434

She went back and sat down, and managed to doze for an hour or so. She was awakened by a nurse coming to check up on Anna.

'No change,' she whispered, and left again. Meredith looked at her watch: 5 a.m. It was that horrible time between night and day. Please let Anna open her eyes when it was daylight. Somehow, the idea that her daughter could wake and leave the night behind was a comfort to Meredith. She would help her forward.

Anna called her name. 'Mum, are you there? Can I have a drink of water?'

Meredith gave her the water and was overcome with sadness as she looked down at her daughter drinking from the hospital beaker, like a little girl again. Waking up in the night and wanting her mum. If only Meredith could make it better.

'He's dead, isn't he, Mum.' Her voice was tiny. 'I didn't dream it. Alfie is dead.'

'Yes, dear, I am so sorry.' Meredith held her hand.

'Why? Did I do something wrong? Is it my fault?' Anna's eyes were pleading.

'No, no way. You must never think that. You had a condition called eclampsia.' Meredith sighed. 'It is very rare and not treatable. I am so sorry, darling. It is just a terrible tragedy and I don't know why it had to happen to you.'

'You were right all along. I should never have had the baby. I should have got rid of it.' Anna sounded so bitter.

'Stop it, Anna. I never said to get rid of your baby. I admit I was upset and I didn't want you to keep it, but I soon changed my mind. Please don't say things like this, he was your beloved baby. Your son, Alfie.' She was losing her control.

'Alfie, yes. My boy Alfie. Why did he have to die, Mum? What a waste of nine months!' Anna was gripping Meredith's hand so hard that her nails were biting into the flesh. 'Why was he born if he had to die!' She wailed and caught her breath and started to sob.

'Anna, come on, let it out. You should cry for him and rant and rave. It is so fucking unfair, but there is always a reason for everything. You must trust me on this. Everything that happens to us in our lives happens for a reason.' Meredith climbed onto the bed and lay down next to her daughter. She lifted her arm with the drip out of the way, and held her as tight as she dared. Anna felt so small and frail in her arms. *She is not going to break,* Meredith said to herself. *I am going to hold her forever if needs be, until she is better.*

Anna wept and wept and Meredith just held her. Finally she fell asleep again and her mother was able to lay her back down and extricate herself. It was starting to get light: Meredith could see through the blinds the early pale pink of a frosty morning. They had got through this first, terrible night and now they would move forward together.

The nurse came in again and Meredith took the chance to nip to the loo. There was a trolley going round with morning tea for the wards and the lady saw Meredith was in need; she handed her a cup with a big smile and a 'There you go, darlin', get that down you. Cup of tea always does the trick!' She shuffled off, pushing her trolley and humming to herself.

When she came back, Meredith found the nurse making Anna's bed.

'Hey, are you awake, darling?' she asked. Anna opened her eyes and stared blankly at her mother, as if she had shut down.

'Do you want a cup of tea?' Meredith started to hand hers over to her daughter but Anna pushed her away and turned her face to the wall.

Meredith put the cup and saucer down and took Anna's hand. 'Come on, Anna, we are going to beat this. Your baby must not die in vain. We must be strong for him.'

436

'Why? What does it matter now? He is dead. I have nothing to live for any more.' Her words cut through Meredith like a knife.

'That's not true, and you know it. You have a family who love you, a boyfriend who needs you more than ever, and you have your whole life in front of you. I know it is hard to see this now, but you will do so in time. You will remember your baby and thank him for what he has done for you.'

'Mum, what are you talking about? What has this to do with Alfie dying? He is dead. End of story. Please just go away and leave me alone.'

Meredith could hold back no longer. Taking Anna by both shoulders, she hauled her up so she was sitting directly in front of her.

'Look at me!' Meredith fought back the tears. 'Your baby brought us together as a family and made us whole again. You found your father and I found the man I love. You and I have found our family. We can move on and be a unit and be strong and look after each other. You are seventeen and beautiful, and you will have other babies and you will tell them all about their brother Alfie and how he had an incredibly short life, but he did live and he did exist, and he knew your love for him was the greatest thing in the world. You are so lucky, Anna, because once you get beyond your grief you will be able to see just how wonderful it is to love another human being with all your heart and soul, and you will never settle for second-best like lots of people do. You know what to look for, and you will find it again. Trust me, please, trust me. Alfie has given you the greatest gift you can imagine. Love in your heart.'

Meredith could not stop the tears, and it was Anna's turn to hold her mother until she was all cried out.

The two women sat together for a long time, just holding each other.

Chapter Twenty-Nine

Alfie Neil was buried in Highgate Cemetery on 2 January 1998. There was a short burial service at the Church of England church in Highgate. The vicar had a daughter the same age as Anna who had been at school with her. It was a very simple ceremony. Meredith helped Anna choose two hymns: 'Jesus Wants Me for a Sunbeam' and 'All Things Bright and Beautiful', and Tom and Anna both read a piece from the Bible.

Anna was incredibly brave and Meredith was immensely proud of her. She stood through the ceremony, and at the grave, between Meredith and Jack, and after they had thrown a white rose each onto the tiny white coffin and started to walk away, Anna linked her arms in each of theirs and whispered, 'Thank you, Mum and Dad. I love you very much.'

It was a very hard start to the New Year. Meredith was trying to be there for Anna but at the same time she had the series to produce. As usual, her life was going on hold for the sake of her job. Then one morning as she was rushing round getting ready to go to Marsh Hall the phone rang. It was only seven in the morning and her heart missed a beat. What now?

'Meredith?' It was Jack.

'Yes – what is it?' she said sharply, daring fate to hand her another piece of bad news.

'It's OK, don't panic. I just wanted to catch you before you set off. Look, I need to talk to you. Can you postpone driving up to Burslet until tomorrow?' he asked.

'Well, I don't know. There is so much going on up there and the crew are all back from holiday today and—'

'Stop right there and just listen to me, please. This is important,' Jack interrupted. 'I am coming round to your place this minute, so wait in for me.' The phone went dead.

Meredith let out a sigh of exasperation. He could be so bossy sometimes. She went to the kitchen and put the kettle on to make some more coffee and then phoned her mother. She knew that Jane would be up already. She didn't sleep much these days.

'Mum, it's Meredith. Look, can you do me a huge favour? Can you call Frank and tell him to explain to Bill and the crew that I will not be there today, as I have been detained. And could Bill ring me as soon as he gets this message?'

'I'll phone Frank the minute we say goodbye. How's it all going? How is Anna?' Jane sounded concerned.

They were all aware that Anna was in a very fragile state of mind and that it might take many months for her to recover. There was no question of her going back to school to join the Sixth Form. The therapist she was seeing had told Meredith that Anna was young and strong and that her relationship with Tom was very positive. The boy had shown remarkable strength of character. He hardly left Anna's side. He would take her for long walks on the Heath and they would often go to the cemetery and spend a whole morning there. Tom was teaching Anna to draw and she was really rather good at it. She seemed to find great comfort in sketching nature. She was still very thin and hardly ate anything, but her eyes were slowly losing the haunted look of a young doe and she was able to talk to Meredith sometimes about her feelings.

Meredith tried to be there as much as she could, but it was proving very difficult. She was feeling tired and stressed and grey. All her hopes for her family reunion had been dashed. *It is not about you, Meredith*, she said to herself. *Shut up!*

The bell rang and she opened the door to a very harassed-looking Jack. He brushed past her and went straight into the kitchen and poured himself a cup of coffee.

'Help yourself to coffee, why don't you?' muttered Meredith, following him in.

'Meredith, we have to make serious changes to our lives. Your daughter needs you with her and you are not around most of the time because of your fucking TV commitments. You are going to have to make time for her!'

Meredith stared at him across the kitchen table. 'Now just hang on a minute. Who the hell are you to march in here and tell me how to look after my daughter? How dare you, Jack!' Meredith could feel the rage gathering.

'I have a right as her father to suggest to you that you are not doing the right thing by Anna. She is only a kid, for Christ's sake! She needs you!'

Meredith could not believe what she was hearing.

'I know how old my daughter is, thank you. I know how young she is too – and I bloody well know what she feels like. Well, actually I don't, because I have never lost a child, but I damn well know a lot more about her than you do, you arrogant bastard. It is none of your bloody business to come here and tell me what to do.'

Jack stood and came straight up to Meredith so they were practically nose to nose.

'Don't you dare tell me it is not my business! You tried to leave me out from day one, remember? Slept with me and then

440

got pregnant and didn't respect me enough to have the decency to tell me. How incredibly fucking selfish is that? Sixteen – no, nearly seventeen years you kept me away from my daughter, Meredith. Seventeen years. Then you have the bloody cheek to condescend to let me join in your jolly Happy Families.'

'How can you say these things?' Meredith could not believe what she was hearing. 'You walked out of my life that morning after saying there was no way you were interested in having a relationship with me. Every time I saw you, you were with some woman. What was I supposed to do? Tap you on the shoulder and say "Hi, remember me? I had your baby. Are you free now to whisk me away and live happily ever after?"'

Meredith turned away but Jack grabbed her arm and pulled her back to face him.

'Get your hand off my arm,' she said very slowly and quietly.

Jack stepped away. 'OK, OK, sorry, but please, Meredith, listen to what I am trying to say. I have been thinking about this for the last few days. I am on my own now and I don't want to lose touch with Anna – or Harry, for that matter. God knows what is going on in his head. I know I am fucked up, but I don't want to hurt any more people ...'

'Hang on just a minute, Jack. What are you talking about? Who have you hurt, can I ask?' It was Meredith's turn to grab Jack's arm, but he didn't pull away.

'I broke it off with Mo the night we came back from Wiltshire. She knew it wasn't working long before that, but I kept trying to keep it going because I couldn't face the truth. Then suddenly I just couldn't pretend any more. I was stringing her along and it was not right.' Jack looked wiped out.

'What is the truth?' asked Meredith.

He stood in the middle of her kitchen like a lost boy. He started to speak, then just turned and left.

Meredith didn't try to follow or call after him because she was dumbstruck. The whole incident had lasted about five minutes and she had no idea what it had all been about. What was Jack trying to achieve? She started to feel the anger rising again. The nerve of him, telling her what she could and couldn't do. Anna was her daughter, and she knew what was best for her. She was her mother, for goodness' sake. Just then, the phone rang.

'Hello,' she answered rather abruptly.

'Meredith, it's Bill – I got your message. Look, don't worry about rushing down here today. We can't do any more filming until the foundations have been laid in the main house. As you know, Christmas rather got in the way of that moving forward. I shall be doing some pick-up shots around the farm, et cetera, so we are not wasting time, but realistically you will not be missed until after this weekend.'

Meredith suddenly relaxed. 'Oh thanks, Bill, that is good news in a way. I need some time to sort a couple of things down here so I will take your advice and come up to the Hall at the weekend. Thanks so much for letting me know the score.'

Meredith put the phone down and then picked it up again straight away. 'Mum, it's me again. Can I ask you another favour? May I come down now with Anna and stay with you until the weekend?'

'Of course you can, it would be a pleasure to have you both. I will go and make up the beds now. What time do you think you will get here?'

'About five, I reckon, if I get a move on. Lots of love and see you later.' Meredith ran upstairs to wake Anna. In fact, the girl was already awake and dressed.

'How do you fancy a couple of days on Malthouse Farm with me and your gran?' Meredith asked her. 'I thought we could make it a Girls Only few days. What do you think?'

Anna looked at her mother and said, 'What was Jack shouting about? I heard you rowing. What's the matter?'

'Oh, nothing really, he was just in a bad mood. I'll tell you later. Now, are you up for this trip or what?' Meredith wanted to get going. Now she had a plan in her head she was a woman on a mission.

'Well, I had better ring and check that Tom doesn't mind.' Anna picked up her mobile phone. 'I will talk to him now and be down in a minute, Mum.' She waited for Meredith to leave the room before she dialled. Taking the hint, Meredith left, thinking to herself, Why can't she ask him in front of me? What's so difficult?

She went to her bedroom and started to lay clothes out on the bed to be packed. Anna came in five minutes later and said, 'Tom is very happy for me to go. He thinks it is a great idea. So what time do you want to leave?'

'Right this minute. Let's hurry up – I feel the need for fresh air,' announced her mother.

But by the time the two of them had gathered themselves together, it was almost lunchtime. They spent the journey singing terrible pop songs and sucking sweets.

Jane came out to meet them. She was still sprightly for a woman in her seventies.

They all trundled into the warmth of her little cottage, which had received a facelift as well as the farmhouse, and flung themselves down in front of a roaring fire.

'Oh Granny, this is fantastic!' exclaimed Anna. 'I love this room. Look, Mum, Gran has got a real rocking horse.' She got up and went over to the beautiful horse. It was a dappled grey with a long flowing mane of real horse hair and a silky black tail to match.

'Yes, I bought it for—' Jane stopped and gasped. 'Oh – what am I saying? Anna, dear, please forgive me. I just didn't think.' The old lady's eyes filled with tears.

Anna stroked the horse's mane in silence for a moment and then she said, 'Please don't be upset, Gran. Alfie would have loved this, but so would any child – so you can look after it until we have a new child to love it.' She then walked back to the fire and sat down.

Meredith's heart ached for her daughter. 'Mum, have you got crumpets by any chance?' she asked. Jane pulled herself together and took her cue.

'Yes, I have – and some scones I made after lunch, with jam and cream – and meringues!' They all laughed.

She hurried out to fetch the feast, and Meredith went and sat next to her daughter. 'OK?' she asked, putting her arm round her.

Anna sat staring into the fire. 'I am getting better every day, Mum,' she said quietly. 'Alfie is in my heart and I think about him every second, but the pain is getting less. It is so lovely to be here with you and Gran. I feel as if I have joined the club. Does that make sense?' She gave a sad little laugh.

'Yes, it absolutely does,' said Meredith. 'And you are a worthy member.'

They ate their tea in front of the fire and watched TV until they all started to fall asleep so they trooped off for a nap. Jane had made up beds in her two-spare rooms. They each had a beautiful handmade quilt and cushions.

'Mum, you are clever,' said Meredith, admiring the embroidery on her bedspread. She crossed to a beautiful antique chair which was facing the window.

'I thought you could sit and ponder,' Jane said fondly.

'I do need to ponder,' replied Meredith. 'There are a few things I have to think about.' She almost said this to herself.

Jane gave her a look but said nothing. She led Anna into her room and showed her the doll on the top of her quilt.

'Do you remember April?' she asked. 'You used to play with her when you were little.'

Anna let out a shriek of delight. 'Oh, I used to love this doll. I didn't know you still had her, Gran.'

'Neither did I,' said Meredith, following them in and looking at her mother. 'You have made her a new dress, Mum.'

'Yes. Well, it is a new era so a new outfit. I am glad you remember her, Anna. She is yours for now, as you are the youngest in line. Dear April is quite elderly now. Let's see, she must be getting on for eighty years old!' she laughed. They all hugged and went their separate ways for the rest of the afternoon.

The next day, Meredith and Anna went for a long walk, ending up at the site. Meredith took Anna through all her plans for the place.

'It is so brilliant, Mum,' she said excitedly. 'But will you live down here when it's finished?'

'I haven't really got that far,' replied Meredith. 'I realise I will have to be pretty full-on to start with, because it is such a personal venture. It is my vision so I must oversee it. But I'm not sure I want to give up all my TV stuff completely.' Meredith thought about how she had always hoped that she and Jack might get back together and live in the countryside. Anna seemed to read her mother's mind.

'What about Jack, Mummy? Do you ever wish you could have got together?' she asked shyly. 'I always hoped you would.'

'Oh, I don't know. It's all very complicated. I don't think he is the kind of man who wants to get tied down for life, and I have never lived with anyone apart from Oliver for longer than a few weeks. Can you imagine me and Jack trying to fit in together?'

'Yes, I can actually. I just think you are both so pig-headed you can't see it!' was her daughter's astonishing response.

'Whatever made you think like this? You have never mentioned any of this before.' Meredith was amazed at what went on in the girl's head. 'Have you ever said anything like this to Jack?'

'No, don't be daft. Tom says it is better to let him work it out for himself.' Anna smiled cheekily.

'You talk to Tom about me and Jack?' demanded Meredith with a feeble attempt at outrage.

'Well, it just seems so obvious to us,' Anna said simply. 'Come on, let's go and find Gran. I'm starving.'

That night Meredith sat in the chair in the window, pondering. She had been so busy worrying about Anna that she had not given much thought to her situation with Jack. Now she was beginning to digest his comments from the other morning, and to comprehend what he was trying to say. She hated to admit that he was right to a certain degree: she was selfish. Not in her intentions towards her daughter, since she wanted more than anything to make things right for her, but Meredith was incessantly moving forward with her life – and for what? What was she chasing? Her life was right in front of her, or rather next door in bed. Her daughter needed her. Her mother would soon need her. Jane was getting older.

Meredith realised she should stop chasing a dream. She had found it. It wasn't about money, since even before Myles left her his fortune she had made enough. No, she was chasing something to fill up her life. So she didn't have a husband, so what? Lots of women didn't. She had wonderful friends like Oliver and Michael and an equally wonderful family. Her brother Frank and his wife Jenny were a fine example of family life. Their children had flown the nest and they were working towards old age together. They would run the farm as a team and that would be it for the rest of their lives.

Meredith didn't want that exactly: she loved her role as a mother, and now as the owner of a soon-to-be luxury spa. She had so many ideas for books she wanted to write and she loved it here. Maybe Anna and Tom could move here as well. When they finally had children, it would be an ideal place to bring them up. She had nothing more to prove. She thought of her darling dad, of how he would have loved his daughter to return to the nest.

Meredith stood up, full of determination. She was going to put a few things in place – and she didn't just mean building foundations.

Over the next two days, Meredith really opened up and talked to Anna about her life. She told her about Jack and how she had felt that evening after Pamela's funeral. Jane had given her permission for Meredith to tell Anna her story, and also her great-grandmother Mary Hughes's story. Anna was enthralled and saddened at the same time by these stories.

'It must have been so frightening to find yourself pregnant back then,' she said. 'And terribly lonely too. Gosh, I am the only one who has fallen pregnant and stayed with the father!' she gasped. 'How weird is that? Long live women's liberation!'

It was after dinner on the Saturday night when the three women had sat down together.

'Hear, hear!' said the others, and they were clinking glasses as the phone rang.

'I'll get it.' Anna jumped up and went to the phone. 'Hello, the Lee residence? Hey, Dad, how are you?' She was obviously thrilled to hear Jack's voice. 'We are all fine, having a girls' night in. Yes, of course, hang on ... By the way, are you coming down any time soon? You can handle three women, Dad!' She chuckled, handing the phone to Meredith.

'Hi,' said Meredith carefully. 'How are you?'

'I am fine. Look, I am sorry for my outburst, but I was very stressed. I was wondering if I might be permitted to come up and take you all out for Sunday lunch tomorrow, to make amends.' Jack sounded very subdued.

'I am sure that would be fine.' Meredith turned to Jane.

'Mum, Jack would like to come down tomorrow and take us out for lunch. Is that OK with you?'

'Of course it is. It would be lovely to see him. Shall we ask Frank and Jenny as well?'

'Can Frank and Jenny come?' asked Meredith.

'Of course they can, and ask my daughter if she wants me to bring her young man. He is going stir crazy without her.'

Anna was listening in to this conversation. She clapped her hands with glee and screeched down the phone, 'Oh yes, please! Is that all right, Gran? Sorry, I forgot where I was. We can help you with the beds and everything,' she offered.

'That is fine. It will be delightful to have you all,' Jane beamed.

'So that is definitely a yes. We will see you tomorrow, Jack. Bye.'

'Goodnight – and don't you girls get too drunk,' said Jack and hung up.

When they went up to bed, Meredith kissed her mum, and then went to Anna's room to say goodnight. Her daughter was sitting up in bed writing in a diary.

'I started it after Alfie died,' she explained. 'The therapist suggested it. I write to him, so one day everything will be in here for my other children to read. He will never be forgotten,' she said simply.

Meredith sat on the bed and passed Anna a package wrapped in tissue.

'What's this?' the girl asked.

'Open it,' replied Meredith.

It was the prayer book that Anna had found in the attic.

'I want you to keep it now,' Meredith told her.

Anna opened it and read down the inscriptions. Written at the bottom in her bold handwriting Meredith had added:

To dearest Anna, my lovely daughter.
Always keep love in your heart.
You are the best thing that ever happened to me.
Your loving Mother,

1998

Anna hugged her mother and they stayed like that on the bed until the clock chimed midnight.

'Oh my goodness – pumpkin-time,' said Meredith. 'Go to sleep. We are very busy tomorrow and your Prince Charming is coming.'

'So is yours, Mum,' said Anna, and she giggled.

Jack tipped up the next day and the whole family adjourned to the local pub for a roast dinner. There was no time for Meredith to be on her own with Jack, which was just as well because she wasn't sure what she felt about him at the moment. Several times over lunch she caught him watching her and looked away. He was on good form and making everyone laugh. He stayed close to Anna, and Meredith could see how much he obviously cared about his daughter.

When everyone went back to the house, Frank and Jenny left to go and start the afternoon milking. Anna decided to go and lie down and Jane took Tom off for a walk. Meredith had declined as she needed to go and check up on the site and, of course, Jack was coming with her. They walked around for the first half an hour inspecting drains and comparing plans, and then Bill arrived back and they went through a shooting schedule for the coming week.

Bill finally left and Meredith and Jack were left standing in the rubble facing each other.

'Alone at last,' he joked. Meredith did not laugh. 'Look,' he went on, 'I want to apologise for shouting at you the way I did.

There was no excuse, except none of us are perfect, not even me!' Meredith still did not crack a smile.

It was starting to spot with rain and she picked her way across the piles of rubble to the front door, leading into what would eventually be the grand hall.

'Do we need our hard hats, I wonder?' said Jack, still trying hard to lighten the mood. Then: 'I have done a lot of thinking these past two weeks and discovered some interesting facts about myself.' He paused as if waiting for Meredith to interrupt but she was not able to find words. There was something different about Jack. He was vulnerable and Meredith was not sure whether this was a good thing or a bad thing. She wanted to ask so many questions, but instinct was telling her to keep quiet and wait.

'I spoke to Harry a couple of days ago and it made me aware how much I miss him. God knows, I never thought I would say that.' Jack shook his head disbelievingly. 'Do you know, it is actually the first time we have ever been apart for any length of time? I hadn't realised how much I relied on him.'

Jack sat in silence for a long time. Meredith was aware of the stillness around them, interrupted only by the odd bleating of a sheep or the cows mooing outside the cowshed, waiting to be milked. It felt calm and safe here, and very comforting.

'I love Anna very much, Meredith, and I will never be able to thank you enough for bringing her into my life. When I first found out, I was angry because I felt that my wife had been betrayed. Not by you, but life. Why could she not have given me a daughter? It is what she always wanted more than anything for us. Adopting Harry was a solution, but not the problem. I was happy – thought I was happy – until Anna appeared in my life. It has taken all these months for me to absorb my emotions. I was so frightened that I would love Anna more than Harry because she is my blood. I felt guilty even thinking these thoughts. Then at Christmas when Harry

450

behaved so stupidly, I panicked. I suddenly thought that maybe Harry had hidden traits in his genetic history that I did not know about and would not be able to cope with. That somehow he would grow into a monster adult and I would not be there for him. I had all this to deal with – and you.'

Jack sighed. 'I am a poor male of the species, Meredith, and it was too much for a man who had happily lived without any commitment, except to his offspring, for twenty years. I was freaking out. Mo is not a stupid woman and I realise now she could see the writing on the wall when I went to Malaysia with you. But I hadn't really thought anything through. Yes, I fancied you – who wouldn't? – and in a sense we had unfinished business, but I didn't expect after all these years to fall in love. But I did, head over heels, and just could not deal with it at all. Then suddenly Anna lost her baby and I seriously thought that any iota of control I might have had over my life was gone forever. I hit out at everything and everybody – Harry, Mo and finally you – but never Anna, darling Anna who has had to bear so much pain. You, however, were fair game. I am truly sorry. You are an amazing woman, Meredith, a wonderful mother and—'

Meredith stopped him. 'Jack, enough, for heaven's sake! You were right. I did not appreciate my life. I was obsessed with moving on all the time in my career. Sadly, that is what has defined me but also kept me going all these years. But as you said, Anna did need me, and I have recognised that and this week we have become so very close. I have realised there is more to life than the next project.'

She paused as Jack came and stood in front of her and took her hands.

'It is going to be OK. Don't get your knickers in a twist.' Jack smiled and took her face in his hands. He kissed her tenderly and clasped her in his arms.

'What is going to happen to us, Jack?' she mumbled into his shoulder.

'It's simple, you numpty. We are going to get married, have lots of sex and live happily ever after.'

When they got back to the house, Meredith went to find Anna. 'You were right,' she told her. 'I have found my Prince Charming, after all!'

Anna and Tom decided to drive back that night with Jack, while Meredith would stay on for a couple of days and get the filming started.

As he kissed her goodbye, Jack whispered in her ear, 'Just you wait till I get you alone.'

Jane and Meredith waved them off and went back into the warm, whereupon Jane ventured to ask, 'Got any news to tell me, Meredith, love?'

'Oh Mum, Jack has just told me he has split up with Mo and we are going to try and make a go of it as a couple. I just hope we can. Nothing would make me happier. But I am also going to make sure I am around more for Anna. Work is not the be-all and end-all, is it?' She put her arm round Jane. 'My family should be number one.'

'I am very happy for you,' Jane said sincerely. 'You and Anna and Frank and Jenny and Sam and Mary are all so precious to me. I will die a happy woman knowing you are all safe and well.'

'Oh Mum, that is no way to talk,' chided Meredith. 'You have years to go yet.'

'Hmm, that's as maybe but it is jolly good to know you are all settled. Now off you go to bed, and sweet dreams.'

Meredith lay awake in bed for a long time that night, thinking about Jack and Anna, and how life was going to change. She was suddenly filled with great hopes for the future.

Chapter Thirty

When Meredith got back to London there was a message from Anna to ring her as soon as possible.

'What's happened? What's wrong?' she asked urgently, as Anna answered her mobile.

'Don't panic, Mum, nothing has happened. Well, actually, that's not true: something has happened – something wonderful – and I want to tell you all about it. Can we meet for lunch today, or are you too busy?'

Meredith had a mountain of things to do, but bearing in mind her new resolution to put family first she answered, 'Of course I am. Where do you want to meet?'

'What about La Gaffe?' Anna suggested. 'Bernardo is such a lovely man and he is always so pleased to see us.'

'Fine, I will be there at twelve thirty. I will walk up so I can have a glass of wine, or four.' Meredith loved La Gaffe, the Italian restaurant in Hampstead's Heath Street; Bernardo Stella the proprietor was appropriately named 'Stella', since he truly was a star. 'See you there, darling. Bye.' Meredith put down the phone, which rang again immediately.

'Hello, how's it going?' It was Jack. 'I was wondering if you might be free for lunch.'

'I am afraid you have been pipped at the post by your daughter,' Meredith told him. 'She has something to tell me, apparently. You can come too, if you'd like.'

'No, you're all right. I can wait – just,' he added. 'Well, what about dinner then?'

'Perfect. Shall we talk later? I had better get on now or I shall be late.'

Meredith went to hang up but stopped as Jack said, 'I am looking forward to seeing you very much. It is like starting again from the beginning.'

'Yes, it is,' she said softly. 'See you later. Bye.' She hung up and stood looking out of the window for a moment, savouring the quiver of excitement in her belly.

Anna was already sitting at their reserved table chatting to Bernardo when Meredith arrived.

'*Bellissima Signora Lee, come va?* It is wonderful to see you – it has been too long. *Giovanni, una bottiglia di Amarone per le signore, per favore.*' Bernardo fussed around them, making them feel special. When he had taken their order and presented the beautiful bottle of ruby red wine, he was off to the next customer.

'So come on, tell me – what is your news?' said Meredith, tearing open a packet of breadsticks.

Anna laughed. 'Oh Mum, you are like a child. You have no patience at all. Very well, I will put you out of your misery.' She looked her mother in the face and announced: 'Tom and I are going to live in Paris.'

'Paris!' Meredith gasped. 'Why? What on earth has brought this on?' She took a large swig of wine.

'Well, the thing is, as you know, Tom always wanted to finish his education in Paris but that all fizzled out when I got pregnant. His dad has a very old friend called Gerard who runs a gallery there, and this guy has been staying with the family recently. He has suggested that Tom goes and spends a year at a very prestigious art school on the Left Bank. He will help him apply for the place and everything. It is private, so Tom's parents will have to pay the fees, but Tom will contribute by working for Gerard. It is the perfect opportunity for Tom to get fluent in French, but most of the clients are American anyway.'

Anna paused to take a sip of wine and Meredith seized the chance to interrupt.

'That is all wonderful for Tom, but what about you, my darling? What are you going to do in the meantime? You could start your A-levels again in September. You will only be a year behind.' Meredith could hear her voice rising and tried to slow down. Now was not the time to wade in with her size nines.

'I know you still want me to go to university, Mum, but since I have been drawing with Tom and spending time in the Neils' gallery, I have realised how much I love art and design. I am wondering whether I might be able to get a job in an art gallery myself or something similar, so I can contribute to the bills and be learning something at the same time. The Louvre does courses on the History of Art and I could try and get on one of those. Robert Neil is going to help me, and Gerard has offered to find out about other courses.'

Anna said gently, 'Mum, please don't look like that. I am really fired up about this. I can still have a wonderful career without going to uni. Lots of people do, you know.'

Meredith was saved a response, as just then her mushroom risotto arrived. Suddenly she was not feeling very hungry.

'Please at least think about it,' her daughter urged. 'Tom and I want to try for another baby as well, soon. It just seems so right, Mum. I can't explain it but we both feel so strongly that

455

we want to have children. I am sorry if that is disappointing to you, but I must follow my instincts. When Alfie died, I thought I would never find anything to be joyful about again. But now I am so happy, and I know I want to make my life with Tom.'

Anna stopped talking as Meredith reached over and took her daughter's hand.

'I cannot imagine what grief you have suffered, and I want you to be happy more than anything in the world, but do you not think you might be rushing things? Maybe this is all part of your grieving process and in a few months you will feel quite differently.' Meredith was struggling to keep her emotions in check. She was horrified at the thought of her little girl going off to set up home in a tatty flat in some dodgy area of Paris.

'Mum, please, we have really thought this through. I would like to talk to Jack as well, and see what he thinks.'

Anna sounded very determined, and as Meredith could not bear the thought of any more family dissension, she decided to leave it for the moment and talk to Jack herself tonight.

'OK, darling,' she said. 'Now come on, let's tuck in. This risotto is to die for.'

That evening, Meredith and Jack were once more plunged into a big discussion. She had rung him with the news the moment she got home from La Gaffe, and now they were sitting in Meredith's local Chinese restaurant not quite sure where to begin.

Jack had greeted her with a big hug and then seemed taken with a fit of shyness. They did not kiss and Meredith was aware that she was nervous too.

'I feel like celebrating,' Jack told her.

'Celebrating!' Meredith exclaimed. Then she said: 'Sorry,

Jack, I'm feeling a bit on edge this evening and not really in a mood to celebrate. My daughter – sorry, *our* daughter – has decided she wants to go and live in Paris. She is only seventeen, for heaven's sake. I cannot get my head around it.'

Jack took her hand. 'Whoa, hold on, girl. We are going to work this out. In the meantime, I just thought it would be nice for you and me to celebrate the beginning of a beautiful friendship. Again.' He smiled tenderly at her.

Meredith felt her heart jump. Was this really going to be the start of the rest of their lives together? *Oh, please let it be so*, she prayed.

'You are quite right, Mr Blatchford. I apologise. Now get some prawn crackers ordered, and let's waste no more time. I am starving.'

They laughed and the ice was broken. A lovely dinner followed, full of jokes and animated conversation. It really was like a first date, thought Meredith happily. They decided to continue their evening at her place.

Once inside the front door Jack took Meredith in his arms and kissed her passionately. He cradled her face in his hands and looked deeply into her eyes, saying, 'I have missed you so much – you have no idea. I am just not used to this turmoil of being in love, Meredith. I can't say I am really enjoying it much. I feel out of control all the time and I just can't stop thinking about you and making love to you. Come here, my lover, I have waited long enough.'

Jack picked Meredith up and practically threw her over his shoulder as he made for the stairs, Meredith too surprised to utter a word. Upstairs, Jack slid her down onto her bed and they made wonderful love to each other. Each felt that it was like coming home, an affirmation of a love that had been denied expression for far too long. Now, at last, they could be together.

Except, of course, that nothing is that simple – and soon they were sitting up in bed like an old married couple discussing their teenage daughter.

'She is too young to go off to Paris,' fretted Meredith. 'What are Tom's parents thinking of, encouraging them like this? I suppose it is different for a boy, but even so, Tom is only seventeen. Actually, I have a feeling he is eighteen very soon. But that's not the point, is it? Oh Jack, what are we going to do?' she wailed.

'I think we should check out this art course, have a word with Robert's friend Gerard and talk to Anna and Tom. And stop panicking.' Jack turned to see the effect of his words. Meredith was stunned into silence.

'Shall I take that as a yes then?' he asked with a twinkle in his eye.

Meredith let herself be wrapped in Jack's arms and slowly began to relax. He just had this ability to make her feel safe. She closed her eyes and before she knew it, the night was over . . . and the alarm was going off.

'Help! Time to go,' said Jack, waking up. 'I have a meeting in the City in an hour. Come on, woman, move your arse and make me a cup of tea.' He leaped out of bed and made for the bathroom. Half an hour later he left with a promise to meet for dinner with Anna and Tom at the Neils' flat. He was like a whirlwind through the house, leaving a scented trail of Floris behind him.

That evening, Meredith let Jack do most of the talking. He sat next to Anna on the sofa, and Meredith was struck by how alike father and daughter had become. They both leaned forward to make their points and had a way of running their hand through their hair. The Neils were the same as ever. Meredith always felt so inadequate in front of them. They gave off this aura of calm and worldly understanding of some higher order. It was very irritating, and she was gratified to see that even Mr Positive Jack Blatchford was frustrated by their laidback attitude.

'Yes, I understand where you are coming from, Robert,' Jack was saying with just a hint of annoyance, 'but I repeat: how are they going to survive financially?'

It was Gerard who answered. 'I can assure you, Jacques,' Meredith noted the very sexy French accent, 'I will find them somewhere to live, and my wife and I will always be around in case of emergencies. Tom will be earning enough to pay the bills anyway – I will make sure of that. Anna can work if she wants to, but if she chooses simply to study, that will be fine. She will have a qualification at the end of the year which will serve her well to get almost any job in the art world, should she want to work.'

Meredith chipped in: 'Yes, that is all very well and we appreciate all you are doing, but these qualifications are not the same as our English A-levels and they are what count in the UK. What happens if you decide to come back to London and work, Anna?'

'Mum, why can't I worry about that when the time comes? I want to learn as much as I can first about painting and design. That is my ambition. Please try and understand this.' She sighed. 'Jack, do you understand what I am saying? Please can't you make Mum accept that this is what Tom and I want to do with our lives?'

Everybody sat in silence for a good five minutes.

Finally Jack stood up, saying, 'OK, look, it's getting late. Thank you, guys, for having this discussion. I reckon the best thing to do is for Meredith and me to go and have a think about it all, and come back to you tomorrow evening. Don't look so worried, Anna, I am sure we can work something out. Are you coming back with us or staying here?'

'I will stay here tonight, because Tom and I are going to meet a gallery-owner tomorrow morning with Gerard.' She kissed Jack. 'Thanks for all your help, Dad.' She then turned to Meredith, giving her a hug and whispering, 'Are you OK, Mum? I do love you.'

'I know, darling. I am just worried about you, that's all,' said Meredith, giving her a squeeze. 'We will talk tomorrow. Goodnight, everyone, and thank you again for having us all tonight.'

Driving home, Meredith turned to Jack and said, 'I think I am wasting my time trying to persuade Anna to stay, don't you?'

'Yes, I am afraid you are, my lover. But listen to me – it is not all bad. They are a very sensible couple, and they have been through so much together already, more than many older couples ever have to face, in fact. I have had a thought about the living arrangements. Why don't you go over with Anna for a long weekend and see what there is to buy? You can afford it, God knows, and it would be a good way of sussing out the property over there. You might love it. You have told me before now that France is the one place you have always wanted to live. If you help Anna and Tom to buy a place, you can charge them a nominal rent and away you go.'

He looked so pleased with himself that Meredith burst out laughing. 'I have no answer to that,' she told him.

The next morning, she rang Anna and put Jack's plan to her.

'Oh my God, that is the most wonderful idea in the whole world and you are the most wonderful parents. Do you mean it? Oh Mum, that is the answer to all my prayers. Thank you so much.' Anna was thrilled with the idea but also, more importantly, to have her parents onside.

'All right, I will sort out a trip for us for next month. I have quite a lot to organise with the filming before then, and I take it you would like to be here for Tom's birthday. I tell you what, why don't we go the weekend of the twentieth of March? Let's invite Gran as well. It can be a girls' weekend, if Tom doesn't mind, and we can celebrate Mother's Day in Paris – how about that?' Meredith was suddenly very excited about her plan.

'Perfect!' squeaked Anna. 'I can't wait to tell Tom. I am sure he won't mind about our trip. I'll take loads of photos to show him. Speak later, bye.' And she was gone.

Well, here we go again, said Meredith to herself. *Another adventure. Onwards and upwards!*

EPILOGUE

Meredith planned their trip away with military precision. She pored over a map of Paris with Gerard, who showed her exactly where the college was, and his gallery, and the Louvre. The three formed a triangle, so it seemed logical to Meredith to find somewhere within or close to that triangle.

As she was going through the list of relevant properties that had been sent to her by all the leading estate agents in Paris, she suddenly remembered Mademoiselle Lamarr, Myles's mistress. Where was her flat, Place de l'Opera? She looked it up on the map and decided that the area was well suited as their base. She found a small boutique hotel on the internet and reserved three rooms.

When she rang and told her mother that she was going to take the three of them to Paris for Mother's Day, Jane was very excited.

'I have never been abroad, Meredith. This is so wonderful of you. Are we going by plane or train?' Jane hadn't been on a plane before, either, and wasn't quite sure if this was a good idea at this late stage in her life.

'I thought it might be more fun to go on Eurostar. You see more, once you get through the tunnel,' said Meredith.

'Oh yes, I think you are right, dear. Oh, this is so exciting. I must get a passport!' Jane exclaimed. 'I have never had need of one before.'

'It's OK, I am ahead of you. Jenny has collected the form to fill in, and we'll get it processed express at the Passport Office in Victoria. I had to check Anna's as well. So that is fine then. I will organise it all and pop up to see you in case you need to sign anything. Lots of love.' Meredith hung up and carried on with her arrangements.

Jack thought it was a fantastic idea to take Jane. 'It is perfect and your mum will remember it for the rest of her life,' he said.

On the day of departure, Jack took them to Waterloo International and waved them off. They had first-class tickets, so as soon as they were seated, the champagne arrived, and the croissants and orange juice. Jane was beside herself. 'Oh I say, drinking champagne at eight thirty in the morning – how decadent. I must eat a croissant immediately to mop up the alcohol.' She beamed and they all laughed.

It was a wonderful journey on this bright March morning, with a clear blue sky and not a cloud to be seen. As they whizzed through France, Jane watched the French countryside fly by, her face lit up like a child's.

They took a taxi from the Gare du Nord to Avenue de l'Opera. Their hotel was in a wonderful eighteenth-century building overlooking a tranquil square. All their rooms had balconies and everything was very French and chic. The beds were incredibly high and the three of them got hysterical watching Jane trying to clamber up on to hers. She kept sliding down the gorgeous silk coverlet. Anna finally brought her a chair and she climbed up using that as a ladder, then lay on her back exhausted, like a beetle, while her daughter and granddaughter wiped tears of laughter from their eyes.

Meredith could hardly drag her mother away from the

balcony for dinner. Jane would have been perfectly happy to sit there all through this unusually mild March night, looking out at the landmarks of the City of Lights. Meredith and Anna had an early start the next day. Jane was well briefed with sights to see for the day; she had brought along the mobile Frank had got her, and promised to keep it switched on, so they could reach her at any time and vice versa. Meredith too had given in and got herself a mobile; she was quite enjoying using it.

Meredith and Anna saw five apartments in all on their first day. It was exhausting and depressing.

'It's just like London, Mum. The prices are ridiculously inflated and the flats are all so small,' complained Anna.

'Well, tomorrow may be better,' said Meredith, sounding more optimistic than she felt. She had better increase the sum of money she was willing to spend on the property, since what they had seen so far was simply dire. Also, she was wondering how she could slip away privately and find Mademoiselle Lamarr's apartment.

Her opportunity came over supper when Anna said, 'Tomorrow, could I go with Gran to see the Sacre Coeur and Montmartre? I'd love a look at the Place du Tertre and all the other famous streets where the artists lived and worked. If we do our viewings first thing, Mum, then I could meet Gran up there. Well, I mean we both could,' she added.

'That is an excellent idea, Anna. I won't join you as I have to do a business visit tomorrow, so it works out well. You go with Gran and then we can join forces later.'

The next morning, Meredith and Anna trawled up and down the streets and in and out of some dingy apartments, none of which appealed.

'Don't worry, something will turn up, it always does,' Meredith consoled her daughter. 'You go and meet Gran and I will catch you later.'

She watched Anna set off down into the Metro then hailed a taxi, and in a few minutes she was back in the Opera district outside the block of apartments where Mademoiselle Lamarr lived. She checked the number of the apartment and rang the bell. Several seconds passed then a clipped French voice said, *'Oui, qui est là?'*

'Oh um, bonjour. Je m'appelle Meredith Lee et je suis la fille de Myles Harrison. Puis-je parler avec vous un moment, s'il vous plaît?'

The heavy iron door clicked and swung open, and Meredith entered a very grand vestibule. A gleaming mahogany staircase wound its way up to a domed glass roof. The apartment was on the first floor, so, ignoring the very ornate antique lift, Meredith started up the stairs. Mademoiselle Lamarr was waiting at the top. She was incredibly beautiful, tall and slim with jet-black hair drawn back in a chignon at the nape of her swanlike neck. She had French 'chic' in spades. This was evident in her clothes: a perfectly fitted white shirt tucked into a grey pencil skirt, cinched in at the waist with a thin black crocodile belt which matched her crocodile court shoes; the latter were just high enough to show off her perfect pins encased in silk stockings. She seemed a silk-stocking kind of girl, thought Meredith to herself. She was also much younger than Meredith had imagined – probably only in her early forties. Lucky Myles!

'Good morning. It is very nice to meet you,' the woman said. She had a soft low voice, and her English was perfect. A great deal better than Meredith's French.

'Please come in.' She indicated that Meredith should follow her through the door into her apartment. The place had a classic French décor and spoke of luxury and taste. The armchairs and sofas were upholstered in soft cream silks and brocade, which harmonised with the exquisite carpets and drapes.

'You have a beautiful home,' murmured Meredith, taking a

seat on a Louis XV chair. An avid watcher of *Antiques Roadshow*, she had acquired a little knowledge along the way.

'*Alors*, to what do I owe this visit, Madame Lee?' asked Ms Lamarr, crossing her model girl legs.

Meredith tried to sound diplomatic. 'I appreciate that you must think it strange to see me here, but I happened to be in Paris and thought I would make your acquaintance. You see, I inherited my father's estate and I was informed in his will of your circumstances.'

Mademoiselle Lamarr smiled rather coolly and said, 'So you thought you would take a look at your father's mistress, *n'est-ce pas?*' She got up and went to the mantelpiece of the marble fireplace, took a cigarette from a pretty box and lit it, blowing a thin stream of blue smoke into the air. Meredith thought she had never seen anyone make lighting a cigarette look so sexy!

'I am very grateful to you for permitting me to stay in my home, Meredith. It is acceptable to call you Meredith?' she asked.

'Yes, please do. Mademoiselle, I have no idea of the relationship you had with Myles. He was my father but we hardly knew each other. My mother was not married to him. It is a long story ...' Meredith did not want to bring Jane into it at all. 'Anyway, I only discovered he was my father a few years ago and I have hardly seen him since, and then I discovered he had left his entire fortune to me. It is hard to understand why, really. So I hold you no grudge or anything. I do feel sorry for my Aunt Pamela, Myles's wife. It is not easy, I imagine, to be married to a man who considers it his right to take a mistress. But then in French culture it is much more acceptable, isn't it?' Meredith knew she was rambling but couldn't help herself. This woman was mesmerising.

'Please do not trouble yourself to explain, Meredith. I understand completely. As I said, I am very grateful to have my home.

Now if you will excuse me, I must ask you to leave as I have an appointment in five minutes.' She rose in one fluid movement, took Meredith by the hand, kissed her on both cheeks and led her to the door.

'*Au revoir – et mille remerciements,*' she said, and even as Meredith was saying goodbye the door clicked expensively in the lock.

Nice to see you too! thought Meredith sarcastically. Well, that told her all right.

As she began to walk back down the street towards the hotel, her phone rang and she answered it to a very excited Anna. 'Mum, we have found an apartment to rent!' her daughter said breathlessly. 'It's in Montmartre of all places – can you believe it? You have to come and see it right this minute because the landlord is only here till six. Ask the taxi driver to drop you at Chez Louis in the rue du Chevalier. Have you got that, Mum?'

'For rent? But we are looking for somewhere to buy, Anna.'

'I know, but there is a chance you will be able to buy this eventually. It is above a patisserie and the owner, Louis De Rosier, has recently lost his wife. He wants to keep the building for a bit until he decides what he wants to do with his life. Maybe go back to Burgundy to be with his family. He is so sweet, Mum – you will really like him, and the rent is so cheap. It works out at about £400 a month.'

'Well, that is not exactly cheap,' Meredith said cautiously. 'Let me have a quick word with your gran. Give her your phone. Mum? What do you think of this place?'

Jane sounded as excited as Anna. 'It is so beautiful!' she said. 'How I wish I were younger. I would come and live in it myself and learn French, and drink red wine all day and watch the people walk by. Meredith, it is perfect for them.'

'In that case,' Meredith said, 'I think I'd better get there as soon as I can. Hang on and I'll meet you at Chez Louis in about quarter of an hour. Grab me a seat! And I hope he has some nice *gateaux*!'

The taxi dropped her on the rue du Chevalier in the very heart of Montmartre. The narrow cobbled streets were full of shoppers, tourists and locals drinking cognac. Everywhere you looked there were easels and painters. The *quartier* throbbed with life. Meredith looked up at Chez Louis, an impossibly picturesque patisserie. There were tables outside with checked tablecloths and big umbrellas with *Chez Louis* written on them.

It's like a film set, she thought.

Anna appeared and dragged her mother through the tiny baker's shop then out to the back where a rather attractive man was sitting at a desk in a small office.

'*Monsieur Du Rosier, ici ma mere et ma grandmere.* Mum, he doesn't speak much English, but he seems to understand me. And, by the way, he managed to tell me that his name means "rosebush". I love it.'

Meredith shook hands with the proprietor.

'*Enchanté, madame,*' said the very handsome Frenchman. '*Vous avez une fille très belle, et elle a une mere vraiment charmante.*' He said all this with a wicked twinkle in his eye.

'Well, *merci beaucoup,*' smiled Meredith, flattered. '*Est il possible de voir la maison, appartement,* whatever?'

'*Bien sûr. Anna, vas-y, ma fille. Je vous attends ici.*' And Monsieur Du Rosier resumed his seat to carry on with his paperwork.

'Come on, Mum, Gran and I will show you round.' And they set off up the stairs.

The apartment was on two floors above the shop. It had a light and airy living room on the first floor with a good-sized kitchen equipped with all mod cons, and there was a small cloakroom as well, with a washing machine. Up on the second floor were two double bedrooms, both with built-in cupboards and large French-sized double beds. A gorgeous bathroom looked out onto the little garden at the back, filled with pots of herbs, shrubs and a fig tree. The bath was free-standing and one could sit in it and gaze out of the window. It was enchanting. Meredith fell instantly in love with it.

'Oh Anna, you are right – this is wonderful. How did you find it?' she asked.

'Gran spotted it on a noticeboard where we were having a coffee. Isn't she amazing?' said Anna, giving Jane a beaming smile.

'So can she have it, Meredith?' Jane enquired.

'Please, Mum,' joined in her daughter. 'It is everything we could wish for and it is so easy to get down into Paris from here. There are loads of buses and metro stations on the boulevard, and there may even be a job for me part-time in the bakery.'

Meredith had to agree it all seemed perfect. She had just decided to telephone Jack and see what he thought when, as if by magic, her mobile rang.

'Jack, you are psychic. I was just about to ring you,' Meredith gabbled. 'Anna and Jane have found the most lovely flat. Unfortunately, the kids can only rent it at the moment, but it may well be up for sale at a later date. It could be the perfect answer. I mean, if they decide to come home after six months we haven't got embroiled in a whole load of property stuff and contracts, et cetera. Jack, would you be able to get over here and take a look?'

She stopped to draw breath and became aware of Jack laughing on the other end of the line.

'Christ, woman, what are you like? Calm down. As a matter of fact, I am at your hotel waiting for you, and—'

He was stopped by Meredith shrieking into the phone: 'You are here in Paris?'

'Yes, and I have brought Tom with me as I figured he had a right to a say in where he lives,' Jack went on.

This time it was Anna shrieking down the line, 'Dad, you are amazing. I love you!'

Meredith took the phone. 'We all love you.' She gave him the address of Chez Louis. 'Hurry up. We will be here waiting for you both.'

Jane decided she would love to have a cup of tea and one of the delicious pastries on sale. So they adjourned to a vacant table under an umbrella. Monsieur Du Rosier was charming. He tried hard to make himself understood, and between his pidgin English and Meredith's school French and Anna's enthusiasm, he nearly succeeded.

By the time Jack and Tom arrived, the deed was all but done; they were just waiting for the chaps to see the place for themselves and give the go-ahead. Of course they agreed – and Tom was over the moon. The owner went into his office and spent half an hour arranging the paperwork and organising a time to sign on Monday morning, the day after Mother's Day. It was fortunate that Meredith had booked a late train on the Monday, so there would be time to finalise everything before they left.

There was lots of handshaking and kissing on both cheeks, and finally the five of them set off past the famous vineyard at the rear of the Montmartre Museum, and while the three older members of the family hailed a taxi back to the more opulent surroundings of the Opera district, Tom and Anna went off to explore Montmartre – their future home – on their own.

'I am absolutely exhausted,' announced Jane when the taxi drew up at the hotel. 'Would you mind if I went to bed early, you two? I don't think I want anything else to eat tonight after that beautiful tea. The Chez Louis cakes were very filling.'

'You may have a point, Mother. Perhaps we should follow

suit. We need to be fresh for tomorrow as I have booked a special lunch at La Coupole down in Montparnasse; it's a very famous Parisian brasserie, and we are going to raise our glasses to Mother's Day there.'

Jack and Meredith retired to her room and ordered a light supper of a plate of *moules* and a glass of chilled white wine.

'You never told me how come you are here at all,' said Meredith.

'It's because I wanted to be with you tomorrow, if you must know. It was going to be a surprise for all three of you. So don't ask me any more – OK? Be a good girl and come to bed, and tomorrow we will celebrate.'

The next morning, Meredith, Anna and Jane were all awoken by breakfast in bed on a silver tray, with a single red rose. That was the first treat of the day. Several hours later, the whole party were seated in the comfort and vibrant atmosphere of La Coupole. It was raining outside, but nobody cared.

Meredith looked around the table at her beloved mother and daughter, then at Tom, whose eyes were alight with love for her Anna, and finally at Jack. She wished that Harry was with them, to complete the circle.

Her heart was so full that when she tried to speak, her voice trembled too much to go on.

Jack put his fingers to her lips. 'Ssh,' he whispered. 'No time for tears now, my lover.'

Raising his glass of champagne, he proposed a toast: 'To mothers and daughters, where would we be without you?'

He then leaned across, held her tight and murmured in Meredith's ear, 'I love you, and I always will. Happy Mother's Day, my darling.'

Hotels with personality

WIN a 2-night break worth £1,000 at the Best Western hotel of your choice!

Lapping water that massages your feet as you float on air... Crisp English wines made from grapes grown yards from the hotel are ripe for the pouring... Settling down for a classic afternoon tea in the exact same spot as Miss Jean Brodie...

There are thousands more stories like these just waiting to happen at over 275 characterful and unique hotels across Great Britain whether you're enjoying a well deserved weekend break away or a short break in the countryside.

The lucky winner and a guest will be treated to two nights at a Best Western hotel of their choice in Great Britain, including breakfast and dinner daily plus spending money and tickets to an attraction or show in their chosen location up to the value of £1000.

To enter simply visit http://pages.simonandschuster.co.uk/bestwestern/

Best Western Hotels has teamed up with Simon & Schuster to give YOU 15% off! (see the link above for terms and conditions)

Freshly baked bread with homemade jam, views as far as the eye can see, cosy four-posters, melt-in-your-mouth cuisine, and 15% off the lot.

To book, simply call 0845 263 7402, or book online by visiting www.bestwestern.co.uk and entering the Customer Code TELLME into the search box and following the online booking process.

We look forward to welcoming you soon!